Also by Michel Houellebecq

Whatever
Atomised
Platform
Lanzarote
H.P. Lovecraft: Against the World, Against Life

THE POSSIBILITY
OF AN ISLAND

MICHEL HOUELLEBECQ

Translated from the French by Gavin Bowd

Weidenfeld & Nicolson
LONDON

First published in Great Britain in 2005
by Weidenfeld & Nicolson

First published in France in 2005 by Éditions Fayard

1 3 5 7 9 10 8 6 4 2

A CIP catalogue record for this book is available
from the British Library

ISBN 0 2978 5098 9 (hardback)
0 297 85100 4 (trade paperback)

Typeset at The Spartan Press Ltd,
Lymington, Hants

Printed in Great Britain by
Clays Ltd, St Ives plc

Weidenfeld & Nicolson
An imprint of the Orion Publishing Group
Orion House, 5 Upper St Martin's Lane, London WC2H 9EA

www.orionbooks.co.uk

For Antonio Muñoz Ballesta and his wife, Nico,
without whose friendship and great kindness
this novel could not have been written.

Welcome to eternal life, my friends.

This book owes its existence to Harriet Wolff, a German journalist I met in Berlin a few years ago. Before putting her questions to me, Harriet wanted to recount a little fable. For her, this fable encapsulated my position as a writer.

I am in a telephone box, after the end of the world. I can make as many telephone calls as I like, there is no limit. I have no idea if anyone else has survived, or if my calls are just the monologues of a lunatic. Sometimes the call is brief, as if someone has hung up on me; sometimes it goes on for a while, as if someone is listening with guilty curiosity. There is neither day nor night; the situation is without end.

Welcome to eternal life, Harriet.

Who, among you, deserves eternal life?

My current incarnation is deteriorating; I do not think it will last much longer. I know that in my next incarnation I will be reunited with my companion, the little dog Fox.

The advantage of having a dog for company lies in the fact that it is possible to make him happy; he demands such simple things, his ego is so limited. Possibly, in a previous era, women found themselves in a comparable situation – similar to that of domestic animals. Undoubtedly there used to be a form of domotic happiness, connected to the functioning of the whole, which we are no longer able to understand; there was undoubtedly the pleasure of constituting a functional organism, one that was adequate, conceived with the purpose of accomplishing a discrete series of tasks – and these tasks, through repetition, constituted a discrete series of days. All that has disappeared, along with the series of tasks; we no longer really have any specific objective; the joys of humans remain unknowable to us, inversely, we cannot be torn apart by their sorrows. Our nights are no longer shaken by terror or by ecstasy. We live, however; we go through life, without joy and without mystery; time seems brief to us.

The first time I met Marie22 was on a cheap Spanish server; the connection times were appallingly long.

> *The weariness brought on*
> *By the old dead Dutchman*
> *Is not something attested*
> *Well before the master's return.*

2711, 325104, 13375317, 452626. At the address indicated I was shown an image of her pussy – jerky, pixellated, but strangely *real*. Was she alive, dead or an intermediary? Most likely an inter-mediary, I think; but it was something you did not talk about.

Women give an impression of eternity, as though their pussy were connected to mysteries – as though it were a tunnel opening on to the essence of the world, when in fact it is just a hole for dwarves, fallen into disrepair. If they can give us this impression, then good for them; my words are meant sympathetically.

> *The immobile grace,*
> *Conspicuously crushing,*
> *Flowing from the passage of civilisations,*
> *Does not have death as corollary.*

I should have stopped. Stopped the game, the intermediation, the contact; but it was too late. 258, 129, 3727313, 11324410.

The first sequence was filmed from a hill. Immense sheets of grey plastic covered the plain; we were north of Almeria. The harvesting of the fruit and vegetables that grew beneath the plastic used to be done by agricultural labourers – most often of Moroccan origin. After mechanisation was introduced, the workers evaporated into the surrounding sierras.

In addition to the usual equipment – electric generator powering the protective fence, satellite network, sensors – the unit Proyecciones XXI.13 also benefited from a generator of mineral salts and its own source of drinking water. It was far away from the main thoroughfares, and did not figure on any of the recent maps – its construction came after the last surveys. Since the cessation of all air traffic and the permanent jamming of satellite transmission frequencies, it had become virtually impossible to locate.

The following sequence could have been a dream. A man with my face was eating a yoghurt in a steel mill; the manual for the machine tools was written in Turkish. It was unlikely that production would start up again.

12, 12, 533, 8467.

The second message from Marie22 was worded thus:

> *I am alone like a silly cunt*
> *With my*
> *Cunt*

245535, 43, 3. When I say 'I', I am lying. Let us posit the 'I' of perception – neutral and limpid. Put it next to the 'I' of intermediation – when you look at it this way, my body belongs to me; or, more exactly, I belong to my body. What do we observe? An absence of contact. Fear what I say.

I do not want to keep you outside this book; living or dead, you are *readers*. Reading is done outside of me; and I want it to be done – in this way, in silence.

> *Contrary to received ideas,*
> *Words don't create a world;*
> *Man speaks like a dog barks*
> *To express his anger, or his fear.*
>
> *Pleasure is silent,*
> *Just like the state of happiness.*

The self is the synthesis of our failures; but it is only a partial synthesis. Fear what I say.

This book is intended for the edification of the Future Ones. Men, they will tell themselves, were able to produce this. It is not nothing; it is not everything; we are dealing with an intermediary production.

Marie22, if she exists, is a woman to the same extent that I am a man; to a limited, refutable extent.

I too am approaching the end of my journey.

No one will be present at the birth of the Spirit, except for the Future Ones; but the Future Ones are not beings, in our sense of the word. Fear what I say.

PART ONE

COMMENTARY
OF DANIEL24

Now, what does a rat do when it's awake? It sniffs about.
Jean-Didier – biologist

How vividly I remember the first moments of my vocation as a clown! I was seventeen at the time, and spending a rather dreary month in an *all-inclusive* resort in Turkey – it was, incidentally, the last time I was to go on holiday with my parents. My silly bitch of a sister – she was thirteen at the time – was just beginning to turn the guys on. It was at breakfast; as usual in the morning, a queue had formed in front of the scrambled eggs, something the holiday-makers seemed incredibly fond of. Next to me, an old English woman (desiccated, nasty, the kind who would cut up foxes to decorate her living room), who had already helped herself copiously to eggs, didn't hesitate to snaffle up the last three sausages on the hotplate. It was five to eleven, the breakfast service had come to an end, it was inconceivable that the waiter would bring out any more sausages. The German who was in the queue behind her became rigid; his fork, already reaching for a sausage, stopped in mid-air, and his face turned red with indignation. He was an enormous German, a colossus, more than two metres tall and weighing at least 150 kilos. I thought for a moment that he was going to plant his fork in the octogenarian's eyes, or grab her by the neck and smash her head on to the hotplates. She, with that senile, unconscious self-ishness of old people, came trotting back to her table as if nothing had happened. The German was angry, I could sense that he was incredibly angry, but little by little his face grew calm, and he went off sadly, sausageless, in the direction of his compatriots.

Out of this incident I composed a little sketch about a bloody revolt in a holiday resort, sparked by the tiny details that contra-dicted the *all-inclusive* formula: a shortage of sausages at breakfast, followed by a supplemental charge for the mini-golf. That evening, I performed this sketch at the 'You have talent!' soirée (one evening every week the show was made up of turns done by the holiday-makers, instead of by professionals); I played all the characters, thus taking my first steps down the road of the one-man show, a road I scarcely left throughout my career. Nearly everyone came to the after-dinner show, as there was fuck-all to do until the discotheque opened; that meant an audience of 800 people. My sketch was a resounding success, people cried with laughter, and there was noisy applause. That very evening, at the discotheque, a pretty brunette called Sylvie told me I had made her laugh a lot, and that she liked boys with a sense of humour. Dear Sylvie. And so, in this way, my virginity was lost and my vocation decided.

After my baccalaureate, I signed up for acting lessons; there follow-ed some inglorious years, during which I grew nastier and nastier and, as a consequence, more and more caustic; thanks to this, success finally arrived – on a scale which surprised me. I had begun with small sketches on reunited immigrant families, journal-ists for *Le Monde* and the mediocrity of the middle classes in general – I successfully captured the incestuous temptations of mid-career intellectuals aroused by their daughters or daughters-in-law, with their bare belly-buttons and thongs showing above their trousers. In short, I was a *cutting observer of contemporary reality*; I was often compared to Pierre Desproges. While con-tinuing to devote myself to the one-man show, I occasionally accepted invitations to appear on television programmes, which I chose for their big audiences and general mediocrity. I never forgot to emphasise this mediocrity, albeit subtly: the presenter had to feel a little endangered, but not too much. All in all, I was a good professional; I was just a bit overrated. I was not the only one.

I don't mean that my sketches were unfunny; they *were* funny. I was, indeed, a *cutting observer of contemporary reality*; it was just that everything now seemed so elementary to me, it seemed that so few things remained that could be observed in contemporary re-ality: we had simplified and pruned so much, broken so many barriers, taboos, misplaced hopes and false aspirations; truly, there was so little left. On the social level, there were the rich and the poor, with a few fragile links between them – the *social ladder*, a subject on which it was the done thing to joke; and the more serious possibility of being ruined. On the sexual level there were those who aroused desire, and those who did not: a tiny mechanism, with a few complications of modality (homosexuality, etc.), that could nevertheless be easily summarised as vanity and narcissistic competition, which had already been well described by the French moralists, three centuries before. There were also, of course, the *honest folk*, those who work, who ensure the effective production of wealth, also those who make sacrifices for their children – in a manner that is rather comic or, if you like, pathetic (but I was, above all, a comedian); those who have neither beauty in their youth, nor ambition later, nor riches ever; but who hold on wholeheartedly, and more sincerely than anyone, to the values of beauty, youth, wealth, ambition and sex; those who, in some kind of way, *make the sauce bind*. Those people, I am afraid to say, could not constitute a *subject*. I did, however, include a few of them in my sketches to give diversity, and the *reality effect*; but I began all the same to get seriously tired. What's worse is that I was considered to be a *humanist*; a pretty abrasive humanist, but a humanist all the same. To give some context, here is one of the jokes that peppered my shows:

'Do you know what they call the fat stuff around the vagina?'
'No.'
'The woman.'

Strangely, I managed to throw in that kind of thing, whilst still getting good reviews in *Elle* and *Télérama*; it's true that the arrival of the Arab immigrant comedians had validated macho excesses once more, and that I was genuinely excessive, albeit with grace: going close to the bone, repeatedly, but always staying in control. Finally, the benefit of the humorist's trade, or more generally of a *humorous attitude* in life, is to be able to behave like a complete bastard with impunity, and even to profit hugely from your depravity, in terms of sexual conquests and money, all with general approval.

My supposed humanism was, in reality, built on very thin foundations: a vague outburst against tobacconists, an allusion to the corpses of negro clandestines cast up on the Spanish coasts, had been enough to give me a reputation as a *lefty* and a *defender of human rights*. Me, a lefty? I had occasionally been able to introduce a few, vaguely young, anti-globalisation campaigners into my sketches, without giving them an immediately antipathetic role; I had occasionally indulged in a certain demagogy: I was, I repeat, a good professional. Besides, I looked like an Arab, which helps; the only residual ideological content of the left, in those days, was anti-racism, or more precisely anti-white racism. I did not in fact know the origins of these Arab features, which became more pronounced as the years went by: my mother was of Spanish origin and my father, as far as I know, was Breton. For example, my sister, that little bitch, was undoubtedly the Mediterranean type, but she wasn't half as dark as me, and her hair was straight. One had to wonder: had my mother always been scrupulously faithful? Or had I been engendered by some Mustapha? Or even – another hypothesis – by a Jew? Fuck that: Arabs came to my shows in droves – Jews also, by the way, although in smaller numbers; and all these people paid for their tickets, at the full price. We all worry about the circumstances of our death; the circumstances of our birth, however, are less worrisome to us.

As for *human rights*, quite obviously I couldn't give a toss; I could hardly manage to be interested in the rights of my cock.

In that particular respect, the rest of my career had more or less confirmed my first success at the holiday club. Women in general lack a sense of humour, which is why they consider humour to be one of the virile qualities; throughout my career, opportunities for placing my organ in one of the appropriate orifices were never lacking. To tell the truth, such intercourse was never up to much: women who are interested in comedians are getting old, nearly forty, and are beginning to suspect that things are going to turn bad. Some of them had fat asses, others breasts like flannels, sometimes both. In other words, there was nothing arousing about them; and, anyway, when it's more and more difficult to get a hard-on, the interest goes. They weren't all that old, either; I knew that as they approached fifty they would once again long for something reassuring, easy and false – and of course they wouldn't find it. In the meantime, I could only confirm to them – completely unintentionally, believe me, it's never a pleasure – the decline of their erotic value; I could only confirm their first suspicions, and instil in them, despite myself, a despairing view of life: no, it was not maturity that awaited them, but simply old age; there was not a new blossoming at the end of the road, but a bundle of frustrations and sufferings, at first insignificant, then very quickly unbearable; it wasn't very healthy, all that, not very healthy at all. Life begins at fifty, that's true; insomuch as it ends at forty.

Look at the little creatures moving in the distance; look. They are humans.

In the fading light, I witness without regret the disappearance of the species. A last ray of sunlight skims over the plain, passes over the mountain range barring the horizon to the east, and colours the desert landscape with a red halo. The metal trellises of the protective fence around the residence sparkle. Fox growls softly; no doubt he can sense the presence of the savages. For them I feel no pity, nor any sense of common belonging; I simply consider them to be slightly more intelligent monkeys, and, for this reason, more dangerous. There are times when I unlock the fence to rescue a rabbit, or a stray dog; but never to bring help to a human.

I would never contemplate coupling with a female of their species. Whilst the interspecies barrier is often territorial among invertebrates and plants, among the higher vertebrates it is more a question of behaviour.

A being is fashioned, somewhere in the Central City, that is similar to me; at least he has my features, and my internal organs. When my life ceases, the absence of a signal will be registered in a few nanoseconds; the manufacture of my successor will begin immediately. The next day, or the day after at the latest, the protective fence will be reopened; my successor will settle within these walls. This book will be addressed to him.

Pierce's first law identifies personality with memory. Nothing exists, in the personality, outside what is memorisable (be this memory cognitive, procedural or emotional); it is thanks to memory, for example, that the sense of identity does not dissolve during sleep.

According to Pierce's second law, language is a suitable carrier for cognitive memory.

Pierce's third law defines the conditions for an unbiased language.

Pierce's three laws were going to put an end to the hazardous attempts at memory downloading through the intermediary of a data carrier, in favour of, on the one hand, direct molecular transfer, and, on the other, what today we call *life story*, initially conceived as a simple complement, a provisional solution, but which was, following the work by Pierce, to become considerably more important. Thus, curiously, this major logical advance resulted in the rehabilitation of an ancient form that was basically quite close to what was once called *autobiography*.

Concerning the life story, there are no precise instructions. The beginning can start at any point in time, just as a first glance can alight on any point within a painting; what matters is that, gradually, the whole picture re-emerges.

When you see the success of the car-free Sundays in Paris, and
the walkway along the banks of the Seine, then you can easily
imagine what comes next
Gérard – taxi driver

Today it's almost impossible for me to remember *why* I married my
first wife; if I was to come across her in the street, I don't even think
I'd be able to recognise her. You forget certain things, you forget
them totally; it is wrong to suppose that all things are stored in the
sanctuary of memory; certain events, the majority of them even, are
well and truly *erased*, there remains no trace of them, and it is
absolutely as if they had never happened. To return to my wife, or
rather my first wife, we undoubtedly lived together for two or three
years; when she became pregnant, I ditched her almost immediately. I was having no success at the time, and she received
only a miserable alimony.

On the day of my son's suicide, I made a tomato omelette. 'A
living dog is worth more than a dead lion,' as Ecclesiastes rightly
says. I had never loved that child: he was as stupid as his mother,
and as nasty as his father. His death was far from a catastrophe; you
can live without such human beings.

After my first show, ten years passed, punctuated by short and
unsatisfying affairs, before I met Isabelle. I was then thirty-nine and
she thirty-seven; I was already something of a celebrity. When I
earned my first million euros (I mean, when I had really earned
them, after tax, and placed them in a safe haven), I realised that I
was not a Balzacian character. A Balzacian character who has just
earned his first million euros would, in most cases, figure out a way
to reach the second – with the exception of those few people
who will immediately begin to dream of the moment when they

can count them in tens. For my part, I wondered above all whether I could bring my career to a halt – before concluding no.

During the first phases of my rise to fortune and glory, I had occasionally tasted the joys of consumption, by which our epoch shows itself so superior to those that preceded it. You could quibble forever over whether men were more or less happy in past centuries. You could comment on the disappearance of religions, the difficulty of feeling love, discuss the disadvantages and advantages of both; you could mention the appearance of democracy, the loss of our sense of the sacred, the crumbling of social ties. I myself had done such things, in a lot of sketches, though in a humorous way. You could even question scientific and technological progress, and be under the impression, for example, that the improvement of medical techniques had been at the cost of increasing social control and an overall decrease in *joie de vivre*. But it remains the case that, on the level of consumption, the pre-eminence of the twentieth century was indisputable: nothing, in any other civilisation, in any other epoch, could compare itself to the mobile perfection of a contemporary shopping centre functioning at full tilt. I had thus consumed, with joy, shoes most notably; then, gradually, I had grown weary, and I had understood that my life, without this daily input of basic, renewable pleasures, was going to stop being simple.

When I met Isabelle, I must have been worth six million euros. A Balzacian character, at this stage, buys a sumptuous apartment, which he fills with artworks, and then ruins himself for a dancer. I lived in a banal three-room flat, in the fourteenth arrondissement, and I had never slept with a top model – I hadn't even felt the desire to. At one point it had seemed the right thing to do to copulate with a B-list model; I did not keep an imperishable memory of it. The girl was all right, with rather big breasts, but no bigger than those of others; I was, when you think of it, less overrated than her.

The interview took place in my dressing room, after a show that must be described as a *triumph*. Isabelle was then the editor-in-chief of *Lolita*, after a long spell working at *20 Ans*. At first, I wasn't really up for this interview; whilst flicking through the magazine, I had, however, been surprised by the level of sluttishness that publications for young girls had stooped to: T-shirts cut to fit ten-year-olds, skintight white shorts, thongs showing everywhere, the knowing use of Chupa-Chups, it was all there. 'Yes, but they have a bizarre product positioning . . .' the press officer had insisted. 'And then the fact that the editor-in-chief moves around a lot herself, I think that's a sign . . .'

There are, it seems, people who do not believe in *love at first sight*; without giving the expression its literal sense, it is obvious that mutual attraction is, in all cases, very quick; from the first minutes of my encounter with Isabelle I knew that we were going to share a love story, and that this love story would be long; and I knew that she herself was aware of this. After a few opening questions, on my methods of preparation, etc., she fell silent. I flicked again through the magazine pages.

'These are not really Lolitas . . .' I observed, finally. 'They are sixteen, seventeen years old.'

'Yes,' she said. 'Nabokov was five years out. What most men like is not the moment that precedes puberty, but the one immediately after. Anyway, he wasn't a very good writer . . .'

I too had never been able to bear that mediocre and mannered pseudo-poet, that clumsy imitator of Joyce, who had never been lucky enough to possess the energy that sometimes enabled the insane Irishman to rise above his ponderous prose.

A collapsed pastry, that was what Nabokov's style had always made me think of.

'But exactly,' she continued. 'If a book that is so badly written, and, what's more, is handicapped by a gross mistake concerning the age of the heroine, manages despite everything to be a very good book, to such an extent that it constitutes a lasting myth, and enters everyday speech, then the author has stumbled upon something essential.'

If we agreed on everything, the interview risked being rather flat. 'We could continue over dinner . . .' she proposed. 'I know a Tibetan restaurant in the rue des Abbesses.'

Naturally, as in all serious love stories, we slept together on the first night. At the moment when she undressed, she seemed slightly uneasy, then proud: her body was incredibly firm and supple. It was much later that I learned she was thirty-seven; at that moment, I would have said thirty at most.

'What do you do to keep yourself fit?' I asked her.

'Classical dance.'

'No stretching or aerobics, none of that stuff?'

'No, that's all nonsense; believe me, I've been working in women's magazines for ten years. The only thing that really works is classical dance. Only it's hard, it demands real discipline; but that suits me. I'm rather psychorigid.'

'You, psychorigid?'

'Yes, yes . . . You'll see.'

As time goes on, what strikes me, when I remember Isabelle, is the incredible frankness of our relations, from the very first moment, even in regard to subjects about which women usually prefer to retain a certain mystery, in the mistaken belief that mystery adds a touch of eroticism to the relationship, when on the contrary, most men are violently excited by a direct sexual approach.

'It's not very difficult to make a man come . . .' she had told me, wryly, during our first dinner in the Tibetan restaurant. 'That's to say, I've always managed to.' She was speaking the truth. She was also speaking the truth when she said that there was nothing extraordinary or strange about the secret. 'You need only remember,' she continued with a sigh, 'that men have balls. Women are aware that men have a cock, arguably they are all too aware, because ever since men were reduced to the status of a sexual object, women have been literally obsessed with their cocks; but when they make love they forget, nine times out of ten, that the balls are a sensitive zone. Whether it's for masturbation, penetration or a blowjob, you must, from time to time, put your hand on the man's balls, either to lightly caress them, or to apply greater pressure, and soon you'll realise that they are more or less hard. There you go. That's all.'

It must have been five in the morning, and I had just come inside her, and things were good, really good, everything was comforting and tender, and I was feeling as though I was on the threshold of a happy phase in my life, when I noticed, for no particular reason, the bedroom's decor – I remember that at that moment the moonlight was falling on an engraving of a rhinoceros, an old engraving, of the kind you find in animal encyclopaedias of the nineteenth century.

'Do you like my place?

'Yes. You've got taste.'

'Are you surprised I've got taste, since I work for a shitty magazine?'

I could tell it was going to be hard to hide my thoughts from her. This remark, curiously, filled me with a certain joy; I suppose that is one of the signs of true love.

'I'm well paid . . . You know, often, that's enough reason to take a job.'

'How much?'

'Fifty thousand euros a month.'

'That's a lot; but at the moment I earn more.'

'That's to be expected. You're a gladiator, in the middle of the arena. It's no surprise you're well paid: you risk your neck, you can fall at any moment.'

'Ah . . .'

There, I wasn't completely in agreement; I remember feeling joy again. It's good to be in perfect harmony, to agree on every subject, in the first instance it is even indispensable; but it is also good to have small differences of opinion, if only to be able to resolve them through gentle discussion.

'I suppose you must have slept with a lot of girls who came to your shows . . .' she continued.

'A few, yes.'

Not as many as that, in reality: there had perhaps been fifty, or a hundred at the absolute maximum; but I refrained from articulating that the night that we had just spent together was far and away the best; I felt that she knew it. Not through boastfulness, or exaggerated vanity: simply through intuition, through an understanding of human relations; through an accurate appreciation, also, of her own erotic value.

'If girls are sexually attracted to guys who get up on stage,' she continued, 'it's not simply that they are seeking fame; it's also that they feel an individual who gets up on stage risks his neck, because the public is a big dangerous animal that can annihilate its creation, hunt it down, and force it to flee, booed off in shame. The reward these girls can offer to the guy who risks his neck by going on stage is their body; it's exactly the same thing with a gladiator, or a matador. It would be stupid to imagine that these primitive mechanisms have disappeared; I know them, I use them, I earn my living from them. I understand exactly the erotic attraction of the rugby player, the rock star, the theatre actor or the racing driver: all this follows ancient patterns, with small variations according to fashion or epoch. A good magazine for young girls is one that knows how to anticipate – subtly – these variations.'

I thought for well over a minute; I had to make her understand my point of view. It was important, or maybe not – let's just say I wanted to make her understand.

'You're completely right . . .' I said. 'Except that, in my case, I'm not risking anything.'

'Why?'

She had sat up in bed and was looking at me with surprise.

'Because, even if the public suddenly felt like getting rid of me, it couldn't; there is no one to put in my place. I am, very precisely, irreplaceable.'

She frowned and looked at me; dawn had now broken, and I saw her breasts moving to the rhythm of her breath. I felt like taking one of them in my mouth, sucking it, and emptying my mind; but I told myself I should let her reflect a bit. That didn't take her more than thirty seconds; she really was an intelligent girl.

'It's true,' she said. 'There's a completely abnormal frankness about you. I don't know if it's owing to a particular event in your life, a consequence of your education or what; but there is no chance that the phenomenon could reproduce itself in the same generation. In fact, people need you more than you need them – people of my age, at least. In a few years' time, that'll all change. You know the magazine I work for: all we're trying to do is create an artificial mankind, a frivolous one that will no longer be open to seriousness or to humour, which, until it dies, will engage in an increasingly desperate quest for *fun* and sex; a generation of definitive *kids*. We are going to succeed, of course; and, in that world, you will no longer have your place. But I suppose it's not too bad, you must have had time to put some money away.'

'Six million euros,'

I had replied, automatically, without even thinking; there was another question that had been pestering me for several minutes. 'Your magazine . . . Actually, I don't resemble your readership at all. I am cynical, bitter, I can only interest people who are a bit inclined towards doubt, people who already feel that they've reached the end of the line; this interview can't fit in with your editorial policy.'

'That's true,' she said calmly, with an astonishing calm when I thought about it later – she was so transparent and so frank, with no talent for lying. 'There won't be any interview; it was just a pretext for meeting you.'

She was looking me straight in the eye, and I was in such a state that her words alone were enough to give me a hard-on. I think that she was moved by such a sentimental, such a human erection; she stretched out beside me, placed her head upon my shoulder and began to wank me slowly, squeezing my sex and my balls. I relaxed, and gave myself to her caress. She lived in the sixteenth arrondissement, at the top of Passy; in the distance an overground metro was crossing the Seine. Day was beginning, the murmur of traffic was becoming louder; sperm spurted on her breasts. I took her in my arms.

'Isabelle,' I said into her ear. 'I would like you to tell me how you came to work for this magazine.'

'It's been hardly a year, *Lolita* is only at issue fourteen. I stayed a very long time at *20 Ans*, I occupied all the posts; Germaine, the editor-in-chief, relied completely upon me. At the end, just before the magazine was bought up, she made me assistant editor-in-chief; it was the least she could do; for ten years I had been doing all the work in her place. That didn't stop her hating me; I remember the hatred in her eyes when she handed me Lajoinie's invitation. You know who Lajoinie is, does that ring any bells?'

'Vaguely something . . .'

'Yes, he's not that well known to the general public. He was a shareholder of *20 Ans*, a minority shareholder, but he is the one who pushed for the sale; an Italian group bought it. Obviously, Germaine was fired; the Italians were prepared to keep me, but Lajoinie inviting me to brunch at his house on a Sunday morning could only mean he had something else in mind for me; Germaine could sense this, of course, and that's what made her mad with rage. He was living in Le Marais, just by the Place des Vosges. Still, when I arrived, I was shocked: there was Karl Lagerfeld, Naomi Campbell, Tom Cruise, Jade Jagger, Björk . . . In other words, not the type of people I was used to meeting.'

'Wasn't he the one who created that gay magazine that's doing very well?'

'Not exactly. At the beginning, *GQ* was not targeted at gays, rather it was *ironically macho*: bimbos, motors, a bit of military news; it's true that after six months they noticed that loads of gays were buying it, but it was a surprise, I don't think they've ever really understood the phenomenon. Anyway, shortly afterwards he sold up, and it's that which greatly impressed those in the trade: he sold *GQ* when it was at the top, and when many had thought it could go even higher, and he launched *21*. Since then, *GQ* has collapsed, I think they've lost 40 per cent in terms of national sales, and *21* has become the first monthly for men – they've just overtaken *Le Chasseur Français*. Their formula is very simple: strictly metrosexual. Fitness, beauty care, trends. Not a hint of culture, not an ounce of current affairs, no humour. In short, I had no idea what he was going to propose to me. He greeted me very nicely, introduced me to everyone, and sat me down in front of him. "I have a lot of respect for Germaine . . ." he began. I tried not to lose my cool: no one could have respect for Germaine, that old alcoholic could inspire contempt, compassion, disgust, and all sorts of other things, but never respect. Later I would become aware of his methods for managing personnel: speak ill of no one, under no circumstances, ever; on the contrary, always shower other people with praise, however undeserved – without, obviously, omitting to fire them at the appropriate moment. All the same, I was a bit annoyed, and I tried to divert the conversation to *21*.

' "We mu-st" – he spoke bizarrely, detaching each syllable,

almost like he was speaking in a foreign language – "my coll-eagues are, it is my im-pre-ssion, much too pre-occ-up-ied by the Am-er-ic-an press. We re-main Eur-o-pe-ans . . . Our ref-er-ence point, is what happ-ens in Eng-land . . ."

'All right, *21* was obviously copied from an English format, but so was *GQ*; that did not explain why he'd felt he had to move from one to the other. Had there been studies done in England, a shift in readership?

'"Not to my know-ledge . . . You are very pretty . . ." he continued, without any apparent connection to what he'd said before. "You could be more med-i-a friend-ly . . ."

'I was sitting right next to Karl Lagerfeld, who was eating constantly: he used his bare hands to serve himself from a plate of salmon, dipped the pieces in the cream-and-dill sauce and stuffed them down. From time to time, Tom Cruise threw him distraught looks. Björk, on the other hand, seemed absolutely fascinated – it has to be said that, although she always tried to play with the poetry of the sagas, Icelandic energy, etc., she was in fact conventional and mannered to the extreme; she must have been fascinated to find herself in the presence of a real savage. I suddenly realised that you needed only to take off the couturier's frilly shirt, his tie and silk-lined smoking jacket, and cover him with animal skins: he would have been perfect in the role of a primitive Teuton. He speared a boiled potato and smothered it with caviar, before saying to me: "You must be media-friendly, even if it's just a little bit. I, for example, am *very* media-friendly. I am a big cheese in the media." I think he must have just given up on his second diet in any case, he had already written a book on the first one.

'Someone put on some music, the crowd stirred slightly, and I think Naomi Campbell began to dance. I continued to stare at Lajoinie, waiting for his proposal. In despair, I started a conversation with Jade Jagger, we must have talked about Formentera or something of that kind, an easy subject, but she made a good impression on me, she was an intelligent girl, without airs and graces; Lajoinie's eyes were half-closed, he seemed to have dozed off, but I think now that he was observing how I behaved with the others – that too was part of his method of personnel management.

At one point he grumbled something, but I couldn't hear what, the music was too loud; then he threw an irritated look to his left: in a corner of the room, Karl Lagerfeld had begun to walk on his hands; Björk stared at him, laughing her head off. Then the couturier came and sat down again, giving me a big slap on the shoulders, screaming: "You all right? Everything all right?" before swallowing three eels one after the other. "You're the most beautiful woman here! You wipe the floor with them!" then he seized the cheese board; I believe that he had really taken a shine to me. Lajoinie watched with incredulity as he devoured the livarot. "You really are a big cheese, Karl," he said in one breath; then he turned to me and pronounced: "Fifty thousand euros." And that's all; that's all he said to me that day.

'The following morning, I passed by his office, and he explained a little bit more. The magazine was to be called *Lolita*. "It's a question of a gap in the market . . ." he said. I understood more or less what he meant: *20 Ans*, for example, was bought mainly by fifteen- or sixteen-year-old girls, who wanted to be emancipated in all things, sex in particular; with *Lolita*, he wanted to find the opposite gap in the market. "Our target readership starts at ten years old . . ." he said, "but there is no upper limit." His bet was that, more and more, mothers would tend to copy their daughters. Obviously there's something ridiculous about a thirty-year-old woman buying a magazine called *Lolita*; but no more so than her buying a clinging top, or hot-pants. His bet was that the feeling of ridiculousness, which had been so strong among women, and French women in particular, was going to gradually disappear and be replaced by pure fascination with limitless youth.

'The least you can say is that his gamble paid off. The average age of our readers is twenty-eight – and that increases a little every month. For the advertisers, we are becoming *the* women's magazine – I am telling you what I've been told, and I've some difficulty believing it. I am steering, I am trying to steer, or rather I'm pretending to steer, but basically I don't understand anything any more. I am a good professional, that's true, I told you I was a bit psychorigid – it stems from that: there are never any typos in the magazine, the photos are well laid out, we always publish on the scheduled date; but the content . . . It's understandable that people are afraid of getting old, especially women, that's always been true, but in this case . . . It's gone beyond anything you could imagine; I think women have gone completely mad.'

Now that everything is appearing, in the clarity of emptiness, I am free to watch the snow. My distant predecessor, the unfortunate comedian, chose to live here, in the residence that once stood – excavations prove it, as do photographs – on the site of the unit Proyecciones XXI,13. Back then it was – it is strange to say, and also a little sad – a seaside residence.

The sea has disappeared, and with it the memory of waves. We possess audio and visual documents; none of them enable us to truly experience the tenacious fascination that gripped man, revealed in so many poems, in the face of the apparently repetitive spectacle of the ocean crashing upon the sand. Nor are we able to understand the thrill of the chase, the pursuit of prey; nor religious feeling, nor that kind of immobile, objectless frenzy that man called *mystical ecstasy*.

Before, when humans lived together, they gave each other mutual satisfaction through physical contact; we understand that, for we have received the message of the Supreme Sister. Here is the message of the Supreme Sister, in its intermediary formulation:

> Admit that men have neither dignity nor rights; that good and evil are simple notions, scarcely theorised forms of pleasure and pain.
>
> Treat all men as animals – deserving understanding and pity, for their souls and their bodies.
>
> Remain on this noble and excellent path.

By turning from the path of pleasure, without managing to find an alternative, we have only prolonged the latter tendencies of mankind. When prostitution was definitively outlawed, and the ban effectively applied across the entire surface of the planet, men entered the *grey age*. They were never to leave it, at least not before the sovereignty of the species had disappeared. No truly convincing theory has been formulated to explain what bears all the hallmarks of mass suicide.

Android robots appeared on the market, equipped with a versatile artificial vagina. A high-tech system analysed in real time the configuration of male sexual organs, arranged temperatures and pressures; a radiometric sensor allowed the prediction of ejaculation, the consequent modification of stimulation, and the prolonging of intercourse for so long as was wished. It had a curiosity value for a few weeks, then sales collapsed completely: the robotics companies, some of whom had invested hundreds of millions of euros, went bankrupt one by one. The event was commented on by some as a desire to return to the natural, to the truth of human relationships; of course, nothing could be further from the truth, as subsequent events would clearly demonstrate: the truth is that men were simply giving up the ghost.

A drinks machine dispensed an excellent hot chocolate. We swallowed it in one go, with unconcealed pleasure.
Patrick Lefebvre – Ambulance driver for animals

The show *We Prefer the Palestinian Orgy Sluts* was undoubtedly the pinnacle of my career – from a media point of view, I mean. I briefly migrated from the 'Theatre' pages to 'Home Affairs'. There were complaints from Muslim associations, bomb threats; in other words, a bit of action. I was taking a risk, it's true, but a calculated one; the Islamic fundamentalists, who had appeared in the 2000s, had suffered more or less the same fate as the punks. At first they had been made obsolete by the appearance of polite, gentle and pious Muslims from the Tabligh movement – a kind of equivalent of New Wave, to continue the analogy; the girls at this time still wore the veil, but it was pretty, decorated, with lace and see-through material, rather like an erotic accessory, in fact. And of course, subsequently, the phenomenon had progressively died out: the expensively built mosques were deserted, and the Arab immigrant girls were once again available in the sexual marketplace, like everyone else. It was something of a done deal, when you bear in mind the society we lived in, it could hardly have been otherwise; nevertheless, in the space of one or two seasons, I had found myself cast in the role of a *hero of free speech*. Personally, as regards freedom, I was *rather against*; it's amusing to observe that it's always the enemies of freedom who find themselves, at one moment or another, most in need of it.

Isabelle was at my side, and she gave me acute advice.
  'What you must do,' she said from the outset, 'is have the rabble on your side. With the rabble on your side, no one can get at you.'
  'They *are* on my side,' I protested; 'they come to my shows.'

'That's not enough; you've got to go further. What they respect is dosh. You've got dosh, but you don't show it off enough. You've got to blow it a bit more.'

On her advice, I therefore bought a Bentley Continental GT, a 'magnificent and racy' coupé which, according to *L'Auto-Journal*, 'symbolised the return of Bentley to its original vocation: offering sports cars of very high standing'. A month later, I was on the cover of *Radikal Hip-Hop* – or rather, my car was. Most of the rappers bought Ferraris, some of the more original ones bought Porsches; but a Bentley completely trounced them. They had no culture, those little cunts, even when it came to cars. Keith Richards, for example, had a Bentley, like all serious musicians. I could have chosen an Aston Martin, but it was dearer, and anyway the Bentley was better, the bonnet was longer, you could have lined up three sluts on it with no problem. For one hundred and sixty thousand euros, it was almost a bargain; in any case, as far as credibility among the rabble goes, I think I made a good profit from the investment.

That show also marked the beginning of my brief – but lucrative – movie career. I had inserted a short film into the performance; my initial project, entitled *Let's Drop Miniskirts on Palestine!* already had that tone of light Islamophobic burlesque which was later going to contribute so much to my renown; but, on Isabelle's advice, I had had the idea of introducing a touch of anti-Semitism, aimed at counterbalancing the rather anti-Arab nature of the show; it was a wise route to take. I therefore finally opted for a porn film, or rather a parody of a porn film – a genre that, it's true, is easy to parody – entitled *Munch on my Gaza Strip (my huge Jewish settler)*. The actresses were authentic Arab immigrant girls, guaranteed to originate from the hardest Parisian suburbs – sluts but veiled, just the right type; we had filmed the outside shots at the Sea of Sand, in Ermenonville. It was comical – a rather elevated form of comedy, that's true. People had laughed; or at least most people. In an interview with Jamel Debbouze, he described me as a 'super-cool dude'; you couldn't have asked for more. In fact, Jamel had told me just before the programme: 'I can't wind you up, dude. We've got the same audience.' The TV presenter Marc Fogiel, who had organised the meeting, quickly realised our complicity, and began to shit his pants; I have to admit that for a long time I had been wanting to eviscerate that little prick. But I contained myself: I was very good, *super-cool*, in fact.

The producers of the show had asked me to cut a part of my short film – a part that, in fact, was not very funny; it had been filmed in a block of flats being demolished in Franconville, but was supposed to take place in East Jerusalem. It involved a dialogue between a terrorist from Hamas and a German tourist that took the form of, at one moment, Pascalian dialectics on the foundations of human identity, and, at another, a meditation on economics – a bit *à la* Schumpeter. The Palestinian terrorist began by establishing that, on the metaphysical level, the value of the hostage was nil – because he was an infidel; it wasn't, however, negative – as would have been the case, for example, of a Jew; his destruction was therefore not desirable, it merited simply indifference. On the economic level, however, the value of the hostage was considerable – as he belonged to a rich nation known for showing solidarity with its citizens. Having made these introductory remarks, the Palestinian terrorist carried out a series of experiments. First, he tore out one of the hostage's teeth – with his bare hands – before observing that his negotiable value had remained unchanged. Then he proceeded to do the same operation on a fingernail – with the help, this time, of pincers. A second terrorist intervened, and a brief discussion took place between the two Palestinians, on a more or less Darwinian basis. In conclusion, they tore off the hostage's testicles, without omitting to carefully sew up the wound to avoid a premature death. By mutual agreement, they concluded that the biological value of the hostage was the only value to emerge modified from the operation; his metaphysical value remained nil, and his negotiable value very high. In short, it became more and more Pascalian – and, visually, more and more unbearable; incidentally, it was a surprise to me to realise how inexpensive the special effects used in gore movies really were.

The uncut version of my short film was screened a few months later at the 'Festival of Strangeness', and it was then that the movie proposals began to flood in. Curiously, I was contacted once again by Jamel Debbouze, who wanted to break out of his usual character type to play a bad boy, a real villain. His agent quickly made him see that it would be an error, and finally nothing was done, but the anecdote seems significant to me.

To contextualise it better, you must remember that in those years – the last years of an economically viable French cinema industry – the only attestable successes of French production, the only ones that could pretend to, if not rival American productions, then at least more or less cover their costs, belonged to the *comedy* genre – subtle or vulgar, they all managed to work. On the other hand, artistic recognition, which enabled both access to the last remaining public subsidies and decent coverage in the respectable media, went first of all, in cinema as in the other arts, to productions that praised evil – or, at least, that challenged moral values conventionally described as 'traditional', in a sort of institutionalised anarchy perpetuating itself through mini-pantomimes whose repetitive nature did not blunt their charms in the eyes of the critics, all the more so as they facilitated the writing of reviews which were predictable and clichéd, yet in which they were still able to present themselves as groundbreaking. The putting to death of morality had, on the whole, become a sort of ritual sacrifice necessary for the reassertion of the dominant values of the group – centred for some decades now on competition, innovation and energy, more than on fidelity and duty. If the fluidification of forms of behaviour required by a developed economy was incompatible with a normative cata-logue of restrained conduct, it was, however, perfectly suited to a perpetual celebration of the will and the *ego*. Any form of cruelty, cynical selfishness or violence was therefore welcome – certain subjects, like parricide or cannibalism, in particular. The fact that a comedian, who was known as a comedian, was able to move easily into the domains of cruelty and evil, was therefore necessarily going to constitute, for the profession as a whole, an electric shock. My agent greeted what can truly be described as a *stampede* to his door – in less than two months, I received forty different script proposals – with qualified enthusiasm. I was certainly going to earn a lot of money, he said, and he was going to as well; but, in terms of notoriety, I was going to lose. The scriptwriter may well be an essential element in the making of a film, but he remains, first of all, absolutely unknown to the general public; and anyway, second of all, writing scripts represented a lot of work, which risked distracting me from my career as a showman.

If he was right on the first point – my participation, as scriptwriter, co-scriptwriter or simply consultant on the credits of around thirty films was not going to add one iota to my notoriety – he made a wild overestimate on the second. Film-makers, I quickly realised, are not very intelligent: you need only bring them an idea, a situation, a fragment of story-line, all the things they would be incapable of thinking up themselves; you add a bit of dialogue, three or four silly witticisms – I was capable of producing about forty pages of script per day – you present the product, and they are thrilled. Then they change their minds all the time, on everything – them, the production, the actors, anyone. You need only go to the meetings, tell them they are completely right, that you will rewrite according to their instructions, and Bob's your uncle; never had I known such easy money.

My biggest success as a principal scriptwriter was certainly *Diogenes the Cynic*; contrary to what the title might suggest, it was not a costume drama. The cynics, and it is a generally forgotten point of their doctrine, instructed children to kill and devour their own parents as soon as the latter, becoming unsuitable for work, represented useless mouths to feed; a contemporary adaptation about the problems posed by the development of the fourth age was scarcely difficult to imagine. At one point I had the idea of offering the lead role to the philosopher Michel Onfray, who, naturally, was enthusiastic; but the indigent graphomaniac, so at ease in front of television presenters, or before reasonably amicable students, completely collapsed when faced with a camera, and it was impossible to get anything out of him. The producers returned, wisely, to more tried and tested formulae, and Jean-Pierre Marielle was, as usual, masterly.

At about the same time, I bought a second home in Andalusia, in a zone that was then very wild, a little north of Almeria, called the Cabo de Gata Nature Reserve. The architect's plan was sumptuous, with palm trees, orange trees, jacuzzis and cascades – which, given the climate (it was the driest region in Europe), could be interpreted as slightly mad. I didn't know it at all, but this region was the only one on the Spanish coast up until then to have been spared by tourism; five years later, the land prices had trebled. In short, in those years, I was a bit like King Midas.

It was then that I decided to marry Isabelle; we had known each other for three years, which placed us precisely in the average of premarital association. The ceremony was discreet, and a little sad; she had just turned forty. It seems obvious to me today that the two events are linked; that I wanted, as a proof of affection, to minimise her shock at turning forty. Not that it manifested itself in complaints, or a visible anguish, or anything clearly definable; it was both more fleeting and more poignant. Occasionally – especially in Spain, when we were preparing to go to the beach, and she was putting on her swimsuit – I could feel her, at the moment when I glanced at her, wincing slightly, as if she had felt a punch between the shoulder blades. A quickly stifled grimace of pain distorted her magnificent features – the beauty of her fine, sensitive face was of the kind that resists time; but her body, despite the swimming, despite the classical dance, was beginning to suffer the first blows of age – blows which, she knew all too well, were going to multiply rapidly, leading to total degradation. I didn't fully know what it was that happened to my facial expression in those moments which made her suffer so much; I would have given a great deal to avoid it, for, I repeat, I loved her; but manifestly that wasn't possible. Nor could I reiterate that she was still as desirable, still as beautiful; I never felt, in the slightest way, capable of lying to her. I recognised the look she wore afterwards: it was that humble, sad look of the sick animal that steps away from the pack, puts its head on its paws and sighs softly, because it feels itself wounded and knows that it can expect no pity from its fellow creatures.

The cliffs tower above the sea, in their vertical absurdity, and there will be no end to the suffering of man. In the foreground I see rocks, sharp and black. Further, pixellated slightly on the surface of the screen, is a muddy, indistinct area that we continue to call the sea, and which was once the Mediterranean. Creatures advance in the foreground, along the crest of the cliffs, like their ancestors did, several centuries before; they are less numerous and more dirty. They fight, try to regroup, form packs or hordes. Their faces are now just a surface of red flesh, bare and raw, attacked by worms. They shiver with pain at the slightest breath of wind, which sweeps up gravel and sand. Occasionally they throw themselves on each other, fight and wound each other with their blows or their words. One by one they detach themselves from the group, their pace slows, they fall on their backs. Elastic and white, their backs can withstand contact with the rock; they then resemble upturned turtles. Insects and birds land on bare flesh, peck at it and devour it; the creatures still suffer a little, then are still. The others, a few feet away, continue their struggles and little games. From time to time they come closer to watch the agony of their companions; in these moments their eyes express only an empty curiosity.

I quit the surveillance program; the image disappears, returns to the tool bar. There is a new message from Marie22:

> *The enumerated lump*
> *Of the eye that closes*
> *In the squashed space*
> *Contains the last term.*

247, 214327, 4166, 8275. Light appears, grows and rises; I rush into a tunnel of light. I understand what man felt, when he penetrated woman. I understand woman.

Since we are men, it is right, not to laugh at the misfortunes of mankind, but to lament them.
Democritus of Abdera

Isabelle was growing weaker. Of course, it wasn't easy, for a woman already wounded in the flesh, to work for a magazine like *Lolita*, where every month there arrived new tarts who were always younger, sexier and more arrogant. I remember I was the first to touch on the question. We were walking along the top of the cliffs of Carbonera, which plunged, pitch-black, into sparkling blue water. She didn't seek any escape route, she didn't evade the issue: indeed, indeed, in her line of work you had to maintain a certain atmosphere of conflict, of narcissistic competition, but of which she felt more incapable with every passing day. 'Life debases,' Henri de Régnier once noted; life wears you out, above all – there doubtless remains in some people an undebased core, a kernel of being; but what weight does this residue carry, in the face of the general decay of the body?

'I'll have to negotiate my redundancy compensation,' she said. 'I don't see how I'm going to be able to do that. The magazine is doing better and better, as well; I don't know what pretext to invoke for my departure.'

'Go and see Lajoinie, and explain to him. Simply tell him what you told me. He's old already, I think he can understand. Of course, he's a man of money, and power, and those are passions that die slowly; but, after all you've told me, I think he's a man who can be sensitive to burn-out.'

She did what I proposed, and her conditions were accepted in their entirety; of course, the magazine owed her almost everything. For my part, I couldn't yet call a halt to my career – not completely. Bizarrely entitled 'Forward Snowy! Onwards to Aden!', my last

show was subtitled '100% hateful' – the inscription was emblaz-
oned across the poster, in Eminem-style handwriting; it was in no
way hyperbole. From the outset, I got on to the subject of the
conflict in the Middle East – which had already brought me a few
significant media successes – in a manner which, wrote the *Le
Monde* journalist, was 'singularly abrasive'. The first sketch, entitled
'The Battle of the Tiny Ones', portrayed Arabs – renamed 'Allah's
vermin' – Jews – described as 'circumcised fleas' – and even some
Lebanese Christians, afflicted with the pleasing sobriquet of 'Crabs
from the Cunt of Mary'. In short, as the critic for *Le Point* noted,
the religions of the Book were 'played off against each other' – in
this sketch at least; the rest of the show included a screamingly
funny playlet entitled 'The Palestinians are Ridiculous', into which I
slipped a variety of burlesque and salacious allusions about sticks of
dynamite that female militants of Hezbollah put around their waists
in order to make mashed Jew. I then widened this to an attack on all
forms of rebellion, of nationalist or revolutionary struggle, and in
reality against political action itself. Of course, I was developing
throughout the show a vein of *right-wing anarchy*, along the lines of
'one dead combatant means one less cunt able to fight', which, from
Céline to Audiard, had already contributed to the finest hours of
French comedy; but beyond that, updating St Paul's premise that all
authority comes from God, I sometimes elevated myself to a sombre
meditation, not unlike that of Christian apologetics. I did it, of
course, by evacuating any theological notion and developing a
structural and essentially mathematical argument, based notably on
the concept of 'well-ordering'. All in all, this show was a classic, and
was heralded as such overnight: it was, without a shadow of doubt,
my biggest critical success. According to the general view, my
comedy had never attained such heights – or had never plumbed
such depths – that was another way of looking at it, but in the end
it meant much the same thing; I found myself being frequently
compared to Chamfort, or even La Rochefoucauld.

In the public arena, success was a little slower to arrive, until, that
is, Bernard Kouchner declared himself 'personally sickened' by the
show, which enabled me to sell out the remaining weeks. On
Isabelle's advice, I wrote a little response to him in the 'Right to

Reply' section of *Libération*, which I entitled 'Thanks, Bernard'. So things were going well, really well, which put me in a state that was all the more curious, because I was sick of it all, and, truth be told, only a hair's breadth away from giving up – if things had turned bad, I believe I would have taken off without a word. My attraction to film as a medium – i.e. a dead medium, as opposed to what they pompously called at the time a *living spectacle* – had undoubtedly been the first sign in me of a disinterest in, even a disgust for the general public – and probably for mankind in general. I was working at that time on my sketches with a small video camera, fixed on a tripod and linked to a monitor on which I could control in real time my intonations, funny expressions and gestures. I had always had a simple principle: if I burst out laughing at a given moment it was this moment that had a good chance of making the audience laugh as well. Little by little, as I watched the cassettes, I became aware that I was suffering from a deeper and deeper malaise, sometimes bordering on nausea. Two weeks before the première, the reason for this malaise became clear to me: what I found more and more unbearable wasn't even my face, nor was it the repetitive and predictable nature of certain standard impersonations that I was obliged to do: what I could no longer stand was *laughter*, laughter in itself, that sudden and violent distortion of the features that deforms the human face and strips it instantly of all dignity. If man laughs, if he is the only one, in the animal kingdom, to exhibit this atrocious facial deformation, it is also the case that he is the only one, if you disregard the natural self-centredness of animals, to have attained the supreme and infernal stage of *cruelty*.

The three-week run was a permanent calvary; for the first time, I truly experienced those notorious, atrocious *tears of the clown*; for the first time, I truly understood mankind. I had dismantled the cogs in the machine, and I knew how to make it work, whenever I wanted. Every evening, before going on stage, I swallowed an entire sheet of Xanax. Every time the audience laughed (and I could predict it, I knew how to dose my effects, I was a consummate professional), I was obliged to turn away so as not to see those *hideous* faces those hundreds of faces moved by convulsions, agitated by hate.

This passage from the narration by Daniel1 is undoubtedly, for us, one of the most difficult to understand. The video cassettes he alludes to have been retranscribed and annexed to his life story. I have had the opportunity to consult these documents. Being genetically descended from Daniel1, I have, of course, the same features, the same face: most of our gestures and expressions, even, are similar (although my own, living as I do in a non-social environment, are naturally more limited); but that sudden expressive distortion, accompanied by the characteristic chuckles, which he called *laughter*, is impossible for me to imitate; I cannot even imagine its mechanism.

The notes made by my predecessors from Daniel2 to Daniel23 generally indicate the same incomprehension. Daniel2 and Daniel3 assert that they are still able to reproduce the phenomenon, under the influence of certain liqueurs; but for Daniel4, already, it is an inaccessible reality. Several studies have been done on the disappearance of laughter among the neo-humans; all concur that it happened quickly.

A similar, though slower, evolution can be observed for *tears*, another characteristic trait of the human species. Daniel9 notes that he cried, on a very precise occasion (the accidental death of his dog Fox, electrocuted by the protective fence); but from Daniel10 onwards, there is no more mention of it. Just as laughter is rightly considered by Daniel1 to be symptomatic of human cruelty, tears seem in this species to be associated with compassion. 'We never cry for ourselves alone,' notes an anonymous human author somewhere. These two emotions, cruelty and compassion, evidently no longer hold much meaning in the conditions of absolute solitude in which we lead our lives. Some of my predecessors, like Daniel13, display in their commentary a strange nostalgia for this double loss; then this nostalgia itself disappears, giving way to a more and more fleeting curiosity; one can now, as all my contacts on the network corroborate, consider it practically extinct.

*I relaxed by doing a bit of hyperventilation; and yet, Barnaby, I
could never stop dreaming of the great mercury lakes on Saturn.*
Captain Clark

Isabelle worked out her three months' notice, and her last issue of
Lolita appeared in December. A small cocktail party was organised
in the magazine offices. The atmosphere was a little tense, in so far
as all the guests were asking themselves the same question without
being able to say it out loud: who was going to replace her as editor-
in-chief? Lajoinie appeared for quarter of an hour, ate three blinis,
and gave out no useful information.

We left for Andalusia on Christmas Eve; then followed three
strange months, spent in almost complete solitude. Our new residence was sited just south of San Jose, near Playa de Monsul. My
agent thought this period of isolation was a good thing; it was good,
he said, that I step back a little, in order to stoke up the curiosity of
the public; I didn't know how to confess to him that I intended to
drop it all.

He was about the only one who knew my telephone number; I
couldn't say that I had made many friends during my years of
success; I had, on the other hand, lost a lot of them. The only thing
that can rid you of your last illusions about mankind is to earn a
large sum of money very quickly; then you see them emerge, the
hypocritical vultures. For your eyes to be opened thus, it is essential
to *earn* this sum of money: the truly rich, those who are born rich,
and have never breathed any atmosphere other than wealth, seem
inoculated against the phenomenon, as if they have inherited with
their wealth a sort of unconscious, unthinking cynicism, which
makes them aware from the outset that they will have to encounter
people whose only aim is to wrest their money from them, by any
conceivable means; they behave, therefore, with prudence, and

generally keep their capital intact. For those who are born poor, the situation is much more dangerous; speaking for myself, I was enough of a cynical bastard to understand the situation, I had succeeded in avoiding most of the traps; but as for friends, no, I no longer had any. The people I associated with in my youth were for the most part actors: future failed actors; but I don't think the situation would have been different in another milieu. Isabelle didn't have friends either, and, especially in the final years, she had been surrounded only by people who dreamed of taking her place. Thus we never had anyone to invite round to our sumptuous residence; no one with whom to share a glass of Rioja while watching the stars.

What could we do, then? We asked ourselves the question while crossing the dunes. Live? It's precisely in this kind of situation that, crushed by the sense of their own insignificance, people decide to have children; this is how the species reproduces, although less and less, it must be said. Isabelle was something of a hypochondriac, and she'd just turned forty; but antenatal examinations had made a lot of progress, and I felt that the problem wasn't one of age; the problem was me. There was not only in me that legitimate disgust that seizes any normal man at the sight of a *baby*; there was not only that solid conviction that a child is a sort of vicious dwarf, innately cruel, who combines the worst features of the species, and from whom domestic pets keep a wise distance. There was also, more deeply, a horror, an authentic horror at the unending calvary that is man's existence. If the human infant, alone in the animal kingdom, immediately manifests its presence in the world through incessant screams of pain, it is, of course, because it suffers, and suffers intolerably. Perhaps it's the loss of fur, which makes the skin so sensitive to variations in temperature, without really guarding against attacks by parasites; perhaps it's an abnormal sensitivity of the nervous system, some kind of design fault. To any impartial observer it appears that the human individual *cannot* be happy, and is in no way conceived for happiness, and his only possible destiny is to spread unhappiness around him by making other people's existence as intolerable as his own – his first victims generally being his parents.

Armed with these scarcely humanist convictions, I laid down the foundations of a script, with the working title 'The Social Security Deficit', which addressed the main elements of the issue. The first fifteen minutes of the film consisted of the unremitting explosion of babies' skulls under the impact of shots from a high-calibre revolver – I had envisaged it in slow-motion, then with slight accelerations – anyway, a whole choreography of brains, in the style of John Woo; then, things calmed down a little. The investigation, led by a police inspector with a good sense of humour, but rather conventional methods – I was thinking of Jamel Debbouze again – unearthed the existence of a network of child killers, brilliantly organised and inspired by ideas rooted in Deep Ecology. The MED (Movement for the Extermination of Dwarves) called for the disappearance of the human race, which it judged irredeemably harmful to the balance of the biosphere, and its replacement by a species of bears of superior intelligence – research had been done in the meantime to develop the intelligence of bears, and notably to enable them to speak (I thought of Gérard Depardieu in the role of the chief of the bears).

Despite the convincing casting, and despite also my notoriety, the project never saw the light of day; a Korean producer declared an interest, but proved incapable of securing the necessary finance. This uncommon failure could have awoken the sleeping moralist in me (peacefully asleep in general): if there was a failure, and the project was rejected, it was because there still existed *taboos* (in this case the killing of children), and perhaps, for this reason, all was not lost forever. The thinking man, however, was not slow to take over from the moralist: if there was a taboo, that meant there was, in fact, a *problem*; it was during those same years that there appeared in Florida the first 'childfree zones', high-quality residences for guilt-less thirty-somethings who confessed frankly that they could no longer stand the screams, dribbles, excrement and other environ-mental inconveniences that usually accompany *little brats*. Entry to the residences was therefore, quite simply, forbidden to children younger than thirteen; hatches were installed, like those in fast-food restaurants, to enable contact with families.

An important breakthrough had been made: for several decades, the depopulation of the West (which in fact was not specific to the West; the same phenomenon could be seen in any country or culture once a certain level of economic development was reached) had been the subject of vaguely hypocritical and suspiciously unanimous lamentation. For the first time, young, educated people, in a good position on the socio-economic scale, declared publicly that they *did not want* children, that they felt no desire to put up with the bother and expense associated with bringing up offspring. Such a casual attitude, obviously, could only inspire imitation.

Familiar with the suffering of man, I contribute to the decoupling, I accomplish the return to calm. When I kill a savage who, more audacious than the others, lingers too long at the protective fence – it is usually a female, with prematurely sagging breasts, brandishing her baby like a supplication – I have the sensation of accomplishing a necessary and legitimate act. The similarity of our faces – all the more striking as the majority of those who wander in the region are of Spanish or North African origin – is for me the sure sign of their death sentence. The human species will disappear, it must disappear so that the words of the Supreme Sister can be accomplished.

The climate is mild in the north of Almeria, the great predators rare; it is no doubt for these reasons that the density of savages remains high, albeit in constant decline – a few years ago I even saw, not without horror, a herd of some hundred individuals. My correspondents note the contrary, almost everywhere across the globe: in very general terms, the savages are on the road to extinction; in numerous sites, their presence has not been signalled for several centuries; some of us have even come to consider their existence a myth.

There is no strict limit to the domain of the intermediaries, but there are some certainties. I am The Door. I am The Door, and The Guardian of The Door. The successor will come; he must come. I maintain the presence, to make possible the coming of the Future Ones.

DANIEL1, 6

There are excellent toys for dogs.
Patricia Dürst-Benning

Living together alone is hell between consenting adults. In the life
of a couple, most often there will be at the beginning certain
details, certain discordances about which it is decided to say
nothing, in the enthusiastic certainty that love will end up solving
all problems. These problems grow little by little, silently, before
exploding a few years later and destroying all possibility of living
together. From the beginning, Isabelle had preferred that I take her
from behind; every time I tried another approach she went along
with it at first, then turned around, as if in spite of herself, with an
uneasy half-laugh. During all those years I had attributed this
preference to a peculiarity of her anatomy, an inclination of the
vagina or something along those lines, one of those things that men
can never, despite all their good will, be exactly conscious of. Six
weeks after our arrival, while I was making love to her (I usually
penetrated her from behind, but there was a big mirror in our
bedroom), I noticed that as she approached her climax she closed
her eyes, and only reopened them a long time afterwards, once the
act was finished.

I thought of it again throughout the night whilst emptying two
bottles of pretty disgusting Spanish brandy: I relived our acts of
love, our embraces, all those moments that had united us: I saw her
again looking away each time, or closing her eyes, and I began to
cry. Isabelle let herself come, she made you come, but she did not
like to come, she did not like the outward signs of orgasm; she
didn't like them in me, and no doubt she liked them even less in
herself. Everything coincided: each time I had seen her marvel at
the plastic expression of beauty, it was over painters like Raphaël,
and especially Botticelli: something occasionally tender, but often

cold, and always very calm; she had never understood the absolute admiration I had for Greco, she had never appreciated ecstasy, and I cried profusely because this animal side, this limitless surrender to pleasure and ecstasy was what I liked best in myself, whilst I had only contempt for my intelligence, sagacity and humour. We would never know that infinitely mysterious double look of the couple united in happiness, humbly accepting the presence of organs, and limited joy; we would never truly be lovers.

What was worse, however, was that this ideal of plastic beauty, to which she could never again have access, was going to destroy Isabelle before my very eyes. First of all, there were her breasts, which she could no longer stand (and it's true they were beginning to droop a bit); then her buttocks, which were following the same course. More and more often, it became necessary to turn off the light; then sexuality itself disappeared. She could no longer stand herself; and, consequently, she could no longer stand love, which seemed to her to be false. I could, however, at the beginning, still get a hard-on, at least a little bit; that too disappeared, and from that moment on, it was over; all that remained was a memory of the deceptively ironical words of the Andalusian poet:

Oh, the life men try to live!
Oh, the life they lead
In the world they live in!
The poor souls, the poor souls . . . They don't know how to love.

When sexuality disappears, it's the body of the other that appears, as a vaguely hostile presence; the sounds, movements and smells; even the presence of this body that you can no longer touch, nor sanctify through touch, becomes gradually oppressive; all this, unfortunately, is well known. The disappearance of tenderness always closely follows that of eroticism. There is no refined relationship, no higher union of souls, nor anything that might resemble it, or even evoke it allusively. When physical love disappears, everything disappears; a dreary, depthless irritation fills the passing days. And, with regard to physical love, I hardly had any illusions. Youth, beauty, strength: the criteria for physical love are exactly the same as those of Nazism. In short, I was in the shit.

One solution presented itself, on a link road of the A2 motorway, between Saragossa and Tarragon, a few dozen metres from a service station where Isabelle and I had stopped to have lunch. The existence of pets is relatively recent in Spain. A country with a traditionally Catholic, macho and violent culture, Spain, until only a little while ago, treated animals with indifference, and occasionally with a dark cruelty. But standardisation was doing its work, on this level as on others, and Spain was approaching European, and especially English, norms. Homosexuality was more and more widespread and accepted; vegetarian food was becoming increasingly available, as were New Age baubles; and pets, here given the pretty name of *mascotas*, were gradually replacing children in the family. However, the process had only just begun, and there were many failures: often a puppy, given as a toy at Christmas, was abandoned by the roadside a few months later. Thus, on the central plains, there formed packs of stray dogs. Their existence was brief and miserable. Infested with scabies and other parasites, they found their food in the dustbins of service stations, and generally ended their days under the wheels of a lorry. They suffered terribly, and above all, from the absence of human contact. Having abandoned the pack millennia before, having chosen the company of men, the dog has never been able to re-adapt to the wild. No stable hierarchy established itself in the packs, fights were constant, whether for food or for the possession of females; the pups were abandoned, and occasionally devoured by their older brothers.

I was drinking more and more during this time, and it was after my third anis, on stumbling towards the Bentley, that I was astonished to see Isabelle pass through an opening in the fence, and approach a group of about ten dogs who were stationed on a piece of wasteland near the car park. I knew that she was naturally rather timorous, and that these animals were generally considered dangerous. The dogs, however, watched her approach without aggression or fear. A little white-and-ginger mongrel, with pointed ears, aged about three months at most, began to creep towards her. She stooped, took it in her arms, and returned to the car. This is how Fox entered our lives; and, with him, unconditional love.

The complex interweaving of proteins constituting the nuclear envelope among primates made human cloning, for several decades, dangerous, risky and, at the end of the day, almost impracticable. The operation was, on the other hand, an immediate and total success with the majority of pets, including – though with a slight delay – dogs. It is therefore exactly the same Fox who rests at my feet as I write these lines, adding my commentary, according to tradition, as my predecessors have done, to the life story of my human ancestor.

I live a calm and joyless life; the surface of the residence permits short walks, and a complete array of equipment enables me to tone my muscles. As for Fox, he is happy. He gambols around the residence, content with the imposed perimeters – he quickly learned to keep away from the protective fence; he plays with the ball, or with one of the small plastic animals (I have several hundred of them, bequeathed to me by my predecessors); he really likes musical toys, especially a duck made in Poland, which emits various tuneful quacks. Above all, he likes me to take him in my arms, and rest like that, bathed in sunshine, his eyes closed, his head placed on my knees, in a happy half-sleep. We sleep together, and every morning is a festival of licks and scratches from his little paws; it is an obvious joy for him to be reunited with life and daylight. His joys are identical to those of his ancestors, and they will remain identical among his descendants; his nature in itself contains the possibility of happiness.

I am only a neohuman, and my nature includes no possibility of this order. Humans, or at least the most advanced among them, already knew that unconditional love is the condition for the possibility of happiness. A full understanding of the problem has not yet enabled us to advance towards some kind of solution. The study of the lives of the saints, on whom some based so much hope, has shed no light. Not only did the saints, in their quest for salvation, obey motives that were only partially altruistic (even though submission to the will of the Lord, which they professed, must have often been simply a convenient way of justifying to others their natural altruism), but prolonged belief in a manifestly absent divine entity provoked in them displays of idiocy incompatible in the long term with the maintenance of a technological civilisation. As for the hypothesis of a gene for altruism, it caused so many disappointments that no one dares today to openly put it forward. It has certainly been demonstrated that the centres of cruelty, moral judgement and altruism were situated in the pre-frontal cortex; but research has not enabled us to go beyond this purely anatomical observation. Since the appearance of the neohumans, the thesis of the genetic origin of moral sentiments has given rise to at least three thousand scientific papers, emanating each time from the most authoritative scientific milieus; but not one has been able yet to cross the barrier of experimental verification. What's more, the Darwinian theories explaining the appearance of altruism by a selective advantage that might result for the whole of the group from it, have been the object of imprecise, multiple and contradictory calculations, which finally sank into confusion and oblivion.

Goodness, compassion, fidelity and altruism therefore remain for us impenetrable mysteries, contained, however, within the limited space of the corporeal exterior of a dog. It is on the solution to this problem that the coming, or not, of the Future Ones depends.

I believe in the coming of the Future Ones.

Play entertains.
Patricia Dürst-Benning

Not only are dogs capable of love, but the sex drive does not seem to pose them any insurmountable problems: when they meet a female in heat, she is ready for penetration; when the contrary is true, they seem to feel neither desire nor a lack of it.

Not only are dogs in themselves a subject of permanent wonderment, but they constitute for humans an excellent *subject of conversation* – international, democratic and consensual. It is thus that I met Harry, a German ex-astrophysicist, accompanied by Truman, his beagle. A peaceful naturist, around sixty years old, Harry devoted his retirement to the observation of the stars – the sky of the region was, he explained to me, exceptionally unpolluted; in the daytime he did some gardening, and a little tidying up. He lived alone with his wife, Hildegarde – and, naturally, Truman: they hadn't had children. It is glaringly obvious that without dogs I would have had nothing to say to this man – even with a dog, as it was, the conversation dragged a little (he invited us to dinner the following Saturday; he lived five hundred metres away, he was our closest neighbour). Fortunately he didn't speak French, any more than I spoke German; the fact of having overcome the *language barrier* (a few phrases in English, a smattering of Spanish) gave us therefore, in the end, the sensation of a *successful evening*, when in fact we had only, for two hours, shouted banalities (he was pretty deaf). After the meal, he asked me if I wanted to observe the rings of Saturn. Of course, of course, I wanted to. Well it was indeed a wonderful spectacle, of natural or divine origin – who knows? – offered for contemplation by man: what more could be said? Hildegarde played the harp, I guess she played it *marvellously*, but frankly I don't know if it's possible to play the harp badly – I mean that the way it's constructed, the instrument has always seemed to me incapable of making anything other than melodious sounds. Two things, I think, stopped me getting angry: for one thing, Isabelle was wise enough to pretend to be tired, and to want to return home early, at least once I'd finished the bottle of kirsch; for another, I had noticed in the Germans' house a complete, bound edition of the works of Teilhard de Chardin. If there is one thing that has always plunged me into sadness or compassion, I mean into a state that excludes all manner of nastiness or irony, it is the existence of Teilhard de Chardin – not only his existence, but the very fact that he has, or could have had, readers, however small the number. In the presence of a reader of Teilhard de Chardin I feel disarmed, nonplussed, ready to break down in tears. At the age of fifteen I had fallen by chance on *The Divine Milieu*, left by a presumably disgusted reader on a bench at the railway station in Étréchy-Chamarande. In the space of a few pages, the book had torn screams from me; out of despair, I had smashed my bicycle pump against the walls of the cellar. Teilhard de Chardin was, of course, what one properly calls a *first-class fanatic*; this didn't make him any less totally depressing. He resembled a little those German Christian Scientists, described by Schopenhauer in his time, who, 'once they have put down retort or scalpel, start philosophising on concepts they received at their first communion'. There was also within him this illusion common to all left-wing Christians, or rather centrist Christians, let's say to Christians contaminated by progressive thought since the Revolution, based on the belief that concupiscence is a venal thing, scarcely important, unfit to turn man away from the path to salvation – that the only true sin is the sin of pride. Where, in me, was concupiscence? Or pride? And was I a long way from salvation? The answers to these questions, it seems to me, were not very difficult; Pascal would never, for example, have stooped to such absurdities: you felt when you read him that the temptations of the flesh were not foreign to him, that libertinage was something that he could have felt; and that if he chose Christ over fornication or cards it was neither through distraction nor incompetence, but because Christ seemed to be definitively more *acid*; in short, he was a *serious* author. If *erotica* had been found on Teilhard de Chardin I believe that would have reassured me, in a sense; but I didn't believe it for a second. What had he ever experienced, who had he ever associated with, this pathetic Teilhard, in order to have such a benign and naive understanding of mankind – while at the same time, in the same country, bastards as considerable as Céline, Sartre or Genet were running wild? Through his dedications, the addresses on his correspondence, one could manage little by little to divine who they were: posh Catholics, those who were more or less aristocratic, and, frequently, Jesuits. Innocents.

'What are you muttering about?' interrupted Isabelle. I then became conscious that we had left the Germans' house, that in fact we were going along the coast, and that we were about to arrive home. She informed me that for two minutes I had been talking to myself, and she had understood almost nothing. I made a summary of the main elements of the problem.

'It's easy to be an optimist . . .' I concluded bitterly, 'it's easy to be optimistic when you are content to have a dog, and haven't had children.'

'You are in the same situation, and frankly that hasn't made you optimistic . . .' she remarked. 'What it is, is that they are old . . .' she continued indulgently. 'When you grow old you need to think of reassuring and gentle things. You need to imagine that something beautiful awaits us in heaven. In fact we train ourselves for death, a little. When we're not too stupid, or too rich.'

I stopped and considered the ocean and the stars. Those stars to which Harry devoted his waking nights, while Hildegarde gave herself up to free classical improvisations on Mozart themes. The music of the spheres, the starry sky; the moral law in my heart. I considered the trip, and what separated me from it; the night was so mild, however, that I placed a hand on Isabelle's backside – I could feel its shape easily, through the light fabric of her summer dress. She stretched out on the dune, took off her panties, and opened her legs. I penetrated her – face to face, for the first time. She looked straight into my eyes. I remember clearly the movements of her pussy, her little cries at the end. I remember it all the better as it was the last time we made love.

A few months passed. Summer returned, then autumn; Isabelle didn't seem unhappy. She played with Fox, and tended the azaleas; I devoted myself to swimming and re-reading Balzac. One evening, while the sun fell behind the residence, she looked me straight in the eye and told me softly: 'You are going to ditch me for someone younger . . .'

I protested that I had never been unfaithful.

'I know . . .' she replied. 'At one moment, I thought you were going to be: that you'd shag one of the sluts who hung around the magazine, then come back to me, shag another slut, and so on. I would have suffered greatly, but perhaps it would have been better like that, at the end of the day.'

'I tried once; the girl turned me down.' I remembered passing the morning in front of the lycée Fénelon. It was between classes, the girls were fourteen, fifteen and all of them more beautiful and desirable than Isabelle, simply because they were younger. No doubt they were themselves engaged in a ferocious narcissistic competition – between those considered cute by boys their age, and those considered insignificant or, frankly, ugly; all the same, for any one of those young bodies a fifty-something would have been ready to risk his reputation, his freedom and even his life. How simple, indeed, existence was! And how devoid it was of any way out! Once, on passing by the magazine's offices to pick up Isabelle, I had chatted up a sort of Belorussian, who was waiting to pose on page eight. The girl had accepted my invitation for a drink, but had asked for five hundred euros for a blowjob; I had declined. At that time, the judicial arsenal aimed at repressing sexual relations with minors was getting tougher; crusades for chemical castration were multiplying. To increase desires to an unbearable level whilst making the fulfilment of them more and more inaccessible: this was the single principle upon which Western society was based. I knew all this, I knew it inside out, in fact I had used it as material for many a sketch; this did not stop me succumbing to the same process. I woke up in the middle of the night, and downed three glasses of water. I imagined the humiliations I would have to endure to seduce any teenage girl; the painfully extracted consent, the girl's shame as we went out together in the street, her hesitation to introduce me to her friends, the carefree way in which she would ditch me for a boy of her age. I imagined all this, over and over again, and I understood that I could not survive it. In no way did I pretend to escape from the laws of nature: the inevitable decrease of the erectile capacities of the penis, the necessity of finding young bodies to jam that mechanism . . . I opened a packet of salami and a bottle of wine. Oh well, I told myself, I will pay; when I reach that point, when I need tight little asses to keep up my erection, then I'll pay. I'll pay the market price. Five hundred euros for a blowjob, who did that Slav girl think she was? It was worth fifty, no more. In the vegetable drawer, I discovered an opened chestnut mousse. What seemed shocking to me, at this stage in my reflection, was not that there were young girls available for money, but that there were some who *are not* available, or only at prohibitive prices; in short, I wanted a regulation of the market.

'That said, you did not pay . . .' Isabelle pointed out. 'And, five years later, you still haven't made your mind up about doing it. No, what's going to happen is that you'll meet a young girl – not a Lolita, rather a girl aged twenty, twenty-five – and you will fall in love with her. She'll be intelligent, a nice girl, no doubt very pretty. A girl who could have been a friend . . .' Night had fallen, and I could no longer make out the features of her face. 'Who could have been me . . .' She spoke calmly, but I did not know how to interpret this calm, there was something rather unusual in the tone of her voice and I had, after all, no experience of the situation, I had never been in love before Isabelle and no woman had been in love with me either, with the exception of Fat Ass – but that was another issue, she was at least fifty-five years old when I met her, at least that's what I believed at the time, she could have been my mother, it was not a question of love on my part, the idea hadn't even crossed my mind. And love without hope is something else, something painful certainly, but something that never generates the same sense of closeness, the same sensitivity to the intonations of the other, even in the one who loves without hope, they are too lost in vain and frenetic expectation to retain even the smallest amount of lucidity, to be able to interpret any signal correctly; in short I was in a situation that had, in my life, no precedent.

'No one can see above himself,' writes Schopenhauer to make us understand the impossibility of an exchange of ideas between two individuals of too different an intellectual level. At that moment, obviously, Isabelle could see *above me*; I had the prudence to stay quiet. After all, she told me, I might just as easily not meet the girl; given the thinness of my social relations, this was the most likely scenario.

She continued to buy French newspapers, although not that often, not more than once a week, and from time to time she would hand me an article with a sniff of contempt. It was around this time that the French media began a big campaign to promote friendship, probably launched by *Le Nouvel Observateur*. 'Love can break your heart, friendship never will', that was more or less the theme of the articles. I didn't understand why they were interested in spouting such absurdities; Isabelle explained that it was an old chestnut, that we were simply dealing with an annual variation on the theme: 'How to break up and remain good friends'. According to her, this would last another four or five years before we could admit that the passage from love to friendship, i.e. from a strong feeling to a weak one, was patently the prelude to the disappearance of all feeling – on the historical level, I mean, for on the individual one, indifference was by far the most favourable situation: once love had broken down, it was generally not transformed into indifference, and even less frequently into friendship. On the basis of this remark, I laid the foundations of a script entitled *Two Flies Later*, which was to constitute the apex – and end – of my cinematic career. My agent was delighted to learn that I was getting back to work – two and a half years' absence was a long time. He was less delighted when he held the finished product in his hands. I had not hidden from him the fact that it was a film script, which I aimed to produce and act in myself; that wasn't the problem, on the contrary he said, people have been waiting for a long time, it's good they're going to be surprised, it could have cult status. The content, however . . . Frankly, was I not going a bit too far?

The film related the life of a man whose favourite pastime was killing flies with an elastic band (hence the title); in general, he missed them – you were, however, talking about a three-hour long feature. The second-favourite pastime of this cultivated man, a great reader of Pierre Louÿs, was having his cock sucked by little prepubescent girls – well, fourteen at the oldest; he had more success with this than with the flies.

Contrary to what has since been repeated by media hirelings, this film was not a monumental flop; it was even a triumph in certain foreign countries, and made a considerable profit in France, without, however, reaching the numbers that one could have expected, given the until then vertiginous rise of my career; that's all.

Its failure with the critics, on the other hand, was real; to this day I still think it was undeserved. 'An undistinguished knockabout farce', was the headline in *Le Monde*, differentiating itself from its more moralistic peers, who raised, especially in their editorials, the question of banning it. It was certainly a comedy, and most of the gags were very obvious, if not vulgar; but there were certain passages of dialogue, in certain scenes, which seem to me, with hindsight, to be the best thing I ever produced. In particular in Corsica, in the long sequence filmed on the slopes of Bavella, where the hero (played by me) shows the little Aurore (nine years old), whom he has just conquered over a Disney tea at Marineland in Bonifacio, around his second home.

'There's no point in living in Corsica,' she hurled insolently, 'if it means living on a bend in the road.'

'To see cars pass,' he (I) replied, 'is already to live a little.'

No one had laughed; neither during the screen test, nor at the comic film festival in Montbazon. And yet, and yet, I told myself, never had I reached such heights. Could Shakespeare himself have produced such dialogue? Could he have even imagined it, the sad git?

Beyond the hackneyed subject of paedophilia, this film strove to be a vigorous plea against *friendship*, and more generally against all *non-sexual* relationships. What in fact could two men *talk about*, beyond a certain age? What reason could two men find for being together, except, of course, in the case of a conflict of interests, or of some common project (overthrowing a government, building a motorway, writing a script for a cartoon, exterminating the Jews)? After a certain age (I am talking about men of a certain level of intelligence, not aged brutes), it's quite obvious that *everything has been said and done.* How could a project as intrinsically empty as two men *spending some time together* lead to anything other than boredom, annoyance and, at the end of the day, outright hostility? Whilst between a man and a woman there still remained, despite everything, something: a little bit of attraction, a little bit of hope, a little bit of a dream. Speech, which was basically designed for controversy and disagreement, was still scarred by its warlike origins. Speech destroys, separates, and when it is all that remains between a man and a woman then you can consider the relationship over. When, however, it is accompanied, softened and in some way sanctified by caresses, speech itself can take on a completely different meaning, one that is less dramatic but more profound, that of a detached intellectual counterpoint, free and uninvolved in immediate issues.

Launching an attack not only on friendship, but on all social relationships as soon as they are unaccompanied by physical contact, this film thus constituted – only the magazine *Slut Zone* had the perspicacity to notice this – an indirect eulogy to bisexuality, if not hermaphroditism. All in all, I was harking back to the Ancient Greeks. When you get old, you always hark back to the Ancient Greeks.

The number of human life stories is 6174, which corresponds to Kapreker's first constant. Whether they come from men or women, from Europe or Asia, America or Africa, whether they are complete or not, all agree on one point, and one point only: the unbearable nature of the mental suffering caused by old age.

It is no doubt Bruno1, with his brutal succinctness, who gives us its most striking image when he describes himself as 'full of a young man's desires, with the body of an old man'; but I repeat, all the testimonies concur, whether it is that of Daniel1, my distant predecessor, or of Rachid1, Paul1, John1, Felicity1, or that particularly poignant one of Esperanza1. At no moment in human history does growing old seem to have been a pleasure cruise; but, in the years preceding the disappearance of the species, it had manifestly become atrocious to the point where the level of voluntary deaths, prudishly renamed *departures* by the public-health bodies, was nearing 100 per cent, and the average age of departure, estimated at sixty across the entire globe, was falling towards fifty in the most developed countries.

This figure was the result of a long evolution, scarcely begun at the time of Daniel1, when the average age at death was much higher, and suicide by old people was still infrequent. The now-ugly, deteriorated bodies of the elderly were, however, already the object of unanimous disgust, and it was undoubtedly the heatwave of summer 2003, which was particularly deadly in France, that provoked the first consciousness of the phenomenon. 'The Death March of the Elderly' was the headline in *Libération* on the day after the first figures became known – more than ten thousand people, in the space of two weeks, had died in the country; some had died alone in their apartments, others in hospital or in retirement homes, but all had essentially died because of a lack of care. In the weeks that followed, that same newspaper published a series of atrocious reports, illustrated with photos that were reminiscent of concentration camps, relating the agony of old people crammed into communal rooms, naked on their beds, in nappies, moaning all day without anyone coming to rehydrate them or even to give them a glass of water; describing the rounds made by nurses unable to contact the families who were on holiday, regularly gathering up the corpses to make space for new arrivals. 'Scenes unworthy of a modern country', wrote the journalist without realising that they were in fact the proof that France was *becoming* a modern country, that only an authentically modern country was capable of treating old people purely as rubbish, and that such contempt for one's ancestors would have been inconceivable in Africa, or in a traditional Asian country.

The obligatory indignation aroused by these images quickly faded, and the development of active euthanasia – or, increasingly often, active voluntary euthanasia – would, in the course of the following decades, solve the problem.

It was recommended to humans, wherever possible, that they end up with a *complete* life story, before they died, in accordance with the belief, widespread at the time, that the last moments of life might be accompanied by some kind of *revelation*. The example cited most often was that of Marcel Proust, whose first reflex upon sensing death's approach, was to rush to the manuscript of *In Remembrance of Things Past* in order to note his impressions of dying.

Very few, in practice, had this courage.

All in all, Barnaby, we would need a powerful ship, with a
thrust of three hundred kilotons. Then we could escape the
earth's gravity and make for the satellites of Jupiter.
                                                    Captain Clark

Preparation, filming, post-production, a limited promotional tour
(*Two Flies Later* had been released simultaneously in most of the
European capitals, but I restricted myself to France and Germany):
in all, I had stayed away from home for just over a year. The first
surprise awaited me at Almeria airport: a compact group of around
fifty people, massed behind the barriers at the exit, were brandishing diaries, T-shirts and posters of the film. I already knew this
much from the early viewing figures: the film, which had modest
takings in Paris, had been a hit in Madrid – as well as, I might add,
in London, Rome and Berlin; I had become a star in Europe.

Once the group had dispersed, I noticed Isabelle, on a seat at the
back of the arrivals hall. That too was a shock. Dressed in trousers
and a shapeless T-shirt, she screwed up her eyes in my direction
with a mixture of fear and shame. When I was a few metres away
from her she began to cry, the tears streamed down her cheeks
without her trying to wipe them away. She had put on at least
twenty kilos. Even her face, this time, had not been spared: puffy
and blotchy, her hair greasy and unkempt, she looked awful.

Obviously Fox was overjoyed, jumped in the air, licked my face
for a good quarter of an hour; I sensed easily that that was not going
to be enough. She refused to undress in my presence, and reappeared dressed in a flannelette tracksuit that she wore to bed. In
the taxi from the airport, we did not exchange a word. Empty
bottles of Cointreau were scattered on the bedroom floor; that said,
the house had been tidied.

In the course of my career, I had blethered enough about the opposition between eroticism and tenderness, and I had played the roles of all the characters: the girl who goes to gang-bangs and yet seeks a very chaste, refined and sisterly relationship with the true love of her life; the half-impotent simpleton who accepts her; the gang-banger who takes advantage. Consummation, forgetting, misery. I had made entire theatres laugh their heads off with these kinds of themes; and they had earned me considerable sums of money. Nevertheless, this time they concerned me directly, and this opposition between eroticism and tenderness appeared to me as it really is: one of the worst examples of bullshit of our time, one of those that signs, definitively, the death warrant of civilisation. 'The laughing's over, you little bugger . . .' I repeated to myself with disturbing gaiety (because at that time the sentence turned over and over in my head, I couldn't stop it, eighteen tablets of Atarax made no difference, and I ended up resorting to a Pastis-Tranxene cock-tail). 'But the one who loves someone for her beauty, does he love her? No: for the pox, which will kill beauty without killing the person, will make him stop loving her.' Pascal did not know Cointreau. It is also true that, living in a time when bodies were less on show, he overestimated the importance of the beauty of the face. The worst part of it is that it was not her beauty, in the first place, that I had found attractive in Isabelle: intelligent women have always turned me on. To tell the truth, intelligence is not very useful in sexual intercourse, and it serves really only one purpose: to know at which moment you should put your hand on a man's cock in a public place. All men like this, it's the monkey's sense of domina-tion, residual traces of that kind of thing, and it would be stupid not to realise it; the only issue is the choice of the time, and the place. Some men prefer that the indecent gesture is witnessed by a woman; others, probably those who are a little gay or very domi-nant, prefer it to be another man; others still find nothing pleases them as much as a couple giving them a complicit look. Some prefer trains, others swimming pools, others nightclubs or bars; an intelli-gent woman knows this. Anyway, I still had good memories of being with Isabelle. At the end of each night I could conjure up sweeter and quasi-nostalgic thoughts; at this point, at my side, she would be snoring like a cow. Dawn approached, and I realised that these memories, also, would vanish quite quickly; it was then that I opted for the Pastis-Tranxene cocktail.

On the practical level, there was no immediate problem: we had seventeen bedrooms. I moved into one of those overlooking the cliffs and the sea; Isabelle, apparently, preferred to contemplate inland. Fox went from room to room, it amused him a lot; he suffered no more from it than a child from the divorce of his parents, rather less I'd say.

Could things continue in this way for a long time? Well, unfortunately, yes. During my absence, I had received seven hundred and thirty-two faxes (and I must acknowledge, there too, that Isabelle had regularly changed the paper tray); I could spend the rest of my days running from one festival invitation to the next. From time to time, I'd stop by: a little caress for Fox, a little bit of Tranxene, and Bob's your uncle. For the moment, however, I was in need of a complete rest. I therefore went to the beach, on my own, obviously – I wanked a little on the terrace whilst ogling naked teenage girls (I too had bought a telescope, but it wasn't for looking at the stars, ha ha ha); in short, I was muddling through. I muddled more or less well; although, all the same, I almost threw myself off the cliff three times in two weeks.

I revisited Harry, and he was on form; Truman, however, had aged. We were invited again to dinner, this time in the company of a Belgian couple who had just settled in the region. Harry had introduced the man as a *Belgian philosopher*. In reality, after completing his doctorate in philosophy, he had passed the civil service exam, then led the dreary life of a tax inspector (with conviction, however, for, as a socialist supporter, he believed in the benefits of high taxation). He had published, here and there, a few philosophical articles in journals of a materialist bent. His wife, a sort of gnome with short white hair, had also spent her life as a tax inspector. Oddly, she believed in astrology, and insisted on doing my horoscope. I was Pisces with Gemini in the ascendant, but for all I fucking cared I could well have been Poodle with Mechanical Digger in the ascendant, ha ha ha. This witty remark won me the esteem of the philosopher, who liked to smirk at his wife's fads – they had been married for thirty-three years. He, for his own part, had always fought obscurantism; he came from a very Catholic family, and this, he assured me, with a little quaver in his voice, had been a great obstacle to his sexual development. 'Who *are* these people? Who *are* these people?' I repeated to myself in despair as I fiddled with my herrings. (When he became nostalgic for his native Mecklenburg, Harry bought his food in a German supermarket in Almeria.) Evidently, the two gnomes had not had any sex life, other than, perhaps, one that was vaguely procreative (subsequent events, in fact, were to reveal that they had begotten a son); they simply did not belong to that group of people who have access to sexuality. This did not prevent them from becoming indignant, criticising the pope, bemoaning an AIDS virus that they would never have the chance to catch; all this made me feel like dying, but I restrained myself.

Fortunately Harry intervened, and the conversation was raised to more transcendent subjects (the stars, infinity, etc.), which allowed me to tuck into my plate of sausages without trembling. Naturally, there too the materialist and the Teilhardian were in disagreement – I became conscious at that moment that they must have met up with each other often, drawing pleasure from this exchange, and that this could go on for thirty years, to their mutual satisfaction. We got on to the subject of death. After having fought all his life for a sexual liberation he had never experienced, Robert the Belgian now fought for euthanasia – which he had, on the contrary, every chance of experiencing. 'And the soul? What about the soul?' gasped Harry. All in all, their little double-act was running smoothly; Truman fell asleep at about the same time as me.

Hildegarde's harp brought everyone into harmony. Ah yes, music; especially when the volume is down. There wasn't even material here for a sketch, I told myself. I could no longer laugh at the idiotic militants of immorality, at the kind of remark: 'It is, all the same, more pleasant to be virtuous when you have access to vice,' no I couldn't. Nor could I laugh any more at the terrible distress of cellulite-ridden fifty-something women, and their unful-filled desire for passionate love; nor at the handicapped child they had succeeded in procreating by half raping an autistic man ('David is my sunshine'). All in all, I couldn't laugh at anything any more; I had reached the end of my career, that was clear.

There was no love-making, that evening, as we went home through the dunes. We had to put an end to it all, however, and a few days later Isabelle announced her decision to leave. 'I don't want to be a burden,' she said. 'I wish you all the happiness you deserve,' she said as well – and I still wonder to this day if it was a bitchy remark.

'What are you going to do?' I asked.

'Go back to my mother's, I suppose . . . it's what women generally do in my situation, no?'

It was the only moment, the only one, when she let a little bitterness show. I knew that her father had left her mother, ten years before, for a younger woman; the phenomenon was certainly becoming more widespread, but of course, there was nothing new about it.

We behaved like a civilised couple. In all, I had earned forty-two million euros. Isabelle was happy with half of our assets, and she did not demand any compensation. This still added up to seven million euros; she wouldn't be joining the ranks of the poor.

'You could do a bit of sex tourism . . .' I proposed. 'In Cuba, there are some very nice men.'

She smiled and nodded. 'They prefer Soviet poofters . . .' she said light-heartedly, furtively imitating the style of my glory days. Then she became serious again and looked me straight in the eye (it was a very still morning; the sea was blue and slack).

'Have you still not fucked any whores?' she asked.

'No.'

'Well, me neither. So,' she continued, 'you haven't fucked for two years?'

'No.'

'Well, me neither.'

Oh, we were little darlings, sentimental little darlings; and it was going to kill us.

*

There was still the last morning, and the last walk; the sea was as blue as always, the cliffs just as black, and Fox trotting along beside us. 'I'm taking him,' Isabelle had said abruptly. 'It's to be expected, he's been with me longer; but you can have him when you want.' As civilised as you could get.

Everything was already packed, the removal lorry was going to pass by the following day to transport her things to Biarritz – although a retired schoolteacher, her mother had bizarrely chosen to end her days in this region full of ultra-rich bourgeois women who had nothing but contempt for her.

We waited together another fifteen minutes for the taxi that would take her to the airport. 'Oh, life will pass quickly . . .' she said. It seemed to me that she was speaking mostly to herself; I said nothing in reply. Once she was in the taxi, she gave me a last wave with her hand. Yes; now, things were going to be very calm.

It is not general practice to shorten human life stories, whatever the repugnance or boredom they may inspire in us. It is precisely this repugnance and boredom that we must cultivate, in order to distinguish ourselves from the species. It is on this condition, the Supreme Sister warns us, that the coming of the Future Ones will be made possible.

If I am deviating here from this rule, in accordance with tradition uninterrupted since Daniel17, it is because the following ninety pages of the manuscript of Daniel1 have been made completely obsolete by scientific development.[1] At the time when Daniel1 was alive, male impotence was often attributed to psychological causes; we know today that it was essentially a hormonal phenomenon, in which the psychological causes played only a small, and always reversible, part.

A tormented meditation on the decline of virility, intercut with the at once pornographic and depressing description of failed attempts with various Andalusian prostitutes, these ninety pages contain, however, a lesson perfectly summed up for us by Daniel17 in the following lines, which I have extracted from his commentary:

> The ageing of the human female encompassed, in fact, the degradation of such a large number of characteristics, as aesthetic as they were functional, that it is very difficult to determine which was the most painful, and it is almost impossible, in the majority of cases, to cite a single cause behind the choice of suicide.
>
> The situation seems to be very different in the case of the human male. Subject to aesthetic and functional degradations as much as, if

---

[1] However, the curious reader will be able to find these pages in the annex to the commentary by Daniel17, at the same IP address.

not more than, the female, he nevertheless managed to overcome them for as long as the erectile capacities of the penis were maintained. When these disappeared forever, suicide generally followed within two weeks.

It is no doubt this difference that explains a curious statistical observation, already made by Daniel3: whilst in the last generations of the human species, the average age for departure was 54.1 years among women, it rose to 63.2 years among men.

DANIEL 1, 9

What you call dreaming is very real for the warrior.
André Bercoff

I sold the Bentley, it reminded me too much of Isabelle, and its ostentation was beginning to annoy me, in order to buy a Mercedes 600 SL – a car that in reality was just as expensive, but more discreet. All the rich Spaniards drove Mercedes – they weren't snobs, the Spanish, they showed off in a conventional way; and also a cabriolet is better for the babes – known locally as *chicas*, a word I liked. The classified ads in *Voz de Almeria* were explicit: *piel dorada, culito melocotón, guapisima, boca supersensual, labios expertos, muy simpática, complaciente.* A very beautiful and expressive language, naturally suited to poetry – you can rhyme almost everything. There were brothel bars, as well, for those who had difficulty visualising the descriptions. Physically, the girls were in good shape, they corresponded to the wording of the ad, and they kept to the advertised price; as for the rest, well . . . They turned the television or CD player up too loud, turned the light down to a minimum, in other words they tried to cut themselves off; they hadn't the vocation for it, that was clear. Obviously, you could *oblige* them to turn the volume down and turn the lights up; after all, they expected a tip, and every little thing counts. There are certainly people who get off on this kind of intercourse, and I could easily imagine the type; but I was quite simply not one of them. What's more, most of the girls were Romanian, Belorussian and Ukrainian, in other words from one of those absurd countries that emerged from the implosion of the Eastern bloc; and one cannot say that Communism has particularly fostered sentimentality in human relations; it is, on the whole, *brutality* that is predominant among the ex-Communists – in comparison, Balzacian society, which emerged from the decomposition of royalty, seems a miracle of charity and gentleness. It is good to distrust doctrines preaching fraternity.

It was only after Isabelle left that I truly discovered the *world of men*, in the course of pathetic wanderings along the virtually deserted motorways of central and southern Spain. Except for the weekends and the start of the holidays, when you encounter families and couples, the motorways are an almost exclusively male universe, populated by salesmen and lorry drivers, a sad and violent world where the only publications available are porn mags and magazines for car maintenance, where the plastic revolving stand presenting a choice of DVDs under the title *Tu mejor peliculas* generally only enables you to complete your collection of *Dirty Debutantes*. This universe is not much talked about, and it's true that there's not much to say about it; no new form of behaviour is experimented with in it, it can't provide any valuable fodder for colour supplements, in short it is a little-known world, and it gains nothing from being so. I formed no virile friendship, and more generally I felt close to no one during those few weeks, but that wasn't a problem, in this universe no one is close to anyone, and even the smutty complicity of the tired waitresses who had pressed their sagging breasts into a 'Naughty Girl' T-shirt could, I knew, only lead to copulation that came at a price, and was always too brief. I could, if push came to shove, start a fight with a heavy-goods lorry driver and get my teeth smashed in in a parking lot, amid the gasoline fumes; that was basically the only possibility of adventure on offer in this universe. I lived in this way for a little more than two months, I burned thousands of euros on glasses of French champagne for mindless Romanian girls who, after all that, would still refuse, ten minutes later, to suck me off without a condom. It was on the Autovia Mediterraneo, precisely at the exit for Totana Sur, that I decided to put an end to this dismal ride. I had parked my car in the last available space in the parking lot of the hotel and restaurant Los Camioneros, where I went in to have a beer; the atmosphere inside was exactly what I'd come to expect over the previous weeks, and I stayed for ten minutes without really fixing my attention on anything, only conscious of a general, muffled weariness that made my movements more uncertain and tired, and of a certain gastric heaviness. On leaving I realised that a carelessly parked Chevrolet Corvette was blocking in my car. The prospect of returning to the bar and searching for the owner was enough to plunge me into a discouraged gloom; I leaned back against a concrete wall, trying to get the whole picture of the situation, but mostly smoking cigarettes. Out of all the sports cars available on the market, the Chevrolet Corvette, with its uselessly and aggressively virile lines, with its absence of true mechanical nobility wedded to its overall modest price, is undoubtedly the one that corresponds best to the notion of *pimpmobile*; what sort of sordid Andalusian macho type was I going to bump into? Like all individuals of his kind, the man undoubtedly had a solid understanding of cars, and was therefore perfectly poised to recognise that my car, being more discreet than his, cost three times more. To the act of virile self-assertion he had made by parking in such a way as to block me in, was therefore added, undoubtedly, an undercurrent of social hatred, and I was right to fear the worst. It took me three-quarters of an hour, and half a packet of Camels, to pluck up the courage to return to the bar.

I immediately identified the individual, slouched at the end of the counter in front of a saucer of peanuts, letting his beer go warm while he shot, from time to time, desperate looks at the giant television screen where girls in hot-pants gyrated their pelvises to a fairly slow groove; it was obviously a *foam party*, the outline of the girls' buttocks became clearer and clearer, as they were moulded by the hot-pants, and the man's despair was increasing. He was small, pot-bellied and bald, doubtless around fifty years old, dressed in a jacket and tie, and a wave of sad compassion crashed over me; his Chevrolet Corvette was certainly not going to help him to *pick up babes*, it would just make him look, at best, like a *fat old fart*, and I found myself admiring the quotidian courage that made it possible, despite everything, for him to drive a Chevrolet Corvette. How could a suitably young and sexy girl do anything other than *snigger* at the sight of that little man getting out of his Chevrolet Corvette? I had to put a stop to this, despite everything, and I went over to him with all the smiley indulgence I could muster. As I had feared, he was combative at first, and tried to get the waitress to act as a witness – she didn't even raise her eyes from the sink where she was washing glasses. Then he gave me a second look, and what he saw must have calmed him down – I myself felt so old, weary, unhappy and mediocre: for obscure reasons, he must have concluded that the owner of the Mercedes SL was also a loser, almost a companion in misfortune, and he tried then to establish a male bond, offered me a beer, then a second one, and proposed that we end the evening at the New Orleans. To get out of it, I pretended that I still had a long road ahead of me – it is an argument that men generally respect. I was in reality less than fifty kilometres from my house, but I had just realised that I might as well continue my *road movie* at home.

In fact, there was a motorway a few kilometres from my residence, and beside it there was a similar kind of establishment. After leaving Diamond Nights, I drove, as usual, across the beach of Rodalquilar. My Mercedes 600 SL coupé skimmed over the sand; I activated the door-opening mechanism: in twenty-two seconds it transformed into a cabriolet. It was a splendid beach, almost completely deserted, of a geometrical flatness, with immaculate sand, and surrounded by cliffs with strikingly black vertical faces; a man graced with a real artistic temperament would undoubtedly have been able to make the most of this solitude, this beauty. For my part, I felt myself faced with infinity like a flea on a sheet of flypaper. I couldn't give a fuck about this beauty, this geological transcendence, in fact I even found it all vaguely menacing. 'The world is not a panorama,' notes Schopenhauer, dryly. I had probably placed too much importance on sexuality, in fact, that's indisputable; but the only place in the world where I felt good was snug in the arms of a woman, snug inside her vagina; and at my age I saw no reason for that to change. The existence of the pussy was already in itself a blessing, I told myself, the simple fact that I could be in there, and feel good, already constituted sufficient reason for prolonging this dismal journey. Others hadn't had this chance. 'The truth is that nothing could suit me on this Earth,' noted Kleist in his diary just before he committed suicide on the banks of the Wannsee. I often thought of Kleist, in those days; some of his verse had been engraved on his tomb:

Nun
O Unsterblichkeit
Bist du ganz mein.

I had gone there in February, I had made the pilgrimage. There was twenty centimetres of snow, naked, black branches twisted beneath the grey sky, the atmosphere seemed filled with creeping movements. Every day, a fresh bouquet was placed on his grave; I had never met the person who did this. Goethe had come across Schopenhauer, then Kleist, without really understanding them; pessimistic Prussians, that's what he must have thought, in both cases. The Italian poems of Goethe have always made me puke. Did you have to be born under a completely grey sky to understand? I didn't think so; the sky was a brilliant blue, and no vegetation crept over the cliffs of Carboneras; this didn't make much difference. No, I was certainly not exaggerating the importance of woman. And what's more, coupling . . . geometrical perfection.

I had told Harry that Isabelle was 'on her travels'; that was already six months ago, but he didn't show surprise, and he seemed to have forgotten she even existed; basically, I think he wasn't very interested in human beings. I attended another debate with Robert the Belgian, under almost the same conditions as the first; then a third, but this time the Belgians were flanked by their son Patrick, who had come to spend a week's holiday, and his girlfriend Fadiah, a stunning negress. Patrick looked about forty-five and he worked in a bank in Luxemburg. I immediately formed a good impression of him, in any case he seemed less stupid than his parents – I learned later that he had important responsibilities, and that a lot of money was channelled through him. As for Fadiah, she couldn't be more than twenty-five, and with her it was difficult to go beyond the level of strict erotic judgement; but, this didn't seem to bother her much. A white bandeau partially covered her breasts, she wore a tight miniskirt, and that was about all; that said, I didn't get a hard-on.

The couple were Elohimites, that is to say they belonged to a sect that worshipped the Elohim, extraterrestrial creatures responsible for the creation of mankind, and they were waiting for their return. I had never heard this kind of nonsense before, so I listened, during dinner, with a bit of attention. Essentially, according to them, everything boiled down to an error of transcription in the Book of Genesis: the creator, Elohi, was not to be taken in the singular, but in the plural. There was nothing divine or supernatural about our creators; they were simply material beings, more evolved than us, who had learned how to master space travel and the creation of life; they had also defeated ageing and death, and asked only to share their secret with the most deserving among us. Ah ha, I said to myself; there's the carrot.

In order for the Elohim to return, and reveal to us how to escape death, we (that is to say mankind) had first to build an embassy for them. Not a palace of crystal with walls of hyacinth and beryl, no, no, something simple, modern and nice – suitably comfortable; the prophet believed he knew they liked jacuzzis (for there was a prophet, who came from Clermont-Ferrand). For the location of the embassy he had thought first, quite classically, of Jerusalem; but there were some problems, a few neighbourly disputes, in short it wasn't the right moment. An animated discussion with a rabbi from the Messiahs Commission (an Israeli body that specialised in this kind of case) had given him another lead. The Jews, obviously, were badly situated. When Israel was established, the Jews' thoughts had turned to Palestine, but also to other places like Texas or Uganda – which were also a bit dangerous, but not quite as much; in short, the rabbi concluded good-naturedly, they shouldn't focus too much on the geographical aspects. God is everywhere, he exclaimed, His presence fills the Universe (I mean, he corrected himself, in your case the Elohim).

In fact the prophet thought not: the Elohim were situated on the planet of the Elohim, and from time to time they travelled, that's all; but he abstained from entering into a new geographical con-troversy, for the conversation had edified him. If the Elohim had travelled as far as Clermont-Ferrand, he told himself, there had to be a reason for it, probably linked to the geological character of the place; volcanic zones pulsate a lot, everyone knows that. That's why, Patrick told me, the prophet had, after a brief enquiry, opted for the island of Lanzarote, in the Canary islands. The land was bought, all that remained was for construction to begin.

Was he, by any chance, suggesting to me that this was the moment to invest? No, no, he reassured me, from this point of view we're clear, the subscriptions are minimal, and anyone can come and verify the accounts when they want to. If you knew what I do, in Luxemburg, sometimes, for other clients . . . no really, if there is one point on which we can't be attacked it is this.

On finishing my glass of kirsch, I told myself that Patrick had opted for an original synthesis of the materialist convictions of his dad and the astral fads of his mum. There was then the traditional harp 'n' stars session. 'Waaooh! Wicked! . . .' exclaimed Fadiah on seeing the rings of Saturn, before stretching out on her deckchair. Indeed, indeed, the region's sky was very pure. Turning round to grab the bottle of kirsch, I saw that she had spread her thighs, and it seemed in the darkness that her hand was thrust up under her skirt. A little later, I heard her panting. So, while observing the stars, Harry thought of Christ Omega; Robert the Belgian thought of I know not what, perhaps helium in fusion, or intestinal problems; as for Fadiah, she was masturbating. To each according to their character.

A kind of joy descends from the physical world. I am attached to the Earth.

The rocks, completely black, today plunge through vertical stages to a depth of three thousand metres. This vision, which terrifies the savages, inspires no terror in me. I know that there is no monster hidden in the abyss; there is only fire, the original fire.

The melting of the ice occurred at the end of the First Decrease, and reduced the population of the planet from fourteen billion to seven hundred million.

The Second Decrease was more gradual; it happened throughout the whole of the Great Drying Up, and continues to this day.

The Third Decrease will be definitive; it is yet to come.

No one knows the cause of the Great Drying Up, or at least its efficient cause. It has, of course, been demonstrated that it was owing to the modification of the axis of rotation of the Earth on the plane of its orbit; but the event is considered highly improbable, in quantum terms.

The Great Drying Up was a necessary parable, teaches the Supreme Sister; a theological condition for the Return of the Humid.

The duration of the Great Drying Up will be long, the Supreme Sister also teaches.

The Return of the Humid will be the sign of the coming of the Future Ones.

God exists. I walked into him.
Anon

From my first stay with the Very Healthy Ones, I recall in particular a ski-lift in the mist. The summer course was being held in Herzegovina, or in some such region, known primarily for the conflicts that had once drenched it in blood. It was, however, very pretty: the chalets, the inn, all made of dark wood, with red-and-white checked curtains, and heads of boars and stags decorating the walls, all of it done with a Central European kitsch that I've always liked. 'Ach, war, the madness of men, Gross Misfortune . . .' I mentally repeated to myself, imitating involuntarily the intonation of Francis Blanche. For a long time I had been the victim of a sort of mental echolalia, which in my case did not apply to famous songs, but to the phrases used by classic comedians: when, for example, I began to hear Francis Blanche repeating: 'KOL-LOS-SAL SHOOT-ING!' as he does in *Babette Goes off to War* I had a lot of difficulty getting it out my head, I had to make an enormous effort. With de Funès, it was even worse: his vocal shifts, his funny expressions, his gestures, I suffered them for hours at a time, it was as if I were possessed.

Basically I had worked hard, I told myself, I had spent my life working endlessly. The actors I knew at the age of twenty had had no success, it's true, most had even completely given up the trade, but it must also be said that they had done fuck-all, they had spent their time drinking in bars or trendy clubs. During this time I was rehearsing, alone in my bedroom, I spent hours on each intonation and each gesture; and I *wrote* my sketches as well, I really wrote them, it took me years before that became easy. If I worked so hard, it was probably because I wouldn't actually have been capable of enjoying myself; I wouldn't have been very at ease in the bars and trendy clubs, at the parties organised by couturiers, in the VIP sections: with my ordinary physique and my introverted temperament, I had, from the outset, very little chance of being *the life of the party*. So I worked, for want of anything else; and I have had my revenge. In my youth, basically, I was in the same state of mind as Ophélie Winter when she ruminated, thinking about her entourage: 'Have a good laugh, my little cunts. Later I'll be the one on the podium and I'll give you all the finger.' She had declared that in an interview with *20 Ans*.

I had to stop thinking about *20 Ans*, I also had to stop thinking about Isabelle; I had to stop thinking about almost everything. I stared at the moist, green slopes, I tried to see only the mist – mist had always helped me. Ski-lifts in the mist. Thus, between ethnic wars, they found the means to go ski-ing – you have to work your abductors, I said to myself, and I outlined a sketch in which two torturers exchanged fitness tips in a weights room in Zagreb. It was over the top, I couldn't help it: I was a clown, I would remain a clown and I would die like a clown – with hate, and in convulsions.

If I privately referred to the Elohimites as the Very Healthy Ones, it was because they were, in fact, very healthy. They did not want to grow old; and with this goal in mind, they forbade themselves from smoking, and took anti-radicals and other such things that you generally find in parapharmacy shops. Drugs were rather frowned upon. Alcohol was permitted, in the form of red wine – limited to two glasses a day. They were slightly *Cretan Diet*, if you like. These instructions, insisted the prophet, had no moral significance. Health was the objective. All that was healthy, and therefore, in particular, all that was sexual, was permitted. You could see this at once, on looking at the website and in the brochures: a pleasant and slightly insipid erotic kitsch, sort of pre-Raphaelite with big tits, *à la* Walter Girotto. Male or female homosexuality was also present in the illustrations, in smaller doses: strictly heterosexual himself, the prophet had nothing of the homophobe about him. The ass, the cunt: according to the prophet, everything was good. He was there in person, all dressed in white, to greet me with an outstretched hand at Zwork airport. I was their first real VIP, and he had wanted to make an effort. Up until then, they had only had one very minor VIP, a Frenchman as well, an artist called Vincent Grelsamer. He'd had, nonetheless, an exhibition at the Pompidou Centre – of course, even Bernard Branxène has had an exhibition at the Pompidou Centre. So he was a half-pint VIP, a Plastic Arts VIP. A nice boy, by the way. And, I was immediately convinced on seeing him, probably a good artist. He had a sharp, intelligent face, and a strangely intense, almost mystical look in his eyes; that said, he expressed himself normally, with intelligence, weighing his words. I had no idea what he did, whether it was video art, installations or what, but you got the feeling that this guy *really* worked. We were the only two declared smokers – which, in addition to our VIP status, brought us closer. We did not, however, go as far as smoking in the presence of the prophet; but, from time to time, during the lectures, we went outside for a quick smoke, which was quite soon tacitly accepted. Ah, VIPness.

I hardly had time to settle in, and make myself an instant coffee, before the first lecture began. To attend the 'teachings' you were supposed to put on, over your usual clothes, a long white tunic. I obviously felt a little ridiculous when I pulled the thing on, but it didn't take long for the point of the accoutrement to become clear to me. The layout of the hotel was very complex, with glass passages linking the buildings, half-levels and underground galleries, all with signs written in a bizarre language that was vaguely reminiscent of Welsh, which in any case I didn't understand a word of, so much so that it took me half an hour to find my way back. During this lapse of time, I came across about twenty people who were making their way, like me, down the deserted corridors and who were wearing, like me, long white tunics. On arriving in the lecture room, I had the impression that I'd started off on a spiritual path – even though this word had never made the slightest sense to me. It made no sense, but there I was. You could indeed judge me by my appearance.

The day's orator was a very tall, thin, bald guy, impressively serious – when he tried to be funny, it was quite frightening. I called him

Knowall, and he was in fact a professor of neurology at a Canadian university. To my great surprise, what he had to say was interesting, and even fascinating in places. The human mind, he explained, developed by the creation and progressive chemical reinforcement of neural networks of variable length, from two to fifty neurones, if not more. As a human brain contained several billion neurones, the number of combinations, and therefore of possible circuits, was staggering – it went way beyond, for example, the number of molecules in the universe.

The number of circuits used varied greatly from one individual to the next, which sufficed, according to him, to explain the countless gradations between idiocy and genius. But, even more remarkably, a frequently used neuronal circuit became, as a result of ionic accumulations, easier and easier to use – there was, in short, progressive self-reinforcement, and that applied to everything: ideas, addictions and moods. The phenomenon was proven for individual psychological reactions as well as for social relations: to conscientise mental blocks only reinforced them; trying to settle a conflict between two people generally made it insoluble. Knowall then launched a pitiless attack on Freudian theory, which was not only based on no consistent physiological foundations, but also led to dramatic results that were directly contrary to the chosen goal. On the screen behind him, the succession of diagrams that had punctuated his speech stopped and was replaced by a brief and poignant documentary devoted to the mental – and sometimes unbearable – sufferings of Vietnam veterans. They couldn't forget, had nightmares every night, could no longer even drive or cross the street without assistance, they lived constantly in fear and it seemed impossible for them to re-adapt to a normal social life. It focused then on the case of a stooped, wrinkled man who had only a thin crown of dishevelled red hair and who seemed to be truly reduced to a wreck: he trembled constantly, could no longer leave his house and was in need of permanent medical assistance; and he suffered, suffered without end. In the cupboard of his dining room he kept a little jar, filled with soil from Vietnam; every time he opened the cupboard and took out the jar, he broke down in tears.

'Stop,' said Knowall. 'Stop.' The image froze on the close-up of the old man in tears. 'Stupidity,' continued Knowall. 'Complete and utter stupidity. The first thing this man should do is take his bottle of Vietnamese soil and throw it out of the window. Every time he opens the cupboard, every time he takes out the bottle – and sometimes he does it up to fifty times a day – he reinforces the neuro-circuit, and condemns himself to suffer a little more. Similarly, every time that we dwell on the past, that we return to a painful episode – and this is more or less what psychoanalysis boils down to – we increase the chances of reproducing it. Instead of advancing, we bury ourselves. Whenever we experience sadness, disappointment, something that prevents us from living, we must start by moving out, burning photos, avoiding talking to anyone about it. Repressed memories disappear; this can take some time, but they disappear in the end. The circuit deactivates itself.'

'Any questions?' No, there were no questions. His presentation, which had lasted more than two hours, had been remarkably clear. As I went into the dining hall I saw Patrick coming towards me, all smiles, stretching out his hand. Had I had a good journey, was I settled in, etc.? While we conversed pleasantly, a woman embraced me from behind, rubbing her pubis against my backside, placing her hands on my belly. I turned around: Fadiah had taken off her white tunic and put on a sort of vinyl leopard-patterned body; she looked in rude health. Whilst continuing to rub her pubis against me she too asked me about my first impressions. Patrick regarded the scene good-naturedly. 'Oh, she does this with everyone . . .' he told me as we made for a table where a man of about fifty, strongly built, with thick grey hair in a crewcut, was already sitting. He stood up to greet me and shook my hand, observing me closely. During the meal, he didn't say much, contenting himself from time to time with adding a point of detail on the logistics of the course, but I could sense that he was studying me. He was called Jérôme Prieur, but straight away I baptised him Cop. He was in fact the right-hand man of the prophet, the Number 2 of the organisation (although they used a different phrase, and had a whole load of titles along the lines of 'archbishop of the seventh rank', but that was what they really meant). You progressed according to seniority and merit, as in all organisations, he told me without smiling; according to seniority and merit. Knowall, for example, although he had only been an Elohimite for five years, was Number 3. As for Number 4, I absolutely had to be introduced to him, insisted Patrick, he really appreciated what I did, he himself had a great sense of humour. 'Oh, humour . . .' I stopped myself replying.

The afternoon lecture was given by Odile, a woman of around fifty who had had the same kind of sex life as Catherine Millet, and who incidentally looked a bit like her. She seemed a sympathetic woman, without problems – again like Catherine Millet – but her presentation was a bit woolly. I knew that there were women like Catherine Millet, who shared the same kind of tastes – I estimated the number at around one in a hundred thousand, this didn't seem to me to have varied throughout history, and was unlikely to evolve. She became somewhat animated when outlining the probability of contamination by the AIDS virus in relation to the various orifices – this was obviously her hobby horse, she had gathered a whole heap of figures. She was in fact vice-president of the association Couples Against AIDS, which tried to provide intelligent information on this subject – that is to say, enabling people to only use a condom when it was strictly necessary. For my part, I had never used a condom, and with the development of tritherapies, I wasn't going to start now – supposing I ever had chance to fuck again; for me, at that point, even the prospect of fucking, and of fucking with pleasure, seemed to be more than sufficient motivation for putting an end to it all.

The main objective of the lecture was to set out the restrictions and constraints that the Elohimites imposed on sexuality. It was quite simple: there were none – between *consenting adults*, as they say.

This time, there were questions. Most of them dealt with paedophilia, a subject on which Elohimites had had legal disputes – come to think of it, who hasn't gone on trial for paedophilia nowadays? The position of the prophet, as Odile reminded us here, was crystal-clear: there exists a moment in human life called *puberty*, when sexual desire appears – the age, varying according to the individual and the environment, was somewhere between eleven and fourteen.

To make love with someone who was unwilling, or who was not able to formulate a clear consent, *ergo* a prepubescent, is *evil*; as for what might happen after puberty, that was evidently situated out-side any moral judgement, and there was almost nothing else to say. The end of the afternoon became mired in common sense, and I was beginning to feel the need for an aperitif; they were, it must be said, a bit of a pain in the ass when it came to that. Fortunately, I had supplies in my suitcase, and as a VIP I had a single room, of course. Sinking after the meal into a mildly drunken state, alone between the immaculate sheets of my king-size bed, I drew up a sort of balance-sheet for this first day. Surprisingly, many of the adher-ents had forgotten to be twats; and, even more surprisingly, many women had forgotten to be ugly. It's true, also, that they didn't miss any opportunity to do themselves up. On this subject, the teachings of the prophet were consistent: if man was to make an effort to repress his masculine side (machismo had shed too much blood in the world, he exclaimed with emotion in the different interviews I had seen on his website), woman could on the contrary give free rein to her femininity and the exhibitionism that is consubstantial with her, through all kinds of sparkling, transparent or skintight clothing that the imagination of various couturiers and creators had put at her disposal: nothing could be more pleasant and excellent, in the eyes of the Elohim.

That's what the women did, then, and at the evening meal there was a certain erotic tension: it was light, but constant. I sensed that this was only going to grow stronger, as the week wore on; I also sensed that I was not really going to suffer from it, and that I would content myself with getting peacefully plastered whilst watching the banks of mist drift in the moonlight. The freshness of the pastures, the Milka cows, the snow on the summits: a very beautiful place for forgetting, or for dying.

The next morning, the prophet himself made an appearance for the first lecture: dressed all in white, he leaped on to the stage, under the light of the projectors, amidst enormous applause – straight away there was a standing ovation. Seen from afar, it struck me that he looked a bit like a monkey – undoubtedly owing to the relationship between the length of his front and back limbs, or his general posture, I don't know, it was very difficult to pin down. That said, he didn't look like an evil monkey: a monkey with a flat skull, a sensualist, nothing more.

He also resembled, indisputably, a Frenchman: the ironic look, sparkling with malice and mocking, you could absolutely have imagined him in a Feydeau farce.

He didn't look his sixty-five years at all.

'What will be the number of the Elect?' the prophet asked straight away. 'Will it be 1729, the smallest number that can be broken down in two different ways to the sum of two cubes? Will it be 9240, which possesses 64 dividers? Will it be 40,755, simultaneously triangular, pentagonal and hexagonal? Will it be 144,000, as our friends the Jehovah's Witnesses desire – a truly dangerous sect, I might add in passing?'

As a professional, I have to admit it: he was very good on stage. I wasn't completely awake, and the hotel coffee was awful; but he had grabbed me.

'Will it be 698,896, a palindromic square?' he continued. 'Will it be 12,960,000, the second geometrical number of Plato? Will it be 33,550,336, the fifth perfect number, written by an anonymous scribe in a medieval manuscript?'

He held himself still exactly in the centre of the spotlight, and took a long pause before speaking again: 'The Elect will be whoever wishes for it in his or her heart' – a shorter pause – 'and has behaved accordingly.'

He went on, fairly logically, about the conditions for election, before turning to the building of the embassy – a subject which was, visibly, close to his heart. The lecture lasted a little over two hours, and frankly it was well done, a good job, and I was not the last to applaud. I was sitting next to Patrick, who whispered in my ear: 'He's truly in very good form this year . . .'

As we left the lecture hall to go to lunch, we were intercepted by Cop. 'You are invited to the table of the prophet,' he told me gravely. 'You too, Patrick . . .' he added; Patrick blushed with pleasure, whilst I did a bit of hyperventilating to relax. Whatever Cop did, even when he was conveying good news, he did it in such a way that it made you shit your pants.

An entire wing of the hotel was reserved for the prophet, where he had his own dining room. Whilst waiting in front of the entrance where a young girl was exchanging messages over her walkie-talkie, we were joined by Vincent, the Plastic Arts VIP, led by one of Cop's subordinates.

The prophet painted, and the whole of the wing was decorated with his works, which he had had brought over from California for the duration of the course. They represented exclusively women, nude or dressed in suggestive clothing, in the middle of various landscapes, from the Tyrol to the Bahamas; I understood then where all the website and brochure illustrations had come from. As I crossed the corridor I noticed that Vincent was averting his gaze from the canvasses, and that he had difficulty repressing a spasm of disgust. I approached them in my turn before recoiling, nauseated: the word kitsch would have been too weak to describe these productions; close up, I think I had never seen anything quite as ugly.

The highlight of the exhibition was situated in the dining room, an immense space lit by windows looking out on to the mountains: behind the prophet's chair, a painting, eight metres by four, showed him surrounded by twelve young women dressed in see-through tunics, who stretched out towards him, some with expressions of adoration, others with clearly more suggestive ones. There were Whites, Blacks, an Oriental and two Indians; at least the prophet wasn't racist. He was, however, manifestly obsessed with big breasts, and he liked pretty thick pubic hair; in short, this man had simple tastes.

While we waited for the prophet Patrick introduced me to Gérard, the joker, and Number 4 in the organisation. He owed this privilege to the fact that he was one of the first of the prophet's companions. He had already been at his side when the sect was created, thirty-seven years before, and he had remained faithful to him, despite the latter's sometimes surprising about-turns. Of the four 'companions of the first hour', one was dead, another an

Adventist, and the third had left a few years earlier when the prophet had called on them to vote for Jean-Marie Le Pen against Jacques Chirac in the second round of the presidential elections, with the aim of 'accelerating the decomposition of France's pseudo-democracy' – a little like the Maoists, in their heyday, calling for a vote for Giscard against Mitterrand in order to aggravate the contradictions of capitalism. So there remained only Gérard, and this seniority gave him certain privileges, like having lunch every day at the table of the prophet – which was not the case with Knowall or even Cop – or occasionally to make funny remarks about his physical characteristics – to talk for example about his 'fat ass' or his 'eyes like cock-slits'. It emerged in the course of the conversation that Gérard knew me well, that he had seen all my shows, that he had in fact been following me since the beginning of my career. Living in California, totally indifferent moreover to any production of a cultural order (the only actors he knew by name were Tom Cruise and Bruce Willis), the prophet had never heard of me; it was therefore to Gérard, and Gérard alone, that I owed my VIP status. It was also he who dealt with the press, and with media relations.

Finally the prophet appeared, bouncing, freshly showered, dressed in jeans and a 'Lick my balls' T-shirt, and carrying a shoulder bag. Everyone stood up; I copied them. He came to me, holding out his hand, all smiles: 'Well? How did you find me?' I was gobsmacked for a few seconds before I realised that the question was not designed to trap me: he was addressing me exactly like one of the *brothers*. 'Er . . . good. Frankly, very good . . .' I replied. 'I particularly appreciated the opening material about the number of the elect, with all the figures.' 'Ah, ha ha ha . . .' He took a book out of his bag, *Funny Mathematics*, by Jostein Gaarder. 'It's all in there!' He sat down rubbing his hands, and tucked into his grated carrots straight away; we copied him.

Probably in my honour, the conversation turned quickly to comedians. Joker knew a lot about the subject, but the prophet, too, had a few notions, he had even known Coluche in his early days. 'We were in the line-up for the same show, one evening, in Clermont-Ferrand . . .' he told me nostalgically. In fact, in the period when the record companies, traumatised by the arrival of rock music in France, had recorded anything, the prophet (he was not yet a prophet) had cut a 45 under the stage name of Travis Davis; he had toured a little in the Central region, and things had been left at that. A little later, he had tried to break into racing cars – without much success there either. All in all, he had taken some time to find himself; the encounter with the Elohim had come at the right moment: without it, we might have had a second Bernard Tapie on our hands. Today, he hardly sang at all, but he had retained a real taste for fast cars, which had enabled the media to allege that he maintained, in his property in Beverly Hills, a veritable racing-car stable at the expense of his followers. This was completely untrue, he told me. First, he didn't live in Beverly Hills, but in Santa Monica; secondly, he possessed only a Ferrari Modena Stradale (a slightly souped-up version of the ordinary Modena, and made lighter by the use of carbon, titanium and aluminium) and a Porsche 911 GT2; in short, rather fewer than a middling Hollywood actor. It's true he planned to replace his Stradale with an Enzo, and his 911 GT2 with a Carrera GT; but he wasn't sure he'd have the means.

I was tempted to believe him: he gave me the impression of being a womaniser rather than a money man, and the two are compatible only up to a certain point – from a certain age, two passions are too much: happy are those, nevertheless, who manage to keep hold of one of them; I was twenty years younger than him, and it was evident that I was already close to zero. To feed the conversation, I mentioned the Bentley Continental GT that I had just traded in for a Mercedes 600 SL – which, I was conscious, could be read as a sign of gentrification. If there weren't any cars, you have to really ask yourself what men could possibly talk about.

In the course of the lunch, not one word was pronounced on the subject of the Elohim, and, as the week went on, I began to ask myself: did they really believe in them? Nothing is more difficult to detect than a light cognitive schizophrenia, and with the majority of the followers I was unable to make a judgement. Patrick, clearly, believed in them, which, moreover, was a little worrying: here was a man who held an important post in his Luxemburg bank, through whom sums of money occasionally exceeding a billion euros passed, who believed in fictions that directly contradicted the most elementary Darwinian arguments.

A case that intrigued me even more was that of Knowall, and I ended up asking him the question directly – with a man of such intelligence, I felt incapable of playing games. His reply, as I expected, was perfectly clear. One, it was completely possible, and even probable, that some living species, sufficiently intelligent to create or manipulate life, had appeared somewhere in the Universe. Two, man had well and truly come into being by means of evolution, and his creation by the Elohim was therefore to be taken only as a metaphor – however, he warned me against too blind a belief in the Darwinian vulgate, which was being abandoned more and more by serious researchers; the evolution of species in reality owed far less to natural selection than to genetic drift, that is to say pure chance, and to the appearance of geographical isolates and separate biotopes. Three, it was totally possible that the prophet had met, not an extraterrestrial, but a man from the future; some interpretations of quantum mechanics in no way excluded the possibility of the movement of information, if not material entities, in the opposite direction to time's arrow – he promised to provide me with documentation on the subject, which he did not long after the end of the course.

Emboldened, I then led him on to a subject that, since the beginning, had bothered me: the promise of immortality made to the Elohimites. I knew that a few cells had been taken from each follower, and that modern technology allowed their unlimited conservation; I had no doubts about the fact that the minor difficulties preventing human cloning at that current time would sooner or later be overcome; but personality? How would the new clone have the memory, however small, of his ancestor's past? And to what extent, if his memory was not preserved, would he feel like the same being, reincarnated?

For the first time I sensed something in his eyes besides the cold competence of a mind used to rational notions, for the first time I had the impression of an excitement, an enthusiasm. This was his subject, the one he had devoted his life to. He invited me to accompany him to the bar; he ordered a very creamy hot chocolate for himself, I took a whisky – he didn't even seem to notice this violation of the sect's rules. A few cows approached the bay windows, and stopped, as if observing us.

'Some interesting results have been obtained from certain nemathelminth worms,' he began, 'through simple centrifugation of the implicated neurone, and an injection of the proteic isolate into the brain of the new subject: you obtain a renewal of avoidance reactions, in particular those related to electric shocks, and even of routes followed in some simple mazes.'

I had the impression, at that moment, that the cows were nodding their heads; but he didn't notice the cows either.

'Evidently, these results do not translate to vertebrates, and even less to evolved primates like man. I suppose you remember what I said, on the first day of the course, concerning the neuro-circuits. Well, the reproduction of such a mechanism is possible, not in computers as we know them, but in a certain type of Turing machine, which we can call fuzzy automata, on which I am working at the moment. Unlike classical calculators, fuzzy automata are capable of establishing variable, evolving connections between adjacent calculating units; they are therefore capable of memorisation and apprenticeship. There is no *a priori* limit to the number of calculating units that can be linked, and therefore to the complexity of possible circuits. The difficulty at this stage, and it is considerable, consists of establishing a bijective relation between the neurons of a human brain, taken in the few minutes following its death, and the memory of a non-programmed automaton. The lifespan of the latter being almost limitless, the next step will be to reinject the information in the opposite direction, towards the brain of the new clone; this is the *downloading* phase which, I am convinced, will present no particular difficulty once the *uploading* has been perfected.'

Night was falling; the cows gradually turned away, returning to their pastures, and I could not prevent myself from thinking that they were distancing themselves from his optimism. Before leaving, he gave me his card: Professor Slotan Miskiewicz, from the

University of Toronto. It had been a pleasure to talk with me, he said, a real pleasure; if I wanted complementary information, I shouldn't hesitate to send him an e-mail. His research was progressing apace at that moment, and he hoped to make significant progress in the year to come, he repeated with a conviction that seemed to me a little forced.

A veritable delegation accompanied me to Zwork airport on the day of my departure: in addition to the prophet there was Cop, Know-all, Joker, and other less heavyweight members, including Patrick, Fadiah and Vincent, the Plastic Arts VIP, with whom I had got on pretty well – we exchanged addresses, and he invited me to come to see him when I was next in Paris. Of course, I was invited to the winter course, which would be held in March in Lanzarote and which would, the prophet warned me, take on an extraordinary dimension: this time, members from across the entire globe were invited.

I have certainly made only friends this week, I thought as I passed through the metal detector. No action, mind you; it's true I didn't exactly have the looks for that. Nor did I, needless to say, intend to join their movement; what had attracted me to it, at its core, was *curiosity*, that old curiosity that had been mine since childhood, and which, apparently, outlived desire.

The plane had two propellers, and gave the impression of being about to blow up at any moment during the flight. As we flew over the pastures, I became conscious that during this course, people, not to mention me, hadn't fucked much – as far as I knew, and I think I probably would have known, I was really good at that type of observation. Couples had stayed as couples – I hadn't got wind of any orgy, nor even a banal threesome; and those who came alone (the great majority) remained alone. In theory it was all extremely open, all forms of sexuality were permitted, even encouraged, by the prophet; in practice, the women wore erotic clothing, there was a lot of rubbing, but things went no further. That's what is curious, and would be interesting to delve into, I told myself before falling asleep on my meal tray.

After three changes, and an extremely unpleasant journey overall,

I landed at Almeria airport. It was about 45°C: that was thirty degrees more than in Zwork. It was good, but still not enough to stop the rise in anxiety. Crossing the tiled corridors of my house, I switched off the air conditioners one by one that the warden had switched on the day before my return – she was an old and ugly Romanian, her teeth in particular were very rotten, but she spoke excellent French; I had complete confidence in her, as they say, even if I had stopped giving her housework to do, because I couldn't stand a human being looking at my personal objects – it was quite funny, I told myself occasionally whilst wiping the floor, to do the housework myself, with my forty million euros; but that was how it was, I could do nothing about it: the very idea that a human being, however insignificant, could contemplate the details of my existence, and its emptiness, had become unbearable to me. On passing in front of the mirror in the main living room (an immense mirror, which covered an entire wall; you could, with a woman you loved, have made love there whilst contemplating your reflections, etc.) I was shocked to see my face: I had become so thin I looked almost translucent. A ghost, that's what I was becoming, a ghost of the sunny lands. Knowall was right: you had to move out, burn photos, and all the rest.

Financially, moving would have been an interesting operation: the price of land had almost trebled since my arrival. I still had to find a buyer; but rich people were plentiful, and Marbella was beginning to become rather saturated – the rich certainly like the company of the rich, no doubt it calms them, it's nice for them to meet beings subject to the same torments as they are, and who seem to form a relationship with them that is not totally about money; it's nice for them to convince themselves that the human species is not uniquely made up of predators and parasites; when you reach a certain density, however, there is a saturation point. For the moment, the density of rich people in the province of Almeria was rather too low; one needed to find a rich person who was quite young, pioneering and intellectual, possibly with ecological sympathies, a rich person who could take pleasure in observing pebbles, someone who had made a fortune in information technology, for example. In the worst-case scenario, Marbella was only one hundred and fifty kilometres away, and the plans for a new motorway were progressing quickly. No one, in any case, would miss me around here. But where would I go? And to do what? The truth is, I felt ashamed – ashamed of confessing to the estate agent that I had separated from my partner, that I didn't have any mistresses either, who could have put a bit of life into this immense house, and ashamed finally of confessing that I was alone.

Burning photos, however, was feasible. I devoted an entire day to gathering them together, there were thousands of snaps, I had always had a thing about souvenir photos; I only made a rapid selection, it is possible that some incidental mistress disappeared on this occasion. At sunset, I took all of them, in a wheelbarrow, out to a sandy area next to the terrace, poured a jerrycan of petrol over them and lit a match. It was a splendid fire, several metres high, which must have been visible kilometres away, perhaps even on the Algerian coast. The pleasure was strong, but incredibly fleeting: around four in the morning I woke up again, with the impression that thousands of worms were swarming under my skin, and the almost irresistible desire to tear at myself until I bled. I telephoned Isabelle, who picked up the phone after the second ring – so she was not sleeping either. We agreed that I would stop by to take Fox in the following days, and that he would remain with me until the end of September.

As with all Mercedes above a certain power, with the exception of the SLR McLaren, the speed of the 600 SL is electronically limited to 250 km/h. I don't think I dipped particularly below this speed between Murcia and Albacete. There were a few long and very open bends; I had an abstract sense of power – that, no doubt, of a man indifferent to death. A trajectory remains perfect, even one that concludes in death: there can be a lorry, an overturned car, an imponderable; this takes nothing away from the beauty of the trajectory. A little after Tarancon, I slowed down somewhat to turn on to the R3, then the M45, without really going below 180 km/h. I went back up to maximum speed on the R2, which was completely deserted, and which bypassed Madrid at a distance of around thirty kilometres. I crossed Castille along the N1 and I kept at 220 km/h until Vitoria-Gasteiz, before embarking on the more sinuous roads of the Basque country. I arrived in Biarritz at eleven in the evening, and took a room at the Sofitel Miramar. I met Isabelle the following morning at ten in the Silver Surfer. To my great surprise she had grown thinner, and I even had the impression she had shed all her excess kilos. Her face was slim, a little wrinkled, ravaged by sadness too, but she had become elegant and beautiful again.

'What have you done to stop drinking?' I asked.

'Morphine.'

'You haven't had problems getting supplies?'

'No, no, on the contrary, it's very easy here; there's a network in all the tearooms.'

So all the old biddies of Biarritz were shooting up with morphine; it was a scoop.

'It's a question of generation . . .' she told me. 'Now it's posh, rock-'n'-roll old biddies; inevitably they have other needs. That said,' she added, 'don't be under any illusions: my face has returned more or less to normal, but the body has completely collapsed, I don't even dare show you what's underneath my tracksuit' – she pointed to a sea-blue item, with white stripes, chosen three sizes too big – 'I don't do any dance, no more sport, nothing; I don't even go swimming any more. I do an injection in the morning, one in the evening, and in between I look at the sea, that's all. I don't even miss you, at least not often. I want for nothing, Fox plays a lot, he's very happy here . . .'

I nodded, finished my hot chocolate, and left to settle my hotel bill. An hour later, I was overlooking Bilbao.

A month's holiday with my dog: throwing the ball down the stairs, running together on the beach. Living.

On 30 September, at five in the afternoon, Isabelle parked in front of the residence, She had chosen a Mitsubishi Space Star, a vehicle classed by *L'Auto-Journal* in the category of 'ludospaces'. Following the advice of her mother, she had opted for the 'Box Office' model.

She stayed about forty minutes before driving back to Biarritz. 'Ah yes, I'm turning into a little old woman . . .' she said, putting Fox in the back seat. 'A nice little old lady in her Mitsubishi Box Office.'

For a few weeks now, Vincent27 has been seeking to establish contact. I had had only brief relations with Vincent26; he hadn't informed me of the proximity of his death, nor of his passing to the intermediary stage. Between neohumans, the phases of inter-mediation are often brief. Each can, if he likes, change digital address, and make himself undetectable; for my part I have de-veloped so few relationships that I have never considered it neces-sary. Sometimes entire weeks pass without me connecting myself, which exasperates Marie22, my most assiduous interlocutor. As Smith has already acknowledged, the subject–object separation is triggered, in the course of cognitive processes, by a convergent mesh of failures. Nagel notes that the same applies to separation between subjects (except that failure is not this time of an empirical order, but rather an affective one). It is in failure, and through failure, that the subject constitutes itself, and the passage of humans to neohumans, with the disappearance of all physical contact that is its correlative, has in no way modified this basic ontological given. We, like humans, have not been delivered from our status as *individuals*, and the dull dereliction that accompanies it; but unlike them, we know that this status is only the consequence of a failure in perception, another name for nothingness, the absence of the Word. Penetrated by death and formatted by it, we no longer have the strength to enter into the Presence. Solitude could, for certain human beings, have represented a joyful escape from the group; but as such, it involved, for each of these solitary beings, abandoning their original sense of belonging in order to discover other laws, and another group. Now that all the groups have disappeared, and every tribe has dispersed, we know ourselves isolated but similar to each other, and we have lost the desire to unite.

*

For three consecutive days, I received no message from Marie22: this was unusual. After having turned it over in my mind, I sent her a coding sequence that linked into the video surveillance camera of the unit Proyecciones XXI,13; she replied within a minute, with the following message:

> *Beneath the sun of the dead bird,*
> *Spreads infinitely the plain;*
> *There is no death more serene:*
> *Show me some of your body.*

4262164, 51026, 21113247, 6323235. At the address indicated there was nothing, not even an error message; a completely blank screen. So she wanted to pass into non-coding mode. I hesitated as, very slowly, on the blank screen, the following message formed: 'As you have probably guessed, I am an intermediary.' The letters disappeared, and a new message appeared: 'I am going to die tomorrow.'

With a sigh, I plugged in the video mechanism and zoomed in on my naked body. 'Lower, please,' she wrote. I suggested we pass into vocal mode. After a minute, she replied: 'I am an old intermediary, nearing the end; I don't know if my voice will be pleasant. But, if you prefer, yes . . .' I then understood that she would not want to show me any part of her anatomy; degradation, at the intermediary stage, is often very sudden.

In fact, her voice was almost entirely synthetic; there remained, however, some neo-human intonations, especially in the vowels, some strange slips towards softness. I took a slow panoramic shot down to my belly. 'Lower still . . .' she said in an almost inaudible voice. 'Show me your sex, please.' I obeyed; I masturbated my virile member, following the rules taught by the Supreme Sister; certain intermediary women feel a nostalgia at the end of their days for the virile member, and they like to contemplate it during the final minutes of actual life; Marie22 was apparently one of these women – this did not really surprise me, given the exchanges we had had in the past.

*

For three minutes, nothing happened; then I received a final message – she had returned to non-vocal mode: 'Thank you, Daniel. I am now going to disconnect myself, put the last pages of my commentary in order, and prepare for the end. In a few days Marie23 will move in here. She will receive her IP address from me, and an invitation to stay in contact. Some things have happened, through our partial incarnations, in the period following on from the Second Decrease; other things will happen, through our future incarnations. Our separation does not have the character of a farewell; I can sense that.'

We're like all artists, we believe in our product.
Début de soirée – the group

In the first days of October, under the influence of an attack of resigned sadness, I went back to work – since, undoubtedly, that was all I was good for. Well, the word *work* is perhaps a bit strong for my project – a rap record entitled *Fuck the Bedouins*, with 'Tribute to Ariel Sharon' as the subtitle. It was a big critical success (I was again on the cover of *Radikal Hip-Hop*, this time without my car), but the sales were average. Once again, in the press, I found myself portrayed as a paradoxical paladin of the free world; but even so, the scandal was less intense than during the days of *We Prefer the Palestinian Orgy Sluts* – this time, I told myself with a vague nostalgia, the radical Islamists had truly lost it.

The relative lack of success in sales terms was doubtless attributable to the mediocrity of the music; you could hardly call it rap, I had settled for sampling my sketches over some drum and bass, adding a few vocals here and there – Jamel Debbouze took part in one of the choruses. I had, however, written an original track, 'Let's fuck da niggahs' anus' that I was quite pleased with: 'anus' rhymed with 'cunnilingus', 'fuck' with 'suck', 'niggah' with 'mafia'; pretty lyrics that could be read on all sorts of levels – the journalist from *Radikal Hip-Hop*, who himself rapped in his spare time, without daring to tell the editor, was visibly impressed, in his article he even compared me to the sixteenth-century poet Maurice Scève. At last, potentially, I had a hit, and what's more, there was a good buzz about me; it really was a shame that the music wasn't up to it. I had heard lots of good things about a sort of independent producer, Bertrand Batasuna, who fiddled around on cult records, because they were no longer available on the market, for an obscure label; I was bitterly disappointed. Not only was this guy totally sterile creatively – he spent all his time, during the recording sessions, snoring on the carpet and farting every quarter of an hour – but he was, in private, very unpleasant, a real Nazi – I later learned that he had in fact been a member of the National and European Federation for Action. Thank God, we weren't paying him much; but if this was the best 'new French talent' Virgin could come up with, they rightly deserved to be gobbled up by BMG. 'If we had used Goldman or Obispo, like everyone else, we wouldn't be in this situation . . .' I ended up saying to Virgin's artistic director, who let out a long sigh; basically, he agreed, besides, his last project with Batasuna, a chorus of Pyrenean ewes sampled with hardcore techno, had been a dismal commercial failure. It was just that he had his budget, he couldn't take the responsibility of exceeding it, it was necessary to consult the group's headquarters in New Jersey, in short I dropped it. One does not travel second class.

That said, my time in Paris during the recording was almost pleasant. I was staying in the Lutétia, which reminded me of Francis Blanche, the German High Command, my best years in fact, when I was ardent, hateful, with a future ahead of me. Every evening, to send myself to sleep, I re-read Agatha Christie, especially the early works, the last ones were too overwhelming for me. Don't even mention *Endless Night*, which plunged me into stupors of unhappiness, but I had also not once managed to prevent myself from crying at the end of *Curtain: Poirot's Last Case*, whenever I read the farewell letter from Poirot to Hastings.

But now I am very humble and I say like a little child, 'I do not know . . .'

Goodbye, cher ami. I have moved the amyl nitrate ampoules away from beside my bed. I prefer to leave myself in the hands of the bon Dieu. May his punishment, or his mercy, be swift!

We shall not hunt together again, my friend. Our first hunt was here – and our last . . .

They were good days.

Yes, they have been good days . . .

With the exception of the Kyrie Eleison from the Mass in C, and perhaps Barber's *Adagio*, I couldn't imagine very much else that could put me in such a state. Infirmity, sickness, forgetting, that was good; that was *real*. No one before Agatha Christie had been able to portray in such a heart-rending way the sadness of physical decrepitude, of the gradual *loss* of all that gave life meaning and joy; and no one since has succeeded in equalling her. For a few days I almost felt like returning to a real career, doing serious things. It was in this state of mind that I telephoned Vincent Greilsamer, the Elohimite artist; he seemed happy to hear from me, and we agreed to go for a drink that very evening.

I arrived ten minutes late at the brasserie of the Porte de Versailles where we had arranged to meet. He got up and waved to me. Anti-sect associations encourage you to resist the favourable impression that forms after a first meeting or an initiation course, during which the sinister aspects of the doctrine may well have been silently diffused. In fact, so far, I couldn't see where the trap might be; this guy, for example, seemed normal. A bit introverted, granted, doubtless a bit isolated, but no more than me. He expressed himself directly, straightforwardly.

'I don't know much about contemporary art,' I said apologetically. 'I've heard of Marcel Duchamp, and that's all.'

'He is certainly the one who's had the greatest influence on twentieth-century art, yes. One thinks less frequently of Yves Klein; yet all the people who do performance art and "happenings", who work on their own bodies, refer more or less consciously back to him.'

He was silent. Aware that I had offered no reply, and that I didn't even look like I understood what he was talking about, he spoke again:

'Roughly speaking, you have three big trends. The first, and most important one, the one that gets 80 per cent of the subsidies, whose pieces go for the most money, is gore in general: amputations, cannibalism, enucleation, etc. All the collaboration work done with serial killers, for example. The second is the one that uses humour: there's irony directed at the art market, *à la* Ben; or at finer things, *à la* Broodthaers, where it's all about provoking uneasiness and shame in the spectator, the artist, or in both, by presenting a pitiful, mediocre spectacle that leaves you constantly doubting whether it has the slightest artistic value; then there's all the work on kitsch, which draws you in, which you come close to, and can empathise with, on the condition that you signal by means of a meta-narration that you're not fooled by it. Finally, there is a third trend, this is the virtual: it's usually young artists, influenced by manga and by heroic fantasies; many of them start like that, then fall back to the first trend once they realise they can't make their living on the Internet.'

'I suppose you don't belong to any of the three trends.'

'I like kitsch sometimes, I don't particularly feel the desire to mock it.'

'The Elohimites go a bit far in that direction, don't they?'

He smiled. 'But the prophet does that with complete innocence, there's no irony in him, it's much healthier . . .' I noticed in passing that he'd said 'the prophet' absolutely naturally, without any particular inflection in his voice. Did he really believe in the Elohim? His disgust for the pictorial productions of the prophet must have sometimes bothered him, all the same; there was something in this boy that eluded me, I was going to need to pay particular attention if I wanted not to get his back up; I ordered another beer.

'Basically, it is a question of degree,' he said. 'Everything is kitsch, if you like. Music as a whole is kitsch; art is kitsch, literature itself is kitsch. Any emotion is kitsch, practically by definition; but any reflection also, and even in a sense any action, the only thing that is not absolutely kitsch is nothingness.'

He let me meditate a little on these words before continuing: 'Would you be interested in seeing what I do?'

Obviously, I accepted. I arrived at his place the following Sunday, in the early afternoon. He lived in a house in Chevilly-Larue, right in the middle of a zone that was undergoing a phase of 'creative destruction', as Schumpeter would have said: muddy wastelands, as far as the eye could see, sprouting with cranes and fences; a few carcasses of buildings, in varying states of completion. His burrstone house, which must have dated from the thirties, was the only survivor from that era. He came to the doorstep to greet

me. 'It was my grandparents' house . . .' he told me. 'My grand-
mother died five years ago; my grandfather followed her three
months later. He died of a broken heart, I think – I was surprised
he even held on for three months.'

On entering the dining room, I had a sort of shock. I wasn't really
working class, despite what I liked to bang on about in all my
interviews; my father had already climbed up the first, and most
difficult, half of the social ladder – he had become an *executive*.
Nevertheless I *knew* the working class, I had had the occasion
throughout my childhood, at my uncles' and aunts' houses, to be
immersed in it: I knew their sense of family, their naive sentimentality, their taste for alpine chromolithographs and collections of
great authors bound in imitation leather. All this was there, in
Vincent's house, right down to the photos in their frames, to the
green velvet phone cover: he had visibly changed nothing since the
death of his grandparents.

Somewhat ill at ease, I allowed myself to be led to an armchair
before I noticed, hanging on the wall, perhaps the only decorative
element that did not date from the previous century: a photo of
Vincent sitting next to a big television set. In front of him, on a low
table, had been placed two quite crude, almost childish, sculptures
representing a loaf of bread and a fish. On the television screen, in
giant letters, was displayed the message: FEED THE PEOPLE.
ORGANISE THEM.

'It was the first piece of mine that really had any success . . .' he
commented. 'In my early years I was strongly influenced by Joseph
Beuys, and especially by the happening: "Ich Führe Baadermeinhof
Durch Dokumenta". It was the middle of the seventies, at the time
when the terrorists of the Rote Armee Fraktion were being hunted
throughout Germany. The Dokumenta de Kassel was then the most
important exhibition of contemporary art in the world; Beuys had
displayed this message at the entrance to indicate his intention of
showing Baader or Meinhof around the exhibition, on a day that
suited them, in order to transmute their revolutionary energy into a
positive force, utilisable by the whole of society. He was completely
sincere, that was the beauty of the thing. Of course, neither Baader
nor Meinhof turned up: on the one hand, they considered

contemporary art to be one of the manifestations of bourgeois decomposition, on the other they feared a trap by the police – which was, by the way, perfectly possible, the Dokumenta not enjoying any special status; but Beuys, in the megalomaniac delirium he was in at the time, had probably not even given the slightest thought to the police.'

'I remember something about Duchamp . . . A group, a banner with a phrase like: "The Silence of Marcel Duchamp is Overestimated".'

'Exactly; except that the original phrase was in German. But that illustrates the very principle of the intervention art: create an effective parable that is taken up and narrated in a more or less distorted way by third parties, in order to indirectly modify the whole of society.'

I was naturally a man who knew about life, society and things; I knew an everyday version of them, limited to the most common motivations that set the human machine in motion; my vision was that of a *cutting observer of social issues*, a Balzacian-lite; it was a world view in which Vincent had no assignable place, and for the first time in years, in reality for the first time since my initial encounter with Isabelle, I began to feel slightly destabilised. His words had made me think of the promotional material for *Two Flies Later*, in particular the T-shirts. Printed on each of them was a quotation from the *Manual of Civility for Young Girls for use by Educational Establishments*, by Pierre Louÿs, the bedside reading of the hero of the film. There were a dozen different quotations; the T-shirts were made of a new kind of fibre that sparkled and was a little transparent, very light, which could be fitted into a plastic envelope to be slipped into the pages of the issue of *Lolita* that preceded the release of the film. I had by then met Isabelle's successor, an incompetent *groovy chick*, who could scarcely remember the password for her computer; but that didn't stop the magazine from selling. The quotation I had chosen for *Lolita* was: 'To give ten cents to a poor man because he hasn't any bread is perfect; but to suck his dick because he hasn't any bread, that would be too much: you're not obliged.'

When you think of it, I said to Vincent, I had done *intervention art* without knowing it. 'Yes, yes . . .' he replied uneasily. I noticed then, a little uncomfortably, that he was *blushing*; it was touching, and a bit unhealthy. I became conscious at the same time that probably no woman had ever set foot in this house; the first act of a woman would have been to change the decoration, to tidy away at least a few of these objects, which contributed to the not only old-fashioned, but frankly quite funereal atmosphere.

'It's no longer that easy to have relationships, after a certain age, I find . . .' he said, as if he had read my thoughts. 'We no longer really have the opportunity to go out, nor the taste for it. And then there are lots of things to do, formalities, steps to take . . . the shopping, the laundry. We need more and more time to look after our health, as well, simply to maintain the body in more or less working order. After a certain age, life becomes administrative – more than anything.'

Since Isabelle had left I was not that used to speaking to people more intelligent than I, capable of divining my train of thought; what he had just said, especially, was crushingly true, and there was a moment of unease – sexual subjects are always a bit heavy, and I thought it right to talk politics to add a bit of banter, and, staying on the theme of intervention art, I recounted how Workers' Struggle, a few days after the fall of the Berlin Wall, had plastered Paris with dozens of posters proclaiming: 'Communism Remains the Future of the World'. He listened to me with that attentiveness, that childlike seriousness that was beginning to wring my heart before he con-cluded that although the act had real power, it had, however, no poetic dimension, when you bear in mind that Workers' Struggle was, above all, a party, an ideological machine, and that art was always *cosa individuale*; even when it was a protest, it only had value if it was a solitary protest. He apologised for his dogmatism, smiled sadly, and suggested: 'Shall we go and see what I do? It's down-stairs . . . I think that things will be more concrete afterwards.' I got up from the armchair, and followed him to the stairway that opened on to the hall. 'By knocking down the partitions, that's given me a cellar of twenty metres on each side; four hundred square metres is good for what I'm doing at the moment . . .' he continued in an uncertain voice. I felt more and more ill at ease: people had often spoken to me about show-business, media projects, and micro-sociology; but art, never, and I was filled with the presentiment of something novel, dangerous and probably fatal; from a domain where there was – a bit like in love – almost nothing to win and almost everything to lose.

I placed a foot on the level ground beneath the last step, and let go of the banister. It was totally dark. Behind me, Vincent flicked a switch.

Forms appeared at first, blinking, vague, like a procession of mini-ghosts; then a zone lit up, a few metres to my left. I didn't understand the direction of the lighting at all; the light seemed to come from the space itself. 'LIGHTING IS A METAPHYSICS . . .'; the phrase turned over in my head for a few seconds, then disappeared. I approached the objects. A train was entering a spa in central Europe. The snowclad mountains, in the distance, were bathed in sunshine; lakes sparkled, there were high mountain pastures. The girls were ravishing, they wore long dresses and veils. The gentlemen smiled as they greeted them, doffing their top hats. Everyone seemed happy. 'THE BEST IN THE WORLD . . .': the phrase sparkled for a few instants, then disappeared. The locomotive was gently steaming, like a big, gentle animal. Everything seemed balanced, *in its place*. The lights dimmed slowly. The windows of the casino reflected the setting sun, and every pleasure bore the imprint of Germanic honesty. Then it became completely dark, and a sinuous line appeared in the space, formed of translucent, red, plastic hearts, half-filled with a liquid that beat against their sides. I followed the line of hearts, and a new scene appeared: this time it consisted of an Asian wedding, celebrated perhaps in Taiwan, or Korea, in a country anyway that had only recently known wealth. Pale-pink Mercedes dropped the guests off in the square in front of a neo-Gothic cathedral; the husband, dressed in a white smoking jacket, advanced through the air, a metre above the ground, his little finger entwined with that of his betrothed. Some pot-bellied Chinese Buddhas, surrounded by multicoloured electric bulbs, quivered with joy. A flowing, bizarre music became slowly louder, whilst the married couple were lifted into the air before hanging over the assembled guests – they were now as high as the rose window of the cathedral. They exchanged a long kiss, both virginal and labial, to the applause of the guests – I saw little hands moving. In the background, caterers lifted the lids off steaming plates, on the surface of the rice the vegetables produced little spots of colour. Fireworks exploded, and there was a fanfare of trumpets.

Again it went dark, and I followed a more indistinct path, as if trekking through woods, I was surrounded by green-and-gold rustlings. Dogs were frolicking in the clearing of the angels, they were rolling around in the sun. Later, the dogs were with their masters, protecting them with loving looks, and later still they were dead, and little stelae sprouted up in the clearing to commemorate love, walks in the sunshine, and shared joy. No dog was forgotten: their embossed photos decorated the stelae at the foot of which the masters had left their favourite toys. It was a joyful monument, from which all tears were absent.

In the distance, as if suspended from trembling curtains, some words in gilded letters took shape. There was the word 'LOVE', the word 'GOODNESS', the word 'TENDERNESS', the word 'FIDELITY', the word 'HAPPINESS'. Coming out of the total darkness, they evolved, from nuances of matt gold through to blinding luminosity; then they fell back alternately into the night, but at the same time following one another in their rise towards the light, in such a way that they seemed, somehow, to create one another. I continued my path across the cellar, guided by the light that shone sequentially on all the corners of the room. There were other scenes, other visions, so many that I gradually lost any notion of time, and only recovered full consciousness once I had gone back upstairs, and was seated on a wicker garden bench in what could once have been a terrace or a winter garden. Night was falling on the waste-ground landscape; Vincent had lit a big lamp. I was visibly shaken, and he served me a glass of cognac without my needing to ask.

'The problem . . .' he said, 'is that I can no longer really exhibit, there are too many regulations, and it's almost impossible to transport. Someone came from the Delegation for Plastic Arts; they plan to buy the house, and maybe make videos and sell them.'

I understood that he was touching on the practical and financial side of things purely through politeness, in order to allow the conversation to return to a normal footing – it was very obvious that in his situation, at the extreme emotional limit of survival, material questions could no longer carry more than a limited weight. I failed to reply to him, nodded and served myself another glass of cognac; his self-control at that moment seemed terrifying to me. He spoke again:

'There is a famous phrase that divides artists into two categories: revolutionaries and decorators. Well, I didn't have much of a choice, the world decided for me. I remember my first exhibition in New York, at the Saatchi gallery, for the happening "Feed the People. Organise Them". I was quite impressed, it was the first time in a long time that a French artist was exhibiting in an important New York gallery. I was also a revolutionary then, and convinced of the revolutionary value of my work. It was a very cold winter in New York, and every morning you found tramps in the streets who had frozen to death; I was convinced that people were going to change their attitude as soon as they saw my work: that they were going to go out into the street and follow exactly the instruction on the television screen. Of course, none of that happened: people came, nodded, exchanged intelligent words, then left.

'I suppose that the revolutionaries are those who are capable of coming to terms with the brutality of the world, and of responding to it with increased brutality. I simply did not have that kind of courage. I was ambitious, however, and it is possible that the decorators are fundamentally more ambitious than the revolutionaries. Before Duchamp, the artist had as his ultimate goal a world view that was at once personal and accurate, that is to say moving; it was already a huge ambition. Since Duchamp, the artist no longer contents himself with putting forward a world view, he seeks to create his own world; he is very precisely the rival of God. I am God in my basement. I have chosen to create a small, easy world where you only encounter happiness. I am perfectly conscious of the regressive nature of my work; I know that it can be compared to the attitude of adolescents who, instead of confronting the problems of adolescence, dive headfirst into their stamp collection, their herbarium or whatever other glittering, limited, multicoloured little world they choose. No one will dare say it to my face, I get good reviews in *Art Press*, as in the majority of the European media; but I could read the contempt in the eyes of the girl who came from the Delegation for Plastic Arts. She was thin, dressed in white leather, with an almost swarthy complexion, very sexual; I understood at once that she considered me to be a little invalid child, and very sick. She was right: I am a tiny little invalid child, very sick, who cannot live. I can't come to terms with the brutality of this world; I just can't do it.'

Back at the Lutétia, I had some difficulty getting to sleep. Obviously, Vincent had left someone out of his categories. Like the revolutionary, the comedian came to terms with the brutality of the world, and responded to it with increased brutality. The result of his action, however, was not to transform the world, but to make it acceptable by transmuting the violence, necessary for any revolutionary action, into *laughter* – in addition, also, to making a lot of dosh. To sum up, like all clowns since the dawn of time, I was a sort of *collaborator*. I spared the world from painful and useless revolutions – since the root of all evil was biological, and independent of any imaginable social transformation; I established clarity, I forbade action, I eradicated hope; my balance-sheet was mixed.

In a few minutes I reviewed the whole of my career, especially the movie one. Racism, paedophilia, cannibalism, parricide, acts of torture and barbarism: in less than a decade, I had creamed off all the lucrative niches. It was, however, curious, I told myself again, that the alliance between nastiness and laughter had been considered so innovative in movie circles; they can't have read Baudelaire in their profession.

There remained pornography, on which everyone had broken their teeth. The thing seemed up till now to resist all attempts at sophistication. Neither the virtuosity of the camera movements, nor the refinement of the lighting brought about the slightest improvement: they seemed instead to constitute handicaps. A more 'Dogma'-style attempt, with DV cameras and CCTV images, hadn't proved any more successful: people wanted clear images. Ugly, but clear. Not only had attempts at 'quality pornography' collapsed into farce, but they had also been unalloyed commercial fiascos. All in all, the old adage of the marketing directors, 'It's not because people prefer the basic products that they will not buy our luxury products,' seemed in this case to be demolished, and the sector, one of the most lucrative in the profession, remained in the hands of shady Hungarian, or even Latvian, jobbers. At the time when I was making *Munch on my Gaza Strip* I had, one afternoon, for research purposes, visited the set of one of the last French producers who was still active, a Ferdinand Cabarel. That hadn't been a waste of an afternoon – on the human level, I mean. Despite his very south-west surname, Ferdinand Cabarel looked like a former roadie for AC/DC: whitish skin, greasy, dirty hair, a 'Fuck your cunts' T-shirt, death's head rings. Straight away I told myself I had rarely seen such a twat. He only managed to survive thanks to the ridiculous work rate he imposed on his crew – he canned about forty usable minutes per day, whilst also doing promotional photos for *Hot Video*, and even passed for an intellectual in the profession, asserting that he 'worked with a sense of urgency'. I'll spare you the dialogue ('I excite you, eh, my little slut' – 'Yes, you excite me, my little bastard') and the puny stage directions ('now, a double' obviously indicated, to everyone, that the actress was going to be the object of a double penetration), what struck me above all was the incredible contempt with which he treated his actors, particularly the male ones. Without the slightest irony, or the slightest humour, Cabarel would scream into his megaphone things like: 'If you don't get a hard-on, guys, you won't be paid!', or 'If the other guy ejaculates, he's out the door . . .' At least the actress had a fake fur coat to cover her nakedness between shots; if the actors wanted to keep warm, they had to bring their own blankets. After all, it was the actress who the male viewers would go to see, she was the one who would perhaps be on the cover of *Hot Video*; as for the actors, they were just treated like cocks on legs. I also learned (with a bit of difficulty – the French, as we know, don't like to talk about their salaries) that the actress was paid five hundred euros per day of shooting, whilst they had to be content with one hundred and fifty.

They weren't even in it for the money: incredible and pathetic as it may seem, they did this job *in order to fuck girls*. I remembered in particular the scene in the underground parking lot: they were shivering, and, as I looked at those two guys, Fred and Benjamin (one was a lieutenant in the fire brigade, the other an administrator) who wanked melancholically to keep themselves ready for 'the double', I had said to myself that, sometimes, men could truly be courageous beasts, so long as it was regarding pussy.

This far from brilliant memory led me, at the end of the night, after suffering near-total insomnia, to lay the foundations of a script with the provisional title 'Motorway Swingers', which would allow me to cleverly combine the commercial advantages of pornography and ultra-violence. In the morning, as I devoured brownies in the bar of the Lutétia, I wrote the pre-credits sequence.

An enormous black limousine (perhaps a Packard from the sixties) was driving slowly along a country road, bounded by prairies and bright-yellow broom bushes (I thought of filming in Spain, probably the Hurdas region, which is very pretty in May); as it moved, it emitted a low rumble (like a bomber returning to base).

In the middle of a prairie, a couple were making love amidst nature (it was a prairie full of flowers, with high grass, poppies, cornflowers and yellow flowers whose name escaped me for the moment, but I noted in the margin: 'Force her on the yellow flowers'). The girl's skirt was hitched up, her T-shirt lifted above her breasts, in short she looked a *right tart*. Having unbuttoned the man's trousers, she was gratifying him with fellatio. A tractor's engine slowly running in the background let you believe that you were dealing with a couple of farmhands. A little blowjob between ploughing, the *Rite of Spring*, etc. A tracking outwards informed us, however, that the two lovebirds were getting it on in front of a camera, and that in fact we were looking at the making of a pornographic film – probably quite a high-quality one, since there was a complete crew.

The Packard limousine stopped, overlooking the prairie, and two executioners got out, dressed in black double-breasted suits. Pitilessly, they machine-gunned the young couple and the crew. I hesitated, then scored out 'machine-gunned': it was better to use more original equipment, for example a launcher of sharp steel discs, which would spin around in the atmosphere before cutting flesh into pieces, particularly that of the two lovers. There wouldn't need to be any skimping, the cock could be severed when it was in the girl's throat etc.; all in all, it needed what my production director on *Diogenes the Cynic* would have called *quite cool images*. I noted in the margin: 'foresee a ball-ripping machine'.

At the end of the sequence, a fat man with very black hair, a face that was shiny and pockmarked by syphilis, and who also wore a black double-breasted suit, got out of the back of the car, accompanied by a skeletal and sinister old man, looking a bit like William Burroughs, whose body floated inside a grey raincoat. The latter contemplated the carnage (fragments of red flesh in the prairie, yellow flowers, men in black suits), sighed gently and turned round to his companion, saying: 'It's a moral duty, John.'

Eventually, after various massacres had been perpetrated, most often on young, if not teenage, couples, it emerged that these rather unsavoury characters were members of an association of Catholic fundamentalists, perhaps affiliated to Opus Dei; this dig at the return of the moral order was, in my mind, going to win me the sympathy of left-wing critics. A little later, it appeared, however, that the killers had themselves been filmed by a second crew, and that the true aim of the whole business was the commercialisation not of porn films, but of ultra-violence. Plot within a plot, film within a film, etc. A watertight project.

In a nutshell, as I said to my agent that very evening, I was making progress, I was working, in other words I was getting back to my old rhythm; he declared himself happy, and confessed that he had been worried. Up to a certain point, I was sincere. It was only two days later, as I boarded the plane for Spain, that I realised I would never finish the script – not to mention produce it. There is a certain social agitation in Paris that gives you the illusion of having plans; back in San Jose, I knew I was going to freeze completely. Try as I might to play at being elegant, I was shrivelling like an old monkey; I felt myself worn down, diminished beyond redemption; my mutterings and murmurs were those of an old man. I was now forty-seven, it was thirty years since I had started making my peers laugh; now I was finished, washed-out, inert. The spark of curiosity that remained in my vision of the world was soon going to be extinguished, and then I would be as dead as the stones, only with some vague suffering on top of that. My career had not been a failure, at least not on the commercial level: if you attack the world with sufficient violence, it ends up spitting its filthy lucre back at you; but never, never will it give you back joy.

No doubt like Marie22 at the same age, Marie23 is a playful and graceful neohuman. Even if ageing does not have for us the tragic character it had for humans of the last period, it is not without certain forms of suffering. These are moderated, as are our joys; but there still remain variations between individuals. Marie22, for example, seems to have been at times strangely close to mankind, as shown by the message below, which is not at all neohuman in tone, and which in the end she did not send (it is Marie23 who found it yesterday whilst consulting her archives):

An old woman in despair,
With a hooked nose,
In her raincoat crosses
St Peter's Square.

37510, 236, 43725, 82556. Bald, old, reasonable human beings, dressed in grey, crisscross one another, a few metres apart, in their wheelchairs. They move around in an immense grey empty space – there is no sky, no horizon, nothing; there is just greyness. Each one mutters to himself, head sunk into shoulders, without noticing the others, without even paying attention to the space around them. A closer examination reveals that the surface on which they move is slightly sloping; small variations in level form a network of curves that guide the movement of the wheelchairs, and normally prevent any possibility of them bumping into one another.

I have the impression that Marie22 wanted, in creating this image, to express what humans of the old race would feel if they found themselves confronted with the objective reality of our lives – this is not the case with the savages: even if they move between our residences, they quickly learn to keep their distance, nothing allows them to imagine the real technological conditions of our existence.

Marie22's commentary shows that, at the end, she seems to have begun to feel a certain sympathy for the savages. This could bring her close to Paul24, with whom, incidentally, she had engaged in a continual correspondence; but whilst Paul24 adopts Schopenhauerian accents to evoke the absurdity of the savages' existence, devoted entirely to suffering, and calls for them to be blessed with a swift death, Marie22 goes as far as imagining that their fate could have been different, and that they could, in certain circumstances, have known a less tragic end. It has, however, been shown countless times that the physical pain that accompanied the existence of humans was consubstantial with them, that it was the direct consequence of an inadequate organisation of their nervous system, just as their inability to establish inter-individual relations in a mode other than that of confrontation resulted from a relative insufficiency of their social instincts in relation to the complexity of the societies that their intellectual means enabled them to found – that was already patently true in the case of a medium-sized tribe, not to mention those giant conglomerations that remain associated with the first stages of the effective disappearance.

Intelligence permits the domination of the world; this can appear only within a social species, and through the medium of language. This same sociability, which had enabled the appearance of intelligence, was later to hinder its development – once technologies of artificial transmission had been perfected. The disappearance of social life was the way forward, teaches the Supreme Sister. It is no less the case that the disappearance of all physical contact between neohumans has been able to have, and sometimes still has, the character of an asceticism; moreover, this is precisely the term that the Supreme Sister uses in her messages, at least in their intermediary formulation. In my own messages to Marie22, there were some that owe much more to the affective than to the cognitive or propositional. Without going as far as feeling for her what humans described as *desire*, I was sometimes able to briefly slide down the slope of *feeling*.

The fragile, hairless, badly irrigated skin of the humans was terribly sensitive to the lack of caresses. Better circulation of the cutaneous blood vessels and a slight decrease in the sensitivity of type L nervous fibres have both allowed, from the first neohuman generations onwards, a decrease in the suffering linked to absence of contact. The fact still remains that I would have difficulty imagining a day of my life spent without running my hand through Fox's coat, without feeling the warmth of his little loving body. This necessity does not diminish as my strength wanes, I even have the impression that it becomes more and more pressing. Fox can feel it, asks less to play, presses against me, lays his head on my knees; we spend whole nights in this position – nothing equals the sweetness of sleep when it happens in the presence of the loved one. Then dawn returns and rises over the residence; I prepare Fox's bowl and I make myself a coffee. I now know that I will not finish my commentary. I will leave with no real regret an existence that brought me no real joy. Considering death, we have reached a state of mind that was, according to the monks of Ceylon, the one sought by the Buddhists of the Lesser Vehicle; our life at the moment of its end 'is like blowing out a candle'. We can also say, to use the words of the Supreme Sister, that our generations follow one another 'like flicking the pages of a book'.

Marie23 sends me a few messages, then I leave without reply. It will be the role of Daniel25 to prolong contact, if he so wishes. A slight cold has invaded my extremities; it is the sign that I am entering the final hours. Fox senses it, moans softly, licks my toes. I have already seen Fox die several times, before being replaced by his replica; I have known the closing of his eyes, the cardiac rhythm which stops without altering the profound, animal peace of those beautiful brown eyes. I cannot attain that wisdom, no neohuman will be able to attain it really; I can only get closer to it, and slow down voluntarily the rhythm of my breath and my mental projections.

The sun rises again, and reaches its zenith; however, it becomes colder and colder. Some vague memories appear briefly, then disappear. I know that my asceticism will not have been in vain; I know that I will be part of the essence of the Future Ones.

The mental projections also disappear. There probably remain only a few minutes. I feel nothing but a very slight sadness.

PART TWO

COMMENTARY
OF DANIEL25

During the first part of your life, you only become aware of happiness once you have lost it. Then an age comes, a second one, in which you already know, at the moment when you begin to experience true happiness, that you are, at the end of the day, going to lose it. When I met Belle, I understood that I had just entered this second age. I also understood that I hadn't reached the third age, in which anticipation of the loss of happiness prevents you from living.

With regard to Belle, I will just say, without exaggeration or metaphor, that she gave life back to me. In her company, I lived moments of intense happiness. It was perhaps the first time I had had the opportunity to utter this simple sentence. I lived moments of intense happiness; inside her, or just next to her; when I was inside her, or just before, or just after. Time, at this stage, stayed always in the present; there were long moments when nothing moved, and then everything fell back again into an 'and then there was'. Later, a few weeks after we met, these happy moments fused, became joined; and my whole life, in her presence, before her eyes, became happiness.

Belle, in reality, was called Esther. I have never called her Belle out loud – never in her presence.

It was a strange story. Heart-rending, so heart-rending, my Belle. And undoubtedly the strangest thing is that I wasn't really surprised. Undoubtedly, I had had the tendency, in my relations with people (I almost wrote: 'in my official relations with people'; and it was a bit like that, in fact), undoubtedly, I had had the tendency to overestimate my state of despair. Something in me therefore knew, had always known that I would end up finding love – I'm talking about reciprocated love, the only one that counts, the only one that can effectively lead us to a different order of perception, where individuality fissures, where the conditions of the world appear modified, and its continuation legitimate. I was not, however, naive; I knew that the majority of people are born, grow old and die without having known love. Not long after the epidemic of 'mad cow disease', new measures had been introduced to ensure that people knew where their beef had come from. In the meat section of supermarkets, in fast-food establishments, small labels appeared, generally worded thus: 'Born and raised in France. Slaughtered in France.' A simple life, in fact.

If you look at the circumstances, the beginning of our love story was extremely banal. I was forty-seven when we met, she was twenty-two. What's more, she was an actress, and it's well known that film producers sleep with their actresses; some films, even, appear to only have been created for that purpose. That said, could I be considered a *film producer*? As producer I only had *Two Flies Later* to my name, and I was about to give up producing *Motorway Swingers* – in fact, I had already given up on it the moment I returned from Paris; when the taxi pulled up in front of my residence in San Jose I sensed infallibly that I no longer had the strength, and that I was not going to pursue this project, nor any other. Nonetheless, things had followed their usual course, and waiting for me were about ten faxes from European producers, who wanted to know a bit more about it. My treatment kept itself to one sentence: 'To bring together the commercial advantages of pornography and ultra-violence.' This was not a treatment, at most it was a pitch, but it was good, my agent had told me, lots of young producers proceeded like that today, I was, without knowing it, a modern professional. I had also been sent three DVDs from the main Spanish artistic agents; I had begun to prospect for potential actors, indicating that the film had a 'possible sexual content'.

And so, that was how the greatest love affair of my life started: in a predictable, conventional and even if you like, vulgar way. I put a plate of Arroz Tres Delicias in the microwave, put a DVD at random into the player. As the meal heated up, I had the time to eliminate the first three girls. After two minutes, the machine beeped, I took the meal out of the oven, and added some Suzi

Weng pepper purée; at the same time, on the giant screen at the back of the living room, Esther's trailer was beginning.

I skipped rapidly over the first two scenes, taken from some sitcom and what was undoubtedly an even more mediocre police series; however, my attention had been attracted by something, I had my finger on the remote, and at the moment of the second change of scene I pressed immediately to return to normal speed.

She was naked, standing in a room that was difficult to make out – no doubt an artist's atelier. In the first image, she was being splattered with a jet of yellow paint – the one who was throwing the paint was out of shot. Then you found her stretched out in the middle of a dazzling pool of yellow paint. The artist – you could see only his arms – was pouring a bucket of blue paint on to her, then spreading it over her belly and breasts; she looked in his direction with trusting amusement. He guided her by taking her hand, she turned over on her front, he poured some more paint on the small of her back, spread it all over her back and her ass; her ass moved, accompanying the movement of the hands. There was in her face, in each of her gestures, a deeply moving innocence and sensual grace.

I knew the work of Yves Klein, I had done research since my meeting with Vincent, I knew that there was nothing original or interesting about this happening on an artistic level; but who still thinks of art when happiness is possible? I watched the clip ten times in a row: I had a hard-on, sure, but I think I understood a lot of things, as well, from those first minutes onwards. I understood that I was going to love Esther, that I was going to love her violently, without caution or hope of return. I understood that this affair would be so strong that it might kill me, that it was even probable that it *was* going to kill me, as soon as Esther ceased loving me, because ultimately there are certain limits – however much any one of us might have a certain capacity for resistance, one always ends up dying of love, or rather of the absence of love, it's inevitably fatal. Yes, a lot of things were already determined, from these first minutes on, the process was already up and running. I could still interrupt it, I could avoid meeting Esther, destroy this DVD, go travelling, very far away, but in actuality I called her agent the following day. Naturally, he was delighted, yes it's possible, I think she's doing nothing at the moment, you know better than me that the current situation is not easy, I think I'm right in saying we have never worked together, it will be a pleasure – *Two Flies Later* had undoubtedly had a certain impact, everywhere other than France; he spoke decent English, and in general Spain was modernising surprisingly quickly.

Our first meeting took place in a bar in the Calle Obispo de Leon, a fairly big, fairly typical bar, with dark-wood panelling and tapas – I was rather grateful to her for not choosing a Planet Hollywood. I arrived ten minutes late, and from the moment she looked up at me there was immediately no longer any question of free will, we were already in the domain of the *given*. I sat down in front of her on the bench, experiencing something like the sensation I had had a few years previously when I went under general anaesthetic: the impression of an easy, approved departure, the intuition that at the end of the day death would be a very simple thing. She was wearing tight, low-cut jeans, and a clinging pink top that left her shoulders uncovered. When she stood up to go and order, I caught sight of her thong, also pink, showing above her jeans, and I began to get hard. When she came back from the counter, I had a lot of difficulty taking my eyes off her belly button. She noticed this, smiled, and sat next to me on the bench. With her light blonde hair and her very white skin, she did not really look like a typical Spanish girl – I would have rather said a Russian. She had pretty, attentive brown eyes, and I no longer really remember my first words but I think I indicated almost immediately that I was going to drop my film project. She looked surprised rather than really disappointed. She asked me why.

Basically I didn't know, and I threw myself into quite a long explanation, which went back to when I was her age – her agent had already told me that she was twenty-two. It emerged from the story that I had led quite a sad and solitary life, marked by hard labour, and intercut with frequent periods of depression. Words came easily to me, I was speaking in English, and from time to time she had me repeat a sentence. All in all I was going to drop not just this film but almost everything, in conclusion I said I no longer felt the least ambition, or rage to win or anything of that kind, it seemed to me that at this point in my life I was truly tired.

She looked at me perplexed, as if the word seemed to her to be badly chosen. Yet that was it, perhaps in my case it was not a physical tiredness, rather a nervous one, but is there actually a difference? 'I've lost faith . . .' I said finally. 'Maybe it's better . . .' she said; then she put a hand on my sex. Nuzzling her head in the hollow of my shoulder, she gently pressed my cock between her fingers.

In the hotel room, she told me a little more about her life. Certainly you could describe her as an actress, she had played in sitcoms and police series – where, generally, she was raped and strangled by more or less numerous psychopaths, and a few advertisements as well. She had even taken the starring role in a Spanish feature film, but it had not yet been released, and anyway it was a terrible film; Spanish cinema, she claimed, was on its last legs.

She could go abroad, I said, in France, for example, they still made films. Yes, but she didn't know if she was a good actress, or, besides, whether she wanted to be an actress. In Spain she managed to work from time to time, thanks to her atypical physique; she was conscious of this blessing, and of its relative nature. Basically she considered her work as an actress to be nothing more than odd-jobbing, better paid than serving pizzas or distributing flyers for a disco night, but more difficult to find. Otherwise, she studied piano and philosophy. And, above all, she wanted to live.

Rather like the studies pursued by an accomplished young lady of the nineteenth century, I told myself mechanically as I unbuttoned her jeans. I have always had trouble with jeans, with their big metal buttons, and she had to help me. However, I immediately felt good inside her, I think that I had forgotten that it was so good. Or perhaps it had never been so good, perhaps I had never felt so much pleasure. At forty-seven; life is strange.

Esther lived alone with her sister, who was forty-four and had been more like a mother to her; her real mother was half-insane. She did not know her father, even by name, she had never seen a photo of him, nothing.

Her skin was very soft.

At the moment when the protective fence closed, the sun pierced between two clouds, and the whole of the residence was bathed in a blinding light. The paint on the outside walls contained a small quantity of slightly radioactive radium, which gave effective protection from the magnetic clouds, but increased the reflectivity of the buildings; the wearing of protective glasses, in the first days, was recommended.

Fox came towards me, weakly wagging his tail. Canine companions rarely survive the disappearance of the neohuman with whom they have spent their lives. Of course, they recognise the genetic identity of the successor, whose body odour is identical, but in the majority of cases this is not sufficient, they stop playing and eating and die quickly, in the space of a few weeks. I thus knew that the beginning of my effective existence would be marked by mourning; I also knew that this existence would unfold in a region distinguished by a large density of savages, where the instructions on protection should be rigorously followed; what's more, I was prepared for the basic elements of a classical life.

What I did not know, however, and which I discovered on entering the office of my predecessor, was that Daniel24 had made some handwritten notes without reporting them to the IP address of his commentary – which was rather unusual. Most of them displayed a curious, disabused bitterness – like this one, scribbled on a page taken from a spiral-bound notebook:

> *Insects bang between the walls,*
> *Limited to their tedious flight*
> *Which carries no message other*
> *Than the repetition of the worst.*

Others seemed marked by a strangely human weariness, a sensation of vacuity:

> *For the past months, not the slightest inscription*
> *And nothing in the world worthy of inscription.*

In both cases, he had proceeded in uncoded mode. Without being directly prepared for this eventuality, I was not totally surprised: I knew that the line of Daniels had, since its founder, been predisposed to a certain form of doubt and self-deprecation. I was, however, shocked to discover this final note, which he had left on his bedside table, and which, given the state of the paper, had to be very recent:

> *Reading the Bible at the swimming pool*
> *In a down-at-heel hotel,*
> *Daniel! Your prophecies drain me*
> *The sky has the colour of drama.*

The humorous levity, the self-irony – as well as, besides, the direct allusion to human elements of life – were here so marked that such a note could easily have been attributed to Daniel1, our distant ancestor, rather than to one of his neohuman successors. The conclusion was unavoidable: by plunging into the at once ridiculous and tragic biography of Daniel1, my predecessor had let himself be gradually impregnated by certain features of his personality; in a sense, this was exactly the goal sought by the Founders; but, contrary to the teachings of the Supreme Sister, he had not been able to keep a sufficient critical distance. The danger existed, it had been noted, and I felt prepared to face it; I knew above all that there was no other way out. If we wanted to prepare for the coming of the Future Ones, we had first to follow mankind in its weaknesses, its neuroses, its doubts; we had to make them entirely ours, in order to go beyond them. The rigorous duplication of the genetic code, meditation on the life story of the predecessor, the writing of the commentary: such were the three pillars of our faith, unchanged since the time of the Founders. Before preparing myself a light meal, I joined my hands for a short prayer to the Supreme Sister and I felt lucid, balanced and active again.

Before falling asleep, I skimmed over the commentary of Marie22; I knew that I would soon get back in contact with Marie23. Fox stretched out beside me and sighed softly. He was going to die next to me, and he knew it; he was already an old dog now; he fell asleep almost immediately.

It was another world, separated from the ordinary world by a few centimetres of fabric – indispensable social protection, since 90 per cent of men who came across Belle would be seized by the immediate desire to penetrate her. Once her jeans were off, I played for a little while with her pink thong, noting that her sex quickly became moist; it was five in the afternoon. Yes, it was another world, and I stayed there until eleven the following morning – it was the cut-off point for breakfast, and I was beginning to get seriously hungry. I had probably slept, for brief periods. For the rest, those few hours justified my life. I was not exaggerating and I was conscious of not exaggerating: we were at that moment in the absolute simplicity of things. Sexuality, or more precisely desire, was of course a theme I had touched on many a time in my sketches; that many things in this world centred around sexuality, or more precisely desire, I was as conscious of as anyone else – and probably more so than many others. In these conditions, as an ageing comedian, I had occasionally let myself be overcome by a sort of sceptical doubt: sexuality was perhaps, like so many other things and perhaps everything in this world, *overrated*; perhaps it was just a banal *ruse*, dreamed up to increase competition among men and the speed at which the whole system functioned. There was maybe nothing more to sexuality than there was in lunch at Taillevent, or in a Bentley Continental GT; nothing that justifies one getting that worked up.

That night would show me that I was wrong, and bring me to a more elementary view of things. The following day, back at San Jose, I went down to the Playa de Monsul. Observing the sea, and the sun sinking into the sea. I wrote a poem. This fact was already curious in itself: not only had I never written poetry before, but I had practically never read any, with the exception of Baudelaire. Besides, poetry, as far as I knew, was dead. I quite regularly bought a quarterly literary review, of rather esoteric tendencies – without truly being part of the literary world, I occasionally felt close to it; after all, I did write my own sketches, and even if I aimed at nothing more than a rough parody of the 'spoken word' I was conscious of how difficult the simple operation of aligning words and organising them into sentences could be without the whole lot collapsing into incoherence, or sinking into tedium. In this review, two years earlier, I had read a long article devoted to the disappearance of poetry – a disappearance that the author judged inevitable. According to him, poetry, as non-contextual language, anterior to the objects–properties distinction, had definitively deserted the world of men. It was situated in a primitive elsewhere to which we would never again have access, because it came before the true formation of object and language. Unfit to transport information more precise than simple bodily or emotional sensations, and intrinsically linked to the magical state of the human mind, it had been rendered irredeemably obsolete by the appearance of reliable procedures of objective proof. I had been convinced by all this at the time, but that morning I hadn't washed, I was still filled with the scent of Esther, and its savours (never with us had there been a question of using a condom, the subject had simply not been touched on, and I think she had never thought of it – I too hadn't thought of it, and that was more surprising because my first sexual experiences had taken place at the time of AIDS, an AIDS that was then inevitably fatal, and this should have left its mark on me). Well, AIDS belonged no doubt to the domain of the contextual, that's what you could say, and in any case I wrote my first poem, that morning, while I was still bathed in the scent of Esther. Here is that poem:

> *At heart I have always known*
> *That I would find love*
> *And that this would be*
> *On the eve of my death.*
>
> *I have always been confident,*
> *I have not given up:*
> *Long before your presence,*
> *You were announced to me.*

> *So you will be the one,*
> *My real presence,*
> *I will be in the joy*
> *Of your non-fictional skin*
>
> *So soft to the caress,*
> *So light and so fine,*
> *Entity non-divine,*
> *Animal of tenderness.*

At the end of that night, the sun had returned to Madrid. I called a taxi and waited a few minutes in the hotel lobby with Esther while she replied to the many messages that had accumulated on her mobile. She had already made numerous calls during the night, and she seemed to have a very rich social life; most of her conversations ended with the expression *un besito*, or sometimes *un beso*. I didn't really speak Spanish, the nuance, if there was one, escaped me, but I became conscious, at the moment when the taxi stopped in front of the hotel, that in practice she did not kiss much. It was quite curious because, by contrast, she liked penetration in all its forms, she presented her ass with a lot of grace (she had pert buttocks rather like those of a boy), and she sucked without hesitation and even with enthusiasm; but every time my lips approached hers she turned away, a little annoyed.

I put my travel bag in the boot; she offered me a cheek, there were two quick kisses, then I got into the car. Whilst moving off down the avenue, a few metres further on, I turned around to wave goodbye; but she was already on the phone, and did not notice my gesture.

As soon as I arrived at Almeria airport I understood how my life was going to be over the following weeks. For some years already, I had left my mobile almost systematically off: it was a question of status, I was a European star; if people wanted to contact me they had to leave a message, and wait for me to reply. This had sometimes been hard, but I had stuck to my rule, and over the years I had been proven right: producers left messages; well-known actors, newspaper editors, they all left messages; I was at the top of the pyramid, and I intended to stay there, at least for a few years, until I officially retired from the stage. This time my first action, on getting off the plane, was to switch on my mobile; I was surprised, and almost terrified by the violence of the disappointment that seized me when I saw that I had no message from Esther.

Your only chance of survival, if you are sincerely smitten, lies in hiding this fact from the woman you love, of feigning a casual detachment under all circumstances. What sadness there is in this simple observation! What an accusation against man! However, it had never occurred to me to contest this law, nor to imagine disobeying it: love makes you weak, and the weaker of the two is oppressed, tortured and finally killed by the other, who in his or her turn oppresses, tortures and kills without having evil intentions, without even getting pleasure from it, with complete indifference; that's what men, normally, call love. During the first few days I went through great moments of hesitation regarding this phone. I walked up and down the rooms, lighting cigarette after cigarette, from time to time I walked to the sea, turned back and realised that I had not seen the sea, that I would have been incapable of confirming its presence in that minute – during these walks, I forced myself to separate myself from my phone, to leave it on my bedside table, and more generally I forced myself to respect an interval of two hours before switching it back on, and seeing once again that she hadn't left any message. On the morning of the third day I had the idea of leaving my telephone on permanently, and of trying to forget to wait for the ring; in the middle of the night, on swallowing my fifth Mepronizine tablet, I realised that this didn't serve any purpose, and I began to resign myself to the fact that Esther was the stronger, and that I no longer had any power over my own life.

On the evening of the fifth day, I called her. She didn't seem at all surprised to hear from me, time seemed to her to have passed very quickly. She happily agreed to come and visit me in San Jose; she knew the province of Almeria, having holidayed there several times as a small girl; for the last few years she had been going instead to Ibiza or Formentera. She could spend a weekend, not the next one, but in a fortnight; I took a deep breath so as not to show my disappointment. '*Un besito*,' she said just before hanging up. We had stepped up another gear.

Two weeks after my arrival, Fox died, just after sunset. I was stretched out on the bed when he approached and tried painfully to jump up; he wagged his tail nervously. Since the beginning, he hadn't touched his bowl once; he had lost a lot of weight. I helped him to settle on my lap; for a few seconds, he looked at me, with a curious mixture of exhaustion and apology; then, calmed, he closed his eyes. Two minutes later, he gave out his last breath. I buried him inside the residence at the western extremity of the land surrounded by the protective fence, next to his predecessors. During the night, a rapid transport from the Central City dropped off an identical dog; they knew the codes and how to work the barrier, I didn't have to get up to greet them. A small white-and-ginger mongrel came towards me wagging its tail. I gestured to him. He jumped on the bed and stretched out beside me.

Love is simple to define, but it seldom happens – in the series of beings. Through these dogs we pay homage to love, and to its possibility. What is a dog but a machine for loving? You introduce him to a human being, giving him the mission to love – and however ugly, perverse, deformed or stupid this human being might be, the dog loves him. This characteristic was so surprising, so striking for the humans of the previous race that most of them – all testimonies agree on this point – came to love the dog back. The dog was therefore a machine for loving, which could also train others to love – its efficiency, however, remained limited to dogs, and never extended to other men.

No subject is more touched on than love, in the human life stories as well as in the literary corpus they have left us; homosexual love like heterosexual love is touched on, without us being able, up until now, to uncover any significant difference; no subject, either, is as discussed, as controversial, especially during the final period of human history, when the cyclothymic fluctuations concerning belief in love became constant and dizzying. In conclusion, no subject seems to have preoccupied man as much; even money, even the satisfaction derived from combat and glory, loses, by comparison, its dramatic power in human life stories. Love seems to have been, for humans of the final period, the acme and the impossible, the regret and the grace, the focal point upon which all suffering and joy could be concentrated. The life story of Daniel1, turbulent, painful, as often unreservedly sentimental as frankly cynical, and contradictory from all points of view, is in this regard characteristic.

I almost rented another car to go and fetch Esther from Almeria airport; I was afraid she would get an unfavourable impression from the Mercedes 600 SL coupé, but also from the swimming pool, the jacuzzis and more generally the display of luxury that characterised my life. I was mistaken: Esther was a realist; she knew that I had had some success and therefore expected, logically, that I would live in fine style; she knew all kinds of people, some very rich, others very poor, and found nothing remarkable in it; she accepted this in-equality, like all the others, with a perfect straightforwardness. My generation was still scarred by different debates around the question of which economic regime one should wish for, debates that always concluded with agreement about the superiority of the market economy – with the sledgehammer argument that populations on which another mode of organisation had been imposed had zealously and even petulantly rejected it, as soon as they had the chance to. In Esther's generation, those debates themselves had disappeared; capitalism was for her a natural habitat, in which she moved with the grace that characterised all the actions in her life; to strike in protest of planned redundancies would have seemed to her as absurd as striking against the weather getting colder, or the invasion of North Africa by crickets. The idea of any form of collective demand was generally foreign to her, it had always seemed obvious to her that, on the financial level as for all the essential questions of life, everyone had to look after themselves, and sail their own ships without relying on help from anyone else. No doubt in order to toughen herself up, she felt compelled to exercise strict financial independence, and although her sister had quite a lot of money, she had, since the age of fifteen, insisted on earning her pocket money herself, buying her own discs and clothes, even if it meant she had to do tedious jobs like distributing brochures or delivering pizzas. She didn't, however, go as far as offering to pay her share in restaurants, or anything like that; but I sensed from the beginning that giving her too sumptuous a gift would have unsettled her, it would have been a slight threat to her independence.

She arrived dressed in a turquoise pleated miniskirt and a Betty Boop T-shirt. In the airport car park, I tried to take her in my arms; she quickly moved away, looking flustered. At the moment when she put her suitcase in the boot, a gust of wind lifted her skirt, and I got the impression that she wasn't wearing anything beneath it. Once I was in front of the wheel, I asked her the question. She nodded with a smile, hitched her skirt up to her waist and parted her thighs a little: the hairs of her pussy formed a small, well-trimmed blonde rectangle.

As I fired the ignition; she pulled her skirt back down: I now knew that she wasn't wearing any panties, the desired effect had been produced, it was enough. We arrived at the residence, and as I was taking her suitcase from the boot, she went ahead of me up the few steps leading to the entrance; as I made out the lower curves of her little ass I grew dizzy and almost ejaculated in my trousers. I caught up with her, and embraced her tightly. 'Open the door . . .' she said rubbing her ass distractedly against my cock. I obeyed, but we were scarcely inside when I pressed against her again; she knelt down on a little rug nearby, putting her hands on the floor. I opened my flies and penetrated her, but unfortunately the car ride had so excited me that I came almost straight away; she seemed a little disappointed, but not too much. She wanted to change and have a bath.

If Stendhal's famous saying, which was also appreciated by Nietzsche, that beauty is a promise of happiness, is in general completely false, it can, however, be applied perfectly to eroticism. Esther was ravishing, but so was Isabelle, in her youth she was probably even more beautiful; Esther, on the other hand, was more erotic, she was incredibly, deliciously erotic, and I became conscious of it again when she came back from the bathroom: immediately after slipping on a large pullover she pulled it down slightly to reveal the straps of her bra, then she readjusted her thong so that it showed above her jeans; she did all these little gestures automatically, without even thinking, with irresistible naturalness and candour.

On waking the following morning, my first joy was the idea that we were going to go down to the beach together. Naturism is tacitly accepted on the Playa de Monsul, as on all the wild, out-of-the-way, almost deserted beaches in the Cabo de Gata Nature Reserve. Of course, nudity is not erotic, at least that's what they say, for my part I've always found nudity *rather* erotic – when the body is beautiful, obviously – let's just say that it is not what is *most* erotic. I had had tedious discussions about this with journalists at the time when I introduced neo-Nazi naturists into my sketches. I knew, anyway, that she had gone to find something; I had only to wait for a few minutes, then she appeared dressed in white hot-pants, with the first two buttons left open, uncovering the start of her pubic hair; over her breasts she had tied a golden shawl, taking care to raise it a bit so that you could see their undersides. The sea was very calm. Once she had sat down, she undressed completely, and opened her thighs wide, offering her sex to the sun. I poured some oil on her belly and began to caress her. I have always been quite gifted at that, at least I know the best way to tackle the inside of the thighs, the perineum, it's one of my little talents. I was right in the middle of this, and noticing with satisfaction that Esther was beginning to display her desire to be penetrated, when I heard 'Hello!' shouted by a strong and joyful voice, a few metres behind me. I turned round: Fadiah was advancing in our direction. She was naked, and carried a white canvas beach bag on her shoulder, adorned with the multicoloured star with curved branches that was the sign of the Elohimites; she certainly had a superb body. I got up, made the introductions, and an animated conversation began in English. The little white ass of Esther was very attractive, but the round and curved one of Fadiah was also tempting, in any case I was growing more and more hard, but for the moment they both acted as if they had not noticed; in porn films there is always at least one scene with two women, I was convinced that Esther had nothing against it, and something told me that Fadiah would be equally up for it. On leaning down to relace her sandals, Esther brushed against my cock, as if inadvertently, but I was certain that she had done it deliberately, I took a step in her direction, my sex was now raised up to her face. Patrick's arrival calmed me down a little; he too was naked, well built but corpulent, I noticed that he was beginning to grow a pot belly, probably thanks to his business lunches, but nonetheless he was a fine medium-sized mammal. I had nothing against a foursome in principle but for the moment my vague sexual desires had somewhat subsided.

We continued to talk, all four of us naked, a few metres from the sea shore. Neither he nor she seemed surprised by the presence of Esther and the disappearance of Isabelle. The Elohimites rarely form stable couples, they can live together for two or three years, sometimes more, but the prophet strongly encourages everyone to keep their autonomy and independence, particularly financial, no one must consent to a durable reduction of their individual freedom, whether through marriage or through a civil union, love must remain open and be able to be constantly renewed, such are the principles decreed by the prophet. Even if she profited from the high earnings of Patrick and the way of life they facilitated, Fadiah probably shared no possessions with him, and they no doubt had separate bank accounts. I asked Patrick for news about his parents, and then he announced some very sad news: his mother had died. This had been very unexpected and brutally sudden: a nosocomial infection contracted in a hospital in Liège, where she had gone for a routine hip operation, to which she had succumbed within a few days. He had been on a work trip to Korea, and hadn't been able, himself, to see her on her death bed, by the time he returned she was already frozen – she had given her body to science. Robert, his father, had difficulty handling the shock, in fact he had decided to leave Spain to move into a retirement home in Belgium; he had left him the property.

In the evening, we dined together in a fish restaurant in San Jose. Robert the Belgian just nodded his head, and took little part in the conversation; he was almost completely sedated by tranquillisers. Patrick reminded me that the winter course was taking place in

Lanzarote in a few months' time, and he strongly hoped that I would be present, the prophet had spoken about this again a week ago, I had made a very good impression on him, and this time it would be truly grandiose, attendees would be coming from across the entire globe. Esther, naturally, was welcome. She had never heard of the sect, so she listened to the presentation of the doctrine with curiosity. Patrick, no doubt warmed up by the wine (a Tesoro de Bullas, from the region of Murcia, a wine that hits you hard), emphasised the sexual aspects in particular, The love taught by the prophet, and which he recommended one practise, was the true, unpossessive, love: if you truly loved a woman, should you not rejoice at seeing her take pleasure with other men? I knew this sort of chat, I had had tedious discussions about it with journalists at the time when I introduced anorexic orgy sluts into my sketches. Robert the Belgian nodded with desperate approval, he who had probably never known any woman other than his wife, now deceased, and who was no doubt going to die quite quickly in his retirement home in Brabant, wallowing anonymously in his urine, still happy to have avoided molestation by the auxiliary nurses. Fadiah too seemed to agree completely, dipped her prawns in the mayonnaise and greedily licked her lips. I had absolutely no idea what Esther might think of it, I imagine she must have found the theoretical discussions on this subject rather stuffy and *dated*, and frankly I could almost agree with her – although for different reasons, linked rather to a general repulsion I felt for theoretical discussions, it was becoming more and more difficult for me to take part in them, or even to feign some kind of interest. Fundamentally I could have certainly formulated some objections, for example the fact that non-possessive love only seemed conceivable if you yourself lived in an atmosphere saturated with delights, from which all fear was absent, particularly fear of abandonment and death, and that it implied at the very least, and among other things, eternity; in short the conditions for it were not reality; a few years earlier I would certainly have argued, but I no longer had the strength for it, and anyway it wasn't too serious, Patrick was a bit drunk, he was listening to himself with satisfaction, the fish was fresh, we were passing what it is conventionally called *a pleasant evening*. I promised to come to Lanzarote, Patrick assured me with an expansive gesture that I would benefit from utterly exceptional VIP treatment; Esther did not know, she would probably be taking exams at that time. As he left us I gave Robert a long handshake, and he muttered something I couldn't understand a word of; he was trembling a little, in spite of the mild temperature. He troubled me, this old materialist, with his features gnawed by sadness, his hair turned white overnight. He had only a few months left, perhaps a few weeks. Who would miss him? Not many; probably Harry, who was going to find himself deprived of pleasing, well-planned, but not too quarrelsome conversations. I then became conscious that Harry would probably bear better than Robert had the death of his wife; he could imagine Hildegarde playing the harp among the angels of the Lord, or, in a more spiritual form, snug in a topological corner of the omega point, something like that; for Robert the Belgian, the situation was hopeless.

'What are you thinking?' asked Esther as we went through the front door. 'Sad things . . .' I replied pensively. She nodded her head, gave me a serious look, and realised that I really was sad. 'Don't worry . . .' she said; then she knelt down to suck me off. She had a very honed technique, doubtless inspired by porn films – it was immediately obvious for she had that gesture, which you learn quickly in films, of throwing back her hair to allow the boy, for want of a camera, to watch you in action. Since their beginnings, fellatio has always been the jewel in the crown of porn films, the only thing that can serve as a useful model for young girls; it was also the only incidence in which you could occasionally find a bit of real emotion in the act, because it is the only incidence in which the close-up is, also, a close-up of the face of the woman, where you can read in her features that joyful pride, that childlike delight she feels when giving pleasure. In fact, Esther told me afterwards that she had refused this caress in her first sexual relationship, and had only decided to launch herself into it after having seen a lot of films. She now did it remarkably well, and took pleasure in her own mastery; later, I never hesitated, even when she seemed too tired or indisposed to fuck, to ask her for a blowjob. Immediately before ejaculation she would back off slightly to receive the jet of sperm on her face or in her mouth, but then she would return to the attack to meticulously lick, right to the last drop. Like many very pretty young girls she became ill easily, and had a delicate stomach and she had at first swallowed reluctantly; but experience had demonstrated to her in the clearest manner possible that she should take advantage of it, that swallowing their sperm was not, for men, an indifferent or optional action, but rather it constituted an irreplaceable personal expression; she now gave herself to it with joy, and I felt immense happiness on coming in her little mouth.

After a few weeks' reflection, I made contact with Marie23, simply leaving her my IP address. She replied with the following message:

> *I saw God clearly*
> *In his nonexistence,*
> *In his precious nothingness*
> *And I grabbed my chance.*

12924, 4311, 4358, 212526. The address indicated was that of a grey, smooth, silky surface, whose thickness was run through with light movements, like a velvet curtain rustled by the wind, to the rhythm of distant brass harmonies. The composition was both calming and slightly intoxicating, and I lost myself for some time in contemplation. Before I had time to reply, she sent me a second message:

> *After the event of leaving the Void,*
> *We shall swim at last in the liquid Virgin.*

51922624, 4854267. In the middle of a blasted landscape composed of carcasses of tall grey buildings, with gaping windows, a giant bulldozer was carrying mud. I zoomed gently into the enormous yellow vehicle, with its rounded forms and its appearance of a remote-controlled toy – there did not seem to be a driver in the cabin. In the middle of the blackened mud, human skeletons were scattered by the bulldozer's blade as it advanced; by zooming in a little more I made out more clearly tibias and skulls.

'It's what I see from my window . . .' Marie23 wrote to me, passing without warning into non-coding mode. I was a bit taken aback; this meant she was therefore one of the rare neohumans living in the old conurbations. It was a subject, I also realised, that Marie22 had never touched on with my predecessor; at least his commentary carried no trace of it. 'Yes, I live in the ruins of New York,' replied Marie23. 'In the middle of what men called Manhattan . . .' she added a little later.

That obviously was of little importance, since it was out of the question that neohumans would venture out of their residences; but I was happy for my part to live in the middle of a natural landscape. New York was not that unpleasant, she replied; since the time of the Great Drying Up there was lots of wind, the sky was constantly changing, she lived high up and spent a lot of time observing the movement of the clouds. Some chemical factories, probably situated in New Jersey, judging from the distance, continued to function, and at sunset the pollution gave the sky strange pink and green hues; and the ocean was still present, far to the east, unless it was an optical illusion, but in good weather you could sometimes make out a vague shimmering.

I asked her if she had had time to finish the life story of Marie1. 'Oh yes . . .' she immediately replied. 'It is very short: less than three pages. She seemed to have an astonishing talent for synthesis.'

That too was original, but possible. On the other hand, Rebecca1 was famous for her life story, which was more than two thousand pages long, and yet covered a period of only three hours. For this, as well, there was no rule.

The sexual life of man can be broken down into two phases: the first when he prematurely ejaculates, and the second when he can no longer manage to get a hard-on. During the first weeks of my relationship with Esther, I noticed that I had returned to the first phase – despite believing, for a long time, that I had begun the second. Sometimes, while walking beside her in a park, or along the beach, I was overwhelmed by an extraordinary drunkenness, I had the impression of being a boy of her age, and I walked more quickly, breathed deeply, walked upright and spoke loudly. At other times, however, on meeting our reflections in a mirror, I was filled with nausea, and, breathless, I shrivelled between the covers; in one fell swoop, I felt so old, so flaccid. On the whole, however, my body wasn't that badly preserved, I didn't have a trace of fat, I even had a few muscles; but my ass sagged, and especially my balls, they sagged more and more, and it was irrevocable, I had never heard of any treatment; yet she licked these balls, and caressed them, without seeming at all bothered. As for her body, it was so fresh and smooth.

Around mid-January, I had to go to Paris for a few days; an intense cold spell had fallen upon France, and every morning homeless people were found frozen on the pavements. I understood perfectly why they refused to go into the shelters opened for them, why they had no desire to mix with their fellows; it was a savage world, populated by cruel and stupid people, whose stupidity, by some peculiar and repugnant fusion, further exacerbated their cruelty; it was a world where you found neither solidarity nor pity – fights, rape and acts of torture were commonplace, it was in fact a world that was almost as hard as the prisons, with the exception that surveillance was almost nonexistent, and danger constant. I visited

Vincent, his house was overheated. He greeted me in slippers and a dressing gown, he screwed up his eyes and took a few minutes to manage to express himself normally; he had lost more weight. I had the impression I was his first visitor in months. He had worked a lot in his basement, he told me, would I like to have a look? I didn't feel I had the courage and left after a coffee; he continued to shut himself up in his marvellous, dreamlike little world, and I realised that no one would ever have access to it again.

As I was in a hotel near the Place de Clichy, I took advantage of this to go into a few sex shops, to buy some sexy underwear for Esther – she had told me she particularly liked latex, that she also liked being masked, handcuffed and wrapped in chains. The salesman seeming to be unusually competent, I spoke to him about my problem with premature ejaculation; he recommended a German cream, recently put on the market, whose composition was complex – it contained sulphate of banzoncaine, some potassium hydrochlorite, and some camphor. By applying it to the glans before sexual intercourse and massaging it in carefully, sensitivity was diminished, and the rise of pleasure and ejaculation happened much more slowly. I tried it on my return to Spain and it was an immediate and total success, I could penetrate her for hours, with no constraints except respiratory exhaustion – for the first time in my life I wanted to stop smoking. Generally, I woke up before her, my first move was to lick her, her pussy would quickly become moist and she would open her thighs to be taken: we made love in bed, on the settees, at the swimming pool, on the beach. Perhaps people live like this for years on end, but I personally had never known such happiness, and I wondered how I had been able to live up until then. She had instinctively the expressions, the little gestures (licking her lips greedily, squeezing her breasts in her palms to push them out towards you) that remind one of a slightly *sluttish* young girl, and that bring a man's excitement to its highest point. To be inside her was a source of infinite joy, I could feel each of the movements of her pussy when she closed it, softly or more strongly, around my sex, for whole minutes I screamed and cried at the same time, I no longer knew where on earth I was, occasionally when she withdrew I noticed that very loud music had been playing, and that I had heard nothing. We rarely went out, sometimes we went to drink cocktails in a lounge bar in San Jose, but there too she would quickly come up to me, lay her head on my shoulder, press my cock with her fingers through the thin fabric, and often we left immediately to fuck in the toilets – I had given up underwear, and she never wore panties. She truly had very few inhibitions: sometimes, when we were alone in the bar, she knelt down between my legs on the carpet and sucked me off whilst finishing her cocktail with little sips. One day, late in the afternoon, we were surprised in this position by the waiter: she withdrew my cock from her mouth, but kept it in her hands, looked up and gave him a big smile whilst continuing to jack me off me with two fingers; he also smiled, collected the bill, and it seemed to me at that moment as if all had long ago been foreseen and arranged by a higher authority, and that my happiness, too, was included in the economy of the system.

I was in paradise, and I would have had no objection to remaining there for the rest of my days, but she had to leave at the end of the week to start her piano lessons again. On the morning of her departure, before she woke up, I carefully massaged my glans with the German cream; then I knelt above her face, parted her long blonde hair and introduced my sex between her lips; she began to suck before even opening her eyes. Later, while we had breakfast, she told me that the more pronounced taste of my sex in the morning, mixed in with that of the cream, had reminded her of cocaine. I knew that after snorting much of their cocaine, a lot of people then liked to lick the remaining grains of powder. She explained to me then that, at certain parties, there was a game in which the girls did a line of coke off the sex of the boys who were there; anyway, she didn't go to this kind of party very often nowadays, it had been mostly when she was sixteen, seventeen.

For me, the shock was quite painful; the dream of all men is to meet little sluts who are innocent but ready for all forms of depravity – which is what, more or less, all teenage girls are. Then, gradually, the girls quieten down, thus condemning men to remain eternally jealous of their depraved pasts as little sluts. To refuse to do something because you've already done it, because you've already *been there*, rapidly leads to the destruction, for yourself as much as for others, of any reason for living, for any possible future, and it plunges you into an oppressive ennui that will eventually transform into atrocious bitterness, accompanied by hatred and rancour towards those who still belong to the land of the living. Esther, thankfully, had not quietened down, but I couldn't stop myself asking her questions about her sex life; she would answer me, as I had expected, candidly, and straightforwardly. She had first made love at the age of twelve, after a night out in a disco, on a language course in England; but it wasn't very important, she told me, rather it was an isolated experience. Then, nothing had happened for about two years. Then she had begun to go out in Madrid, and there, yes, quite a lot of things had happened, she had really discovered sexual games. A few orgies, yes. A bit of S&M. Not really with girls – her sister was completely bisexual but no, she preferred boys. For her eighteenth birthday she had wanted, for the first time, to go to bed with two boys, and she kept an excellent memory of it, the boys were very fit, this threesome had continued for some time; as it went on the boys had gradually specialised, she jerked and sucked both of them off but one would more often penetrate her from the front, the other from behind and this was perhaps what she preferred, he would really bugger her very hard, especially when she had bought poppers. I imagined her, a frail young girl, entering the sex shops of Madrid to ask for poppers. There is a brief ideal period, during the dissolution of societies with strong religious moral strictures, when young people truly desire a free, unbridled and joyful life; then they grow weary, little by little narcissistic competition takes the upper hand, and in the end they fuck even less than at the time of strong religious morality; but Esther still belonged to that brief ideal period, which had come late to Spain. She had been so straightforwardly, so honestly sexual, she had indulged with such grace in all the games, all the experiences in the sexual arena, without ever thinking that there could have been anything *bad* in it, that I didn't even manage to hold it against her. I just had the persistent and tormenting feeling of having met her too late, much too late, and of having wasted my life; that feeling, I knew, would never leave me, quite simply because it was true.

*

We saw each other very often in the following weeks, I spent practically all my weekends in Madrid. I had no idea if she slept with other boys in my absence, I suppose she did, but I managed pretty well to chase the thought from my mind, after all she was always available to me, happy to see me, she always made love with as much candour and as little reserve, and I truly can't see what more I could have asked for. It didn't even cross my mind, or very rarely, to ask what a pretty girl like her could see in me. After all, I was *a laugh*, she laughed a lot in my company, this was perhaps quite simply the only thing that saved me, now as it had with Sylvie, thirty years before when I had started out on a love life that had been, on the whole, unsatisfying and punctuated by long eclipses. It was certainly not my money that attracted her, nor my celebrity – in fact, every time I was recognised in the street when I was with her, she looked rather annoyed. Nor did she particularly like being recognised as an actress herself – this also happened, though more rarely. It is true that she didn't consider herself to be an *actress*; most actors accept being loved for their celebrity without any problem, and why not? After all it's part of themselves, of their most authentic personality, or in any case the one they have chosen for themselves. By contrast, men who can accept that they are loved for their money are rare, in the West at least; the same cannot be said for Chinese shopkeepers. In the simplicity of their souls, Chinese shopkeepers consider that their class S Mercedes, their bathrooms with hydromassage showers and more generally their money are part of themselves, and therefore they have no objection to arousing the enthusiasm of young girls through these material attributes, they have the same immediate, direct relationship with them that a Westerner can have with the beauty of his face – and in fact theirs makes even more sense, since, in a sufficiently stable politico-economic system, if it's often the case that a man is stripped of his physical beauty by illness, if ageing will in any case inevitably strip him of it, it is far less likely that he will be stripped of his villas on the Côte d'Azur, or of his class S Mercedes. It's true, however, that I was a Western neurotic, and not a Chinese shopkeeper, and that in the complexity of my soul I far preferred to be appreciated for my humour than for my money, or even for my celebrity – for I was in no way certain, during an otherwise long and active career, that I had given the best of me, that I had explored all the facets of my personality, I was not an authentic artist in the sense that Vincent, for example, could be, because I knew all too well in my heart of hearts that there was nothing funny about life, but I had refused to take this into account, I had been a bit of a whore, in fact, I had adapted to the tastes of the public, I had never been really sincere, supposing that is possible, but I knew that you had to suppose it, and that if sincerity, in itself, is nothing, it is nevertheless the condition for everything else. Deep down, I knew that not one of my miserable sketches, not one of my lamentable scripts, mechanically stitched together, with the skill of a wily professional, to entertain an audience of bastards and monkeys, deserved to survive me. This thought was, at moments, painful; but I knew that I would succeed, in this as in everything, in chasing it away quite quickly.

The only thing I had difficulty explaining to myself, was the irritation Esther displayed whenever her sister phoned, and she was with me in a hotel bedroom. On thinking of it, I became conscious that whilst I had met some of her friends – essentially homosexuals – I had never met her sister, with whom, moreover, she lived. After a moment's hesitation, she confessed to me that she had never spoken to her sister about our relationship; every time we saw each other she pretended to be with a girlfriend, or another boy. I asked her why: she had never really reflected on the question; she felt that her sister would be shocked, but she did not elaborate on this. It was certainly not the content of my productions, shows or films, that were to blame; she was still only a teenager when Franco died, she had taken an active part in *la movida* that had followed, and led a pretty unbridled life. All drugs had their place in her world, from cocaine to LSD, via magic mushrooms, marijuana and Ecstasy. When Esther was five her sister lived with two men, themselves bisexual; all three of them slept in the same bed, and came to say good night to her, together, before she went to sleep. Later she had lived with a woman, whilst still receiving many lovers, several times she had organised some pretty hot parties in the apartment. Esther would go in to say good night to everyone before returning to her bedroom to read *Tintin*. There were, however, some boundaries, and she had once kicked out a guest who was too heavy-handed in his caressing of the little girl, even threatening to call the police. 'Between free and consenting adults', that was the boundary, and adult life began at puberty, all that was made perfectly clear. I could see very plainly the kind of woman she was, and on the question of art she would certainly have been a supporter of total freedom of expression. As a left-wing journalist she had to respect dosh, *dinero*, so all in all I couldn't see what she could have to reproach in me. There must have been something else, something less respectable, and in the end, to be clear in my own mind I asked Esther directly.

She replied after a few minutes' reflection, in a pensive voice: 'I think she is going to find you too old . . .' Yes that was it, the moment she said it I knew it was true, and the revelation caused me no surprise, it was like the echo of a dull, not unexpected shock. The age difference was the last taboo, the final limit, all the stronger for the fact that it remained the last and had replaced all the others. In the modern world you could be a swinger, bi, trans, zoo, into S&M, but it was forbidden to be *old*. 'She's going to find it unhealthy, abnormal that I'm not with a boy my own age . . .' she continued with resignation. Well, yes I was an ageing man, this was my *disgrace* – to borrow Coetzee's term; it seemed perfect to me, I could think of no better word, and this moral freedom that is charming, fresh and seductive in adolescents could only become in my case, the repellent insistence of an old fart who refuses to *give up the ghost*. There was no escaping what her sister would think, or what almost anyone would have thought in her place – short of becoming a Chinese shopkeeper.

I had decided at that particular time to remain in Madrid all week, and two days later I had a little argument with Esther on the subject of *Ken Park*, the latest film by Larry Clark, which she had been keen to go and see. I had hated *Kids*, and I hated *Ken Park* even more, the scene where this dirty little shit beats up his grandparents was particularly unbearable. That film-maker completely disgusted me, and it was no doubt this sincere disgust that made me incapable of stopping myself from talking about it, whilst I strongly suspected that Esther liked him out of habit and conformism, because it was generally cool to approve of the representation of violence in the arts, and that she liked him without any real discernment, in the same way she liked, for example, Michael Haneke, without even realising that the meaning of those sorrowful and moral films by Michael Haneke was completely different from that of those by Larry Clark. I knew that it would have been better for me to keep quiet, that abandoning my usual comic character could only bring me trouble, but I couldn't, the imp of the perverse was the stronger. We were in a bizarre, very kitsch bar, with mirrors and gold fixtures, full of paroxysmal homosexuals who buggered themselves silly in adjacent backrooms, yet which was open to everyone, with groups of young boys and girls calmly drinking Coca-Colas at neighbouring tables. I explained to her whilst rapidly downing my iced tequila that I had built the whole of my career and fortune on the commercial exploitation of bad instincts, of the West's absurd attraction to cynicism and evil, and that I therefore felt myself ideally placed to assert that among all the merchants of evil, Larry Clark was one of the most common, most vulgar, simply because he unreservedly took the side of the young against the old, because all his films were an incitement to children to treat their parents without the least humanity, the least pity, and that there was nothing new or original about this, it had been the same in all the cultural sectors for the last fifty-odd years, and this supposedly cultural tendency in fact only hid the desire for a return to a primitive state where the young got rid of the old without cere- mony, with no questions asked, simply because they were too weak to defend themselves. It was, therefore, just a brutal regression, typical of modernity, to a stage preceding all civilisation, for any civilisation could judge itself on the fate it reserved for the weakest, for those who were no longer either productive or desirable, in short Larry Clark and his abject accomplice Harmony Korine were just two of the most tedious – and artistically the most miserable – examples of the Nietzschean scum who had been proliferating in the cultural field for far too long, and who could in no way be put on the same level as people like Michael Haneke, or like me, for example – who had always made sure to introduce a certain element of doubt, uncertainty and unease into my shows, even if they were (I was the first to admit it) otherwise repugnant. She listened to me with a sad expression, but with great attention, she hadn't yet touched her Fanta.

The advantage of giving a moral lecture, is that this type of argument has been under such strong censorship, and for so many years, that it provokes an incongruous effect and immediately attracts the attention of the interlocutor; the disadvantage is that the interlocutor never manages to take you completely seriously. The serious and attentive expression on Esther's face threw me for an instant, but I ordered another glass of tequila and ploughed on, whilst becoming conscious that I was getting excited artificially, that there was something false about my sincerity: apart from the patently obvious fact that Larry Clark was just a small, undistinguished merchant and that to cite him in the same sentence as Nietzsche was already in itself something derisory, I felt in my heart of hearts scarcely more concerned about these subjects than by world hunger, human rights or any rubbish of that kind. Nevertheless, I went on, with increasing acrimony, carried away by that strange mixture of nastiness and masochism, which I perhaps hoped would lead me to my destruction, after it had brought me fame and fortune. Not only did the old not have the right to fuck, I continued ferociously, but they no longer had the right to rebel against a world that nevertheless crushed them unsparingly, made them defenceless prey to the violence of juvenile delinquents before dumping them in ignoble twilight homes where they were humiliated and mistreated by decerebrated auxiliary nurses, and despite all this, rebellion was forbidden to them, rebellion too – like sexuality, like pleasure, like love – seemed reserved for the young and to have no point for other people, any cause incapable of mobilising the interest of the young was disqualified in advance, basically, old people were in all matters treated simply as waste, to be granted only a survival that was miserable, conditional and more and more narrowly limited. In my script *The Social Security Deficit*, which hadn't seen the light of day – it was, moreover, the only one of my projects not to see the light of day, and this appeared highly significant to me, I continued, almost beside myself – I incited instead the old to rebel against the young, to use them and to *show them who's boss*. Why for example should male and female adolescents, voracious and sheep-like consumers, always greedy for pocket money, not be *forced into* prostitution, the only means by which they could modestly reimburse the immense efforts and struggles that were made for their well-being? And why, at a time when contraception had been perfected, and the risk of genetic degeneration perfectly localised, should we maintain the absurd and humiliating taboo that is incest? Those are the real questions, the authentic moral issues! I exclaimed angrily; now that was no Larry Clark.

If I was acrimonious, she was sweet; and if I took, unreservedly, the side of the old, she did not take, to the same extent, the side of the young. A long conversation ensued, becoming more and more emotional and tender, first in the bar, then at a restaurant, then in another bar, and finally in the hotel bedroom; we even forgot, for one evening, to make love. It was our first real conversation, and it seemed to me to be the first real conversation I'd had with anyone for years, the last probably took place at some point at the start of my life with Isabelle, I had probably never had a real conversation with anyone other than a woman I loved, and essentially it seemed unsurprising to me that the exchange of ideas with someone who doesn't know your body, is not in a position to secure its unhappiness or on the other hand to bring it joy, was a false and ultimately impossible exercise, for we are bodies, we are, above all, principally and almost uniquely bodies, and the state of our bodies constitutes the true explanation of the majority of our intellectual and moral conceptions. It was only now I learned that Esther had had a very serious kidney illness, at the age of thirteen, which had necessitated a long operation, and that one of her kidneys had remained definitively atrophied, which obliged her to drink at least two litres of water a day, while the second one, saved for the time being, could at any moment show signs of weakness; it seemed obvious to me that this was an essential detail, that it was even no doubt for this reason that she had not *calmed down* on the sexual level: she knew the price of life, and how short it was. I also learned, and this seemed even more important, that she had had a dog, found in the streets of Madrid, and that she had looked after it since the age of ten; it had died the previous year. A very pretty young girl, treated with constant regard and paid enormous attention by the whole of the male population, including those – the huge majority – who no longer have any hope of obtaining sexual favours from her, frankly especially by them, with an abject emulation that with some fifty-somethings borders on senility pure and simple, a very pretty young girl before whom all faces open, all difficulties are ironed out, greeted everywhere as if she were the queen of the world, naturally becomes a sort of monster of egoism and self-satisfied vanity. Physical beauty plays here exactly the same role as nobility of blood in the Ancien Régime, and the brief consciousness that they might have at adolescence of the purely accidental nature of their rank rapidly gives way among very pretty young girls to a sensation of innate, natural and instinctive superiority, which places them completely outside, and far above, the rest of mankind. Everyone around her having as their objective to spare her all difficulties, and to satisfy the least of her desires, a very pretty young girl effortlessly comes to consider the rest of the world as made up of so many *servants*, herself having the sole task of maintaining her own erotic value – in the expectation of meeting a boy worthy of receiving her homage. The only thing that could save her on the moral level, is having a concrete responsibility for a weaker being, to be directly and personally responsible for the satisfaction of its physical needs, for its health and survival – this being could be a brother or a younger sister, a pet, whatever.

Esther was certainly not *well educated* in the normal sense of the term, the thought never crossed her mind to empty an ashtray, or to clear away what was left on her plate, and she didn't mind in the slightest about leaving the lights on behind her in the rooms she had just left (there had been occasions when I, following step by step her journey through my residence in San Jose, had had to flick off seventeen switches); there was also no question of asking her to think of doing the shopping, to bring anything back from a shop that was not intended for her own use, or more generally to do any kind of favour for anyone. Like all very pretty young girls she was basically only good for fucking, and it would have been stupid to employ her for anything else, to see her as anything other than a luxury animal, pampered and spoiled, protected from all cares as from any difficult or painful task so as to be better able to devote herself to her exclusively sexual service. But, nonetheless, she was very far from being that monster of arrogance, of absolute and cold egoism, or, to speak in more Baudelairean terms, that *infernal little bitch* that the majority of very pretty young girls are; there was in her the consciousness of illness, weakness and death. Although beautiful, very beautiful, infinitely erotic and desirable, Esther was no less sensitive to animal infirmities, because she knew them; it was that evening that I became conscious of it, and I began to truly love her. Physical desire, however violent, had, for me, never been enough to lead to love, it had never been able to reach that ultimate stage where it was accompanied, through a strange juxtaposition, by compassion for the one I desired; any living being, obviously, deserves compassion for the simple fact that it is alive, and therefore exposes itself to innumerable sufferings; but, when you're talking about a being that is young and in perfect health, it is a consideration that appears very theoretical. Through her kidney illness, her physical weakness, which was above suspicion yet real, Esther could arouse an unaffected compassion in me, whenever I wanted to feel this way about her. Being herself compassionate, having the same occasional aspirations towards goodness, she could also arouse in me esteem, which completed the edifice, and even though I was able to desire someone completely contemptible, even though I had even found myself on several occasions fucking girls with the sole aim of confirming my power over them and, it's true, to *dominate* them, if I had gone as far as using this unworthy feeling in some sketches, as far as displaying a troubling understanding of rapists who sacrifice their victim immediately after finishing with her body, I had, however, always needed to respect in order to love, never in my heart of hearts had I felt perfectly at ease in a sexual relationship based purely on erotic attraction and indifference to the other, I had always needed, to feel sexually happy, a minimum – for want of love – of sympathy, respect and mutual understanding; no, I had not given up on mankind.

Not only was Esther compassionate and gentle, but she was also intelligent and shrewd enough to put herself, when necessary, in my place. After this discussion in which I had defended with an impetuosity that was wearisome – and, moreover, stupid, since she hadn't even dreamed of putting me in this category – the right to happiness for ageing people, she concluded by saying that she would speak to her sister about me, and would get around to making the introductions very soon.

During that week in Madrid, when I was almost always with Esther, and which remains one of happiest periods of my life, I also realised that if she had other lovers their presence was unusually discreet, and if I wasn't the only one – which was, after all, equally possible – I was no doubt the *favourite*. For the first time in my life I felt unrestrictedly happy to be a man, by this I mean a human being of the masculine sex, because for the first time I had found a woman who opened herself completely to me, who gave me totally, without limits, what a woman can give to a man. For the first time also, I felt moved in regard to others by charitable and friendly intentions: I would have liked everyone to be happy, like I was myself. I was no longer a clown, I had left *the humorous attitude* far behind me; in short I was living again, even if I knew that this would be for the last time. All energy is of a sexual nature, not mainly, but exclusively, and when the animal is no longer good for reproducing, it is absolutely no longer good for anything; it is the same for men. When the sexual instinct is dead, writes Schopenhauer, the true core of life is consumed; thus, he notes in a metaphor of terrifying violence, 'human existence resembles a theatre performance which, begun by living actors, is ended by automatons dressed in the same costumes'. I didn't want to become an automaton, and it was this, that real presence, that taste for *living life*, as Dostoyevsky would have said, that Esther had given back to me. What is the point of maintaining a body that no one touches? And why would you choose a nice hotel bedroom if you have to sleep there alone? I could only, like so many who had finally been defeated despite their sniggers and their grimaces, bow down: immense and admirable, undoubtedly, was the power of love.

During the night that followed my first contact with Marie23, I had a strange dream. I was in the middle of a mountain landscape, the air was so clear that you could make out the slightest detail of the rocks and the ice crystals; the view extended far beyond the clouds, beyond the forests, as far as a line of steep summits, sparkling in their eternal snows. Near me, a few metres below, a small old man, dressed in furs, with a craggy face like that of a Kalmuk trapper, was digging patiently around a picket in the snow; then, armed only with his modest knife, he began to saw through a transparent cord, a metre in diameter, run through with optical fibres. I knew that this cord was one of those that led to the transparent room, the room in the midst of the snows where the leaders of the world gathered. The look on the face of the old man was wise and cruel. I knew that he was going to succeed, for he had time on his side, and that the foundations of the world were going to collapse; he was moved by no precise motivation, but by an animal-like obstinacy; I attributed to him the intuitive knowledge and powers of a shaman.

Like those of the humans, our dreams are almost always re-combinations of various elements of reality that occurred in the waking state; this has led some to see in them a proof of the non-uniqueness of the real. According to them, our dreams could be insights into other branches of the universe, which exist in the sense described by Everett-deWitt, i.e. other bifurcations of observable phenomena that appeared at the same time as certain events in the day; they would thus not be in anyway the expression of a desire or a fear, but rather the mental projection of substantial sequences of events, compatible with the global evolution of the wave function of the universe, but not directly proveable. Nothing in this hypothesis explained what it was that allowed dreams to escape from the usual limitations of the cognitive function, denying a given observer any access to the non-proveable sequences of events in his own branch of the universe; besides I had absolutely no idea what, in my existence, could have given birth to so divergent a branch.

According to other interpretations, some of *our* dreams are of a different order from those experienced by mankind; of artificial origin, they are the spontaneous productions of mental half-forms engendered by the modifiable interweaving of the electronic elements of the network. A gigantic organism could have demanded to be born, to form a common electronic consciousness, but it could only, at that instant, manifest itself by the production of a series of oneiric waves generated by the progressive subsets of the network, and constrained to propagate themselves through the transmission channels opened by the neohumans; it consequently sought to exert control over the opening of these channels. We were ourselves incomplete beings, beings in transition, whose destiny was to prepare for the coming of a digital future. Whatever can be said about this paranoid hypothesis, it is certain that a software mutation had taken place, probably dating from the beginning of the Second Decrease, and that, after first attacking the encoding system, it had gradually extended to all of the software layers of the network; no one knew its extent exactly, but it had to be big, and the reliability of our transmission system had, even in the best of cases, become very uncertain.

The danger of oneiric overproduction had been noted since the time of the Founders, and could also, more simply, be explained by the conditions of absolute physical isolation in which we were called upon to live. No effective treatment was known. The only suggested defence was to avoid sending and receiving messages, cutting off all contact with the neohuman community, and recentring oneself upon the elements of individual physiology. I forced myself to do this, and put in place the main devices for biochemical surveillance: it took several weeks for my oneiric production to return to its normal level, and for me to once again be able to concentrate on the life story of Daniel1, and on my commentary.

*In order to hijack netstat, you have to be injected into it; for that,
you have no other choice than to hijack all userland.*
kdm.fr.st

I had rather forgotten the existence of the Elohimites when I
received a phone call from Patrick, reminding me that the winter
course began in two weeks, and asking me if I still intended
participating. I had received an invitation letter, a VIP letter, he
made clear. I found it easily in my pile: the paper was adorned, as a
watermark, with young naked girls dancing among flowers. His
Holiness the prophet was inviting me, along with other friendly
eminent personalities, to attend, as every year, the celebration of
the anniversary of the 'marvellous encounter' – the one with the
Elohim, I imagined. It would be a special celebration, where previously unknown details concerning the construction of the
embassy would be unveiled, in the presence of believers from
across the globe, guided by their nine archbishops and their forty-
nine bishops – these honorary distinctions had nothing to do with
the real organisational structure; they had been dreamed up by
Cop, who judged them indispensable for the good management of
any human organisation. 'We're going to have a hell of a ball!' the
prophet had added, for my attention, in his own hand.

As she had foreseen, Esther had exams at this time, and could not
accompany me. Nor would she have had much time to see me, so I
accepted without hesitation – after all, I was now retired, I could do
a bit of tourism, sociological excursions, try and live some pictur-
esque or funny moments. I had never dealt with sects in my
sketches despite their being an authentically modern phenomenon;
they were proliferating, regardless of all the rationalist campaigns
and warnings, nothing seemed able to stop them. For some time I

played, quite vainly, with the idea of an Elohimite sketch, then I bought my plane ticket.

The flight stopped over at Gran Canaria, and while we circled waiting for our place in the landing path, I observed the dunes of Maspalomas with curiosity. The gigantic sand formations plunged into a bright-blue ocean; we were flying at low altitude, and I could make out figures forming on the sand, caused by the movement of the wind, sometimes resembling letters, sometimes animals or human faces; you couldn't help seeing signs there, and giving them a divinatory interpretation, and I began to feel oppressed, despite or because of the uniformity of the blueness.

Almost everyone got off at Las Palmas airport; then a few passengers who were shuttling between the islands got on. Most seemed to be long-distance travellers, in the manner of Australian backpackers armed with a *Let's Go Europe* guide and location maps for McDonalds. They behaved quietly, also looking at the landscape, and exchanging intelligent or poetic remarks in hushed voices. A little before landing we flew over a volcanic zone with tortured, dark-red rocks.

Patrick was waiting for me in the arrivals hall of Arrecife airport, dressed in trousers, a white tunic embroidered with the multicoloured star of the sect, and a wide smile on his lips – I had the impression that he had begun to smile five minutes before my arrival, and in fact he continued to, for no apparent reason, as we crossed the car park. He pointed out a white Toyota minibus to me, also adorned with the multicoloured star. I sat down in the front seat: Patrick's face was still lit up by an objectless smile; as he waited in the queue to insert his exit ticket he began to drum his fingers on the steering wheel whilst shaking his head, as if he was possessed by an internal melody.

We were driving across a plain that was intensely black, almost bluish, formed of angular, rough rocks, scarcely shaped by erosion, when he spoke again. 'You'll see, this course is superb . . .' he said in a hushed tone, as if to himself, or as if he was telling me a secret. 'There are special vibrations . . . It's very spiritual, really.' I politely agreed. The remark only half surprised me: in New Age literature it is classically accepted that volcanic regions are moved by telluric currents, to which most mammals – and especially man – are sensitive; they are supposed to incite, among other things, sexual promiscuity. 'That's it, that's it . . .' said Patrick, still ecstatic. 'We are sons of fire.' I abstained from reacting.

Just before arriving we drove along a beach of black sand, scattered with little white pebbles; I must admit that it was strange, and even disturbing. First I looked attentively, then I turned away; I felt a bit shocked by this brutal inversion of values. If the sea had been red, I would no doubt have been able to accept it; but it was still as desperately blue.

The road suddenly branched off inland and five hundred metres further on we stopped before a solid metal barrier, three metres high, flanked with barbed wire, which extended as far as one could see. Two guards armed with machine guns were patrolling behind the gate, which was apparently the only way out. Patrick gestured to them, they unlocked the gate, approached, and looked at me carefully before letting us pass. 'It's necessary . . .' Patrick told me in a voice as ethereal as ever. 'Journalists . . .'

The path, which was quite well tended, crossed a flat dusty zone, covered in small red pebbles. Just as I was able to make out, in the distance, a sort of village of white tents, Patrick turned left in the direction of a sheer rocky escarpment, eroded on one of its sides, made of the same black, probably volcanic rock that I had noticed a little earlier. After two or three bends, he stopped the vehicle on a terreplein and we had to continue on foot. Despite my protests he insisted on taking my suitcase, which was quite heavy. 'No, no, please . . . You are a VIP guest . . .' He had adopted a bantering tone, but something told me that it was in fact much more serious. We passed in front of about a dozen caves dug into the rock, before reaching another terreplein, almost at the top of the hillock. An opening three metres wide and two metres high led to a much vaster grotto; there, too, two armed guards were posted at the entry.

We went first into a square room, about ten metres on each side, with bare walls, furnished solely with a few folding chairs placed along the walls; then, preceded by a guard, we crossed a corridor lit by tall standard lamps in the shape of columns, quite similar to those that were fashionable in the seventies: inside a luminescent viscous liquid, which was yellow, turquoise, orange or mauve in colour, big globules would form and rise up the luminous column before disappearing.

The apartments of the prophet were furnished in the same seventies style. A thick orange carpet, streaked with violet lightning, covered the floor. Low settees, covered with fur, were placed irregularly around the room. At the back, steps led to a pink-leather swivel-reclining chair, with integrated footrests; the chair was empty. Behind it, I recognised the painting that had been in the prophet's dining room in Zwork – in the middle of a supposedly Eden-like garden, twelve young girls dressed in transparent tunics contemplated him with adoration and desire. It was ridiculous if you like, but only to the – essentially fairly feeble – extent that a purely sexual thing can be; humour and a sense of the ridiculous (I was paid, indeed well paid to know it) can only be completely victorious if they attack targets that have already been disarmed such as religiosity, sentimentalism, devotion, a sense of honour etc.; on the contrary, they show themselves impotent when it comes to harming the deep, egoistical and animal determinants of human conduct. Whatever, this painting was so bad that it took me some time to recognise the models in the persons of the young girls seated on the steps, who were trying more or less to replicate their pictorial positions – they must have been told of our arrival – yet were offering only an approximate reproduction of the canvas: whereas some of them had the same vaguely Greek, transparent tunics, lifted up to the waist, others had opted for strapless bras and black latex suspenders; in every case, their sex was exposed. 'They are the fiancées of the prophet,' Patrick told me with respect. He then explained that these elect had the privilege of living in the permanent presence of the prophet; all of them had been given bedrooms in his Californian residence. They represented all the races of the Earth, and had been destined by their beauty for the exclusive service of the Elohim: they could therefore only have sexual intercourse with them – once, of course, they had honoured the Earth with their visitation – and with the prophet; they could also, when the latter expressed the desire, have sexual intercourse with one another. I meditated for a while on this prospect, whilst trying to recount them: there were undoubtedly only ten of them. At that moment, I heard a lapping noise coming from my right. Some halogen lamps situated in the ceiling lit up, revealing a swimming pool hewn into the rock, surrounded by luxurious vegetation; the prophet was bathing naked. The missing two girls waited respectfully near the access ladder, holding a white dressing gown and a towel adorned with the multicoloured star. The prophet was taking his time, rolling around in the water, and drifting lazily as he floated on his back. Patrick grew silent and lowered his head; you could hear nothing but the lapping of the water.

He finally got out and was immediately enveloped in the dressing gown, whilst the second girl knelt to rub his feet; I then noticed that he was bigger, and, above all, more strongly built than I remembered; he had presumably been doing weights to keep himself in shape. He came towards me with arms open wide, and embraced me. 'I am so happy . . .' he said in a deep voice, 'I am so happy to see you . . .' I had wondered several times during the journey what exactly he expected from me; perhaps he had exaggerated my notoriety to himself. Scientology, for example, no doubt benefited from the presence in its membership of John Travolta or Tom Cruise; but I was far below their level. He was too, if the truth be told, and this was maybe the simple explanation: he would take whatever he could get his hands on.

The prophet took his place in his reclining chair; we sat on pouffes down below. At a sign from him, the young girls scattered and returned, carrying stoneware dishes filled with almonds and dried fruit; others carried amphora filled with what turned out to be pineapple juice. So he was dwelling in the Greek style; the stage production, however, left something to be desired, it was a bit annoying to see, on a sideboard table, the wrappings for the Nicenuts television mix. 'Susan . . .' said the prophet softly to a very blonde girl, with blue eyes and a ravishing candid face, who had remained seated at his feet. Obeying without a word, she knelt between his thighs, opened the dressing gown, and began to suck him off; his sex was short and thick. He wanted, apparently, to establish from the outset a clear position of dominance; I wondered in passing if he did it uniquely for pleasure, or if that was part of a plan to impress me. I was in fact completely unimpressed, though I noticed that Patrick seemed bothered, and looked embarrassedly at his feet, he was blushing a little, despite the fact that this was, in principle, absolutely in accordance with the theories he professed. The conversation ranged first over the international situation – characterised, according to the prophet, by grave threats to democracy; the danger represented by Muslim fundamentalism was, he argued, in no way exaggerated, he had heard worrying information from his African followers. I didn't have much to say on the issue, which was no bad thing, as it enabled me to preserve on my face an expression of respectful interest. From time to time he placed his hand on the girl's head, she interrupted her movement; then at another sign, she started sucking him off again. After having monologued for a few minutes, the prophet wanted to know if I wished to rest before the meal, which would be taken in the company of the main leaders; I had the impression that the correct answer was: 'Yes.'

'That went well! That went very well!' Patrick slipped into my ear, quivering with excitement, as we went back up the corridor. His display of submission left me a bit perplexed: I tried to recall what I knew about primitive tribes, hierarchical rituals, but I had difficulty remembering, I had read about it in my youth, at the same time as I took acting lessons; I had convinced myself then that the same mechanisms could be found, scarcely modified, in modern societies, and that knowledge of them could help me write sketches – the hypothesis had more or less proved accurate, Lévi-Strauss having helped me in particular. On emerging on to the terreplein I stopped, struck by the vision of the canvas camp where the followers dwelled, about fifty metres below: there must have been a good thousand igloo tents, very close together, all identical, immaculately white, and laid out so as to form that curved pointed star that was the emblem of the sect. You could make out the design only from above – or from the sky, Patrick suggested. Once built, the embassy would have the same form, the prophet himself had designed the plans, he would certainly want to show them to me.

I had expected a more or less sumptuous meal, punctuated by sybaritic delights; I was quickly disillusioned. When it came to food, the prophet was a devotee of the greatest frugality: tomatoes, mushrooms, olives, couscous – all served in small quantities; a bit of goat's cheese, accompanied by one glass of red wine. Not only was he a Cretan Diet fanatic, he did an hour of gymnastics every day, along the lines of movements precisely designed to tone the cardiovascular system, and took tablets of Pantestone and MDMA, as well as other medication, available only in the USA. He was literally obsessed by physical ageing, and the conversation was almost uniquely about the proliferation of free radicals, the bypass of collagen, the fragmentation of elastin and the accumulation of lipofuscin inside liver cells. He seemed to know his subject from top to bottom, and Knowall intervened only from time to time to clarify a point of detail. The other guests were Joker, Cop and Vincent – whom I saw for the first time since my arrival, and who seemed even more detached than usual: he wasn't listening at all, and appeared to be thinking about private and inexpressible things, his face seemed to quiver with nervous twitches, especially each time Susan appeared – we were served by the fiancées of the prophet, who had put on for the occasion long white tunics slit down the sides.

The prophet didn't take any coffee, and the meal ended with a sort of green-coloured infusion, which was particularly bitter – but which was, he claimed, a remedy for accumulations of lipofuscin. Knowall confirmed the information. We left each other early, the prophet insisting on the necessity of a long and reparatory sleep. Vincent hurried along behind me in the corridor on the way out, I had the impression he was clinging to me, and wanted to talk. The cave that had been allocated to me was slightly more vast than his, it had a terrace that overlooked the canvas camp. It was only eleven in the evening but everything was perfectly calm, no music could be heard, and there were few comings and goings between the tents. I served Vincent a glass of Glenfiddich that I had bought at the duty-free in Madrid airport.

I more or less expected him to start the conversation but he did nothing and contented himself with refilling his glass and turning the liquid around in it. To my questions about his work, he replied only in discouraged monosyllables; he had lost even more weight. In despair, I ended up speaking about myself, in other words about Esther, it was about the only thing in my life recently that seemed worthy of mention; I had bought a new sprinkler system, as well, but I didn't feel able to talk about that subject for long. He asked me to speak again about Esther, which I did with great pleasure; his face brightened up little by little, he said he was happy for me, and I felt he was sincere. Affection between men is a difficult thing, because it cannot materialise into anything, it's something unreal and soft, but always a bit painful, too; he left ten minutes later without revealing anything to me about his life. I stretched out in the darkness and meditated on the psychological strategy of the prophet, which seemed to me obscure. Was he going to make me the offering of a female follower intended to entertain me sexually? He was probably hesitating, he can't have had much experience in the treatment of VIPs. I contemplated the prospect calmly: I had made love with Esther that very morning, it had been even longer and more delightful than usual; I had no desire for another woman, I wasn't even certain, if the case arose, that I'd manage to be interested. Men are generally considered to be cocks on legs, capable of fucking any girl so long as she is sufficiently arousing, without any consideration of feelings coming into the picture; the portrait is more or less accurate, but still a bit forced. Granted, Susan was ravishing, but on seeing her suck the cock of the prophet I had felt no adrenaline rush, no rise in ape-like rivalry, on me the effect had been wasted, and in general I felt myself to be unusually calm.

I woke up at about five in the morning, just before dawn, and had an energetic wash that I concluded with a freezing shower; I had the impression, which was quite difficult to justify and which moreover was going to turn out to be false, that I was preparing to live a decisive day. I made myself a black coffee, and drank it on the terrace whilst observing the canvas camp as it began to wake up; a few followers were making their way towards the communal toilets.

In the rising sun, the stony plain looked dark red. Far towards the east you could see metal protection barriers, the land demarcated by the sect must have been at least ten square kilometres. I suddenly made out Vincent, accompanied by Susan, walking down the winding path, a few metres below. They stopped on the terreplein where we had left the minibus the previous day. Vincent was waving his hands, seemed to be pleading his cause, but speaking softly, I was too far away to understand him; she looked at him calmly, but her expression remained inflexible. Turning her head she saw me looking at them, and put a hand on Vincent's arm to make him shut up; I turned back inside my grotto, pensive. Vincent didn't look like he'd get lucky: with her limpid gaze, untroubled it seemed by anything, her athletic and healthy body of a young Protestant sportswoman, this girl had all the basic elements of a fanatic: you could just as easily have imagined her in a radical evangelical movement, or a small band of serious ecologists; as it turned out she was devoted body and soul to the prophet, and nothing could persuade her to break her vow of exclusive sexual service. I understood then why I had never introduced sects into my sketches: it is easy to make jokes about human beings, to consider them as burlesque mechanisms when they are, banally, moved by cupidity or desire; but when they give the impression of being animated by a deep faith, by something that goes beyond the survival instinct, the mechanism breaks down, and laughter in principle is stopped.

One by one, the followers, dressed in white tunics, came out of their tents, and made their way towards the opening hewn into the base of the rocky peak, which led to an immense natural cave where the teachings took place. Many of the tents looked empty to me; in fact, I was to learn, in a conversation I had a few minutes later with Cop, that the winter course had attracted only three hundred people this year; for a movement that claimed to have eighty thousand members throughout the world, it wasn't much. He attributed this lack of success to the excessively high intellectual level of Miskiewicz's lectures. 'It goes completely over people's heads . . . In a course intended for everyone, it is best to put the emphasis on simpler, more galvanising emotions. But the prophet is completely fascinated by the sciences . . .' he concluded bitterly. I was surprised that he spoke to me with such frankness; the distrust he felt towards me during the course at Zwork seemed to have vanished. Unless he was seeking an ally in me of course; he must have made enquiries, understood that I was a VIP of the first order, perhaps destined to play a role in the organisation, if not to influence the prophet's decisions. His relations with Knowall were not good, that was obvious, the latter considered him to be some sort of junior officer, only good for maintaining order or organising supplies for the meals. During their sometimes caustic exchanges, Joker would be elusive, make gags, avoid taking sides, relying entirely on his personal relationship with the prophet.

The first lecture of the day started at eight o'clock, and it was, of course, a lecture by Miskiewicz, entitled 'The Human Being: Matter and Information'. On seeing him take the podium, emaciated and serious, a bundle of papers in his hand, I told myself that he would, in fact, have been perfectly at home in a seminar of doctoral students, but that here he wasn't quite as comfortable. He quickly greeted the audience before beginning his presentation: no wink to the public nor any trace of humour, not even an attempt to produce a collective, sentimental or religious emotion; nothing except raw, brutal knowledge.

After half an hour devoted to the genetic code – very well explored at the time of speaking – and of the – still little known – modalities of its expression in the synthesis of proteins, there was, nevertheless, a little bit of theatre. Two assistants brought on to the table in front of him, with some difficulty, a container about the size of a bag of cement, made up of plastic pouches which were transparent, juxtaposed, of unequal size and containing various chemical products – the largest, by far, was filled with water.

'This is a human being!' exclaimed Knowall, almost with emphasis – I learned later that the prophet, taking account of Cop's remarks, had asked him to put a little bit of drama into his presentation, and had even signed him up for an accelerated oratory course, with video training and participation by professional actors. 'The container placed on this table,' he continued, 'has exactly the same chemical composition as an adult human being weighing seventy kilos. As you will notice, we are composed primarily of water . . .' He seized a slender probe and pierced the transparent pouch; there was a little jet of water.

'Of course, there are big differences . . .' The show was over, he gradually became his serious self again; the water pouch was becoming flaccid and slowly grew flat. 'These differences, however big they may be, can be summed up in one word: information. The human being is matter plus information. The composition of this matter is now known to us, to the nearest gram: it involves simple chemical elements, found widely in inanimate nature. The information is also known to us, at least in principle: it is based entirely on DNA, that of the nucleus and that of the mitochondria. The DNA contains not only the information necessary for the construction of the whole, for embryo-genesis, but also that which pilots and subsequently commands the functioning of the organism. That being the case, why should we limit ourselves to passing through embryo-genesis? Why not directly manufacture an adult human being, from the necessary chemical elements and the schema provided by the DNA? This is, very obviously, the path of research that we will take in the future. The men of the future will be born directly into an adult body, a body aged eighteen, and this is the model that will be subsequently reproduced, it is in this ideal form that they will reach, that you and I will reach, if my research advances as quickly as I hope, immortality. Cloning is only a primitive method, directly copied from the natural mode of reproduction; the development of the embryo gives us nothing but the possibility of deformations and errors; once we have the construction plan, and the necessary materials, it becomes a useless stage.

'This is not the case,' he continued, 'and this is a point I want to draw your attention to, for the human brain. There is, indeed, some crude prewiring: a few basic elements of aptitudes and character traits are already inscribed in the genetic code; but essentially the human personality, which constitutes our individuality and our memory, forms gradually, throughout our lives, by the activation and chemical reinforcement of neuronal sub-networks and dedicated synapses; individual history, in a word, creates the individual.'

*

After a meal as frugal as the previous one, I took my place next to the prophet in his Range Rover. Miskiewicz got in the front, and one of the guards took the wheel. The path continued beyond the tent village, hewn into the rock; a cloud of red dust quickly enveloped us. After a quarter of an hour the car stopped in front of a parallelepiped of a squared section, immaculately white, devoid of openings, which looked about twenty metres long and ten metres high. Miskiewicz pressed a remote control; a massive door, with invisible hinges, turned in the rock face.

Inside, he explained to me, there reigned, day and night, and throughout the entire year, a uniform and constant temperature and luminosity. A staircase led us to a gangway above that went around the building, serving a succession of offices. The metal wardrobes embedded in the walls were filled with DVDs of carefully labelled data. The lower level contained nothing but a hemisphere with transparent plastic sides, irrigated by hundreds of tubes, likewise transparent, leading to polished-steel containers.

'These tubes contain the chemical substances necessary for the manufacture of a living being,' continued Miskiewicz, 'carbon, hydrogen, oxygen, nitrogen, and the different trace elements . . .'

'It is in this transparent bubble,' added the prophet enthusiastically, 'that the first human conceived in a completely artificial manner will be born; the first real cyborg.'

I looked at the two men attentively: for the first time, the prophet did not seem to be joking at all, he appeared to be impressed, and almost intimidated himself, by the prospects opening up in the future. Miskiewicz, on the other hand, seemed completely sure of himself, and keen to continue his explanations: inside this room, he was the real boss, the prophet no longer had the last word. I then became conscious that the outlay of the laboratory must have been expensive, indeed very expensive, that it was probably through here that the most part of the subscriptions and profits passed, that this room was essentially the true *raison d'être* of the sect. In reply to my questions, Miskiewicz made clear that they were now able to realise the synthesis of the whole of the proteins and complex phospholopids implicated in the functioning of cells; that they had also been able to reproduce all of the organites, with what he considered to be the temporary exception of the Golgi apparatus, but they had run into unforeseen difficulties with the synthesis of the plasmic membrane, and were therefore not yet able to produce an entirely functional living cell. To my question about knowing whether they were ahead of other research teams, he frowned; I had, apparently, not completely understood: it was not simply that they were in advance, they were the *only* team in the world to be working on an artificial synthesis, where DNA no longer provided the development of embryonic layers, but was used uniquely for information concerning the completed organism. It was precisely this that was to enable them to bypass the embryo-genesis stage and directly manufacture adult individuals. So long as you remained reliant upon normal biological development, it would take about eighteen years to construct a new human being; when all of the processes were mastered, he believed he would be able to reduce this time to less than an hour.

In reality, it took three centuries of research to reach the goal that Miskiewicz had set in the first years of the twenty-first century, and the first neohuman generations were created by means of the cloning he'd thought we would have dispensed with far more quickly. It is, however, true that his embryological intuitions turned out, in the long term, to be extraordinarily fertile, although this unfortunately led to the same credit being accorded to his ideas on the modelling of the functioning of the brain. The metaphor of the human brain as a fuzzy Turing machine was finally shown to be completely sterile; there really were in the human mind non-algorithmic processes, as in reality had already been indicated by the existence, established by Gödel from the 1930s onwards, of undemonstrable propositions that could, nevertheless, be unambiguously recognised as *true*. But in this, too, it took three centuries to abandon that direction of research, and to become resigned to using the old mechanisms of conditioning and apprenticeship – improved, however, and made more rapid and reliable by the injection into the new organism of the proteins extracted from the hippocampus of the previous organism. This hybrid method combining the biochemical and the propositional corresponds badly to the desire for rigour expressed by Miskiewicz and his first successors; its only ambition is to represent, according to Pierce's operationalist and ever so slightly insolent formula, 'What we can do best, in the real world, given the current state of our knowledge.'

Once injected into the memory space of the application, it is
possible to modify its behaviour.
kdm.fr.st

The first two days were mainly taken up by Miskiewciz's lectures; the spiritual or emotional aspect was scarcely present, and I began to understand Cop's objections: at no moment in human history had a religion ever extended its influence over the masses by appealing to reason alone. The prophet himself remained slightly in the background, I met him mostly at mealtimes, he stayed in his cave much of the time, and I imagine that the faithful must have been slightly disappointed.

Everything changed on the morning of the third day, which was to be devoted to fasting and meditation. Around seven, I was awoken by the grave and melancholy sound of Tibetan horns playing a simple melody, on three indefinitely held notes. I went out on to my terrace; dawn was breaking on the stony plain. One by one the Elohimites came out of their tents, unrolled a mat on the ground, and stretched out, placing themselves around a platform where the two horn players flanked the prophet who was sitting in the lotus position. Like the followers, he was dressed in a long white tunic; but while theirs were made of ordinary cotton, his was cut from shiny white satin, which sparkled in the dawn light. After a couple of minutes he began to speak in a slow, deep voice, which, well amplified, could be heard easily over the sound of the horns. In simple terms, he incited the followers to become conscious of the earth on which their bodies lay, to imagine the volcanic energy that emanated from the earth, this incredible energy, superior to that of the most powerful atomic bombs; to make this energy theirs, to incorporate it into their bodies, their bodies that were destined for immortality.

Later, he asked them to strip themselves of their tunics, and present their naked bodies to the sun; to imagine, there too, this colossal energy, made up of millions of simultaneous thermonuclear reactions, this energy, which was that of the sun, as of all the stars.

He asked them to go deeper than their bodies, deeper than their skins, to try through meditation to visualise their cells, which contained the DNA that was the repository of their genetic information. He asked them to become conscious of their DNA, to fix the idea firmly in their minds that it contained their blueprint, the blueprint of the construction of their bodies, and that this information, unlike matter, was immortal. He asked them to imagine this information crossing the centuries in expectation of the Elohim, who would have the power to reconstitute their bodies, thanks to the technology they had developed and the information contained in their DNA. He asked them to imagine the moment of the return of the Elohim, and the moment when they themselves, after a period of waiting similar to a long sleep, would come back to life.

I waited for the end of the meditation session to join the crowd that was making towards the cave where Miskiewicz's lectures had taken place; I was surprised by the effervescent, slightly abnormal gaiety that seemed to have seized the participants: many called to one another loudly and stopped to embrace for a few seconds, others advanced skipping and leaping, others sang a joyful threnody as they walked. In front of the grotto a banner had been hung bearing the words: 'Presentation of the Embassy' in multicoloured letters. Near the entrance I bumped into Vincent, who seemed very removed from the prevailing fervour; as VIPs, we doubtless had a dispensation from ordinary religious emotions. We sat down in the middle of the others, and the shouts ceased as a giant screen, thirty metres wide, rolled down the far wall; then it went dark.

The plans for the embassy had been conceived with the help of 3D creation software, probably AutoCad and Freehand; I later learned with surprise that the prophet had done everything himself. Although completely ignorant in almost every field, he was passionate about computers (and not only about video games), he had a good command of the most elaborate tools for graphic creation, and had, for example, created the sect's entire website with the help of Dreamweaver MX, going as far as to write a hundred pages of HTML. With the plans of the embassy, as with the conception of the site, he had in any case given a free rein to his natural taste for ugliness; beside me Vincent emitted a pained groan, then lowered his head and stared obstinately at his knees throughout the entire screening – which lasted slightly over half an hour. Slides followed slides, generally linked by transitions in the form of the explosion and recomposition of the image, all of it to the soundtrack of Wagner overtures sampled with loud techno. Most of the rooms of the embassy assumed the form of perfect solids, from dodeca-hedrons to icosahedrons; gravity, doubtless through artistic con-vention, was abolished there, and the viewpoint of the virtual visitor floated freely up and down rooms separated by jacuzzis overburdened with precious stones, with walls adorned with heartbreakingly realistic pornographic etchings. Some rooms in-cluded bay windows looking out over a landscape of lush prairies, dotted with multicoloured flowers, and I wondered briefly how the prophet intended to go about achieving such a result in the radically arid landscape of Lanzarote; given the hyper-realist rendering of the flowers and blades of grass, I finally concluded that this wasn't the kind of detail that would stop him, and that he would doubtless use artificial prairies.

There followed a *finale* in which the viewer rose into the air, and the entire structure of the embassy was revealed to them – a star with six branches and curved points – then, in a breathtaking tracking out, the Canary Islands, then the whole of the surface of the globe, whilst the first bars of 'Thus Spake Zarathustra' thun-dered in the air. Then silence fell, whilst on the screen vague images of galactic star clusters followed. These images disappeared in their turn and a spotlight fell on the stage to accompany the appearance of the prophet, bounding resplendent in his ceremonial costume of white satin, with yokes that threw off adamantine flashes. An immense ovation rippled through the room, everyone stood up applauding and shouting: 'Bravo!' With Vincent I felt more or less obliged to get up and applaud as well. It lasted at least twenty minutes; sometimes the applause faded, and seemed to die out; then a new, even stronger wave started, originating in particular from a small group down the front gathered around Cop, which spread to the whole of the hall. There were thus five fadings, then five reprises, until the prophet, probably sensing that the phenomenon was eventually going to die a death, opened his arms wide. Silence fell immediately.

In a voice that was deep and, I must admit, quite impressive (but the sound system overdid the echoes and low notes a bit), he sang the first bars of the welcome song for the Elohim. Several people around me repeated the words softly. 'We will re-build the em-bass-y . . .' The prophet's voice began to climb towards the high notes: 'With the he-lp of those who love you.' More and more people around me were singing. 'Its pil-lars and its co-lonn-ades.' The rhythm became more indecisive and slow, until the prophet sang again in a triumphant, powerfully amplified voice, resounding throughout the entire grotto: 'The new Je-ru-sa-lem!' The same myth, the same dream, just as powerful three millennia later. 'And it will wipe every tear from their eyes . . .' A wave of emotion ran through the crowd and everyone repeated after the prophet, on three notes, the chorus, which consisted of a single word, repeated indefinitely: 'Eeee-looo-him! . . . Eeee-looo-him!' Cop, his arms stretched skywards, sang in a stentorious voice. A few metres from me I noticed Patrick, his eyes closed behind his glasses, his hands spread in an almost ecstatic attitude, whilst Fadiah beside him, probably rediscovering the reflexes of her Pentecostalist ancestors, writhed, chanting incomprehensible words.

There was another meditation, this time in the silence and darkness of the cave, before the prophet spoke again. Everyone listened to him not only in veneration, but also with a mute, adoring joy that bordered on pure rapture. I think this was mainly owing to his tone of voice, which was supple and lyrical, here marking tender and meditative pauses, there crescendos of enthusiasm. His speech seemed a bit incoherent at first, starting with the diversity of the forms and colours in animal nature (he invited us to meditate on butterflies, which seemed to have no other reason for being other than to fill us with wonder through their shimmering flight) and going on to the burlesque reproductive customs current among different animal species (he lingered, for example, on a particular species of insect in which the male, fifty times smaller than the female, spends his life as a parasite in her abdomen before leaving it, to fertilise her then die; he must have had a book like *Funny Biology* in his library, I suppose the title existed for all the disciplines). This disorderly accumulation of details built up, however, to a *strong idea*, which he expounded to us immediately afterwards: the Elohim who had created us, us and all life on this planet, were undoubtedly high-powered scientists, and we had to follow their example and revere science, the basis of any practical achievement, we had to respect it and give it the means necessary for its development, and more specifically we had to congratulate ourselves on having among us one of the world's most eminent scientists (he pointed to Mis-kiewicz, who stood up and stiffly saluted the crowd, to thunderous applause); but, if the Elohim held science in great esteem, they were no less, and indeed above all, *artists*: science was only the necessary means for achieving this fabulous diversity of life, which could not be considered as anything other than a work of art, the most grandiose one of all. Only colossal artists had been able to conceive of such admirable luxuriance, diversity and aesthetic imagination. 'It is also, therefore, a huge honour for us,' he went on, 'to have with us two artists of great talent, known the world over . . .' He gestured towards us. Vincent stood up hesitantly; I followed him. After a moment of wavering the people around us moved apart and formed a circle to applaud us, smiling widely. I made out Patrick, a few metres away; he applauded me warmly, and seemed to be growing ever more emotional.

'Science, art, creation, beauty, love . . . Play, tenderness, laugh-ter . . . How beautiful, my friends, life is! How marvellous it is, and how we wish it could go on for eternity! . . . This, my dear friends, will be possible, and possible very soon . . . The promise has been made, and it will be kept.'

After these last tenderly anagogical words, he stopped speaking, and marked a period of silence before singing the welcome song for the Elohim again. This time the entire gathering sang loudly, slowly clapping their hands. Beside me Vincent was singing his head off, and I myself was inches away from feeling a genuine collective emotion.

The fasting ended at ten in the evening, and big tables were set up under the stars. We were invited to place ourselves at random, without taking account of our usual relationships and friendships, something made all the easier as it was almost totally dark. The prophet sat down at a high table, on a platform, and everyone lowered their heads as he said a few words about the diversity of tastes and flavours, and how this was another source of pleasure that the day of fasting would enable us to appreciate even more; he also mentioned the need to chew slowly. Then, changing the subject, he invited us to concentrate on the marvellous human person we were going to find opposite us, on all those marvellous human persons, in the splendour of their magnificently developed individualities, whose diversity, in just the same way, promised us an unheard-of variety of encounters, joys and pleasures.

With a slight whistling noise, and slightly missing their cue, the gas lamps at the corner of each table lit up. I lifted my eyes again: on my plate, there were two tomatoes; in front of me was a young girl of about twenty, with very white skin, and a face whose purity of lines reminded me of Botticelli; her thick, black, tightly curled hair fell down to her waist. She played the game for a few minutes, smiled at me, spoke to me, tried to learn more about the *marvellous human person* I could have been; she was called Francesca, was Italian, more precisely she came from Umbria, but was studying in Milan; she had followed the Elohimite teachings for two years. Quite quickly, however, her boyfriend, who was sitting on her right, intervened in the conversation; he was called Gianpaolo and was an actor – well, he acted in some advertisements, and occasionally a few TV films – he was, in short, at about the same stage as Esther. He too was very handsome, with fairly long, shiny chestnut hair, and a face that one could easily trace back to the primitive Italians whose name escaped me for the moment; he was also quite well-built, his tanned biceps and pectorals could be clearly made out under his T-shirt. Personally he was a Buddhist, and had only come on this course out of curiosity – his first impression, however, was good. They lost interest in me quite quickly, and began a lively conversation in Italian. Not only did they make a splendid couple, but they also seemed to be sincerely in love. They were still in that enchanted moment when you discover the universe of the other, when you feel the need to marvel at what they marvel at, be amused by what amuses them, share in whatever entertains, pleases and offends them. She was looking at him with the tender rapture of a woman who knows herself chosen by a man, who feels joy in it, who has not yet become completely inured to the idea of having a companion at her side, a man for her exclusive use, and who says to herself that life is going to be very sweet.

The meal was as frugal as usual: two tomatoes, some taboulé, a piece of goat's cheese; but once it had been cleared away, the two fiancées made their way between the tables, carrying amphoras that contained a sweet, apple-based liqueur. A communicative euphoria, made up of many light, interspersed conversations, spread among the guests; several of them were singing softly. Patrick came over and crouched beside me, promising that we would see each other often in Spain, that we were going to become true friends, and that I could visit him in Luxemburg. When the prophet stood up to speak again, there were ten minutes of enthusiastic applause; under the spotlights, his silvery silhouette was surrounded by a sparkling halo. He invited us to meditate on the plurality of worlds, to turn our thoughts towards those stars that we could see, each surrounded by planets, and to imagine the diversity of life forms populating those planets, the strange vegetation, the animal species about which we knew nothing, and the intelligent civilisations, some of which, like that of the Elohim, were much more advanced than our own, and only asked to share with us their knowledge, to allow us to come among them, to inhabit the universe in the pleasure of their company, in permanent renewal and in joy. Life, he concluded, was from all points of view marvellous, and it only remained for us to make every instant worthy of being lived.

When he came down from the podium everyone stood up, a line of disciples formed around him as he passed, waving their arms to the sky and repeating rhythmically: 'Eeee-looo-hiiim!'; some were laughing uncontrollably, others burst into tears. Once he reached Fadiah, the prophet stopped and lightly caressed her breasts. She started joyfully and emitted a sort of 'Yeep!' They went off together, through the crowd of disciples who sang and applauded wildly. 'It is the third time! The third time she has had this distinction!' Patrick proudly whispered to me. He then informed me that in addition to his twelve fiancées, the prophet would from time to time give an ordinary female disciple the honour of spending a night in his company. The excitement gradually calmed down, and the followers returned to their tents. Patrick wiped the lenses of his glasses, which were misted over with tears, then put an arm around my shoulders, looking up to the sky. It was an exceptional night, he told me; he could feel the waves coming from the stars even more than normal, the waves full of love that the Elohim were carrying to us; it was on such a night, he was convinced, that they would return among us. I didn't really know what to say in reply. I had not only never held any religious belief, but I hadn't even envisaged the possibility of doing so. For me, things were exactly as they appeared to be: man was a species of animal, descended from other animal species through a tortuous and difficult process of evolution; he was made up of matter configurated in organs, and after his death these organs would decompose and transform into simpler molecules; no trace of brain activity would remain, nor of thought, nor, evidently, of anything that might be described as a *spirit* or a *soul*. My atheism was so monolithic, so radical, that I had never been able to take these subjects completely seriously. During my days at secondary school, when I would debate with a Christian, a Muslim or a Jew, I had always had the impression that their beliefs were to be *taken ironically*; that they obviously didn't believe, in the proper sense of the term, in the reality of the dogmas they professed, but that they were a sign of recognition, a sort of password allowing them access to the community of believers – a bit like grunge music was, or Doom Generation for fans of that game. The weighty seriousness they sometimes brought to debates between equally absurd theological positions seemed to contradict this hypothesis; but the same thing, basically, could be said for the fans of a game: for a chess player, or a participant who is truly immersed in a role-play, the fictional space of the game becomes something completely serious and real, you could even say that nothing else exists for him, for the duration of the game at least.

This annoying enigma of those who believe was therefore being posed to me once again, in practically the same terms, with regard to the Elohimites. Of course in certain cases the dilemma was easy to resolve. Knowall, for example, obviously could not take this twaddle seriously, but he had very good reasons to remain in the sect: given the heterodox character of his research, he would never have been able to obtain as much financial support elsewhere, or a laboratory with as much modern equipment. The other leaders – Cop, Joker, and, of course, the prophet – also drew a material benefit from their membership. The case of Patrick was more curious. Certainly, the Elohimite sect had enabled him to find a lover who was explosively erotic, and probably as hot as she appeared to be – which would not have been so easy in the outside world: the sex life of bankers and business leaders, in spite of all their money, is in general absolutely miserable, they have to content themselves with brief and highly expensive rendezvous with escort girls who despise them and never miss an opportunity to make them feel the physical disgust they inspire. However, Patrick seemed to exhibit a real faith, an unfeigned hope in the eternity of delights that the prophet offered a glimpse of; all the same, in a man whose behaviour bore the imprint of a great bourgeois rationality, it was troubling.

Before falling asleep, I thought again at length about the case of Patrick, and that of Vincent. Since the first evening, the latter had not spoken to me. Waking early the following morning, I saw him again walking down the winding road along the hillside in the company of Susan; they appeared to be plunged once again in an intense and interminable discussion. They separated at the top of the first terreplein, with a nod, and Vincent went back in the direction of his bedroom. I was waiting for him near the entrance; he jumped at the sight of me. I invited him for coffee at my place; taken aback, he accepted. While the water was heating, I put the cups and cutlery on the little garden table on the terrace. The sun was emerging with difficulty between some bumpy dark-grey clouds; a thin violet ray ran just above the line of the horizon. I poured him a coffee; he added a sugar cube, and pensively stirred the mixture in his cup. I sat down in front of him; he remained silent, lowered his eyes, and brought the cup to his lips. 'Are you in love with Susan?' I asked him. He raised an anxious look towards me. 'It's as obvious as that?' he asked after a long pause. I nodded in agreement. 'You should take a step back . . .' I said, and my calm, firm tone gave the impression I had been reflecting on this deeply, earlier, whilst in fact I had only just thought of it for the first time, but I forged ahead:

'We could take a trip around the island . . .'

'You mean . . . leave the camp?'

'Is it forbidden?'

'No . . . No, I don't think so. We'd have to ask Jérôme how we go about it . . .' All the same, the prospect seemed to worry him a little.

'Of course you can! Of course you can!' Cop exclaimed good-humouredly. 'We're not in a prison here! I'll ask someone to drive you to Arrecife; or perhaps to the airport, that'll be more practical for renting a car.'

'But you'll be coming back this evening?' he asked just as we were getting into the minibus. 'It's just so I know . . .'

I had no precise plan, other than to bring Vincent back to the normal world for a day, i.e. almost anywhere; i.e. given the place we were in, it would most likely be the beach. He exhibited a surprising docility and lack of initiative; the car-rental man had provided us with a map of the island. 'We could go to Teguise beach . . .' I said, 'it's the easiest to get to.' He didn't even bother to reply.

He had brought along a pair of trunks and a towel, and he sat placidly between the dunes, he even seemed ready to spend the day there if he had to. 'There are a lot of other women . . .' I said, out of the blue, to begin a conversation, before I became aware that this wasn't that straightforward. It was the low season, there were probably about fifty people in our field of vision: teenage girls with attractive bodies, flanked by *boys*; young mothers whose bodies were already less attractive, accompanied by small children. Our mutual sharing of a common space with them was fated to remain purely theoretical; none of these people belonged to a kind of reality with which we could, in one way or another, interact; in our eyes they had no more existence than if they had been images on a cinema screen, in fact, rather less I'd say. I was beginning to feel that this excursion into the normal world was doomed to failure when I became aware that there was, moreover, a risk of it ending in quite an unpleasant manner.

I hadn't done it deliberately, but we had installed ourselves in the portion of beach that belonged to a Thomson Holidays club. On returning from the sea, which had been rather cold, and which I hadn't managed to get into, I saw that a hundred or so people were thronging around a podium on which a mobile sound system had been set up. Vincent hadn't moved; sitting in the middle of the crowd, he regarded the surrounding agitation with perfect indifference. As I rejoined him, I was able to read 'Miss Bikini Contest' on a banner that hung above the podium. Indeed, about ten little sluts aged thirteen to fifteen waited by one of the stairs to the podium, wiggling and emitting little cries. After a spectacular musical gimmick, a tall Black dressed like a circus chimp bounded onto the podium and invited the girls to come up one by one. 'Ladies and gentlemen, boys and girls,' he shouted in English into his HF microphone, 'welcome to the "Miss Bikini" contest! Have we got some sexy girls for you today!' He turned to the first girl, a leggy red-haired teenager sporting a minimal white bikini. 'What's your name?' he asked her. 'Ilona,' the girl replied. 'A beautiful name for a beautiful girl!' he shouted with gusto. 'And where are you from, Ilona?' She came from Budapest. 'Budaaaa-pest! That city's ho-ooot!' he roared with enthusiasm; the girl burst into nervous laughter. He moved on to the next girl, a platinum-blonde Russian, very curvaceous in spite of her fourteen years, who looked a right tart, then he asked each of the others a couple of questions, bounding around and puffing out his chest in his silver lamé smoking jacket, making essentially more and more obscene remarks. I threw a despairing look at Vincent: he was as much at home in this seaside spectacle as Samuel Beckett in a rap video. Having gone through all the girls, the Black turned towards four paunchy sixty-somethings, seated behind a small table, notebooks in front of them, and made a great show of pointing them out to the public: 'And judging the-eem . . . is our international jury! . . . The four members of our panel have been around the world a few times – that's the least you can say! They know what sexy boys and girls look like! Ladies and gentlemen, a special hand for our experts!' There was some weak applause, during which the ridiculed seniors waved to their families in the audience, then the competition began in earnest: one after the other, the girls took to the stage, in their bikinis, to do a sort of erotic dance: they wiggled their bottoms, smeared themselves with suntan oil, played with their bra-straps, etc. The music was house, played at full volume. And so, that was it: we were in the *normal world*. I thought again of what Isabelle had told me on our first evening together: a world of definitive *kids*. The Black was an adult *kid*, the members of the jury ageing *kids*; there was nothing here that might actually encourage Vincent to return to his place in society. I suggested that we leave at the point when the Russian girl began stuffing her hand down her bikini bottoms; he accepted with indifference.

On a map on the 1:200 000 scale, especially on a Michelin map, the whole world seems happy; on a map of a larger scale, like the one I had of Lanzarote, things deteriorate: you start to make out the hotels, the leisure infrastructures. On a scale of 1:1 you find yourself back in the normal world, which is not very pleasant; but if you increase the scale even more, you are plunged into a nightmare: you start to make out the dust mites, mycoses and parasites that eat away at the flesh. By 2 p.m., we were back at the centre.

'Good timing, that's very good timing,' declared Cop as he welcomed us, jumping with enthusiasm; the prophet had just decided, in an impromptu fashion, to organise a little dinner that evening to bring together the *celebrities* present, that is to say all those who could, in one way or another, provide media contacts or have a public profile. Joker, who was standing next to him, nodded vigorously and winked at me as if to suggest that I didn't have to take it all that seriously. In reality, I think he was counting on me to improve the situation: as the person responsible for public relations, he had up until then only known failure; in the best cases, the sect was portrayed as a bunch of cranks and UFO freaks, and in the worst, as a dangerous organisation propagating ideas that flirted with eugenics, if not Nazism; as for the prophet, he was regularly ridiculed for his successive failures in his previous careers (racing driver, cabaret singer . . .). In short, the presence of a fairly substantial VIP like myself was an unexpected stroke of luck for them, you could say I was extra air in their tyres.

Ten or so people were gathered in the dining room; I recognised Gianpaolo, accompanied by Francesca. He probably owed this invitation to his acting career, however modest; evidently, the term *celebrities* had to be taken in its broadest sense. I also recognised a woman of about fifty, platinum blonde, quite plump, who had performed the welcome song for the Elohim with a scarcely bearable sonic intensity; she introduced herself as an opera singer, or more accurately a choral singer. I had the place of honour, just in front of the prophet; he greeted me cordially, but seemed tense and anxious, and looked nervously around in every direction; he calmed down a little when Joker sat down next to him. Vincent sat on my right, and threw a sharp look at the prophet, who was rubbing bread into little balls and rolling them mechanically on the table; at that instant he seemed tired and distracted, for once he really looked his sixty-five years. 'The media hate us . . .' he said bitterly. 'If I was to disappear now, I don't know what would remain of my work. They would move in for the kill . . .' Joker, who was getting ready to make some witty remark, turned to him, gathered from his tone of voice that he was speaking seriously, and was left gaping. His face, flattened as if by an iron, his small nose, and the few spiky hairs on his head: everything predisposed him to playing the clown, he was one of those unfortunate beings whose very despair cannot be taken completely seriously; the fact remains that, in the event of a sudden collapse of the sect, his fate would not have been an enviable one, I wasn't even sure he had another source of income. He lived with the prophet in Santa Monica, in the same house occupied by the twelve fiancées. He had no sexual life himself, and generally he didn't do much with his days, his only eccentricity was to have garlic sausage flown over from France, the

Californian *delicatessen* shops seeming to him to be insufficient; he also collected fish hooks and appeared on the whole to be quite a miserable puppet, emptied of any personal desire and any living substance, whom the prophet kept at his side more or less out of charity, to basically be used as a foil or a whipping boy when the opportunity arose.

The prophet's fiancées made their appearance, carrying plates of hors d'œuvre; doubtless in homage to the artistic nature of the assembled guests, they had exchanged their tunics for cheeky Mélusine fairy costumes, with conical hats covered in stars and skintight dresses in silvery sequins that exposed their asses. An effort had been made that evening with the food, there were little meat pastries and various zakouskis. Mechanically, the prophet caressed the bottom of the brunette who was serving him zakouskis, but that didn't seem to be sufficient to improve his morale; nervously, he asked that the wine be served immediately, downed two glasses in one go, then slumped back into his chair, looking long and hard at those present.

'We must do something with the media . . .' he said at last to Joker. 'I've just read this week's *Nouvel Observateur*, this systematic smear campaign, it's just not on . . .' The other frowned, then after a minute's reflection, as if stating an utterly remarkable truth, he said: 'It's difficult . . .' in a dubious tone. I thought he was responding with slightly surprising detachment, because he was, after all, officially the only one responsible – and this was all the more obvious as neither Knowall nor Cop were present at this dinner. He was without doubt completely incompetent in this field, as in all others, he had got used to getting bad results, and thought that it would always be thus, that everyone around him had also got used to the results being bad; he too must have been almost sixty-five, and he no longer expected much from life. His mouth opened and closed silently, he was apparently looking for something funny to say, but couldn't find it, he was the victim of a temporary comedy breakdown. He finally gave up: the prophet, he must have thought, was in a bad mood this evening, but he would get over it; he calmly tucked into his meat pastry.

'In your view . . .' The prophet addressed me directly, looking me straight in the eye. '. . . is the hostility of the press truly a long-term problem?'

'On the whole, yes. Of course, by posing as a martyr, by complaining of being unjustifiably ostracised, you can successfully attract a few deviants – Le Pen managed this in his time. But at the end of the day you lose – especially when you want to express a unifying message, that is, from the moment you try to increase your appeal beyond a certain audience.'

'There you go! There you go! . . . Listen to what Daniel has just told me!' He got up in his chair, enlisting the entire table as witnesses. 'The media accuse us of being a sect when they are the ones who stop us becoming a religion by systematically misrepresenting our ideas, by denying us access to the general public, while the solutions we propose are for every human being, regardless of their nationality, race, previous beliefs . . .'

The guests stopped eating; some nodded, but no one could formulate the slightest remark. The prophet sat down again, discouraged, and nodded to the brunette, who served him another glass of wine. After some silence, the conversations round the table started up again: most were about various acting roles, scripts and movie projects. Many of the guests appeared to be actors – novices or D-list; probably as a result of the determining role that chance plays in their lives, actors are often, I had already remarked, easy prey for all kinds of bizarre sects, beliefs and spiritual disciplines. Strangely, none of them had recognised me, which was rather a good thing.

'Harley de Dude was right . . .' the prophet said pensively in English. 'Life is basically a conservative option . . .' I wondered for a while who he was speaking to, before realising that it was me. He stopped, then continued in French. 'You see, Daniel,' he said with genuine sadness, which was surprising for him, 'mankind's only aim is to reproduce, to continue the species. Although this aim is obviously insignificant, mankind pursues it with terrifying relentlessness. Men may well be unhappy, atrociously unhappy, but they resist with all their strength the thing that could change their fate: they want children, and children similar to them, in order to dig their own grave and perpetuate the conditions for unhappiness. When you suggest that they accomplish a mutation, advance along another path, you come to expect ferocious rejection. I have no illusions about the years to come: as the conditions for the technical realisation of the project come closer, opposition will become more and more fierce; and all the intellectual power is in the hands of supporters of the *status quo*. The battle will be tough, very tough . . .' He sighed, finished his glass of wine, and seemed to plunge into a personal meditation, unless he was simply struggling against apathy; Vincent fixed the prophet with an incredibly attentive look as his mood swung between discouragement and unconcern, between a tropism of death and the convulsions of life: he looked more and more like a tired old monkey. After a couple of minutes he stood up from his chair and cast a brighter look over the guests; it was only at that instant, I think, that he noticed Francesca's beauty. He gestured to one of the girls serving, the Japanese one, and said a few words in her ear; she approached the Italian girl and passed on the message. Francesca jumped up, delighted, without even looking at her companion, and came to sit on the prophet's left.

Gianpaolo sat up in his seat, his face completely still; I looked away and, despite myself, noticed the prophet passing a hand through the young woman's hair; her face was full of a happiness that was – how shall I put it? – childlike, senile and moving all at once. I looked down at my plate, but after thirty seconds I got tired of contemplating my pieces of cheese and risked a look to my side; Vincent continued to stare shamelessly at the prophet, with even a certain jubilation, it seemed to me; the latter was now holding the girl by the neck, and she had laid her head on his shoulder. When he put a hand in her blouse, I couldn't help looking over at Gianpaolo: he had raised himself a little more out of his chair, I could see the fury burning in his eyes, and I wasn't the only one, all conversation had ceased; then, defeated, he sat back slowly and lowered his head. Gradually the conversation started up again, first in low voices, then more normally. The prophet left the table in the company of Francesca before the desserts had even arrived.

The next day I came across the young woman as we left the

morning lecture. She was speaking to an Italian girlfriend of hers. I slowed down as I passed, and heard her say: '*Communicare . . .*' Her face was radiant, serene, she seemed happy. The course itself had settled into a rhythm: I had decided to attend the morning lectures, but forego the afternoon workshops. I joined the others for the evening meditation, immediately before the meal. I noticed that Francesca was again beside the prophet, and that they left together after dinner; however, I had not seen Gianpaolo all day.

A sort of herbal tea bar had been set up at the entrance to one of the caves. I came across Cop and Joker sitting in front of some lime tea. Cop was speaking with great animation, emphasising his speech with energetic gestures, he was obviously talking about a subject very close to his heart. Joker did not reply; looking concerned, he nodded vaguely whilst waiting for the other's virulence to burn out. I went over to the Elohimite stationed at the kettles; I didn't know what to order, I have always hated infusions. In despair, I opted for a hot chocolate: the prophet tolerated cocoa, on condition that it was greatly reduced in fat – probably in homage to Nietzsche, whose ideas he admired. When I passed by their table, the two leaders were silent; Cop was staring severely ahead of him. With a sharp hand gesture he invited me to join them, apparently re-dynamised by the prospect of a new interlocutor. ·

'What I was saying to Gérard,' he said (oh yes, even this poor deprived being had a first name, he doubtless had a family, maybe loving parents who had bounced him on their knees; life was truly too hard, if I thought about this kind of thing for too long I would end up blowing my brains out, there was no doubt about it), 'what I was saying to Gérard is that in my view we communicate far too much about the scientific aspect of our teachings. There is a whole New Age, ecologist trend that is frightened off by intrusive tech-nologies, because they take a dim view of man's domination of nature. They are people who strongly reject the Christian tradition, who are often close to paganism or Buddhism; we could have potential sympathisers in them.'

'On the other hand,' Gérard said astutely, 'you attract the techno-freaks.'

'Yes . . .' Cop replied doubtfully. 'But they're mainly in California,

I assure you that in Europe you don't see many of them . . .' He turned to me again: 'What do you think?'

I didn't really have any opinion, it seemed to me that in the long term the supporters of genetic technology would become more numerous than its opponents; I was above all surprised that they were putting me yet again in the role of witness to their internal contradictions. I hadn't yet realised it, but as a showman I was credited by them with a sort of intuitive understanding of the currents of thought, the fluctuations of public opinion; I saw no reason for disabusing them, and after having uttered a few banalities that they listened to respectfully I left the table with a smile, under the pretext of tiredness, slipped out of the cave and walked towards the village of tents, I wanted to see the grass-roots followers at first hand.

It was still early, and no one had gone to bed; most were sitting cross-legged, generally on their own, more rarely in couples, in front of their tents. Many of them were naked (without being obligatory, naturism was widely practised by the Elohimites; our creators the Elohim, who had acquired a perfect mastery of the climate of their planet of origin, went around naked, as was appropriate for any liberated, proud being, having rejected guilt and shame; as the prophet taught, the traces of Adam's sin had disappeared, and now we lived according to the new law of true love). On the whole they were doing nothing, or perhaps they were meditating in their own way – many had their palms open, and their eyes were turned towards the stars. The tents, provided by the organisation, looked like teepees, but the canvas, which was white and slightly shiny, was very modern, of the 'new materials from space research' type. All in all, it was a kind of tribe, a high-tech Indian tribe, I think all the tents had Internet connections, the prophet insisted repeatedly on this, it was indispensable in order for his directives to be instantly communicated to them. I suppose they must have conducted intense social relationships via the Internet, but what struck me on seeing them all together was rather their isolation and silence; each one stayed in front of his tent, without speaking or going to see his neighbours, they were only a few metres from each other but seemed oblivious even to their mutual existence. I knew that most of them didn't have children or pets (it wasn't forbidden, but strongly advised against all the same; the aim was above all to create a new species, and the reproduction of existing species was considered an outmoded and conservative option, proof of a flaky temperament, and one that did not exactly indicate a greater faith; it seemed rather implausible that a father could rise very far in the organisation). I walked down all the pathways and passed in front of several hundred tents without anyone speaking to me; they contented themselves with a nod or a discreet smile. I told myself at first that they were perhaps a bit intimidated: I was a VIP, I had the privilege of direct access to the prophet's conversation; but I quickly realised that when they came across each other on one of the pathways, their behaviour was identical: a smile, a nod, and nothing more. After leaving the village I continued walking, and went for several hundred metres along the stony path before stopping. There was a full moon, and you could make out perfectly the gravel and blocks of lava; far to the east, I could see the weak luminosity of the metal barriers encircling the grounds; I was in the middle of nowhere, the temperature was mild and I would have liked to reach some kind of conclusion.

I must have stayed like that for a while, in a state of great mental emptiness, because on my return the encampment was silent; everyone, apparently, was sleeping. I consulted my watch: it was just after three. A light was still on in Knowall's cell; he was at his desk but he heard my footsteps and signalled for me to enter. The internal decor was less austere than I would have imagined: there was a divan with some quite pretty silk cushions, and rugs with abstract motifs covered the rocky floor; he offered me a glass of tea.

'You must have realised that there was some tension inside the leadership . . .' he said before pausing. I was, obviously, in their view, a *heavyweight*; I couldn't help thinking that they were exaggerating my importance. It's true that I could say anything and the media would always be there to record my words; but to go from there to a point when people would listen to me, and change their point of view, was a rather giant leap: everyone had become used to *celebrities* expressing themselves in the media on the most varied subjects, saying things that were generally predictable, and no one paid them any real attention any more; basically the system of the spectacle, obliged to produce a disgusting consensus, had long since collapsed under the weight of its own meaninglessness. But I did nothing to disabuse him; I acquiesced with that attitude of benevolent neutrality that had served me so well in life, that had enabled me to hear so many intimate confessions, in so many different milieus, which I then re-used, crudely distorted out of recognition, in my sketches.

'I'm not really worried, the prophet trusts me . . .' he continued. 'But our image in the media is catastrophic. We're seen as cranks, yet no laboratory in the world, at the moment, would be capable of producing results like ours . . .' He swept a hand around the room as if all the objects there, the biochemistry works in English from Elsevier Publications, the DVDs of data lined above his desk, the glowing computer screen were there to bear witness to the seriousness of his research. 'I ruined my career by coming here,' he went on bitterly, 'I no longer have access to the top-ranking publications . . .' Society is an accumulation of layers, and I had never introduced scientists into my sketches, theirs was in my view a specific layer, motivated by ambitions and evaluative criteria that could not be transposed to mere mortals, there was no material in it for the general public; however, I listened, as I listened to everyone, motivated by an old habit – I was a sort of ageing spy on mankind, a spy in retirement, but I could still do it, I still had good reflexes, I think I even nodded to encourage him to go on, but I sort of listened without hearing, his words just passed between my ears, I had established involuntarily a sort of filtering function in my brain. I was, however, conscious that Miskiewicz was an important man, perhaps one of the most important men in human history, he was going to change its destiny at the deepest biological level, he had at his disposal the know-how and the procedures, but maybe I was the one who was no longer really interested in human history, I too was a tired old man, and then, just as he was singing the praises of the rigour of his experimental protocols to me, of the seriousness he brought to the establishment and validation of his counterfactual propositions, I was suddenly seized by desire for Esther, for her nice supple vagina, I remembered the little movements of her vagina closing around my cock. I pleaded tiredness and was scarcely outside Knowall's cave before dialling her mobile number but there was no one there, just her voicemail, and I didn't really feel like having a wank, the production of spermatozoids was slower at my age, the recovery period was getting longer, whatever sexual opportunities life had left to offer me were going to become rarer and rarer before they disappeared completely. I was, of course, in favour of immortality, Miskiewicz's research undoubtedly constituted a hope, the only hope in fact, but it wouldn't be for me, nor for anyone of my generation, on this subject I nurtured no illusion, the optimism he displayed with regard to imminent success was, moreover, probably not a lie but a necessary fiction, necessary not only for the Elohimites who financed his projects but also for himself; no human project has ever been undertaken without the hope of its accomplishment in a reasonable time, and more precisely with a maximum time-frame delineated by the foreseeable lifespan of the one who conceived of the project, mankind has never operated according to a team spirit that spreads across generations, even though this is the way things actually happen at the end of the day: you work, you die, and future generations profit from it unless of course they prefer to destroy what you have done, but this thought has never been formulated by any of those who have committed themselves to a project, they have preferred to ignore it, for otherwise they would have simply ceased to act, they would have simply lain down and waited for death. It was for that reason that Knowall, however modern he was on an intellectual level, was still a romantic in my eyes, his life was guided by old illusions, and now I wondered what Esther could be up to, if her little vagina was contracting on other cocks, and I began to seriously want to rip out one or two of my organs, thankfully I had brought along a dozen boxes of Rohypnol – I had thought big – and I slept for more than fifteen hours.

When I awoke the sun was low in the sky, and I immediately sensed that something strange was going on. The weather was stormy, but I knew that it would not break, it never broke, the rainfall on the island was practically nil. A faint yellow light bathed the village of the followers; the openings of a few tents were lightly ruffled by the wind but apart from that the encampment was deserted, no one was on the pathways. In the absence of human activity, the silence was total. As I climbed the hill I passed in front of the bedrooms of Vincent, Knowall and Cop, still without meeting anyone. The prophet's residence was wide open, for the first time since I arrived there were no guards at the entrance. Despite myself, on entering the first room, I muffled the sound of my footsteps. While crossing the corridor that led to his private apartment I heard hushed voices, the sound of a piece of furniture being dragged across the floor, and something that resembled a sob.

All the lights were on in the main hall where the prophet had welcomed me on the day of my arrival, but here too there was no one. I walked around, pushed open a door that led to the office, then turned back. On the right-hand side, near the pool, I bumped into Gérard, who was standing in the doorway leading to the prophet's bedroom. Joker was in a sorry state: his face was even more wan than usual, pitted with dark shadows under the eyes, I had the impression he had not slept all night. 'Something terrible . . . something terrible . . .' His voice was weak and quavering, almost inaudible. 'Something terrible has happened . . .' he finally articulated. Cop joined him and stood in front of me, sizing me up. Joker finally made a kind of plaintive bleating noise. 'Well, now we've reached this point, we might as well let him in . . .' groaned Cop.

The interior of the bedroom was taken up by an immense round bed, three metres in diameter, covered with pink satin; pink-satin pouffes were placed here and there in the room, whose walls were covered on three sides with mirrors; the fourth side was a big bay window overlooking the stony plain and the volcanoes beyond, which were slightly menacing in the stormy light. The bay window had been smashed to pieces, and the corpse of the prophet lay in the middle of the bed, naked, his throat cut. He had lost an enormous amount of blood, the carotid had been cleanly severed. Knowall padded nervously around the room. Vincent, sitting on a pouffe, seemed rather absent, he scarcely looked up on hearing me approach. A young woman with long black hair, whom I recognised as Francesca, was prostrate in a corner of the room, dressed in a white nightdress stained with blood.

'It was the Italian . . .' Cop said dryly.

It was the first time I had seen a corpse, and I wasn't that impressed; I wasn't particularly surprised either. At dinner two days before, when the prophet had set his heart on the Italian girl, I had had the fleeting impression, in the space of a few seconds, on seeing her boyfriend's expression, that this time the prophet had gone too far, and that things weren't going to go as smoothly as usual; and then, when Gianpaolo had finally appeared to submit, I had told myself that he would be crushed like all the others; manifestly, I had been mistaken. Out of curiosity I approached the bay window: the slope was very steep, almost vertical; you could make out a few footholds, and the rock was good, not at all flaky or crumbly, but it was still quite a climb. 'Yes,' Cop commented darkly as he moved closer to me, 'he must have taken it very badly . . .' Then he continued to walk up and down the room, taking care to stay away from Knowall, who was walking on the other side of the bed. Joker remained rooted near the door, opening and shutting his hands mechanically, looking completely haggard, on the edge of panic. I then became conscious for the first time that despite the hedonistic and libertine position assumed by the sect none of the close companions of the prophet actually had any kind of sexual life: in the case of Joker and Knowall this was obvious – one through incapacity, the other through a lack of motivation. Cop, for his part, was married to a woman his age, in her late fifties, which is to say that they could hardly indulge in a *frenzy of the senses* every day; and he took no advantage at all of his lofty position in the organisation to seduce young female followers. The followers themselves, as I had noticed with increasing surprise, were at best monogamous, and for the most part zerogamous – with the exception of the young and pretty female followers on the occasions when the prophet invited them to share his intimacy for one night. Basically, when you thought about it, the prophet had behaved in his own sect like an absolutely dominant male, and he had succeeded in breaking the virility of his companions: not only did the latter no longer have a sexual life, but they did not seek to have one, they forbade themselves any approach to the females, and had integrated the idea that sexuality was the prerogative of the prophet; I then understood why, in his lectures, he indulged in superfluous praise of feminine values and pitiless attacks on machismo: his wish was, quite simply, to castrate his listeners. It's a fact that, among most monkeys, the production of testosterone by the dominated males falls and ends up stopping altogether.

The sky was clearing gradually and the clouds dispersed; a hopelessly clear sky was soon going to illuminate the plain before nightfall. We were right next to the tropic of Cancer – we were there *grosso merdo*, as Joker might have said when he was still in a state to produce witty remarks. 'That has *ass-hole-utely* no importance, I am *a-dick-ted* to muesli for breakfast . . .', that was the witty word-play with which he normally tried to brighten up our days. What was going to become of him, this poor little man, now that Monkey Number One was no more? He flashed terrified looks at Cop and Knowall, respectively Monkey Number 2 and Monkey Number 3, who continued to walk up and down the room, and were beginning to size each other up. When the dominant male is unable to exert his power, the secretion of testosterone resumes, among most monkeys. Cop could count on the loyalty of the military faction of the organisation – he was the one who had recruited most of the guards, and trained them, they obeyed only his orders, while he was alive the prophet relied totally on him for these matters. On the other hand, the lab assistants and all of the technicians responsible for the genetic project looked only to Knowall, to him alone. Basically, we were dealing with a classic conflict between brute force and intelligence, between a basic manifestation of testosterone and a more intellectualised one. Either way, I sensed that it was not going to be over quickly, and I sat on a pouffe near Vincent. He seemed to become aware again of my presence, smiled vaguely and plunged back into his reverie.

About fifteen minutes of silence followed; Knowall and Cop continued to walk up and down the room, the rug muffled their footsteps. Given the circumstances, I felt quite calm; I was conscious that neither Vincent nor I, in the immediate future, had any role to play. In this story we were secondary, honorary monkeys; night was falling, the wind infiltrated the room – the Italian had literally exploded the bay window.

Suddenly, Joker took a digital camera out of his jacket pocket – a Sony DSCF-101 with three million pixels, I recognised the model, I had had the same one before opting for a Minolta Dimage A2, which had eight million pixels, a bridge semi-reflex zoom, and which proved to be more sensitive in fading light. Cop and Knowall stopped, mouth agape, looking at the poor clown zigzagging around the room taking photo after photo. 'Are you OK, Gérard?' asked Cop. In my view, no, he wasn't OK, he was clicking mechanically, without even aiming the camera, and when he approached the window I had the distinct impression that he was going to jump. 'That's enough!' shouted Cop. Joker stopped, his hands were trembling so much that he dropped the camera. Still prostrate in her corner, Francesca sniffed briefly. Knowall also stopped walking, turned to Cop and looked him straight in the eye.

'Now, we are going to have to make a decision . . .' he said in a neutral tone. 'We are going to alert the police, it's the only decision we can take.'

'If we alert the police, it's the end of the organisation. We won't be able to survive the scandal, and you know it.'

'Do you have another idea?'

There was another, clearly more tense silence: the confrontation had begun and I sensed this time it would go on to the bitter end; I even had a quite clear intuition that I was going to witness a second violent death. The death of a charismatic leader is always an extremely difficult moment to manage in a movement of a religious type; when care has not been taken to designate unambiguously a successor, a schism is almost always inevitable.

'He was thinking about death . . .' interrupted Gérard in a tiny, trembling, almost childlike voice. 'He spoke to me about it more and more often; he wouldn't have wanted the organisation to disappear, he was very worried that everything would dissolve after

he had gone. We must do something, we must manage to understand one another . . .'

Cop frowned, vaguely turning his head towards him, as though
reacting to an irksome noise; becoming conscious again of his total
insignificance, Gérard sat back down on a pouffe next to us,
lowered his eyes and calmly placed his hands on his knees.

'May I remind you,' Knowall said calmly, looking Cop straight in
the eyes, 'that for us death is not definitive, this is even our principal
dogma. We possess the genetic code of the prophet, we need only
wait for the procedure to be perfected.'

'Do you really think we're going to wait twenty years for your
thing to work?' Cop retorted violently, without even trying to hide
his hostility any more.

Knowall shivered at the outrage, but replied calmly: 'Christians
have been waiting for two thousand years . . .'

'Maybe, but in the meantime they had to organise the church,
and I'm the best man to do it. When Christ had to designate a
disciple to succeed him, he chose Peter: he wasn't the most brilliant,
the most intellectual nor the most mystical, but he was the best
organiser.'

'If I leave the project, you will have no one to put in my place;
and, in this case, any hope of resurrection vanishes. I don't think
you'll be able to last long in those conditions . . .'

There was silence again, and it became more and more heavy; I
had the impression that they wouldn't be able to come to an
agreement, things had gone too far between them, and for too
long; in the almost total darkness, I saw Cop clench his fists. It was
at this moment that Vincent intervened. 'I want to take the place of
the prophet . . .' he said in a light, almost joyful voice. The others
jumped, Cop bounded to the light switch and then ran over to
shake Vincent: 'What are you talking about? What on earth are you
talking about?' he shouted in his face. Vincent didn't react, he
waited for the other to let go of him before adding, in a voice that
was just as playful: 'After all, I am his son . . .'

The first moment of stupefaction over, it was Gérard who spoke,
plaintively:

'It is possible . . . It is completely possible . . . I know that the prophet had a son, thirty-five years ago, just after the church started, and that he visited him from time to time – but he never spoke about it, even to me. He had him with one of the first female followers, but she committed suicide a little while after the birth.'

'It's true . . .' Vincent said calmly, and there was only the echo of a very distant sadness in his voice. 'My mother couldn't bear his constant infidelities, nor the games of group sex he forced her into. She had burned her bridges with her parents – they were Alsatian Protestant bourgeois, from a very strict family, they had never forgiven her for becoming an Elohimite, in the end she no longer really had contact with anyone. I was brought up by my paternal grandparents, the parents of the prophet; during the first years, I practically didn't see him, he wasn't interested in young children. And then, after I turned fifteen, he visited me more and more frequently: he would debate with me, he wanted to know what I intended to do with my life, finally he invited me to join the sect. It took me about fifteen years to make up my mind. Recently our relationship has been – how shall I put it? – a little calmer.'

I then became conscious of a fact that should have struck me from the beginning, it was that the physical resemblance of Vincent to the prophet was incredibly strong; the expression in their eyes was very different, even totally opposite – it was no doubt this that had prevented me from noticing it – but the main features of their physiognomy – the shape of the face, the colour of the eyes, the position of the eyebrows – were strikingly identical; what's more, they were almost the same height and the same build. Knowall for his part looked at Vincent very attentively, he seemed to come to the same conclusion, and it was finally he who broke the silence:

'Nobody is aware exactly of how far my research has advanced, we have kept it totally secret. We could easily announce that the prophet has decided to abandon his ageing body in order to transfer his genetic code to a new organism.'

'Nobody is going to believe it!' Cop objected violently.

'Very few people, in fact; we can expect nothing from the mainstream media, they're all against us. There will certainly be enormous coverage, and general scepticism; but nobody will be able to prove anything, we are the sole possessors of the prophet's DNA, there is no copy, anywhere. And the most important thing is that the followers are going to believe it; we have been preparing them for years. When Christ rose again on the third day no one believed it, with the exception of the first Christians; this was even precisely the way they defined themselves: those who believed in the resurrection of Christ.'

'What are we going to do with the body?'

'There's no problem if they recover the body, we need only make sure that the wound to the throat is undetectable. For example, we could use a volcanic fissure, and throw it into the molten lava.'

'And Vincent? How do we explain the disappearance of Vincent?' Cop was visibly shaken, his objections were becoming more and more hesitant.

'Oh, I don't know many people . . .' Vincent interjected with levity. 'What's more I was considered suicidal, my death would astonish no one. I think the volcanic fissure is a good idea, that'll remind people of the death of Empedocles . . .' He recited from memory, in a strangely fluid voice: ' "And I will say to you again, prudent Pausanias, that there is no birth for mortal things; there is no baleful end in death; there is only mixing and dissociation of the components of the mixture." '

Cop reflected in silence for a couple of minutes, then threw out: 'We'll also have to deal with the body of the Italian . . .' I knew then that Knowall had won the match. Immediately afterwards Cop called three guards, and ordered them to patrol the grounds, telling them that if they found the body they should bring it back discreetly, wrapped in a blanket, on the back seat of the four-wheel drive. It took them only a quarter of an hour: the poor man had been in such a state of confusion that he had tried to climb the electric fence; he had, of course, been struck down on the spot. They laid the corpse down on the ground, at the foot of the prophet's bed. At that moment Francesca emerged from her stupor, saw the body of her boyfriend and began to make inarticulate, almost animal cries. Knowall approached and slapped her, calmly and firmly, several times; her screams turned into another bout of sobbing.

'We'll have to deal with her as well . . .' Cop remarked darkly.

'I think we have no choice . . .'

'What do you mean?' Vincent turned towards Knowall, suddenly sober.

'I think we would have difficulty counting on her to keep quiet. If we throw the two bodies out of the window they'll be reduced to a pulp after falling for three hundred metres; I'll be amazed if the police will want to do an autopsy.'

'That might work . . .' said Cop after some thought; 'I know the local police chief fairly well. If I tell him that I had come across them climbing the rock face days before, that I had tried to warn them of the dangers, but that they had laughed in my face . . . Besides, it's very plausible, the guy liked extreme sports, I think he went rock-climbing in the Dolomites every weekend.'

'Good . . .' Knowall said. He nodded slightly to Cop, and the two men lifted the body of the Italian, one by the feet, and the other by the shoulders, they took a few steps, then threw it into the abyss; they had moved so quickly that neither Vincent nor I had had time to react. With terrifying energy Knowall returned to Francesca, lifted her by the shoulders and dragged her along the carpet; she had fallen back into apathy, and showed no more reaction than you'd expect from a parcel. As Cop took her by the feet, Vincent screamed: 'Hey!' Knowall put the Italian girl back down and turned to Vincent in annoyance.

'What is it now?'

'You can't do that!'

'And why not?'

'It's murder . . .'

Knowall did not reply, he looked at Vincent and crossed his arms. 'Obviously, it's regrettable . . .' he said finally. 'However, I believe that it's necessary,' he added a few seconds later.

The long black hair of the young woman framed her pale face; her brown eyes settled on each of us in turn, I had the impression that she was no longer in any fit state to understand the situation.

'She is so young, so beautiful . . .' murmured Vincent in a pleading tone.

'I imagine that, in the case of an ugly old woman, elimination would seem more excusable to you . . .'

'No, no,' Vincent protested angrily, 'that's not exactly what I meant.'

'Yes it is,' said Knowall pitilessly, 'it's exactly what you meant; but let's move on. Tell yourself she's just a mortal, a mortal like all of us up until now; a temporary arrangement of molecules. Let's say that in this specific circumstance she is a pretty arrangement; but she has no more substance than a pattern formed by frost, that a simple rise in temperature would reduce to nothing; and, unfortunately for her, her death has become necessary so that mankind can progress. However, I promise you that she will not have to suffer.'

He took an HF transmitter out of his pocket and said a few words in a low voice. A minute later two guards appeared, one of them carrying a soft leather briefcase; he opened it, and took out a small glass bottle and a hypodermic syringe. At a sign from Cop, the two guards withdrew.

'Wait, wait, wait,' I interjected, 'I don't want to be an accomplice to murder either. What's more I don't have any motive.'

'Yes you do,' Knowall dryly riposted, 'you have a very good motive: I can call back the guards. You too are a compromising witness; you are someone famous, no doubt your death would pose more problems; but famous people die too, and anyway we have no other choice.' He was speaking calmly, looking me straight in the eye, I was quite sure he wasn't joking. 'She will not suffer . . .' he repeated softly, and very quickly he leaned over the young woman, found a vein, and injected the solution. Like all the others I had believed that it was a sleeping drug, but in a few seconds she stiffened, her skin turned blue, then her breathing suddenly stopped. Behind me I heard Joker making bestial, plaintive groans. I turned around; he was trembling all over, and could only articulate: 'Ha! Ha! Ha . . .' A stain was forming at the front of his trousers, I realised he had pissed his pants. Furious, Cop got out his own walkie-talkie and barked an order: a few seconds later, five guards appeared, armed with machine guns, and encircled us. On an order from Cop they led us into an adjoining room, furnished with a trestle table and metal filing cabinet, then locked the door behind us.

I couldn't totally convince myself that all this was real, I sent incredulous looks at Vincent, who seemed to be in a similar state of mind, neither of us spoke, the silence was broken only by Gérard's moaning. Ten minutes later Knowall came into the room, and I became conscious that everything was true, that I was looking at a murderer, that he had crossed the line. I considered him with an irrational, instinctive horror, but he seemed very calm, in his eyes he had obviously only carried out a technical act.

'I would have spared her if I could,' he said without addressing any of us in particular. 'But, I repeat, we were dealing with a mortal; and I do not think that morality makes any real sense if the subject is mortal. We are going to attain immortality; and you will be among the first beings to be accorded it; it will, in some way, be the price of your silence. The police will be here tomorrow; you have all night to think about it.'

The days that followed left me with a strange memory, as if we had entered a different space, where ordinary laws were abolished, where everything – the best as well as the worst – could happen at any moment. I must, however, acknowledge in hindsight that there was a certain logic to all this, the logic of Miskiewicz, and that his plan was carried out to the letter, down to the slightest detail. First, the police chief had no doubts about the accidental nature of the death of the young couple. When faced with their disarticulated bodies, their bones in bits, practically reduced to the state of patches of blood spread over the rocks, it was actually very difficult to keep one's cool, and to have any suspicion that their deaths could have had any cause other than the fall. Then, above all, this banal affair was rapidly eclipsed by the disappearance of the prophet. In the remaining hours of the night, Cop and Knowall had dragged his body to an opening that overlooked a small active volcanic crater; the molten lava covered him immediately, special equipment had to be brought from Madrid to recover him, and obviously any autopsy was unthinkable; that very night they had burned the bloodstained sheets, had the bay windows repaired by a workman who looked after maintenance in the grounds, in short they had been impressively active. When the inspector from the Guardia

Civil understood that he was dealing with a suicide, and that the prophet intended to be reincarnated, three days later, in a rejuvenated body, he scratched his chin pensively – he was quite aware of the sect's activities, in fact he believed he was dealing with a group of crazies who venerated flying saucers, his knowledge of them stopped there – and concluded that it would be best to refer the matter to his superiors. This was exactly what Knowall had expected.

From the following day onwards, the affair was on the front pages of the newspapers – not only in Spain, but also in Europe, and soon in the rest of the world. 'The Man Who Thought He Was Eternal', 'The Mad Gamble of the Man-God', those were more or less the headlines. Three days later, seven hundred journalists were camped behind the protective fences; the BBC and CNN had sent helicopters to film the encampment. Miskiewicz selected five journalists from English-speaking science magazines and held a brief press conference. From the outset he excluded the possibility of a visit to the laboratory: official science had rejected him, he said, and forced him to work on the margins; he had taken note of this, and would only communicate his results once he felt the moment was right. From the legal point of view, it was hard to attack his position: it was a private laboratory, privately funded, he was perfectly within his rights to deny access to anyone; the grounds themselves were private, he pointed out, and the flyovers and filming by helicopters seemed to him to be a practice of completely dubious legality. Moreover he was working neither on living organisms, nor even on embryos, but on simple molecules of DNA, and this with the written agreement of the donor. Certainly, reproductive cloning was prohibited or restricted in many countries; but under the circumstance this was not a question of cloning, and no law forbade the artificial creation of life; it was a direction in research that the legislators simply had not dreamed of.

Of course in the beginning the journalists didn't believe it, everything in their training predisposed them to ridiculing the hypothesis; but I realised that they were, despite themselves, impressed by Miskiewicz's personality, by the precision and rigour of his responses; at the end of the interview, I'm convinced, at least two of them had some doubts: it was easy enough for these doubts to spread, amplified, in general-interest magazines.

What amazed me, however, was the immediate, unreserved belief of the followers. On the morning after the death of the prophet, Cop had, in the early hours, called a general meeting. He and Knowall announced that the prophet had decided, in a gesture of oblation and hope, to be the first to keep the promise. He had therefore thrown himself into a volcano, giving his ageing physical body to the flames, in order to be reborn, on the third day, in a renewed body. His last words in his present incarnation, which it was their mission to communicate to the disciples, were the following: 'There where I go, you soon will follow.' I expected some movement in the crowd, a mixture of reactions, maybe some gestures of despair; but none of that happened. As they left, all of them were concentrated and silent, but their eyes gleamed with hope, as if this was the news they had always been waiting for. I had thought that I had a good general knowledge of human beings, but this was based only on their most everyday motives: these people had faith, this was new to me, and it changed everything.

They gathered spontaneously around the laboratory, two days later, leaving their tents in the middle of the night, and waited without saying a word. Among them were five journalists, selected by Knowall, from two press agencies – AFP and Reuters – and three networks, CNN, the BBC and, I think, Sky News. There were also two policemen, from Madrid, who wanted to record a formal statement from the being who was going to emerge from the laboratory – strictly speaking they had nothing on him, but his position was unprecedented: he claimed to be the prophet, who was officially dead, without exactly being him; he claimed to come into the world without a biological father or mother. Lawyers for the Spanish government had examined the question, obviously without finding anything, even in old records, which could apply to the present case; they had therefore decided to content themselves with a formal statement, in which he would confirm in writing his claims, and provisionally accord him the status of a foundling.

At the moment when the doors of the laboratory opened, turning on their invisible hinges, everyone stood up, and I had the impression of an animal panting spreading through the crowd, caused by the sudden acceleration of hundreds of breaths. In the dawning light Knowall's face looked tense, exhausted and closed. He announced that the concluding part of the resurrection operation was running into unexpected difficulties; after having conferred with his assistants, he had decided to extend his deadline by three days; he therefore invited the followers to go back to their tents, remain there as much as possible, and concentrate their thoughts on the transformation, on which the salvation of the rest of mankind depended. He would meet them in three days' time, at sunset, at the foot of the mountain: if everything went well the prophet would have returned to his apartment, and would be in a fit state to make his first public appearance.

Miskiewicz's voice was grave, reflecting the appropriate amount of concern, and this time I noticed an agitation, whispers ran through the crowd. I was quite surprised that he had exhibited such a good understanding of mass psychology. The course was initially scheduled to end the following day, but no one I think seriously thought of leaving: out of three hundred and twelve return flights, there were three hundred and twelve cancellations. As for me, it took me several hours to think of alerting Esther. Once again I got her voicemail, and once again I left a message; I was quite surprised that she didn't call back, she must have been aware of what was happening on the island, the whole world's media was talking about it now.

Of course, the extended deadline increased the incredulity of the media, but curiosity did not abate, instead it increased from hour to hour, and this was what Miskiewicz had intended: he made two brief statements, one each day, this time only to the five science journalists he had chosen as interlocutors, in order to outline the last-minute difficulties he claimed to have run into. He had a perfect mastery of his subject, and I had the impression that the others were beginning to be more and more convinced by him.

I was also surprised by the attitude of Vincent, who was growing progressively into his role. On the level of physical resemblance, the project had raised some doubts in me from the start. Vincent had always been very discreet, he had always refused to speak in public, about his artistic work, for example, on the numerous occasions when the prophet had invited him to; despite this, however, most of the followers had had the occasion to come across him, in the course of the previous years. In a few days, my doubts vanished: I realised to my surprise that Vincent was changing *physically*. First, he had decided to shave his head, and this accentuated his resemblance to the prophet; but the most astonishing thing was that little by little the expression in his eyes was changing, as was his tone of voice. There was now a bright, mischievous gleam in his eyes, which had not been there in all the time I had known him; and his voice was taking on warm, seductive tones, which surprised me more and more. There had always been a gravity to him, a depth that the prophet had never had, but which could also work: the being who was going to be reborn was supposed to have crossed the frontiers of death, you might expect him to come out of the experience as someone more distant, more strange. Cop and Knowall were in any case delighted by the changes in him, I think they had never hoped to obtain so convincing a result. The only one who reacted badly was Gérard, whom I had difficulty now calling Joker: he spent his days wandering around the underground galleries, as if he still hoped to meet the prophet there, he had stopped washing and was beginning to stink. He flashed distrustful and hostile looks at Vincent, like a dog that does not recognise its master. As for Vincent he spoke little, but his eyes were luminous and benevolent, he gave the impression of preparing himself for an ordeal, and of having banished all fear; later he revealed to me that in those days he was already thinking of the construction of the embassy, its decor, he intended to retain nothing of the prophet's plans. He had obviously forgotten the Italian girl, whose death seemed at the time to pose him such painful problems of conscience; and I must confess that I, too, had slightly forgotten her. Perhaps, fundamentally, Miskiewicz was right: a constellation of frost, a pretty but temporary pattern . . . My years in show-business had to some extent weakened my moral sense; however, I still had, I believed, some convictions. Mankind, like all the social species, had built itself on the prohibition of murder within the group, and more generally on the limitation of the level of violence acceptable in the resolution of inter-individual conflicts; civilisation itself had no other real meaning. This idea was valid for all civilisations imaginable, for all the 'rational beings', as Kant would have said, whether mortal or immortal, it was an incontrovertible certainty. After a few minutes' reflection I realised that, from Miskiewicz's point of view, Francesca did *not* belong to the group: what he was trying to do was create a new species, which would have no more moral obligation towards humans than the humans had towards jellyfish or lizards; I realised, above all, that I would have no scruples about belonging to this new species, that my disgust at murder was of a sentimental or emotional, rather than a rational, nature; thinking of Fox, I realised that the murder of a dog would have shocked me as much as that of a man, and probably more so; then, as I had done in all the quite difficult circumstances of my life, I simply stopped thinking.

The fiancées of the prophet had remained ensconced in their bedrooms, and been kept informed of events to exactly the same degree as the other followers; they had greeted the news with the same faith, and confidently expected to find a rejuvenated lover. At one point it struck me that perhaps there would be, in spite of everything, a few difficulties with Susan: she had known Vincent personally, had spoken to him; then I understood that no, she had faith as well, and no doubt more, than all the others, that her very nature excluded the slightest possibility of doubt. In this sense, I told myself, she was very different from Esther, I could never have imagined Esther subscribing to such unrealistic dogmas, and I also realised that since the beginning of this sojourn I had been thinking of her a little less; this was fortunate, moreover, because she still wasn't replying to my messages, I had left about a dozen of them on her voicemail without success, but I wasn't suffering too much, I was in some ways elsewhere, in a space that was still human but utterly different from all I had known before, even some journalists, I realised later when I read their accounts, had been touched by this peculiar atmosphere, this sensation of pre-apocalyptic expectation.

On the day of the resurrection, the faithful gathered from the early hours at the foot of the mountain, even though Vincent's appearance was only scheduled for sunset. Two hours later, the networks' helicopters began to buzz over the area – Knowall had finally given them authorisation to fly over, but he had denied journalists any access to the grounds. For the moment, the cameramen did not have much to pick out – a few images of a peaceful crowd, which waited, without a word or a gesture, for the miracle to happen. When the helicopters returned, the atmosphere became a little more tense – the followers hated the media, which was unsurprising given the treatment they had received from them up until then; but there were no hostile reactions, no threatening gestures or cries.

Around five in the afternoon, a murmur ran through the crowd; some songs were sung, taken up softly by others, then silence reigned again. Vincent, sitting cross-legged in the main cave, seemed not only deep in concentration but in some way outside of time. Around seven, Miskiewicz presented himself at the entrance to the cave. 'Do you feel ready?' he asked him. Vincent nodded without a word, and got up lithely; his long white robe floated on his thinning body.

Miskiewicz was the first to go out, advancing on to the terreplein that overlooked the crowd of the faithful; they all leaped to their feet. The silence was broken only by the regular humming of the helicopters hanging immobile in the air.

'The door has been crossed,' he said. His voice was perfectly amplified, without any distortion or echo, I was sure that with good directional microphones, the journalists would be able to make a good recording of it. 'The door has been crossed in one direction and then in the other,' he continued. 'The barrier of death is no more; that which was foretold has just been accomplished. The prophet has conquered death; he is again among us.' On these words he moved a few metres to one side and bowed his head in respect. There was about a minute's wait that seemed to last forever, no one spoke or moved, all eyes were on the opening of the cave, which faced directly west. At the moment when a ray of the setting sun, through the clouds, illuminated the opening, Vincent came out and advanced onto the terreplein: it was this image, captured by a cameraman from the BBC that would be repeated on televisions across the globe. An expression of adoration filled the faces of the followers, some raised their outstretched arms to the sky; but there was not a cry, not a murmur. Vincent opened his hands and after a few seconds during which he simply breathed into a microphone that captured each of his breaths, he began to speak: 'I breathe, like every one of you . . .' he said softly. 'However, I no longer belong to the same species. I proclaim to you a new mankind . . .' he continued. 'Since its origin the universe has waited for an eternal being, coexistent with it, in which to reflect itself, as in a mirror that is pure and unsullied by time. This being has been born today, just after 5 p.m. I am the Paraclete and the fulfilment of the promise. I am, for the moment, alone, but my solitude will not last, for you will soon join me. You are my first companions, to the number of three hundred and twelve; you are the first generation, the new species called upon to replace man; you are the first neohumans. I am the zero point and you are the first wave. Today, we are entering a different era, where the passing of time no longer has the same meaning. Today, we enter eternal life. This moment will be remembered.'

Daniel1 aside, these crucial days had only three primary witnesses; the life stories of Slotan1 – whom he called 'Knowall' – and of Jérôme1 – to whom he had given the name 'Cop' – converge, fundamentally, with his: the immediate adherence of the followers, their unreserved belief in the resurrection of the prophet . . . The plan seems to have worked from the outset, to the extent that one can actually speak of a 'plan'; Slotan1, as his life story shows, never believed that he was indulging in trickery, persuaded as he was that he would obtain the necessary results within a few years; in his mind, the announcement had simply happened slightly early.

In a very different tone, and with an elliptical brevity that has disconcerted his commentators, the life story of Vincent1 confirms no less precisely what took place, right up to the pathetic episode of the suicide of Gérard, the one whom Daniel1 had nicknamed 'Joker', found hanging in his cell after dragging himself around for a few weeks, and at a point when Slotan1 and Jérôme1 were beginning, for their part, to think of eliminating him. Turning more and more to drink, Gérard became carried away with tearful memories of his youth spent with the prophet and of the 'good tricks' they had played together. Neither of them, it seemed, had believed for a second in the existence of the Elohim. 'It was a just a joke . . .' he repeated, 'a good joke between stoners. We had taken some magic mushrooms, we went for a walk among the volcanoes, and we began to hallucinate the whole thing. I never thought it would go this far . . .' His chatterings were beginning to become embarrassing, for the cult of the Elohim was never officially abandoned, even though it quickly fell into disuse. In their heart of hearts, neither Vincent1 nor Slotan1 placed much importance on this hypothesis of a race of extraterrestrial creators, but both of them concurred with the idea that the human being was going to

214 — The Possibility of an Island

disappear, and that it was necessary to prepare for the advent of its successor. In the mind of Vincent1, even if it were possible that man had been created by the Elohim, recent events proved in any case that he had entered upon a process of Elohimisation, in the sense that he had become, in his turn, a master and creator of life. From this perspective the embassy was becoming a sort of memorial to mankind, destined to bear witness to his aspirations and values in the eyes of the future race; as such it also fitted perfectly into the classical tradition of art. As for Jérôme1, he had become just as completely indifferent to the question of the Elohim, ever since the moment he had been allowed to devote himself to his true passion: the creation and organisation of power structures.

This great diversity of points of view within the triumvirate of the founders certainly played a big role, as has already been emphasised, in the complementary operations that they were able to establish, and in the stunning success of Elohimism in the few years that followed Vincent's 'resurrection'. Moreover, it makes the correlation of their testimonies all the more striking.

DANIEL 1, 18

The complication of the world is unjustified.
Yves Roissy – reply to Marcel Fréthrez

After the extreme tension of the days preceding the resurrection of the prophet in the form of Vincent, after the acme of his media appearance, at the entrance of the cave, in the rays of the setting sun, I am now left with a vague, almost joyful, memory of the days that followed. Cop and Knowall rapidly defined the limits of their respective remits; I realised at once that they would keep to them, and that if no sympathy could emerge between them, they nevertheless functioned efficiently in tandem, for they needed one another, knew it, and shared the same taste for flawless organisation.

After the first evening, Knowall had definitively forbidden journalists access to the grounds, and had, in Vincent's name, refused all interviews; he had even asked for a ban on flyovers – which was immediately granted him by the chief of police, whose aim was to try and calm, as much as possible, the prevailing agitation. By proceeding in this way, Knowall had no specific intention, other than to make it known to the world media that he was in charge of information, that he was at the source of it, and that nothing could happen without his authorisation. The journalists, after having camped unsuccessfully in front of the entrance to the grounds, therefore departed, in smaller and smaller groups, and, by the end of the week, we were alone again. Vincent seemed to have moved definitively into a new reality, and we had no more contact; once, however, on passing by me on the rocky slope that led to our former cells, he invited me to come and see how advanced the plans for the embassy were. I followed him into an underground, white-walled room, lined with loudspeakers and video projectors, then he activated the 'slideshow' program on the computer. It wasn't an embassy, and there weren't really any plans. I had the impression of crossing immense curtains of light, which appeared, formed and vanished all around me. Sometimes I found myself amongst small sparkling, pretty objects, which surrounded me with a friendly presence; then an immense wave of light swallowed everything, and gave birth to a new decor. We were entirely in whiteness, from the crystalline to the milky, from the dull to the dazzling; this bore no relation to any possible reality, but it was beautiful. I told myself that this was perhaps the true nature of art, to show us dreamed-of worlds, impossible worlds, and that it was a thing I had never come close to, that I had never felt myself capable of; I also understood that irony, comedy and humour were going to have to die, for the world to come was the world of happiness, and there would no longer be any place for them there.

Vincent had nothing of the dominant male about him, he had no taste for harems, and a few days after the death of the prophet he had had a long conversation with Susan, following which he had given the other girls back their freedom. I do not know what they had been able to say to one another, I don't know what she believed, if she saw in him the reincarnation of the prophet, if she had recognised him as Vincent, if he had confessed to her that he was his son, or if she had fabricated any in-between conceptions; but I think that for her all this would have been of little importance. Incapable of relativism, and basically quite indifferent to the question of truth, Susan could only live by being entirely in love. Having found a new being to love, perhaps having loved him for a long time already, she had found a new reason for living, and I knew without any danger of being mistaken that they would stay together to the end, until death did them part, as they say, except that perhaps this time death would not occur, Miskiewicz would succeed in reaching his goals, they would be reborn together in renewed bodies, and perhaps, for the first time in the history of the world, they would effectively live a love without end. It's not weariness that puts an end to love, or rather it's a weariness that is born of impatience, of the impatience of bodies who know they are condemned and want to live, who want, in the lapse of time granted them, to not pass up any chance, to miss no possibility, who want to use to the utmost that limited, declining and mediocre lifetime that is theirs, and who consequently cannot love *anyone*, as all others appear limited, declining and mediocre to them.

Despite this new orientation towards monogamy – an implicit orientation, moreover, Vincent had given no directive, the choice he had made of Susan alone was a purely individual choice – the week following the 'resurrection' was marked by a more intense, more liberated and more varied sexual activity, I even heard of some genuine orgies. The couples in the centre did not, however, seem to suffer from this, no break in conjugal relations was observed, nor even a row. Perhaps the closer prospect of immortality had given some substance to that notion of *non-possessive love* that the prophet had preached throughout his life without ever having managed to convince anyone; I think above all that the disappearance of his crushing male presence had liberated the followers, and given them a desire to experience some lighter and more ludic moments.

What awaited me back in my own life had little chance of being as much fun, I could sense it more and more clearly. It was only on the eve of my departure that I managed, at last, to speak to Esther: she explained to me that she had been very busy, that she had been given the main part in a short film, that it had been a stroke of luck, she had been taken on at the last moment, and that the filming had started just after her exams – which she had, incidentally, passed with flying colours; in short, she spoke only about herself. She was, however, aware of the events in Lanzarote and knew that I had been an eye-witness. '*Que fuerte!*' she exclaimed, which seemed a pretty thin comment; I realised then that with her, too, I would keep my silence, and that I would stick to the widely held version of a probable scam, without ever indicating I had been involved up to that point in the events, and that Vincent was the only person in the world with whom, perhaps, I might one day have the chance to speak of them. I then understood why the *éminences grises*, and even the simple witnesses of a historical event whose underlying causes have remained unknown to the general public, feel at some point or another the need to ease their consciences, and to put down on paper what they know.

The next day, Vincent accompanied me to Arrecife airport, he drove the four-wheel drive himself. When we were driving again along that strange beach, its black sand scattered with little white pebbles, I tried to explain this need I felt for a written confession. He listened to me carefully, and after parking just in front of the departure hall, as we smoked, he told me he understood, and gave me permission to write down what I had seen. It was simply necessary that the story be published only after my death, or at least that I would wait before publishing it, or indeed before having it read by anyone, for formal permission from the ruling council of the church – that is to say the triumvirate he formed with Knowall and Cop. Apart from these conditions, which I accepted easily – and I knew he trusted me – I felt he was pensive, as though my request had just thrown him into vague reflections that he was having difficulty disentangling.

We waited for my boarding call in a hall with immense bay windows, overlooking the runways. The volcanoes could be clearly seen in the distance, presences that were familiar and even reassuring under a dark-blue sky. I sensed that Vincent would have liked to make his farewell warmer, from time to time he pressed my arm, or took me by the shoulders; but he couldn't really find the right words, and didn't really know how to make the right gestures. That very evening, a sample of my DNA had been taken, and I was, therefore, officially part of the church. Just as an air hostess announced the boarding for the flight to Madrid, I said to myself that this island, with its temperate stable climate, where sunshine and temperature experienced only minimal variations throughout the year, was truly the ideal place to attain eternal life.

In fact, Vincent1 informs us that it was following this conversation with Daniel1 in the car park of Arrecife airport that he had for the first time the idea of the *life story*, which would be introduced first as an annex, a simple palliative whilst the research of Slotan1 on the cabling of memory networks progressed, but which would assume such great importance following the logical conceptualisations by Pierce.

I had two hours to wait in Madrid airport for the flight to Almeria; these two hours were sufficient to sweep away the state of abstract strangeness in which the time with the Elohimites had left me and plunge me back completely into misery, like venturing, step by step, into ice-cold water; as I got on the plane, in spite of the warmth, I was already literally trembling with anxiety. Esther knew I was leaving that very day, and it had taken an enormous effort not to confess to her that I had a two-hour wait at Madrid airport – the prospect of hearing her tell me that two hours was too short for her to bother making the journey there and back in a taxi, etc., being almost unbearable. Nevertheless during those two hours, wandering between the CD shops, which were shamelessly promoting the new disc from David Bisbal (Esther had figured, scantily clad, in one of the singer's recent videos), the Punta de Fumadores and the Jennyfer clothes shops, I had the increasingly unbearable sensation that I could see her young body, eroticised in a summer dress, crossing the city streets, a few kilometres away, beneath the admiring gazes of boys. I stopped at Tap Tap Tapas and ordered some disgusting sausages, swimming in an incredibly greasy sauce, which I washed down with several beers; I could feel my stomach swell, filling with shit, and the idea crossed my mind of consciously accelerating the process of destruction, of becoming old, repellent and obese to better feel definitively unworthy of Esther's body. Just as I started on my fourth glass of Mahou, a song began playing on the bar radio, I did not know the singer but it wasn't David Bisbal, rather a traditional Latino, with those attempts at vibrato that the young Spaniards now found ridiculous, essentially a singer for housewives rather than a singer for babes, still the refrain was: '*Mujer es fatal*', and I realised that I had never heard this simple and silly thing expressed so accurately, and that poetry when it achieved simplicity was a great thing, undoubtedly *the big thing*. The word 'fatal' in Spanish fitted perfectly, I could see no other that could have better described my situation, it was hell, genuine hell, I had returned to the trap myself, I had wanted to return to it but I didn't know how to get out and I wasn't even sure I wanted to, my soul, in as much as I had one, was growing more and more confused, and my body, because whatever else was true I had a body, was suffering, ravaged by desire.

Back in San Jose I went to bed immediately, after taking a massive dose of sleeping pills. Over the following days, I just wandered from room to room in the residence; it's true, I was immortal but for the moment that didn't change much, Esther still didn't call, and that was the only thing that seemed important to me. Listening by chance to a cultural programme on Spanish television (it was more than by chance; it was a miracle, for cultural programmes are rare on Spanish television, the Spaniards don't like cultural programmes at all, nor culture in general, it's an area that is fundamentally hostile to them, one occasionally has the impression when talking about culture to them that they are sort of personally insulted), I learned that the last words of Immanuel Kant, on his death bed, had been: 'That's enough.' Immediately I had a painful fit of laughter, accompanied by stomach pangs that went on for three days, at the end of which I began to vomit bile. I called a doctor, who diagnosed poisoning, asked me what I had eaten in the last few days and recommended that I buy some dairy products. I bought some dairy products, and that evening returned to the Diamond Nights Bar, which I had remembered as being an honest establishment, where you were not pushed to consume excessively. There were about thirty girls around the bar, but only two male customers. I opted for a Moroccan girl who could have been only seventeen; her big breasts were finely displayed by her décolleté, and I really thought that things were going to go well, but once we were in the bedroom I had to face up to the fact that I wasn't hard enough for her to put a condom on me, under these conditions she refused to suck me off, and so what could we do? She ended up tossing me off, staring obstinately into a corner of the room, she was doing it too hard, it hurt. After a minute there was a small translucent spurt, and she immediately let go of my cock; I pulled my trousers back up before going for a piss.

The following morning, I received a fax from the producer of *Diogenes the Cynic*. He had heard that I was giving up the 'Motorway Swingers' project, he thought it was a real pity; he felt ready to take on the production if I agreed to write the script. He happened to be passing through Madrid the following week, he proposed we meet to talk about it.

I wasn't really in regular contact with this guy, in fact I hadn't seen him for more than five years. On entering the café, I realised that I had completely forgotten what he looked like; I sat at the nearest table and ordered a beer. Two minutes later a man of about forty, with curly hair, dressed in an extraordinary khaki hunting jacket with lots of pockets, stopped in front of my table, smiling widely and holding a glass. He was badly shaven, his face oozed sleaziness and I still didn't recognise him; despite all this, I invited him to sit down. My agent had made him read my treatment and the pre-credits sequence I had developed, he said; he found the project exceptionally interesting. I nodded mechanically whilst looking out of the corner of my eye at my mobile; when I arrived at the airport, I had left a message for Esther telling her I was in Madrid. She called me back at an opportune moment, just as I was beginning to get tangled up in my contradictions, and promised to come by in ten minutes' time. I looked up again at the producer, I still couldn't remember his name but I realised I didn't like him, nor did I like his view of mankind, and more generally I wanted nothing to do with this guy. He was now suggesting that we collaborate on the script; I flinched at this idea. He noticed and back-pedalled, assured me I could absolutely work alone if I preferred, that he had complete trust in me. I had no desire to throw myself into that stupid script, I just wanted to live, to live again a little bit, if such a thing were possible, but I couldn't talk to him about this openly, after all he was a spiteful gossip, the news wouldn't take long to do the rounds in the business, and for obscure reasons – maybe simply through fatigue – it still seemed necessary for me to put people off the scent for a few months. In order to keep the conversation going I told him the story of that German who had eaten another German he had met on the Internet. First he had cut off his penis, then had fried it, with onions, and they had eaten it together. Then he had killed him before cutting him up into pieces, which he then stocked in his freezer. From time to time, he would take out a piece, defrost and cook it, using a different recipe for each occasion. The moment of common manducation of the penis had been an intense religious experience, of real communion between him and his victim, he had stated to the investigators. The producer listened to me with a smile that was both silly and cruel, probably imagining that I intended to integrate these elements into my work in progress, delighting already at the repellent images he would be able to extract from it. Fortunately, Esther arrived, all smiles, her pleated summer skirt twirling around her thighs, and threw herself into my arms with an enthusiasm that made me forget everything. She sat down and ordered a mint Diabolo, waiting politely for our conversation to end. From time to time the producer sent her appreciative looks – she had put her feet up on the chair in front of her, parted her legs, she wasn't wearing any panties and all this seemed natural and logical, a simple consequence of the prevailing temperature, I expected her at any moment to wipe her pussy with one of the bar's paper napkins. Finally he took his leave and we promised to stay in contact. Ten minutes later I was inside her, and I felt good. The miracle happened again, as strongly as on the first day, and I believed again, for the last time, that it was going to last for eternity.

Unrequited love is a haemorrhage. Over the months that followed, as Spain settled into summertime, I could still have pretended to myself that all was well, that we were equally in love; but unfortunately I had never been very good at lying to myself. Two weeks later she visited me in San Jose, and if she still gave me her body with as much abandon, as little restraint as ever, I also noticed that, more and more frequently, she would move a few metres away to speak into her mobile. She laughed a lot during these conversations, more than she did with me, she would promise to be coming back soon, and the idea I had had of proposing that she spend the summer in my company appeared more and more plainly to be senseless; it was almost with relief that I took her back to the airport. I had avoided the break-up, we were *still together*, as they say, and the following week it was I who made the trip to Madrid.

She still went out clubbing a lot, I knew, and sometimes spent the entire night dancing; but she never asked me to accompany her. I imagined her, replying to her friends who asked her out: 'No, not this evening, I'm with Daniel . . .' I now knew most of them, many were students or actors; often of the *groovy* type, with longish hair and comfortable clothes; some by contrast would wittily play up the *macho*, *Latin-lover* style; but all of them, obviously, were *young*, and how could it have been otherwise? How many of them, I sometimes wondered, could have been her lovers? She never did anything that might make me ill at ease; but nor did I ever have the feeling I was part of her group. I remember an evening, it could have been 10 p.m., there were a dozen or so of us in a bar and everyone was talking with great animation about the merits of various clubs, the ones that were more house, the others more trance. For ten minutes, I was dying to say to them that I, too, *wanted* to enter this world, to have fun with them, to stay up all night; I was ready to beg them to take me. Then, by accident, I saw my reflection in a window, and I understood. I looked my forty-something years; my face was careworn, stiff, marked by the experience of life, by responsibilities and sorrows; I didn't look at all like someone you could imagine *having fun*; I was condemned.

During the night, after making love with Esther (and it was the only thing that still worked well, it was without doubt the only youthful, pure thing left in me), contemplating her smooth white body in the moonlight, I thought with pain of Fat Ass. If I was, following the words of the Gospel, to be measured by the measure I had used, then I was in a bad way, for there was no doubt that I had behaved *pitilessly* towards Fat Ass. Not that pity, actually, could have served any useful purpose: there are many things you can do with compassion, but get a hard-on, no, that's not possible.

At the time I had met Fat Ass, I was about thirty, and I was beginning to have some success – not yet with the general public as such, but still a kind of critical success. I noticed immediately this fat and pallid woman who came to all my shows, sat in the front row, and each time handed me her autograph book. It took her almost six months to bring herself to speak to me – come to think of it, no, I believe that, finally, I was the one who took the initiative. She was a cultivated woman, taught philosophy in a Paris university and I really didn't suspect anything. She asked my permission to publish an annotated transcript of some of my sketches in *The Journal of Phenomenological Studies*; naturally, I said yes. I was a little flattered, I must admit, after all I hadn't even sat my baccalaureate and here she was comparing me to Kierkegaard. We exchanged e-mails for a few months, gradually things began to degenerate, I accepted an invitation to dinner at her place, I should have been immediately suspicious when I saw the dress she was wearing indoors, however I managed to leave without humiliating her too much, or at least that's what I had hoped, but the following morning the first pornographic e-mails began. 'Ah, to feel you at last inside me, to feel your stem of flesh opening my flower . . .' It was awful, she wrote like Gérard de Villiers. She really wasn't well preserved, she looked much older, but in reality she was only forty-seven when I met her – exactly the same age as I was when I met Esther. I jumped out of bed the second I became conscious of this, gasping with anxiety, and began running up and down the bedroom – Esther was sleeping peacefully, she had thrown off the blankets, God she was beautiful.

I had imagined then – and fifteen years later I thought of it again with shame and disgust – I had imagined that after a certain age, sexual desire *disappears* and leaves you at least relatively tranquil. How had I, the one who had pretended to himself that he had a caustic and cutting mind, been able to fashion such a ridiculous illusion? I understood life, in principle at least, I had even read some books; and if there was one simple subject, one subject on which, as they say, all the testimonies are in agreement, it was certainly this. Not only does sexual desire not disappear, but with age it becomes even crueller, more and more wrenching and insatiable – and even among those, quite rare, men whose hormonal secretions, erections and all associated phenomena disappear, the attraction to young female bodies does not diminish, it becomes, and this is maybe even worse, *cosa mentale*, the desire for desire.

This is the truth, this is the evidence, this is what, tirelessly, all serious authors have constantly repeated.

At the absolute limit, I could have performed cunnilingus on the person of Fat Ass – I imagined my face venturing between her flabby thighs, their pale rolls of fat, trying to revive her sagging clitoris. But even that, I was sure, would not have been enough – and would perhaps only have aggravated her suffering. She wanted, like all women, to be penetrated, she would not be satisfied with less, it was non-negotiable.

I took flight; like all men put in the same circumstances, I ran away: I stopped replying to her e-mails, I forbade her access to my dressing room. She insisted for years, five, maybe seven, she insisted for a terrifying number of years; I think she insisted right up to the day after my encounter with Isabelle. I had obviously not told her anything, I no longer had any contact; maybe at the end of the day intuition does exist, *female intuition* as they say, it was in any case the moment she chose to disappear, to leave my life, and maybe life itself, as she had, several times, threatened to do.

On the day after that difficult night, I took the first plane to Paris. Esther was slightly surprised, she had thought I would spend the whole week in Madrid, and so had I as that was what I had planned. I didn't fully understand the reason for this sudden departure, maybe I wanted to be *clever*, to show that I too had my life, my activities and my independence – in which case I had failed, she didn't seem upset or destabilised by the news in the slightest, she said: '*Bueno* . . .' and that was that. Above all, I suppose my actions didn't really make any sense, I was beginning to behave like a fatally wounded old animal that charges in all directions, bumps into every obstacle, falls and gets up, more and more furious, more and more weakened, crazed and intoxicated by the smell of its own blood.

I had used as a pretext my desire to see Vincent again, or at least that's what I had explained to Esther, but it was only when I landed at Roissy that I realised how much I really wanted to see him; with this, too, I didn't know why, maybe just to verify that happiness is possible. With Susan he had moved back into his grandparents' house – the house he had, in fact, lived in all his life. It was the end of May but the weather was overcast, and the red-brick exterior rather sinister; I was surprised by the names on the letter box. 'Susan Longfellow' OK, but 'Vincent Macaury'? Well yes, the prophet was called Macaury, Robert Macaury; and Vincent no longer had the right to use his mother's name; the name Macaury had been given to him by the lawyers, because he needed one, whilst awaiting a legal decision. 'I am a mistake . . .' Vincent had once told me alluding to his relationship with the prophet. Maybe; but his grandparents had welcomed him and cherished him like a victim, they had been bitterly disappointed by the hedonistic and irresponsible selfishness of their son – indeed of an entire generation, before things turned bad, and only selfishness remained, hedonism having flown; they had welcomed him in any case, they had opened the doors of their home to him, and this was something, for example, that I would never have done for my own son, the very thought of living under the same roof as that little asshole would have been unbearable, we were simply, he and I, people who *should not have been born.* Unlike, say, Susan, who now lived among these old, cluttered, gloomy furnishings, so far from her native California, and who had immediately felt good there; she had thrown out nothing, I recognised the framed family photos, the grandfather's work medals and the souvenir mechanical bulls bought during a holiday on the Costa Brava; maybe she had let in some fresh air, bought some flowers, I haven't a clue, I've always lived as though I were in a hotel, I don't have the home-making instinct, in the absence of women, I believe I wouldn't even have given it a thought; in any case it was a now a house in which you had the impression that people could be happy, she had the power to do that. She loved Vincent, I realised immediately, it was obvious, but above all she *loved.* It was in her nature to love, as it was for a cow to graze (or a bird to sing; or a rat to sniff about). Having lost her previous master, she had almost instantaneously found another, and the world around her had once again been filled with a positive clarity. I dined with them, and it was a pleasant and harmonious evening, with very little suffering; I did not, however, have the courage to stay the night, and I left at about eleven having reserved a room at the Lutétia.

At Montparnasse-Bienvenue station I thought again about poetry, probably because I had just seen Vincent, and that always brought me back to a clear consciousness of my limits: creative limitations on one hand, but also limitations in love. It must be said that I had just passed by a 'Poetry on the Metro' poster, more precisely the one that reproduced 'Free Love' by André Breton, and, whatever the disgust inspired by the personality of André Breton, whatever the stupidity of the title, its pitiful antinomy, which only demonstrated, in addition to a certain softening of the brain, the instinct for publicity that characterised and ultimately summed up Surrealism, you had to admit it: this idiot had, under the circumstances, written a very beautiful poem. I was not the only one, however, to have some reservations, and two days later, passing by the same poster again, I noticed that it was smeared with graffiti, which said: 'Instead of your stupid poems, give us some trains at rush hour,' which was enough to put me in a good mood for the entire afternoon, and even to give me back some self-confidence: I was only a comedian, I know, but I was still a comedian.

The day after my dinner at Vincent's, I had informed the reception desk at the Lutétia that I would be keeping the room, probably for a few days. They had welcomed the news with a conniving courtesy. After all, don't forget, I was a *celebrity*; I could easily burn my cash by drinking Alexandras at the bar with Philippe Sollers, or Philippe Bouvard – maybe not Philippe Léotard, he was dead; but anyway, given my notoriety, I would have access to these categories of Philippes. I could spend the night with a transsexual Slovenian whore; in short, I could have a *brilliant social life*, it was probably even expected of me, people become famous as a result of one or two talented productions, no more, it's sufficiently surprising that a human being has one or two things to say, after that they manage their decline more or less peacefully, more or less painfully, that's the way it goes.

I did none of that, however, in the days that followed; instead, first thing that morning, I phoned Vincent again. He understood quickly that the spectacle of his conjugal bliss risked hurting me, and suggested that we meet up in the bar of the Lutétia. He really only spoke to me about his embassy project, which had become an installation whose visitors would be the men of the future. He had ordered a lemonade, but didn't touch his drink; from time to time, some *celeb* crossed the bar, noticed me and made me a sign of complicity; Vincent paid no attention. He spoke without looking at me, without even checking that I was listening, in a voice that was both thoughtful and distant, as though he was speaking into a tape recorder, or was testifying at an inquiry. As he explained his idea to me, I became conscious that he was moving little by little further away from his initial plan, that the project was growing more and more ambitious, that his goal was now nothing less than to bear witness to what a pompous author of the twentieth century had felt fit to call the 'human condition'. There were already, he pointed out, many testimonies about mankind, which all agreed in their lamentable assessment; the subject, in short, was *covered*. Calmly, but irreversibly, he was leaving the human shores to sail towards the *absolute beyond*, where I did not feel capable of following him, and no doubt it was the only space where he felt himself able to breathe, no doubt his life had never had any other objective, but it was, of course, an objective he needed to pursue alone; that said, he had always been alone.

We were no longer the same, he insisted in a gentle voice, we had become *eternal*; granted we would need some time to master the idea, to become familiar with it; nevertheless, fundamentally, and from now on, things had changed. Knowall had stayed on Lanzarote after the departure of all the followers, with a few technicians, and he was pursuing his research; he would succeed in the end, there was no doubt about it. Man had a large brain, disproportionate in relation to the primitive demands arising from the struggle to survive, from the elementary quest for food and sex; we were, at last, going to be able to use it. No culture of the mind, he reminded me, had ever been able to develop in societies with a high level of delinquency, simply because physical security is the condition for free thought; no reflection, no poetry nor idea of the slightest creativity has ever been engendered in an individual who has to worry about his survival, who has to be constantly *on his guard*. Once the preservation of our DNA had been ensured, once we had become potentially immortal, we were going, he went on, to find ourselves in conditions of absolute physical safety, in conditions that no human being had ever known; no one could predict what was going to be the result of this, as far as the mind was concerned.

This peaceful, almost disengaged, conversation did me an immense amount of good, and for the first time I began to think of my own immortality, to look at things in a slightly more open manner; but back in my room I found a message on my mobile from Esther, which simply said: 'I miss you', and I felt all over again, incrusted in my flesh, my need for her. Joy is such a rare thing. The following morning, I took the plane back to Madrid.

The incredible importance accorded to sexual matters among humans has always plunged their neohuman commentators into horrified amazement. It was nonetheless painful to see Daniel1 gradually come closer to the *Evil Secret*, as the Supreme Sister calls it; it was painful to feel him gradually overcome by the consciousness of a truth that, once revealed, could only annihilate him. Throughout history, most men have deemed it correct, at a certain point in life, to allude to sexual problems as though they were just trivial childish games, and to assume that the real subjects, the subjects worthy of a man's attention, were politics, business or war, etc. The truth, in Daniel1's time, began to be unearthed; it became more and more clear, and more and more difficult to hide, that the true goals of men, the only ones they would have pursued spontaneously if it were still possible for them to do so, were of an exclusively sexual nature. For us neohumans it is a genuine stumbling block. We can never, the Supreme Sister warns us, get a clear enough idea of it; we will only ever be able to approach an understanding of it by constantly keeping in mind certain regulatory ideas, the most important of which is that in the human species, as in all the animal species that preceded it, individual survival counted for absolutely nothing. The Darwinian fiction of the 'struggle for life' had long hidden this elementary fact that the genetic value of an individual, his power to pass on his characteristics to his descendants, could be summed up, very brutally, by a single parameter: the number of descendants that he was, in the end capable of procreating. Thus it was completely unsurprising that an animal, any animal, was prepared to sacrifice its happiness, its physical well-being and even its life, in the hope of sexual intercourse alone: the will of the species (to speak in finalist terms), a powerfully regulated hormonal system (if you hold to a determinist approach) led them almost inevitably to this choice. The marvellous finery and plumage, the noisy and spectacular parades could easily result in the male animals being spotted and devoured by their predators; such a solution was no less systematically favoured, in genetic terms, as long as it permitted more effective reproduction. This subordination of the individual to the species, based on immutable biochemical mechanisms, was just as strong in the human animal, with the added aggravation that their sexual drives, not limited to the rutting period, could operate permanently – human life stories show us, for example, evidence that maintaining a physical appearance capable of seducing representatives of the opposite sex was the only reason for staying healthy, and that the meticulous care of their bodies, to which Daniel1's contemporaries devoted an increasing proportion of their free time, had no other aim.

The sexual biochemistry of the neohumans – and this was undoubtedly the real reason for the sensation of suffocation and malaise that overcame me as I advanced through Daniel1's story, as I followed the stations of his calvary – had remained almost identical.

Nothingness turns to nothing.
Martin Heidegger

A zone of high pressure had settled, since the start of August, on the central plain, and from the moment of my arrival at Barajas airport I sensed that things were going to turn out badly. The heat was almost unbearable and Esther was late; she arrived half an hour later, naked under her summer dress.

I had left my coitus cream at the Lutétia, and this was my first mistake; I came much too quickly, and, for the first time, I sensed she was a little disappointed. She continued to move, a little, on my sex, which was becoming irredeemably soft, then moved aside with a resigned grimace. I would have given a great deal to get another hard-on; from the moment they are born, men live in a difficult world, a world where the stakes are simplistic and pitiless, and without the understanding of women there are very few who manage to survive. It seemed to me that I understood, from that moment onwards, that she had slept with someone else in my absence.

We took the Metro to have a drink with two of her friends; sweat made the fabric cling to her body, it was easy to make out the aureoles of her breasts, the outline of her ass; all the boys in the carriage, obviously, stared at her; some even smiled at her.

I found it very difficult to take part in the conversation, from time to time I managed to catch a sentence, to offer a few replies, but very soon I was out of my depth and, besides, I was thinking of something else, I felt like I was on a slippery, a very slippery slope. On our return to the hotel, I asked her the question; she acknowledged it without making any excuses. 'It was an ex-boyfriend . . .' she said, in English, as if to convey that it wasn't very important. 'And a friend of his,' she added after a few seconds' hesitation.

So two boys; oh yes, two boys, after all it wasn't the first time. She had met her ex by chance in a bar, he was with one of his friends, one thing led to another, and so, in short, the three of them ended up in the same bed. I asked her how it had been, I couldn't stop myself. 'Good . . . good . . .' she told me, slightly worried by the direction the conversation was taking. 'It was . . . comfortable,' she added, without being able to repress a smile. Yes, comfortable; I could imagine. It took a terrible effort to ask her if she had sucked him off, him, his friend, both of them, if she had been sodomised. I felt the images flood my brain, this must have been obvious because she stopped talking and her forehead became more and more creased with concern. Very quickly she took the only decision possible, to take care of my sex, and she did it with such tenderness, such skill, with her fingers and her mouth, that against all expectation I began to get hard again, and a minute later I was inside her, and it was good, it was good again, I was completely in the moment and so was she, I even believe that she hadn't felt such pleasure in a long time – with me at least, I told myself a couple of minutes later, but this time I managed to chase the thought from my mind, and I held her very tenderly in my arms, with all the tenderness I was capable of, and I concentrated with all my strength on her body, on the actual, warm, living presence of her body.

This little scene, so sweet, so unobtrusive and implicit, had, I now think, a decisive influence on Esther, and her behaviour in the following weeks was guided by only one thought: to avoid hurting me; to try, even, with all the means at her disposal, to make me happy. The means available to her for making a man happy were considerable, and I have the memory of a period of immense joy, irradiated at every moment by a carnal felicity, a felicity I would not have believed could be bearable, nor believed myself capable of surviving. I also retain the memory of her kindness, her intelligence, her compassionate insight and her grace, but, basically, I don't really have what you'd call a memory, or any clear image, I only know that I lived for at least a few days and doubtless a few weeks in a certain *state*, a state of perfection that was sufficient and complete, yet human, of which some men have occasionally sensed the possibility, even though none until now have been able to provide a plausible description of it.

For a long time she had been planning a party for her birthday on 17 August, and she began over the following days to occupy herself with its preparations. She wanted to invite quite a lot of people, about a hundred, and decided to call upon the help of a friend who lived in the Calle San Isidor. He had a big loft on the top floor, with a terrace and a swimming pool; he invited us to talk about it over a drink. He was a big guy called Pablo, with long curly black hair, rather cool; he had slipped on a light dressing gown to let us in, but took it off once he was on the terrace; his naked body was muscled and tanned. He offered us orange juice. Had he slept with Esther? And was I going to ask myself this question, from now on, of all the men I happened to come across? She was attentive, on her guard since the evening of my return; probably spotting a glimmer of concern in my eyes, she turned down the proposition of a little sunbathing by the pool and tried to limit the conversation to the party preparations. There was no question of buying enough cocaine and Ecstasy for everyone; she offered to cover the purchase of a first bag to start the evening, and to ask the dealers to stop by later. Pablo could look after that, he had excellent dealers at the time; he even proposed, in a burst of generosity, to take care of the purchase of some poppers.

On 15 August, the day of the Virgin, Esther made love to me with even more lasciviousness than usual. We were in the Hotel Sanz, the bed faced a big mirror and it was so hot that each movement made us sweat profusely; I had my arms and legs crossed, I no longer felt I had the strength to move, all my senses were concentrated in my sex. For more than an hour she straddled me, going up and down my cock, around which she contracted and relaxed her just-waxed little pussy. Throughout all this time she caressed her breasts (which gleamed with sweat) with one hand, whilst looking me in the eye, smiling and deep in concentration, attentive to all the variations of my pleasure. Her free hand was closed around my balls, which she sometimes pressed gently, sometimes hard, to the rhythm of the movement of her pussy. When she felt me coming she suddenly stopped and pressed sharply with two fingers to stop the ejaculation at its source; then, when the danger had passed, she began to move to and fro again. Thus I spent an hour, perhaps two, on the brink of exploding, at the heart of the greatest joy a man can know, and in the end it was me who asked for mercy, who wished to come in her mouth. She got up, placed a pillow under my backside, and asked if I could see the mirror OK; no, it was better to move a little. I moved to the edge of the bed. She knelt between my thighs, her face level with my sex, which she began to lick methodically, centimetre by centimetre, before closing her lips around my glans; then her hands went into action and she tossed me off slowly, forcefully, as if extracting each drop of sperm from the depths of me, whilst her tongue made rapid movements to and fro. My vision clouded by sweat, having lost all clear notion of space and time, I nevertheless managed to prolong this moment a little, and her tongue had enough time to effect three complete rotations before I came, and it was then as if my whole body, irradiated by pleasure, vanished, sucked in by nothingness, in a release of blessed energy. She kept me in her mouth, almost immobile, sucking my sex slowly, closing her eyes as if to hear more clearly my screams of happiness.

Then she lay down and snuggled in my arms, as night fell rapidly on Madrid, and it was only after half an hour of tender immobility that she told me she had had, for a few weeks now, something to tell me – no one knew about it yet except her sister, she intended to announce it to her friends at the birthday party. She had been accepted by a prestigious piano academy in New York and intended to spend at least the academic year there. At the same time, she had been chosen for a small role in a big Hollywood production about the death of Socrates; she would play a servant of Aphrodite, the part of Socrates would be taken by Robert De Niro. It was only a small part, not more than a week's filming, but it was Hollywood, and the fee was enough to pay for a year's study and maintenance. She would leave at the beginning of September.

It seems to me that I stayed totally silent. I was turned to stone, unable to react, I felt that if I uttered a word I would burst into sobs. '*Bueno* . . . It's a big chance in my life . . .' she concluded by saying plaintively, pressing her head against my shoulder. I almost suggested I go to the United States, to settle there with her, but the words died in me before I could utter them, I fully realised that she had not even imagined this possibility. Nor did she suggest that I visit her: this was a new period in her life, a new departure. I switched on the bedside lamp, and looked at her closely to see if I could make out any trace of fascination with America, with Hollywood, in her; no, there was none, she seemed lucid and calm, she was simply taking the best, most rational decision given the circumstances. Surprised by my lengthy silence she turned to look at me, her long blonde hair fell down on each side of her face, my eyes settled involuntarily on her breasts, I stretched out, switched off the lamp, breathed deeply, I didn't want to make things more difficult, I didn't want her to see me cry.

She spent the next day preparing for the party; in a nearby beauty salon she had a clay mask and a facial scrub. I waited, smoking cigarettes in the hotel bedroom; the following day it was more or less the same thing, after her appointment at the hairdresser she stopped by a few shops, bought some earrings and a new belt. My mind felt strangely empty, rather, I imagined, like that of prisoners on death row: I have never believed that they spend their last hours, with the exception perhaps of those who believe in God, going back over their lives and drawing up a balance sheet; I believe that they simply try to spend the time in the most neutral manner possible; the most fortunate ones sleep, but I wasn't one of those, I don't think I closed my eyes during those two days.

When she knocked on the door of my bedroom, on 17 August, at about eight in the evening, and appeared in the doorway, I understood that I would not survive her leaving. She was wearing a small see-through top, tied beneath her breasts, letting you make out their curves; her golden stockings, held up by garters, stopped a centimetre below her skirt – an ultra-short miniskirt, almost a belt, made of golden vinyl. She wasn't wearing any underwear, and when she leaned down to relace her high boots the movement revealed most of her ass; despite myself I stretched out my hand to caress it. She turned around, took me in her arms and looked at me so compassionately, so tenderly that I thought for an instant she was going to say she had changed her mind, that she was staying with me, now and forever, but this didn't happen and we took a taxi to Pablo's loft.

The first guests arrived around 11 p.m., but the party only really got going after three in the morning. At the start I behaved quite properly, circulating half-nonchalantly around the guests, a glass in my hand; many knew me or had seen me at the cinema, which gave rise to a few simple conversations, the music was too loud anyway and very soon I contented myself with just nodding my head. There were almost two hundred people and I was undoubtedly the only one older than twenty-five, but even that did not manage to de-stabilise me, I was in a strangely calm state; it is true that, in a sense, the catastrophe had already happened. Esther was resplendent, and greeted the new arrivals with effusive kisses. Everybody now knew that she was leaving for New York in two weeks' time, and I had been afraid at the start of feeling a bit ridiculous, after all I was in the position of the guy who *gets dumped*, but no one made me feel that way, people spoke to me as if my situation were unexceptional.

Around ten in the morning, the house music gave way to trance, I had been regularly emptying and refilling my glass of punch, I began to feel a little tired, I told myself it would be wonderful if I could manage to get some sleep, but I didn't really believe this, alcohol had helped to halt the rise in my anxiety but I could still feel that it was there, living inside me, ready to devour me at the slightest sign of weakness. A little earlier, a few people had formed into couples, I had observed movements in the direction of the bedrooms. I chose a corridor at random, and opened a door decor-ated with a poster depicting a close-up of spermatozoids. I had the impression of arriving at the end of a mini-orgy; some half-naked boys and girls were flopped across the bed. In the corner, a blonde teenage girl, her T-shirt pulled up above her breasts, was giving blowjobs; I approached her, but she gestured for me to move away. I sat against the bed, not far from a brunette with dusky skin and magnificent breasts, whose skirt was hiked up around her waist. She seemed fast asleep and didn't react when I parted her thighs, but when I introduced a finger into her pussy, she pushed my hand away mechanically, without fully waking up. Resigned, I sat back down at the foot of the bed and I had been plunged for maybe half an hour into a morose state of exhaustion when I saw Esther come in. She was vivacious, on top form, and accompanied by a male friend – a small homosexual who was very blond and cute, with short hair, whom I knew by sight. She had bought two bags of coke, and knelt down to prepare lines, then put the bit of cardboard she had used on the floor; she had not noticed my presence. Her friend took the first line. When she took her turn to kneel on the floor, her skirt rose very high over her ass. She introduced the cardboard tube into her nostril, and at the moment when she rapidly snorted the white powder, with a well-practised, precise gesture, I knew that I would keep engraved in my memory the image of this little animal, who was innocent, amoral, neither good nor evil, who was simply in search of her ration of excitement and pleasure. Suddenly I thought again of the way in which Knowall had described the Italian girl: a pretty arrangement of particles, a smooth surface, without individuality, whose disappearance would hold no importance . . . and it was this that I had been in love with, that had constituted my only reason for living – and, and this was the worst of it, *still* constituted it. She leaped up, opened the door – the music reached us, much louder – and set off in the direction of the party. I rose reluctantly to follow her; when I got to the main room, she had already started dancing again. I began to dance near her but she didn't seem to see me, her hair twirled around her face, her blouse was soaked with sweat, her nipples were erect under the fabric, the beat became more and more rapid – at least 160 bpm – and I had more and more trouble following it, we were briefly separated by a group of three boys then we were together again back to back, I stuck my ass against hers, and she began to move in response, our asses rubbed against one another harder and harder then she turned around and recognised me. '*Ola*, Daniel . . .' she said smiling before starting to dance again, then we were separated by another group of boys and I suddenly felt extremely tired, about to fall down, I sat on a sofa before pouring myself a whisky but it wasn't a good idea, I was immediately overcome with a horrible nausea, the door of the bathroom was locked and I knocked loudly several times repeating:

'I'm sick! I'm sick!' before a girl came to open it, she had wrapped a towel around her waist, and closed the door again behind me before going back into the bathtub where two guys were waiting for her, she knelt down and one of them penetrated her immediately whilst the other positioned himself to be sucked off, I rushed over to the basin and stuck a hand down my throat, I vomited long and painfully before I felt a bit better, then I went off to lie down in the bedroom, there was no one left except the brunette who had pushed me away earlier, she was still sleeping peacefully, her skirt hiked up to the waist, and despite myself I began to feel terribly sad, so I got up again, went after Esther and attached myself to her, literally and shamelessly, I grabbed her by the waist and begged her to speak to me, to speak to me again, to stay at my side, not to leave me alone, she disengaged with increasing impatience and tried to head towards her friends but I came back at her, took her in my arms, she pushed me away again and I saw their faces close around me, no doubt they were speaking to me as well but I couldn't make anything out, the din of the bass covered everything. I finally heard her saying: 'Please, Daniel, please . . . It's a party!' in an urgent voice, but it did no good, the feeling of being abandoned continued to rise within me, to submerge me, I laid my head back on her shoulder, and at this she pushed me away violently with both arms, shouting: 'Stop that!', now she looked really furious, I turned around and left for the bedroom again, I curled up on the floor, held my head in my hands and for the first time in at least twenty years I began to cry.

The party continued the whole day, at about five in the afternoon Pablo returned with some *pains au chocolat* and croissants, I accepted a croissant, which I dipped in a bowl of café au lait, the music was calmer, it was a kind of melodious and serene chill-out track, several girls were dancing, slowly moving their arms, like big wings. Esther was a few metres away but paid no attention to me when I sat down, she continued to chat with her friends, to evoke memories of other parties, and it was at that moment that I understood. She was leaving for the United States for a year, maybe forever; over there she would make new friends, and, of course, she would find a new boyfriend. I was abandoned, certainly, but in exactly the same way that they were, I had no special status. This feeling of exclusive attachment I had, which was going to torture me until it eventually annihilated me, found no correspondence at all in her, it had no justification, no *raison d'être*: our flesh was distinct, we were unable to experience either the same suffering or the same joy, we were obviously separate beings. Isabelle did not like sexual pleasure, but Esther did not like love, she *did not want* to be in love, she refused this feeling of exclusivity, of dependence, and her whole generation refused it with her. I was wandering among them like some kind of prehistoric monster with my romantic silliness, my attachments, my chains. For Esther, as for all the young girls of her generation, sexuality was just a pleasant pastime, driven by seduction and eroticism, which implied no particular sentimental commitment; undoubtedly love, like pity, according to Nietzsche, had never been anything but a fiction invented by the weak to make the strong feel guilty, to introduce limits to their natural freedom and ferocity. Women had been weak, in particular at the moment of giving birth, early on they had needed to live under the guardianship of a powerful protector, and to this end they had invented love, but now they had become strong, they were independent and free, and they had given up inspiring or indeed feeling a sentiment that no longer had any concrete justification. The centuries-old male project, perfectly expressed nowadays by pornographic films, that consisted of ridding sexuality of any emotional connotation in order to bring it back into the realm of pure entertainment had finally, in this generation, been accomplished. What I was feeling, these young people could not feel, nor even exactly understand, and if they had been able to feel something like it, it would have made them uncomfortable, as if it were something ridiculous and a little shameful, like stigmata in ancient times. They had succeeded, after decades of conditioning and effort, they had finally succeeded in tearing from their hearts one of the oldest human feelings, and now it was done, what had been destroyed could no longer be put back together, no more than the pieces of a broken cup can be reassembled, they had reached their goal: at no moment in their lives would they ever know love. They were free.

*

Around midnight, someone put some techno back on, and people started to dance again; the dealers had left, but there were still quite a lot of Ecstasy and poppers left. Inside my head I wandered around oppressive, claustrophobic zones, which were like a succession of dark rooms. For no precise reason I thought again of Gérard, the Elohimite comedian. 'That has ass-hole-utely no importance . . .' I said at one moment to a girl, a mindless Swede who only spoke English anyway; she looked at me strangely, then I noticed that several people were looking at me strangely, and that I had been speaking to myself, apparently for several minutes. I nodded my head, looked at my watch, then went to sit down on a deckchair by the pool; it was already two in the morning, but the heat was still stifling.

Later I realised I hadn't caught sight of Esther for some time, and I began vaguely to search for her. There weren't many people left in the main room; I stepped over several bodies in the corridor and in the end I discovered her in one of the far bedrooms, stretched out in the middle of a group; she had taken off most of her clothes, and now wore only her gold miniskirt, hiked up around her waist. A boy lying behind her, tall with long curly brown hair, who could have been Pablo, was caressing her ass, and readying himself to penetrate her. She was speaking to another boy, also brown and very muscular, whom I didn't recognise; at the same time, she was playing with his sex, tapping it against her nose and her cheeks and smiling all the while. I closed the door discreetly; I didn't know it yet, but this was to be the last image I would keep of her.

Later still, as dawn was breaking on Madrid, I masturbated quickly near the pool. A few metres away from me there was a girl dressed in black, with a vacant look in her eyes; I thought she wouldn't even notice my presence, but she spat to one side when I ejaculated.

I ended up falling asleep, and I probably slept for a long time, because when I awoke there was nobody left; even Pablo had gone. There was dried sperm on my trousers, and I must have spilt whisky on my shirt, it was reeking. I got up with difficulty, and crossed the terrace amidst piles of food and empty bottles. I leaned against the balcony, and observed the street below. The sun had already begun its descent in the sky, night would not take long to fall, and I knew more or less what awaited me. I was evidently now on the home straight.

Spheres of shiny metal levitated in the atmosphere; they slowly turned around, emitting a lightly vibrant song. The local population's behaviour towards them was strange, a mixture of veneration and sarcasm. This population was undoubtedly composed of social primates – were we dealing here with savages, neohumans, or a third species? Their outfits, consisting of large black capes, black masks with holes pierced in them for the eyes, would not allow this to be determined. The collapsed scenery was made up of references to real landscapes – some views might have recalled the description Daniel1 gives of Lanzarote; I didn't understand exactly where Marie23 was coming from, with this iconographic reconstruction.

> *We bear witness to*
> *The apperceptive centre,*
> *To the emotional IGUS*
> *Surviving the shipwreck.*

Even if Marie23, even if all the neohumans and I were only, as I was beginning to suspect, software fictions, the very pregnancy of these fictions demonstrated the existence of one or several IGUSes, whether they were of a biological, digital or, intermediary nature. The existence in itself of an IGUS was enough to establish that a decrease had taken place, at one point in time, within the field of innumerable potentialities; this decrease was the condition for the paradigm of existence. The Future Ones themselves, if they came to be, would need to make their ontological status conform to the general conditions for the functioning of IGUSes. Hartle and Gell-Mann already establish that the cognitive functioning of the IGUSes (Information Gathering and Utilising Systems) presupposes conditions of stability and the mutual exclusion of sequences of events.

For an IGUS observer, whether natural or artificial, only one branch of universe can be endowed with a real existence; if this conclusion does not exclude in any way the possibility of other branches of universe, it forbids any access to them to a given observer: to use the quite mysterious but synthetic expression of Gell-Mann, 'On every branch, only this branch is preserved.' The very presence of a community of observers, even reduced to two IGUSes, was thus proof of the existence of a *reality*.

According to the current hypothesis, that of an evolution without solution of continuity within a 'carbon biology' lineage, there was no reason to think that the evolution of the savages had been interrupted by the Great Drying Up, nothing indicated however that they had been able, as Marie23 supposed, to gain access to language again, nor that intelligent communities had formed, reconstructing societies of a new type over which neither we, nor the Founders, would have the slightest control.

This theme, regardless, is obviously close to her heart, and she returns to it increasingly often in our exchanges, which are becoming increasingly animated. I sense in her a sort of intellectual ferment, an impatience that is gradually rubbing off on me, although there is nothing, in our external circumstances, that justifies us breaking out of our stasis, and I often quit our intermediation sequences shaken, as if I've been weakened. The presence of Fox, fortunately, soon calms me down, and I settle into my favourite armchair, at the northern extremity of the main room, to await, eyes closed, sitting tranquilly in the light, our next contact.

I took the train to Biarritz that very day; I had to change at Hendaye, some young girls in short skirts and a general holiday atmosphere – which was obviously of little interest to me, but I was still able to note it, I was still human, there were no illusions about that, I was not completely *thick-skinned*, deliverance would never be complete, not until I was effectively dead. On my arrival I took a room at the Villa Eugénie, a former holiday retreat given by Napoléon III to the Empress, which had become a luxury hotel in the twentieth century. The restaurant was also called the Villa Eugénie, and it had a star in the Michelin Guide. I ordered squid with creamy rice, in an ink sauce; it was good. I had the impression that I could order the same thing every day, and, more generally, that I could stay there for a very long time, a few months, all my life, perhaps. The following morning I bought a Samsung X10 laptop and a Canon I80 printer. I more or less had the intention of starting on the project I had talked about to Vincent: to recount, for a yet undetermined audience, the events I had witnessed on Lanzarote. It was only much later, after several conversations with him, after I had explained to him at length the real but weak feeling of calm, the sensation of partial lucidity that this narration gave me, that he had the idea of asking all those aspiring to immortality to devote them-selves to the practice of the *life story*, and to do it in as exhaustive a manner as possible; my own project, as a consequence, bore his influence, and became clearly more autobiographical.

I had of course intended, on coming to Biarritz, to see Isabelle again, but after I moved into the hotel, it seemed to me that, fundamentally, it wasn't all that urgent – quite strange really, because it was already obvious that there was now only a limited amount of time left for me to live. Every day, I went for a walk on the beach, for about quarter of an hour, I said to myself there was a chance I might meet her when she was out with Fox; but this didn't happen, and after two weeks I decided to phone her. After all, maybe she had left town, it was more than a year since we'd last had any contact.

She hadn't left town, but informed me that she was going to as soon as her mother was dead – which would be in a couple of weeks' time, a month at the very most. She didn't seem particularly pleased to hear from me, and I was the one who had to propose we meet. I invited her to lunch at my hotel; it wasn't possible, she told me, because dogs were barred. We finally agreed to meet up as usual at the Silver Surfer, but I immediately sensed that something had changed. It was curious, quite difficult to explain, but for the first time I had the impression that she *had it in for me*. I also realised that I had never spoken to her about Esther, not a word, and I found this difficult to understand because we were, I repeat, civilised, *modern* people; our separation hadn't been marked by any meanness or any financial pettiness in particular, you could say that we had parted *good friends*.

Fox had aged a bit, and put on weight, but he was still as cuddly and playful; you had to give him a bit of help to climb on to your knees, that's all. We spoke about him for more than ten minutes: he delighted the rock-and-roll biddies of Biarritz, probably because the Queen of England had the same dog – and Mick Jagger, too, since his knighthood. He wasn't a mongrel at all, she told me, but a Welsh Pembroke Corgi, the official dog of the Royal Family; the reasons why this little creature of noble extraction had found itself, at the age of three months, incorporated into a pack of stray dogs at the side of a Spanish motorway would forever remain a mystery.

The subject occupied us for nearly a quarter of an hour, then inexorably, as if obeying some natural law, we came to the heart of the matter, and I spoke to Isabelle about my affair with Esther. I told her everything, from the beginning, I spoke for slightly over two hours, and I ended with the account of the birthday party in Madrid. She listened to me carefully, without interrupting, and without showing any real surprise. 'Yes, you always liked sex . . .' she just said briefly, in a low voice, at the point when I was indulging in a few erotic considerations. She had suspected something for a long time now, she said once I had finished; she was happy I had finally decided to talk to her about it.

'Basically, I will have had two important women in my life,' I concluded, 'the first – you – who didn't like sex enough; and the second – Esther – who didn't like love enough.' This time she smiled frankly.

'That's true . . .' she said in a different voice, which was curiously cheeky and juvenile, 'you've had no luck . . .'

She reflected, then added: 'At the end of the day, men are never content with their women . . .'

'Rarely, yes.'

'Doubtless, it's because they want contradictory things. The women as well these days, but that's more recent. Basically, polygamy was perhaps a good solution . . .'

It's sad, the shipwreck of a civilisation, it's sad to see its most beautiful minds sink without trace – one begins to feel slightly ill at ease in life, and one ends up wanting to establish an Islamic republic. Ah well, let's just say it's *slightly sad*; there are always sadder things, obviously. Isabelle had always liked theoretical discussions, it's partly what had attracted me to her; in as much as the exercise is sterile, and can prove fatal when practised for its own sake, it is also profound, creative and tender immediately after making love – immediately after real life. We were looking each other straight in the eye, and I knew, I sensed that something was going to happen, the noises in the café seemed to have hushed, it was as if we had entered a zone of silence, provisional or definitive, I could no longer say, and finally, still looking in my eyes, she told me in a clear and irrefutable voice: 'I still love you.'

I slept at her place that very night, and also the nights that followed – without, however, giving up my hotel room. As I expected, her apartment was tastefully decorated; it was situated in a small residence, in the middle of a park, about a hundred metres from the ocean. It was with pleasure that I prepared Fox's bowl, and took him for his walk; he walked less quickly now, and was less interested in other dogs.

Every morning, Isabelle drove her car to the hospital; she spent most of the day in her mother's bedroom; she was being well looked after, she told me, which had become something exceptional. Like it was every year now, summer was scorching in France, and like every year the old died en masse, owing to lack of care, in their hospitals and retirement homes; but people had long since stopped feeling indignant about this, it had in some way passed into tradition, as though it were a natural means of solving the statistical problem of an increasingly ageing population that was necessarily prejudicial to the economic stability of the country. Isabelle was different, and I became conscious again, by living with her, of her moral superiority over the men and women of her generation; she was more generous, more attentive and more loving. That said, on the sexual level, nothing happened between us; we slept in the same bed without even feeling embarrassed, without even feeling resigned about it. Frankly, I was tired, the heat was overwhelming me as well. I felt about as energetic as a dead oyster; during the day I sat down to write at a small table overlooking the garden but nothing came to me, nothing seemed important or meaningful, I had lived a life that was about to end and that was that, I was like all the others, my career as a showman seemed a long way away now, no trace would remain of any of that.

Sometimes, however, I became conscious again that my narrative originally had another goal; I was well aware that I had witnessed on Lanzarote one of the most important stages, perhaps the decisive stage in the evolution of the human race. One morning when I had a little more energy, I phoned Vincent: they were in the middle of moving house, he told me, they had decided to sell the prophet's property in Santa Monica to transfer the headquarters of the Church to Chevilly-Larue. Knowall had remained on Lanzarote, near the laboratory, but Cop was there with his wife, they had bought a house near to his, and they were building new offices, they were taking on personnel, they were thinking of buying airtime on a television channel devoted to new cults. Manifestly, he was doing fundamental and significant things, at least in his own eyes. However, I couldn't quite bring myself to envy him: throughout my entire life I hadn't been interested in anything other than my cock, now my cock was dead and I was in the process of following it in its deathly decline, I had only got what I deserved I told myself repeatedly, pretending to find in this some morose delectation, whilst in fact my mental state was evolving more and more towards horror pure and simple, a horror made all the worse by the constant brutal heat, by the immutable glare of the blue sky.

Isabelle could sense all this, I think, and would look at me, sighing; after two weeks it was beginning to become obvious that things were going to turn out badly, it would be best for me to leave once again and, let's be honest, for the last time, this time we really were too old, too worn out, too bitter, we could only do ourselves harm, reproach one another with the general impossibility of things. Over our last meal (evening brought a bit of cooler air, we had pulled the table out into the garden, and she had made an effort with the cooking), I spoke to her about the Elohimite Church, and the promise of immortality that had been made on Lanzarote. Of course, she had followed the news a little, but she, like most people, thought that it was all complete bullshit, and she hadn't known that I had been there. I then became conscious that she had never met Patrick, even though she remembered Robert the Belgian, and that basically a lot of things had happened in my life since her departure, it was actually surprising I hadn't spoken to her about it earlier. No doubt the idea was too recent and new; frankly, most of the time I forgot myself that I had become immortal, it took some effort to remember it. I explained it all to her, however, recounting the story from the beginning, with all the requisite clarifications; I emphasised the personality of Knowall, the general impression of competence that he had left me with. Her intelligence, too, was still up to scratch, I think she knew nothing about genetics, she had never taken the time to become interested in it, but she had no difficulty following my explanations, and immediately grasped their consequences.

'Immortality then . . .' she said. 'It would be like a second chance.'

'Or a third chance; or multiple chances, to infinity. Immortality, really.'

'OK; I am happy to leave them my DNA and my estate. You can give me their contact details. I'll do it for Fox as well. For my mother . . .' She hesitated and her tone darkened. 'I think it's too late for her; she wouldn't understand. She's suffering at the moment; I think she really wants to die. She wants nothingness.'

The quickness of her reaction surprised me, and it was from that moment on, I think, that I had the intuition that a new phenomenon was going to manifest itself. The fact that a new religion could be born in the West was already a surprise in itself, bearing in mind that the last thirty years of European history had been marked by the massive and amazingly rapid collapse of traditional religious beliefs. In countries like Spain, Poland and Ireland, social life and all behaviour had been structured by a deeply rooted, unanimous and immense Catholic faith for centuries, it determined morality as well as familial relations, conditioned all cultural and artistic productions, social hierarchies, conventions and rules for living. In the space of a few years, in less than a generation, in an incredibly brief period of time, all this had disappeared, had evaporated into thin air. In these countries today no one believed in God any more, or took account of him, or even remembered that they had once believed; and this had been achieved without difficulty, without conflict, without any kind of violence or protest, without even a real discussion, as easily as a heavy object, held back for some time by an external obstacle, returns as soon as you release it, to its position of equilibrium. Human spiritual beliefs were perhaps far from being the massive, solid irrefutable block we usually imagined; on the contrary, perhaps they were what was most fleeting and fragile in man, the thing most ready to be born and to die.

The majority of testimonies confirm it: it was in fact from this time onwards that the Elohimite Church was to gain more and more followers, and spread unhindered across the whole of the Western world. After having achieved, in less than two years, a takeover of the Western trend towards Buddhism, the Elohimite movement absorbed, with the same ease, the last residues from the fall of Christianity before turning towards Asia, the conquest of which, starting with Japan, was also surprisingly rapid, especially when you consider that this continent had, for entire centuries, victoriously resisted all Christian missionary expeditions. It is true that times had changed, and that Elohimism marched in many respects behind consumer capitalism – which, turning youth into the supremely desirable commodity had little by little destroyed respect for tradition and the cult of the ancestors – in as much as it promised the indefinite preservation of this same youth, and the pleasures associated with it.

Islam, curiously, was a more durable bastion of resistance. Relying on massive and unending immigration, the Muslim religion became stronger in the Western countries at practically the same rate as Elohimism; targeting as a priority the people of the Maghreb and Black Africa, it had no less success with some 'indigenous' Europeans, a success that owed itself uniquely to machismo. If the abandonment of machismo had effectively made men unhappy, it had not actually made women happy. There were more and more people, especially women, who dreamed of a return to a system where women were modest and submissive, and their virginity was preserved. Of course, at the same time, the erotic pressure on the bodies of young girls did not stop growing, and the expansion of Islam was only made possible thanks to the introduction of a series of compromises, under the influence of a new generation of imams who, inspired by Catholic tradition, reality shows and American tele-evangelists' sense of spectacle, developed for the Muslim public an edifying script for life based on conversion and forgiveness of sin, two notions that were, however, relatively foreign to Islamic tradition. In the typical plot-line, which you would find identically reproduced in dozens of *telenovelas* most often filmed in Turkey and North Africa, a young girl, to the consternation of her parents, starts off by leading a dissolute life stained by alcohol, drug-taking and the wildest sexual freedom. Then, shaped by an event that provokes a salutary shock in her (a painful abortion; meeting a pious and upright Muslim boy who is studying to be an engineer), she leaves the world's temptations far behind and becomes a submissive, chaste, veiled wife. The same plot-line existed in its masculine form, this time setting the story around rappers, and emphasising delinquency and the consumption of hard drugs. This hypocritical script was to have a success that was all the more stunning because its designated age for conversion (between twenty-two and twenty-five years old) corresponded pretty accurately to the age when young North African girls, spectacularly beautiful in their teenage years, begin to get fat and feel the need for less revealing clothes. In the space of a couple of decades, Islam thus managed to assume, in Europe, the role that had been Catholicism's in its heyday: that of an 'official' religion, organiser of the calendar and of mini-ceremonies marking out the passage of time, with dogmas that were sufficiently primitive to be grasped by the greatest number whilst preserving sufficient ambiguity to seduce the most agile minds, claiming in principle to have a redoubtable moral austerity whilst maintaining, in practice, bridges across which any sinner could be reintegrated. The same phenomenon occurred in the United States of America, beginning in the Black community in particular – with the caveat that Catholicism, buoyed up by Latin-American immigration, retained important footholds there for a long time.

All this, however, could only go on for so long, and the refusal to grow old, to *settle down* and be transformed into a fat mother was, a few years later, to impact on the immigrant populations in their turn. When a social system is destroyed, this destruction is definitive, and there can be no going back; the laws of social entropy, valid in theory for any human-relational system, were rigorously demonstrated by Hewlett and Dude two centuries later; but they had already, for a long time, been understood intuitively. The fall of Islam in the West curiously echoes that, a few decades earlier, of Communism: in both cases, the phenomenon of decline was to take shape in their countries of origin, and in a few years sweep away the organisations, however powerful and wealthy they were, that had been established in the host countries. When the Arab countries, after years of being insidiously undermined, essentially through underground Internet connections, could at last have access to a way of life based on mass consumption, sexual freedom and leisure, the enthusiasm of their populations was as intense and eager as it had been, half a century earlier, in the Communist countries. The movement started, as is so often the case in human history, in Palestine, more precisely in a sudden refusal by young Palestinian girls to limit their existence to the repeated procreation of future jihadists, and from their desire to take advantage of the moral freedom enjoyed by Israeli women. In a few bursts, the transformation, to the accompaniment of techno music (as rock music, a few years earlier had been the accompaniment to the move towards the capitalist world, and with an effectiveness increased by use of the web) spread to all the Arab countries, which were forced to face a mass revolt by their youth, in the face of which they could obviously do nothing. It then became perfectly clear, in the eyes of the Western populations, that all of the countries of Dar-el-Islam had only been kept in their primitive faith by ignorance and constraint; deprived of their bases in the rear, the Western Islamist movements collapsed at a stroke.

As for Elohimism, it was adapted perfectly to the leisure civilisation in which it had been born. Imposing no moral constraints, reducing human existence to categories of interest and of pleasure, it did not hesitate, for all that, to make its own the fundamental promise at the core of all monotheistic religions: victory over death. Eradicating any spiritual or confusing dimension, it simply limited the scope of this victory, and the nature of the promise associated with it, to the unlimited prolongation of material life, that is to say the unlimited satisfaction of physical desires.

The first fundamental ceremony to mark the conversion of each new follower – the taking of a DNA sample – was accompanied by the signing of a document in which the postulant bequeathed all his possessions to the Church, after his death – the latter reserving the right to invest them, whilst promising to return them to the follower, after his resurrection, in their entirety. This came across as all the less shocking as the objective being pursued was the elimination of all natural bonds, and therefore all systems of inheritance, and because death was presented as a neutral period, simply a stasis in anticipation of a rejuvenated body. After intense lobbying of the American business world, the first convert was Steve Jobs – who requested, and was granted, a partial derogation in favour of the children he had procreated before discovering Elohimism. He was closely followed by Bill Gates, Richard Branson, and then a growing number of leaders of the most important firms in the world. The Church thus became extremely rich, and only a few years after the death of the prophet it was already, in terms of capital invested as well as the number of its followers, the leading religion in Europe.

The second fundamental ceremony was the entry into anticipation of resurrection – in other words suicide. After a period of hesitation and uncertainty, the custom was gradually established of carrying it out in public, according to a simple, harmonious ritual, at a moment chosen by the follower, when he felt that his physical body was no longer in a state to give him the joys he could legitimately expect from it. It was embarked upon with great confidence, in the certainty that resurrection was near – something that was all the more surprising as Miskiewicz, despite the colossal research funding at his disposal, had made no real progress, and, even if he could in fact guarantee the unlimited preservation of DNA, he was for the moment unable to create a living organism more complex than a simple cell. The promise of immortality made at the time of Christianity rested, it must be said, on even shakier foundations. The idea of immortality had basically never been abandoned by man, and even though he may have been forced to renounce his old beliefs, he had still kept, close to him, a nostalgia for them, he had never given up, and he was ready, in return for any explanation, however unconvincing, to let himself be guided by a new faith.

Then, a transformable cult will achieve over a withered dogma the empirical predominance that must prepare the systematic ascendancy attributed by positivism to the emotional aspect of religion.

Auguste Comte – An Appeal to Conservatives

There was so little of the believer in my nature that I was, in reality, almost indifferent to other people's beliefs; it was without any difficulty, but also without attaching any importance to it, that I gave Isabelle the contact details for the Elohimite Church. I tried to make love with her, that last night, but it was a failure. For a few minutes she tried to chew on my cock, but I had the strong sense that she hadn't done this for years, that she didn't believe in it, and anyway, to do this kind of thing properly you need a minimum of faith, and enthusiasm; the flesh in her mouth remained soft and my drooping balls no longer reacted to her half-hearted caresses. She gave up and asked me if I wanted some sleeping pills. Yes I wanted some, it's always a mistake to refuse, in my opinion, it's useless torturing yourself. She was still capable of getting up first and preparing the coffee, that was one thing she could still do. There was a little dew on the lilacs, the temperature was cooler, I had reserved a seat on the 8.32 a.m. train and summer was beginning to loosen its grip.

As usual I took a room at the Lutétia, there too it took me a long time to call Vincent, perhaps a month or two, for no precise reason. I did the same things as before but I did them in slow motion, as if I had to break down the movements in order to carry them out in an almost satisfying manner. From time to time I sat down at the bar, imbibed tranquilly, phlegmatically; quite often, I was recognised by old acquaintances. I made no effort to encourage the conversation, and this didn't bother me at all; truly this is one of the few advantages of being a *star* – or rather a former star, in my case: when you meet someone else and you arrive, as you might normally expect, at a point when you're both bored, even though neither of the two is precisely the cause of it, in some way by *common agreement*, it's always the other who bears the responsibility for it, who feels guilty for not having kept the conversation at a sufficiently high level, for not having known how to establish a sufficiently warm and sparkling atmosphere. This situation is comforting, and even relaxing as soon as one truly begins not to give a fuck. Sometimes, in the middle of a verbal exchange in which I contented myself with nodding my head in a knowing way, I would indulge in involuntary daydreams – moreover, generally rather unpleasant ones. I thought back to those casting sessions when Esther had had to kiss boys, to those sex scenes she had acted out in various short films; I remembered how much I had taken it personally, uselessly as it happens, I could have made a scene or burst into tears but that would have changed nothing, and I was well aware that I could not have survived very long under those conditions anyway, I was too old, I had no strength left; this observation did not, however, diminish my sorrow, because from the place I now found myself in there was no way out other than to go on suffering right to the end, I would never forget her body, her skin nor her face, and I had never felt with such clarity that human relations are born, evolve and die in a totally deterministic manner, as inexorable as the movements of a planetary system, and that it is absurd and vain to hope, however slightly, that you can modify their course.

I could have stayed at the Lutétia for quite some time, perhaps not as long as in Biarritz, because I was starting in spite of everything to drink a bit too much, anxiety was slowly burrowing into my organs and I spent whole afternoons at Bon Marché looking at pullovers, there was no sense in going on like that. One October morning, probably a Monday morning, I phoned Vincent. From the moment of my arrival at the house in Chevilly-Larue I felt as though I was penetrating a termite nest or a hive, an organisation in which everyone had a precisely defined task, and where things had begun to operate at full capacity. Vincent was waiting for me at the door, ready to leave, his mobile in his hand. He got up when he saw me, shook my hand warmly, and invited me to accompany him around their new offices. They had acquired a small office building, the construction was not yet finished, some workers were installing sound-proofed walls and halogen lights, but about twenty people were already settled in their offices: some were answering the telephone, others were typing letters, updating databases or whatever, in short I was in an SME – frankly, it was really a *big* enterprise. If there was one thing I would not have expected from Vincent the first time I met him, it was to see him transform himself into a *business leader*, but after all, anything was possible, and what's more he seemed at ease in the role; sometimes improvements happen, in spite of everything, in the lives of certain people, the process of living cannot simply be reduced to a purely declining trajectory, this would be a deceptive simplification. After introducing me to two of his colleagues, Vincent announced that they had just won an important victory: after several months of legal battles, the Council of State had finally made a judgement authorising the Elohimite Church to buy for its own use the religious buildings that the Catholic Church no longer had the means to upkeep. The only obligation was that which already applied to the previous owners: to maintain, in partnership with the National Office for Historical Monuments, the artistic and architectural heritage in a well-preserved state; but, as far as the nature of the religious celebrations within these buildings went, no limitation had been imposed. Even in eras more aesthetically distinguished than our own, Vincent remarked to me, it would have been unthinkable to bring to fruition in only a few years the conception and realisation of such a display of artistic splendours; this judgement, in addition to putting at the disposal of the faithful a good number of highly beautiful places of worship, was also going to allow them to concentrate their efforts on the building of the embassy.

Just as he was beginning to explain his vision of the aesthetics of the ritual ceremonies to me, Cop entered the office, wearing an impeccable sea-blue blazer; he, too looked in stunning shape, and energetically shook my hand. Undoubtedly, the sect seemed not to have suffered at all from the death of the prophet; on the contrary, even, things seemed to be going better and better. Nothing had happened, it was true, since the staged resurrection at the beginning of the summer on Lanzarote; but the event had had such a media impact that it had proved sufficient, requests for information were continually flooding in, many followed by applications for membership, the numbers of the faithful and of available funds were constantly increasing.

That same evening I was invited to dinner at Vincent's, in the company of Cop and his wife – it was the first time I had met her, and she came across as a level-headed, solid, rather warm person. Once again I was struck by the fact that one could easily have imagined Cop in the guise of a business executive – let's say, a director of human resources – or a civil servant responsible, for example, for the distribution of agricultural subsidies in a high mountain region; nothing about him suggested mysticism or even simple religiosity. In fact, he actually seemed particularly unimpressionable, and it was without any apparent emotion that he informed Vincent of the emergence of a worrying tendency, which had been reported to him from certain zones recently touched by the sect – in particular Italy and Japan. Nothing in the dogma indicated the way that the ceremony of voluntary departure was to proceed; all the necessary information for the reconstruction of the body of the follower being preserved in his DNA, the body itself could be disintegrated or reduced to ashes without this having the slightest impact. An unhealthy theatrical tendency seemed to be gradually developing, in certain cells, around the dispersal of the constitutive elements of the body; particularly implicated were doctors, social workers and nurses. Before taking his leave, Cop passed a file of twenty-odd pages to Vincent, as well as three DVDs – most of the ceremonies had been filmed. I stayed over, and accepted a cognac while Vincent began to read. We were in the living room that had belonged to his grandparents, and nothing had changed since my first visit: the armchairs and the green-velvet settee still had lace antimacassars, the photos of alpine landscapes were still in their frames; I even recognised the philodendron near the piano. Vincent's face darkened rapidly as he went through the file; he gave Susan a summary in English, then quoted a few examples for my attention:

'In the Rimini cell, the body of a follower was entirely drained of its blood; the participants smeared themselves with the blood before eating his liver and sexual organs. In the Barcelona cell, the man had asked to be hung from a butcher's hook in a cellar for a fortnight before being put at the disposal of everyone else: the participants served themselves, cutting off a slice that they consumed between them there and then. In Osaka, the follower had asked that his body be crushed and compacted by an industrial press, until it was reduced to a sphere twenty centimetres in diameter, which would then be covered with a film of transparent silicon, and could be used in a game of bowling; he was apparently a bowling fanatic in his lifetime.'

He stopped, his voice was quavering slightly; he was visibly shocked by the extent of the phenomenon.

'It's a social trend . . .' I said. 'A general trend towards barbarism; there is no reason you should escape it . . .'

'I don't know what to do, I don't know how to put a stop to this. The problem is that we have never talked about morality, at no point . . .'

'There are not a lot of basic socio-religious emotions . . .' Susan interjected in English. 'If you have no sex, you need ferocity. That's all . . .'

Vincent was quiet, he reflected and served himself another glass of cognac; it was at breakfast the following morning that he announced his decision to launch a global campaign: 'Give People Sex. Give Them Pleasure.' In fact, after the first few weeks following the death of the prophet, the sexuality of the followers had rapidly diminished, stabilising at a level roughly equal to the national average, i.e. very low. This decrease in sexuality was a universal phenomenon, common to all the social classes, to all developed nations, which did not spare teenagers or very young adults; homosexuals themselves, after a brief period of frenzy following the liberalisation of their practices, had calmed down a lot, they now aspired to monogamy and a peaceful, settled life, as a couple, devoted to cultural tourism and the discovery of local wines. For Elohimism it was a worrying phenomenon, because, even if it bases itself fundamentally on a promise of eternal life, a religion considerably increases its attractiveness as soon as it is able to give the impression of offering in the here and now a life that is fuller, richer, more exalting and more joyful. 'With Christ, you live more': this had more or less been the constant theme of the advertising campaigns organised by the Catholic Church immediately before its disappearance. Vincent, therefore, had come up with the idea, beyond the Fourierist reference, of reviving a practice of sacred prostitution, classically attested in Babylon, and in the first instance he would appeal to those among the former fiancées of the prophet who might be willing to organise a sort of orgiastic tour, with the aim of setting the followers the example of a permanent sexual gift, and of spreading throughout all the local branches of the Church a wave of lust and pleasure capable of hindering the development of necrophiliac and murderous practices. The idea seemed excellent to Susan: she knew the girls, she could phone them, she was sure that most of them would accept enthusiastically. During the night, Vincent had pencilled a series of sketches intended to be reproduced on the Internet. Openly pornographic (they represented groups of two to ten people, men and women, using their hands, sexes and mouths in almost all manners you could think of), they were nonetheless extremely stylised, with very pure lines, very different from the disgusting photographic realism that characterised the productions of the prophet.

After a few weeks, it became obvious that the campaign was a real success: the prophet's fiancées' tour was a triumph, and, in their cells, the followers strove to reproduce the erotic configurations thrown down on paper by Vincent; they took real pleasure in it, to such a point that, in most countries, the frequency of meetings had multiplied three-fold; the ritual orgy therefore, unlike other sexual propositions of more profane and recent origin, such as swinging, would appear not to be an outdated formula. More significantly still, conversations between followers in everyday life, as soon as they had established a minimum of empathy, were accompanied more and more often by touching, intimate caresses, if not mutual masturbation; the re-sexualisation of human relations, in short, seemed to have been achieved. It was then that we became conscious of a detail that, in the first moments of enthusiasm, had escaped everyone: in his desire for stylisation, Vincent had strayed some way from a realistic representation of the human body. Whilst the phallus still bore some resemblance (although more rectilinear, hairless and devoid of any apparent network of veins), the vulva was reduced in his drawings to a long, narrow slit, devoid of hair, situated in the middle of the body, which prolonged the curve of the buttocks, and which was certainly able to open wide to welcome cocks, but was rather less appropriate for any excretory function. More generally, all the external organs had disappeared, and thus the beings imagined, whilst they were able to make love, were obviously incapable of feeding themselves.

Things could have stayed like this, and been considered a mere artistic convention, were it not for the intervention of Knowall, back from Lanzarote at the beginning of December to present the advances in his research. Even though I still lived at the Lutétia, I spent most of my days in Chevilly-Larue; I wasn't a member of the governing committee, but I was one of the only direct witnesses of the events that had accompanied the death of the prophet, and everyone trusted me, Cop no longer kept any secrets from me. Of course, things were going on in Paris, there were current affairs, a cultural life; nevertheless I was certain that the important and significant things were happening in Chevilly-Larue. I had been persuaded of it for a long time, even if I hadn't been able to translate this conviction into my films or sketches, owing to a lack of real contact with the phenomenon up until now: political or military events, economic transformations, aesthetic or cultural mutations can all play a role, sometimes a very big role, in the life of men; but nothing, ever, can have any historical importance compared to the development of a new religion, or to the collapse of an existing one. To the acquaintances I still sometimes came across at the bar of the Lutétia, I said that *I was writing*; they probably supposed I was writing a novel, and expressed some surprise, I had always had a reputation for being a comedian rather than a 'literary figure'; if they had only known, I said to myself sometimes, if they had only known that this was not a simple work of fiction, but that I was trying to record one of the most important events in human history; if they had only known, I tell myself now, they would not even have been especially impressed. They were, for all their fame, used to a dreary and scarcely changing life, they were used to having little interest in real existence, preferring instead of the real, a commentary on it; I understood them, I had been in the same boat – and I was still there to some extent, maybe even more than they were. Not once, since the 'Give People Sex. Give Them Pleasure' campaign had been launched had I thought of personally taking advantage of the sexual services of the prophet's fiancées; nor had I begged a female member for the alms of a blowjob or a simple handjob, which would have easily been accorded to me. I always had Esther in my head, in my body, everywhere. I said this one day to Vincent, it was late morning, a very beautiful early-winter morning, through the office window I was looking at the trees in the public park: for me it was a 'Your Woman Awaits You' campaign that might have saved me, but things were not turning out this way in the slightest. He looked at me with sadness, he felt sorry for me, he must have had no trouble understanding me, he must have remembered perfectly those still-recent moments when his love for Susan had appeared hopeless. I waved my hand wearily, singing: 'La-la-la . . .' I pulled a grimace, which didn't completely come off as humorous; then, like Zarathustra beginning his descent, I made my way to the staff canteen.

Whatever, I was present at the meeting when Knowall announced that, far from being a simple artist's vision, Vincent's drawings prefigured the man of the future. For a long time animal nutrition had seemed to him to be a primitive system, of mediocre energy efficiency, producing a clearly excessive quantity of waste, waste that not only had to be evacuated, but which in the process provoked a far from negligible wear and tear of the organism. For a long time he had been thinking of equipping the new human animal with that photosynthetic system that, by some curiosity of evolution, was the property of vegetables. The direct use of solar energy was obviously a more robust, efficient and reliable system – as shown by the practically limitless lifespan of plants. What's more, the addition of autotrophic functions to the human cell was far from being as complex an operation as some might imagine; his teams had already been working on the question for some time, and the number of genes involved proved to be astonishingly low. The human being thus transformed would subsist, solar energy aside, on water and a small quantity of mineral salts; the digestive system, just like the excretory system, could disappear – any excess minerals would be easily eliminated, with water, by means of sweat.

Vincent, used to only following Knowall's explanations at some distance, nodded mechanically, and Cop was thinking of something else: it was therefore in this way, in a few minutes, and on the basis of a hasty artist's sketch, that a decision was made on the Standard Genetic Rectification that would be applied, uniformly, to all the units of DNA destined to be called back to life, and to mark a definitive break between the neohumans and their ancestors. The rest of the genetic code remained unchanged; we were dealing with nothing less than a new species and even, strictly speaking, a new kingdom.

It is ironic to think that the SGR, conceived at the outset for reasons of purely aesthetic propriety, is what enabled the neo-humans to survive, without any great difficulty, the climatic catastrophes that were to follow and that no one at the time could have predicted, whilst the humans of the former race would be almost completely decimated.

On this crucial point, the life story of Daniel1, once again, is totally corroborated by those of Vincent1, Slotan1 and Jérôme1, even if they attribute to the event unequal levels of importance. Whereas Vincent1 only alludes to it in a brief paragraph, and Jérôme1 almost completely passes over it, Slotan1, however, devotes tens of pages to the idea of the SGR and the research that would, a few months later, enable its operational realisation. Generally speaking, the life story of Daniel1 is often considered by commentators to be central and canonical. Whilst Vincent1 often places excessive emphasis on the aesthetic meaning of the rituals, whilst Slotan1 devotes himself almost exclusively to the evocation of his scientific research, and Jérôme1 to questions of discipline and material organisation, Daniel1 is the only one who gives us a complete, if slightly detached, description of the birth of the Elohimite Church; whilst the others, caught up in everyday business, only thought of solutions to the practical problems they had to face, he often seems to be the only one to have taken a small step back, and to have really understood the importance of what was happening before his eyes.

This state of things gives me, as it did all my predecessors in the Daniel series, a particular responsibility; my commentary is not and cannot be just an ordinary commentary, since it touches so closely upon the circumstances of the creation of our species, and its system of values. Its central character is further increased by the fact that my distant ancestor was, in the mind of Vincent1 and no doubt in his own, a typical human being, representative of the species, a *human being amongst so many others.*

According to the Supreme Sister, jealousy, desire and the appetite for procreation share the same origin, which is the suffering of being. It is the suffering of being that makes us seek out the other, as a palliative; we must go beyond this stage to reach the state where the simple fact of being constitutes in itself a permanent occasion for joy; where intermediation is nothing more than a game, freely undertaken, and not constitutive of being. We must, in a word, reach the freedom of indifference, the condition for the possibility of perfect serenity.

It was on Christmas Day, mid-morning, that I learned of Isabelle's suicide. I wasn't really surprised by it: I sensed, in the space of a few minutes, that a sort of emptiness was settling inside me; but this was a predictable, anticipated emptiness. I had known, since my departure from Biarritz, that she would end up killing herself; I had known it from a look we had exchanged, on that last morning, as I was going out of the door of her kitchen to get into the taxi that would take me to the railway station. I had also suspected that she would wait until the death of her mother in order to care for her right to the end, and not to cause her pain. I also knew that I too, sooner or later, was going to head towards the same kind of solution.

Her mother had died on 13 December; Isabelle had bought a plot in the municipal cemetery of Biarritz, and dealt with the funeral; she had made her will and put her affairs in order; then, on the night of 24 December, she had injected herself with a massive dose of morphine. Not only had she died painlessly, but she had also probably died joyfully; or, at least, in that state of euphoric relaxation that characterises the product. That very morning, she had put Fox into a kennel; she hadn't left any letter for me, thinking no doubt that it was useless, that I wouldn't understand her well enough; but she had taken the necessary measures to ensure that the dog was passed on to me.

I left a few days later, she had already been cremated; on the morning of 30 December, I went to the 'quiet room' of Biarritz cemetery. It was a large round room, with a ceiling made up of a window that bathed the room in soft grey light. The walls were pierced all over with little cavities into which you could slip parallelepipeds of metal containing the ashes of the deceased. Above each niche a label bore the first and second name of the dead person, engraved in slanted script. In the centre, a marble table, also round, was surrounded by chairs that were made of glass, or rather transparent plastic. After leading me in, the janitor had placed the box containing Isabelle's ashes on the table; then he had left me alone. No one else could enter whilst I was in the room; my presence was signalled by a little red lamp that lit up outside, like those used to indicate action on film sets. I remained in the quiet room, like most people do, for about ten minutes.

I spent a strange New Year's Eve, alone in my bedroom at the Villa Eugénie, turning over simple, morbid, extremely uncontradictory thoughts. On the morning of 2 January, I went to collect Fox. Unfortunately, before I left, I had to return to Isabelle's apartment to fetch the papers necessary for settling the inheritance. From the moment we arrived at the entrance to the residence, I noticed that Fox was quivering with joyful impatience; he had put on even more weight, Corgis are a race with a tendency towards plumpness, but he ran up to Isabelle's door, then, breathless, stopped to wait for me as I walked, much more slowly, up the alley of chestnut trees stripped bare by winter. He let out small impatient yaps as I looked for the keys; poor little fellow, I said to myself, poor little fellow. As soon as I opened the door he rushed inside the apartment, quickly made a tour of it, came back and sent me an inquisitive look. As I looked through Isabelle's desk, he left again, several times, exploring the rooms one by one, sniffing about everywhere then returning, stopping at the bedroom door and looking at me with a vexed expression. The end of any life amounts more or less to a *tidying up*; you no longer feel the urge to throw yourself into a new project, you are content just to dispatch day-to-day matters. All the things you have never done, as anodyne as preparing a mayonnaise or playing a game of chess, little by little become inaccessible, the desire for any new experience as for any new sensation disappears absolutely. Even so, things were *remarkably* tidy, and it took me only a few minutes to find Isabelle's will and the deeds to the apartment; I didn't intend to see the solicitor straight away, I told myself I would return to Biarritz later, whilst knowing that it would be a difficult thing to do, that I would probably not have the courage for it, but that no longer seemed important, nothing seemed very important now. When I opened the envelope, I saw that it would be a futile step; she had left all her estate to the Elohimite Church, and I recognised the standard contract; the legal services would take care of it all.

Fox followed me without difficulty when I left the apartment, probably thinking we were simply going for a walk. In a pet shop near the station, I bought a plastic container in which to transport him during the journey; then I reserved a ticket for the express train from Irun.

The weather was clement in the region of Almeria, a curtain of fine rain enveloped the short days, which gave the impression of never truly beginning, and this funereal peace could have suited me, we could have spent whole weeks like this, my old dog and me, lost in thoughts that were no longer really thoughts, but the circumstances would not unfortunately allow this. Work had begun next to my house on the building of new residences, spreading for kilometres around. There were cranes and cement mixers, it had become almost impossible to get to the sea without having to circumnavigate heaps of sand, piles of metal girders, in the midst of bulldozers and site lorries that charged without slowing down through the middle of geysers of mud. Little by little I lost the habit of going out, apart from twice a day, to walk Fox, which was no longer really pleasant, he would howl and press against me, terrified by the noise of the lorries. I learned from the newsagent that Hildegarde had died, and that Harry had sold his property so he could end his days in Germany. Little by little I even lost the habit of leaving my bedroom, I spent most of my day in bed, in a state of great mental emptiness, which was nonetheless painful. Occasionally, I thought back to my arrival here, with Isabelle, a few years before; I remembered that she had taken pleasure in decorating, and especially in trying to grow flowers and create a garden; we had had, all things considered, a few moments of happiness. I thought back as well to our last moment of sexual union, the night on the dunes, after our visit to Harry's; but the dunes were no longer there, bulldozers had levelled the area: it was now a muddy surface, surrounded by fences. I was going to sell up as well, I had no reason to stay there; I made contact with an estate agent, who informed me that this time the price of land had really increased, and that I could expect to make a considerable profit; I didn't really know in what state I'd die, but in any case I'd die rich. I asked him to try and hurry the sale even if it meant not receiving as high an offer as he hoped, every day, the place became a little more unbearable. I was under the impression that the workers not only had no sympathy for me, but that they were frankly hostile, and deliberately brushed passed me when driving their enormous lorries, spattering me with mud and terrorising Fox. This impression was no doubt justified; I was a foreigner, a man from the North and, what's more, they knew I was richer, much richer, than they were; they felt a veiled, animal hatred towards me, made all the more stronger because it was powerless, the social system was there to protect people like me, and the social system was solid, the Guardia Civil were only a few kilometres away and would patrol more and more often, Spain had just voted for a socialist government that was less open than others to corruption, less linked to the local mafias, and which firmly resolved to protect the cultivated, well-off class that made up most of its electorate. I had never felt much sympathy for the poor, and now that my life was fucked I had less than ever; the superiority my cash gave me over them might even have amounted to a slight consolation: I might have looked at them with contempt as they shovelled their heaps of gravel, backs bent with effort, whilst they unloaded their cargoes of beams and bricks; I might have considered with irony their lined hands, their muscles, the calendars of naked women that decorated their building-site vehicles. These minimal satisfactions, I knew, would not prevent me envying their untroubled, simplistic virility; their youth, also, the brutal evidence of their proletarian, animal youth.

This morning, just before dawn, I received the following message from Marie23:

> *The burdened membranes*
> *Of our waking dreams*
> *Have the muffled charm*
> *Of sunless days.*

399, 2347, 3268, 3846. Displayed on the screen was the image of a vast living room with white walls, furnished with low white leather divans; the carpet, too, was white. Through the bay window, you could make out the tower of the Chrysler Building – I had had the chance to see it in an ancient reproduction before. After a few seconds, a relatively young female neohuman, twenty-five at most, entered the camera's field to position herself in front of the lens. The hair of her head and pubis was curly, thick and black; her harmonious body, with its wide hips and round breasts, gave a strong impression of solidity and energy; physically, she looked like I had imagined. A message scrolled past rapidly, superimposed on the image:

> *And the sea that suffocates me, and the sand,*
> *The procession of each successive moment*
> *Like birds soaring gently over New York,*
> *Like great birds in inexorable flight.*
>
> *Let's go! It's high time we broke the shell*
> *And went towards the sparkling sea*
> *On new paths our feet will recognise,*
> *That we take together, unsure of weakness.*

The existence of defections among the neohumans is not absolutely a secret; even if the subject is not really mentioned, certain allusions and rumours have come to light here and there. No measures are taken against deserters, nothing is done to trace them; the station they occupied is simply and definitively closed down by a team from the Central City; the lineage they represented is declared defunct.

If Marie23 had decided to abandon her post to rejoin a community of savages, I knew that nothing I could say would make her change her mind. For a few minutes, she walked up and down the room; she seemed prey to a restless excitement, and several times almost moved out of the camera's field of vision. 'I don't know exactly what awaits me,' she said finally, turning towards the lens, 'but I know that I need to live more. I have taken some time to make my decision, I have tried to match up all the available information. I have spoken a lot about it with Esther31, who also lives in the ruins of New York; we have even met physically, on two occasions. It's not impossible; there is a big mental strain at the beginning, it's not easy to leave the limits of the station, you feel enormously worried and distressed; but it's not impossible . . .'

I digested the information, and showed by a slight nod that I had understood. 'She is, in fact, a descendant of the same Esther your ancestor knew,' she went on. 'I had thought for a moment that she was going to agree to accompany me; finally, she gave up on the idea, at least for the moment, but I have the impression that she, too, isn't satisfied with our way of life. We spoke about you, several times; I think that she would be happy to enter a phase of intermediation.'

I nodded again. She stared into the lens once more for a few seconds, saying nothing, then, with a bizarre smile, she put a light rucksack on her shoulders, turned around and exited to the left of the camera's field. I remained immobile for a long time in front of the screen as it transmitted the image of the empty room.

After a few weeks of prostration I took up my life story again, but that afforded me only slight relief; I was almost up to the moment of my encounter with Isabelle, and the creation of this attenuated copy of my real existence seemed like a slightly unhealthy exercise to me, I had no impression at all that I was accomplishing something important or remarkable, but Vincent, on the other hand, seemed to attach a great value to it, every week he phoned to find out where I was at, once he even told me that in a way what I was doing was as important as Knowall's research on Lanzarote. He was exaggerating, obviously, nevertheless I returned to the task with more ardour; it was curious how I had come to trust him, to listen to his words as though to an oracle.

Little by little the days grew longer, the weather became warmer and drier, and I began to go out a bit more; avoiding the building site in front of the house, I took the path up through the hills, then I went back down as far as the cliffs; from there I contemplated the sea, which was immense and grey; as flat and as grey as my life. I stopped at each bend, adopting the rhythm of Fox; he was happy, I could tell, with these long outings, even if he now had some difficulty walking. We went to bed early, before sunset; I never watched television, I had omitted to renew my satellite subscription; I no longer read much either, and I had even ended up getting tired of Balzac. Social life concerned me less, without doubt, than at the time when I was writing my sketches; I already knew then that I had chosen a limited genre that would not allow me to accomplish, in all my career, a tenth of what Balzac could do in a single novel. Furthermore, I was completely conscious of what I owed him: I had kept all of my sketches, all of the shows I had recorded, which amounted to about fifteen DVDs; I had never, in the course of those quite interminable days, thought of taking a look at them. I had often been compared to the French moralists, occasionally to Lichtenberg; but never had anyone thought of Molière, or Balzac. Even so, I re-read *Splendeurs et Misères des Courtisanes*, above all for the character of Nucingen. Still, it was remarkable that Balzac had been able to give the character of that lovesick fogey such a pathetic dimension, a dimension that's frankly obvious once you think about it, which is inscribed in its very definition, and which Molière had not dreamed of at all; it's true that Molière was working in comedy, and the same problem always arises: you always end up crashing into the same difficulty, which is that life, fundamentally, *is not* comical.

One April morning, a rainy morning, after wading about for five minutes in some muddy tyre tracks, I decided to stop walking. As I arrived at the door of my residence, I realised that Fox wasn't there; the rain had begun to pour down, you couldn't see further than five metres; I could hear the nearby din of a digger, but I couldn't make it out. I went inside to get a wax coat, then set out in search of him, in the driving rain; one by one, I searched all the places where he liked to stop, whose smells he liked to sniff.

I found him only late that afternoon; he was just three hundred metres from the residence, I must have passed him several times without noticing. Only his head was sticking out of the mud, slightly stained with blood, the tongue protruding, his eyes frozen in a rictus of horror. Scrabbling in the mud with my bare hands, I freed his body, which had burst like a sausage, the intestines had spurted out; he was far off the roadside, the lorry must have veered to run him over. I took off my wax coat to wrap him up and returned home, my shoulders bowed, my face streaming with tears, looking away so as not to see the eyes of the workers who stopped to watch me pass, evil smiles on their lips.

Doubtless I wept for a long time, then I calmed down, night had almost fallen; the site was deserted, but the rain was still falling. I went out into the garden, into what had been the garden, which was now a dusty waste ground in summer and a lake of mud in winter; I had no difficulty digging a grave, at the corner of the house; I put one of his favourite toys on top of it, a small plastic duck. The rain set off another mudslide that in turn engulfed the toy; I began to cry again.

I don't know why but something broke in me that night, like a last protective fence that had not given way at the time of Esther's departure, nor at Isabelle's death. Perhaps because the death of Fox coincided with the moment in my *life story* where I was recounting how we had met him, on the hard shoulder of a motorway between Saragossa and Tarragon; perhaps simply because I was older, and my resistance was diminishing. Still, it was in tears that I phoned Vincent, in the middle of the night, under the impression that my tears would never stop, that I could no longer do anything, till the end of my days, but cry. Such a thing can be observed, I had already observed it in some old people: occasionally their face is calm and static, their mind seems peaceful and empty; but as soon as they regain contact with reality, as soon as they regain consciousness and start thinking again, they immediately start crying – softly, without interruption, for whole days on end. Vincent listened to me attentively, without protesting, despite the late hour; then he promised he would phone Knowall immediately. The genetic code of Fox had been preserved, he reminded me, and we had become immortal; we, but also, if we wished it, our household pets.

He seemed to believe what he was saying; he seemed absolutely to believe it, and I suddenly felt paralysed by joy. By incredulity as well: I had grown up and grown old in the idea of death, and in the certainty of its empire. It was in a strange state of mind, as if I was about to wake up in a magical world, that I waited for the dawn. It broke, colourless, on the sea; the clouds had disappeared, a tiny corner of blue sky appeared on the horizon.

Miskiewicz called a little before seven. Fox's DNA had been preserved, yes, and it was stored under good conditions, there was no reason to worry; unfortunately, for the moment, the cloning operation was as impossible for dogs as it was for humans. But only a few things separated them from their goal, it was only a question of years, probably months; the operation had already been successfully carried out with rats and even – although in an un-reproducible way

– with a domestic cat. Bizarrely, dogs seemed to pose more complex problems; but he promised to keep me informed, and that Fox would be the first to benefit from the technique.

His voice, which I had not heard for a long time, still produced the same impression of technical expertise, of competence, and as I hung up, I felt something strange: this was a failure, right now, it was a failure, and I had no doubt that I was condemned to end my life alone; for the first time, however, I began to understand Vincent, and the other followers; I began to understand the true significance of the Promise; and as the sun emerged and rose above the sea, for the first time, I felt an emotion that, although still obscure, distant and veiled, resembled hope.

The departure of Marie23 troubles me more than I had anticipated; I had become used to our conversations; their disappearance has left a void in me, a sadness, and I can't yet bring myself to resume contact with Esther31.

On the day after her departure, I printed off the topographical maps of the zone Marie23 would have to cross on her way to Lanzarote; I think about her frequently, and imagine her on the stages of her journey. She is no longer a neohuman, she has decided to separate herself from our community, which means her departure was freely chosen and definitive; I must repeat this to myself several times a day to get used to the idea. I also devote an hour every day to reading Spinoza, whom the Supreme Sister recommended in such circumstances.

It was only after the death of Fox that I really became fully conscious of the parameters of the aporia. The weather was changing quickly, it wasn't long before the heat settled on the south of Spain; naked young girls began to tan themselves, especially at weekends, on the beach near the residence, and I began to feel the return, albeit weak and flaccid, of something that wasn't really even desire – for the word would seem to me, despite everything, to imply a minimum belief in the possibility of its fulfilment – but the memory, the phantom of what could have been desire. I could now make out clearly the *cosa mentale*, the ultimate torment, and at that moment I could say at last that I had understood. Sexual pleasure was not only superior, in refinement and violence, to all the other pleasures life had to offer; it was not only the one pleasure with which there is no collateral damage to the organism, but which on the contrary contributes to maintaining it at its highest level of vitality and strength; it was in truth the sole pleasure, the sole objective of human existence, and all other pleasures – whether associated with rich food, tobacco, alcohol or drugs – were only derisory and desperate compensations, mini-suicides that did not have the courage to speak their name, attempts to speed up the destruction of a body that no longer had access to the one real pleasure. Thus human life was organised in a terribly simple fashion, and for twenty years or so, in my scripts and sketches, I had pussyfooted around a reality that I could have expressed in just a few sentences. Youth was the time for happiness, its only season; young people, leading a lazy, carefree life, partially occupied by scarcely absorbing studies, were able to devote themselves unlimitedly to the liberated exultation of their bodies. They could play, dance, love and multiply their pleasures. They could leave a party, in the early hours of the morning, in the company of sexual partners they had chosen, and contemplate the dreary line of employees going to work. They were the salt of the earth, and everything was given to them, everything was permitted for them, everything was possible. Later on, having started a family, having entered the adult world, they would be introduced to worry, work, responsibility and the difficulties of existence; they would have to pay taxes, submit themselves to administrative formalities whilst ceaselessly bearing witness – powerless and shamefilled – to the irreversible degradation of their own bodies, which would be slow at first, then increasingly rapid; above all, they would have to look after children, mortal enemies, in their own homes, they would have to pamper them, feed them, worry about their illnesses, provide the means for their education and their pleasure, and unlike in the world of animals, this would last not just for a season, they would remain slaves of their offspring always, the time of joy was well and truly over for them, they would have to continue to suffer until the end, in pain and with increasing health problems, until they were no longer good for anything and were definitively thrown onto the rubbish heap, cumbersome and useless. In return, their children would not be at all grateful, on the contrary their efforts, however strenuous, would never be considered enough, they would, until the bitter end, be considered guilty because of the simple fact of being *parents*. From this sad life, marked by shame, all joy would be pitilessly banished. When they wanted to draw near to young people's bodies, they would be chased away, rejected, ridiculed, insulted and, more and more often nowadays, imprisoned. The physical bodies of young people, the only desirable possession the world has ever produced, were reserved for the exclusive use of the young, and the fate of the old was to work and to suffer. This was the true meaning of *solidarity between generations*; it was a pure and simple holocaust of each generation in favour of the one that replaced it, a cruel, prolonged holocaust that brought with it no consolation, no comfort, nor any material or emotional compensation.

I myself had betrayed. I had left my wife just after she had become pregnant, I had refused to be interested in my son, I had remained indifferent to his death; I had rejected the chain, broken the endless cycle of the reproduction of suffering, and this was perhaps the only noble gesture, the only act of authentic rebellion in which, after a life that was, despite its apparently artistic character, mediocre, I could take any pride; I had even, albeit for only a short period, slept with a girl who was the same age as my son would have been. Like the admirable Jeanne Calment, once the oldest woman alive, finally dead at one hundred and twenty, who, to the idiotic questions of journalists: 'Come on, Jeanne, don't you believe you're going to see your daughter again? Don't you believe in an *afterlife*?' replied inflexibly, with a magnificent straightforwardness: 'No. Nothing. There is nothing. And I won't see my daughter again, because my daughter is *dead*,' I had maintained to the bitter end the words and attitude of the truth. Incidentally, I had briefly paid homage to Jeanne Calment, in the past, in a sketch that evoked her *moving testimony*: 'I am one hundred and sixteen and I don't want to die.' At the time no one had understood that I was being *doubly ironic*; I regretted this misunderstanding, I regretted above all not having insisted more, not having emphasised sufficiently that her struggle was that of all mankind, that it was basically the only one worth fighting. Of course, Jeanne Calment had died, Esther had left me and biology, generally, had reasserted itself; this had happened all the same, despite us, despite me, despite Jeanne, we had not surrendered, to the end we had refused to collaborate and to accept a system that was designed to destroy us.

Consciousness of my heroism allowed me to while away an excellent afternoon; however, I decided to leave for Paris the following morning, probably because of the beach, and the breasts and bushes of the young girls; in Paris there were also young girls, but you saw less of their breasts and bushes. Anyway, this wasn't the only reason, although I did need to take a step back (from breasts and bushes). My reflections the previous day had plunged me into such a state that I envisaged writing a new show: something hard and radical this time, next to which my previous provocations would look like saccharine humanist blether. I telephoned my agent, and we arranged to meet and talk about it; he was a bit surprised, I had been saying for so long that I was finished, washed-up, dead, that he had ended up believing it. That said, he was pleasantly surprised: I had caused him a few problems, but earned him quite a lot of money: on the whole he liked me.

On the plane to Paris, under the influence of a litre of Southern Comfort bought at the duty-free in Almeria, my hateful heroism turned into a self-pity that was somewhat alleviated by alcohol, and I composed the following poem, which was fairly representative of my state of mind over the preceding weeks, and that I dedicated mentally to Esther:

> *There is no love*
> *(Not really, not enough).*
> *We live unaided,*
> *We die abandoned.*
>
> *The appeal for pity*
> *Resonates in the void,*
> *Our bodies are crippled*
> *But our flesh is eager.*
>
> *Gone are the promises*
> *Of a teenage body,*
> *We enter an old age*
> *Where nothing awaits us*
>
> *But the vain memory*
> *Of our lost days,*
> *A convulsion of hate*
> *And naked despair.*

At Roissy airport, I drank a double espresso, which completely sobered me up, and whilst searching for my credit card I found the poem again. It's impossible, I imagine, to write anything without experiencing a sort of edginess, a nervous excitement, which means that, however sinister the content of what you write might be, you do not immediately find it depressing. With hindsight things look different, and I realised at once that this poem corresponded not simply to my state of mind, but to a starkly observable reality: whatever my convulsions, protestations and side-steps might have been, I had well and truly fallen into the *camp of the elderly*, and there was no hope of return. I ruminated on this distressing thought for some time, as though chewing a meal to get used to its bitterness. It was in vain: the thought was depressing at first, and it remained, on further examination, just as depressing.

The eager welcome I received from the waiters at the Lutétia proved to me in any case that I was not forgotten, that in media terms I was still *in the race*. 'Are you here for work?' the receptionist asked with a knowing smile, it was rather like he was wanting to know whether he should send a whore up to my room; I confirmed with a wink, which provoked another fit of attentiveness and a 'hope you will be fine . . .' whispered like a prayer. It was after this first night in Paris, however, that my motivation started to waver. My convictions remained just as strong, but it appeared derisory to me to return to using an artistic mode of expression whilst somewhere in the world, just around the corner in fact, a *real* revolution was taking place; two days later, I took the train to Chevilly-Larue. When I explained to Vincent my conclusions about the unacceptable character of sacrifice that was now attached to procreation, I noted a sort of hesitation in him, an uneasiness that I had difficulty putting my finger on.

'You know that we are quite involved in the childfree movement . . .' he replied slightly impatiently. 'I must introduce you to Lucas. We have just bought a television programme, or rather part of a television programme, on a channel dedicated to new cults. He is head of programming, we've taken him on to deal with all our communications. I think you'll like him.'

Lucas was a young man of about thirty, with a sharp and intelligent face, who wore a white shirt and a loose-fitting black suit. He, too, listened to me with some unease, before showing me the first of a series of adverts they planned to broadcast, the following week, on most of the global channels. Lasting thirty seconds, it showed, in a single sequence that gave an unbearable impression of veracity, a six-year-old child throwing a tantrum in a supermarket. He was demanding an extra bag of sweets, first in a whining – and already unpleasant – voice then, when his parents refused, by beginning to scream and roll around on the ground, apparently on the verge of apoplexy but stopping from time to time to check, with cunning little looks, that his progenitors were still under his complete mental domination; the other customers flashed indignant looks as they passed by, the checkout staff themselves began to approach the source of trouble, and the parents, growing more and more flustered, ended up kneeling before the little monster and snatching all the packets of sweets within reach to hold out to him, like so many offerings. The image then froze whilst the following message appeared on the screen in capital letters: 'JUST SAY NO. USE CONDOMS.'

The other adverts dwelt once again, with the same strength of conviction, on the main elements of the Elohimite choice of life – sexuality, ageing, death, in short the usual human questions – but the name of the Church itself was not mentioned, except only at the end, in a very brief, almost subliminal insert that simply said: 'Elohimite Church' and a contact telephone number.

'I have found positive adverts to be much harder . . .' Lucas told me in a hushed tone. 'However, I have made one, I think you will recognise the actor . . .' In fact I recognised Cop in the first few seconds, wearing denim dungarees, and busy, in a boatshed by a river, with a manual task that apparently consisted of repairing a canoe. The lighting was superb, shimmering, the pools of water behind him gleamed in a warm mist, it was a bit Jack Daniels-like, but fresher, more joyful, yet without excessive liveliness, like a spring that had acquired the serenity of autumn. He was working calmly, in no hurry, giving the impression of finding pleasure in it and having all the time in the world ahead of him; then he turned towards the camera and smiled broadly as the message: 'Eternity, Tranquilly' was superimposed on the screen.

I then understood the uneasiness they had all, to a greater or lesser extent, been displaying: my discovery about happiness being the exclusive reserve of youth, and about the sacrifice of generations was not actually a discovery at all; everyone here already understood it perfectly; Vincent had understood it, Lucas had understood it, and so too had most of the followers. No doubt Isabelle had also been conscious of it for a long time, and she had committed suicide emotionlessly, under the influence of a rational decision, almost like someone asking to be dealt a second hand when the game of cards has started badly – in those rare games that allow it. Was I more stupid than the average person? I asked Vincent that very evening when I was having an aperitif at his place. No, he replied without emotion, on the intellectual level I was in reality slightly above average, and on the moral level I was the same as everyone else: a bit sentimental, a bit cynical, like most men. I was just very honest, and therein lay my distinction; I was, in relation to the current norms of mankind, almost unbelievably honest. I wasn't to take offence at these remarks, he added, this could all be deduced from the huge success I had had with the public; and it was also what made my life story priceless. Whatever I said to my fellow men would be seen by them as authentic, as *true*; and wherever I went, everyone else, in exchange for a little effort, could follow. If I had converted, it meant that all men, following my example, could convert. He told me all this very calmly, looking me straight in the eye, with an expression of absolute sincerity; and what's more I knew he liked me. It was then I understood, exactly, what he wanted to do; it was then I also understood that he was going to succeed.

'How many members do you have?'

'Seven hundred thousand,' he replied in a second, without thinking. Then I understood a third thing, which was that Vincent had become the true head of the Church, its effective leader. Knowall, as he had always wished, devoted himself exclusively to scientific research; and Cop had lined up behind Vincent, obeyed his orders, and put his practical intelligence and impressive work rate entirely at his disposal. It was Vincent, without a shadow of a doubt, who had recruited Lucas; he was the one who had launched the 'Give People Sex. Give Them Pleasure' campaign; similarly he was the one who had put a stop to it, once the goal had been reached; this time he had well and truly taken the place of the prophet. I then recalled my first visit to the house in Chevilly-Larue, and how he had appeared to me to be on the brink of suicide, or a nervous breakdown. 'The stone that the builders had rejected . . .' I said to myself. 'Oh, subtle priests . . .' I said to myself a little later, in an automatic parody of Nietzschean linguistic quirks that I sensed, however, was actually inappropriate – Vincent's success owed nothing to *the Will*, in the rather silly sense that Nietzsche gives to this term by crudely reducing the ideas of Schopenhauer. I still felt neither jealous nor envious of Vincent; his was of a different essence from mine; I would have been incapable of doing what he did; he had achieved a lot, but he had also gambled a lot, he had gambled his entire being, thrown everything into the balance, and for a long time, indeed since the very beginning, he would have been incapable of proceeding otherwise, there had never been any room at all in him for strategy or calculation. I then asked him if he was still working on the embassy project. He lowered his eyes with unexpected modesty, and told me yes, that he even thought he would finish it soon, that if I stayed on another month or two he could show me; that in fact he wanted me to stay a lot longer, and that I would be the first visitor – immediately after Susan, for it concerned Susan very directly.

Naturally, I stayed; nothing was particularly pressing me to return to San Jose; on the beach there would probably be a bit more breast, a bit more bush, I would be obliged to cope with the situation. I had received a fax from the estate agent, he had had an interesting offer from an Englishman, a rock singer apparently, but I couldn't feel any sense of urgency about that, either, since the death of Fox, I might just as well die there, and be buried beside him. I was at the bar of the Lutétia, and after my third Alexandra this seemed an excellent idea: no I was not going to sell up, I was going to allow the property to fall into decay, and I was even going to forbid its sale in my will, I was going to put some money aside for its upkeep, I was going to make this house into a sort of mausoleum, a mausoleum to shitty things, but a mausoleum nonetheless. 'Mausoleum of shittiness . . .': I repeated the phrase to myself in a low voice, feeling inside me, growing with the warmth of the alcohol, an evil jubilation. In the meantime, to sweeten my final moments, I would invite some whores over. No, not whores, I told myself after a moment's reflection, their performances would undoubtedly be too robotic, too mediocre. I could alternatively proposition the teenage girls who sunbathed on the beach; the majority would refuse, but some might accept, I was certain in any case that they would not be shocked. Obviously, there were a few risks, they might have delinquent boyfriends; there were housemaids I could also try, some were perfectly screwable and perhaps wouldn't say no to the idea of making some extra money. I ordered a fourth cocktail and slowly weighed up the different possibilities as I turned the alcohol in my glass, before realising that I would very probably do nothing, that I would not resort to prostitution now Esther had left me, any more than I had after Isabelle left, and I also understood, with a mixture of terror and disgust, that I would continue (in, I must say, a purely theoretical fashion, because I knew very well that in my case it was all over, that I'd blown my last chance, that I was now ready to depart, that it was necessary to put an end to things, that it was necessary to finish), but that I continued all the same, in my heart of hearts, and in the face of all the evidence, to believe in love.

My first contact with Esther31 surprised me; probably influenced by the life story of my human predecessor, I had expected a young person. Alerted by my request for intermediation, she switched into visual mode: I found myself confronted by a woman with a calm, serious face who must have been just over fifty; she was standing in front of her screen in a tidy little room that must have served as her office, and was wearing spectacles. The fact that she was number 31 was already, in itself, slightly surprising; she explained to me that the line of Esthers had inherited the renal malformation of its founder, and was consequently characterised by shortened lifespans. Of course, she was aware of Marie23's departure: it seemed almost certain to her as well that a community of evolved primates had settled in the place where Lanzarote had once been; that zone of the North Atlantic, she informed me, had suffered a tormented geological fate: after having been completely engulfed at the time of the First Decrease, the island had re-emerged as a result of new volcanic eruptions; at the time of the Great Drying Up it had become an isthmus, and, according to the last surveys, a narrow strip of land still linked it to the African coast.

Unlike Marie23, Esther31 thought that the community that had settled in the zone was not made up of savages, but of neohumans who had rejected the teachings of the Supreme Sister. The satellite images, it's true, left room for doubt: they might, or might not, be beings transformed by SGR; but how could heterotrophs, she pointed out, have survived in a place that supported no trace of vegetation? She was convinced that Marie23, although expecting to meet humans of the previous race, was in fact going to find neohumans who had undertaken the same journey as her.

'Maybe that was, fundamentally, what she was looking for . . .' I said. She reflected for a long time before replying, in a neutral tone: 'That is possible.'

In order to work, Vincent had moved into a windowless hangar, about fifty metres long on either side, situated right next to the Church's offices, and linked to them by a covered passageway. As I passed through the offices, where despite the early hour secretaries, archivists and accountants were busy behind their computer screens, I was struck again by the fact that this powerful spiritual organisation, which was thriving, which already claimed to have, in the countries of Northern Europe, a number of followers equivalent to that of the main Christian denominations, was, in many other respects, organised exactly like an SME. Cop was very comfortable, I could tell, in this hardworking, humble atmosphere that corresponded to his values; the strutting, show-off side of the prophet had always, in reality, deeply displeased him. At ease in his new existence, he behaved like a socially minded employer, listening to his employees, always ready to give them a half-day off or an advance on their salary. The organisation worked wonderfully, the members' legacies came in, after their deaths, and enriched a capital already valued at twice that of the Moonies; their DNA, replicated in five samples, was preserved at low temperature in underground rooms impermeable to most known radiation, which could withstand a thermonuclear attack. The laboratories run by Knowall constituted not only the *nec plus ultra* of current technology; in fact nothing, in the private sector as well as the public, could compare with them, he and his team had acquired, in the field of genetic engineering as well as in that of fuzzy neural networks, an unassailable lead, all done with absolute respect to the legislation that was currently in force, and the most promising students at most of the American and European technological universities now applied to work alongside them.

Once the dogma, ritual and regime had been established, and any dangerous deviations liquidated, Vincent made only brief media appearances, during which he could afford himself the luxury of tolerance, agreeing with representatives of the monotheistic religions on the existence of common spiritual aspirations – without disguising, however, the fact that their objectives were radically different. This strategy of appeasement had paid off; and the two bomb attacks against offices of the church – one, in Istanbul, was claimed by an Islamic group; the other, in Tucson, Arizona, was attributed to a fundamentalist Protestant sect – had aroused universal indignation, and had backfired on their perpetrators. The innovative aspects of the Elohimite proposals for life were now essentially taken on by Lucas, whose incisive communication of them, straightforwardly ridiculing paternity, playing – with a controlled audacity – on the sexual ambiguity of very young girls, and devaluing the ancient taboo of incest without explicitly attacking it, ensured every one of his press campaigns an impact out of all proportion to the investment made, whilst still maintaining the establishment of a broad consensus, through unreserved praise for the dominant hedonistic values and emphatic homage to Oriental sexual techniques, all dressed up visually in a manner that was both aesthetic and very direct, which went on to become seminal (the ad 'Eternity, Tranquilly' had thus been joined by 'Eternity, Sensually' then 'Eternity, Lovingly' which, without a shadow of doubt, innovated the sphere of religious advertising). Without offering any resistance, and without even imagining the possibility of a counterattack, the established churches saw most of their followers, in the space of a few years, disappear into thin air, and their stars wane in favour of the new cult – which, moreover, recruited the majority of its followers from atheistic, well-off, modern milieus – As and B1s, to use Lucas's terminology – to whom they had long since had no access.

Conscious that things were going well, that he was surrounded by the best possible colleagues, Vincent had devoted himself more and more exclusively, over the last few weeks, to his great project, and it was with surprise that I saw again, beneath the mask of the business leader, a man who was fragile, timid and uncertain in speech,

slightly vacant, but at the same time weighed down by a secret
preoccupation. He hesitated for a long time, that morning, before
letting me discover his life's work. We had one coffee, then another,
at the automatic dispenser. Turning the empty cup in his fingers, he
finally said to me: 'I think this will be my last work . . .' before
looking at the floor. 'Susan agrees . . .' he added. 'When the
moment is right . . . I mean, the moment for leaving this world and
beginning the wait for the next incarnation, we will enter this room
together; we will go into the centre of it and there we will take the
lethal mixture together. Other rooms will be built, along the same
model, so that all the followers can have access to it. It seemed to
me . . . it seemed to me that it was useful to formalise this moment.'
He stopped talking, and looked me straight in the eye. 'It was
difficult work . . .' he said. 'I have thought a lot of "The Death of
the Poor", by Baudelaire; that helped me enormously.'

The sublime verses came back to me immediately, as if they had
always been present in a corner of my consciousness, as if my whole
life had only been a more or less explicit commentary on them:

> *Death, alas! consoles and brings to life;*
> *The end of it all, the solitary hope;*
> *We, drunk on death's elixir, face the strife,*
> *Take heart, and climb till dusk the weary slope.*

> *All through the storm, the frost, and the snow,*
> *Death on our black horizon pulses clear;*
> *Death is the famous inn that we all know,*
> *Where we can rest and sleep and have good cheer.*

I nodded my head; what else could I do? Then I went into the
corridor leading to the hangar. As soon as I opened the hermetically
sealed, reinforced door, which led inside, I was dazzled by a blinding light, and for half a minute I couldn't make anything out; the
door closed behind me with a dull thud.

Gradually my eyes became accustomed, and I recognised forms
and contours; it looked a little like the computer simulation I had

seen on Lanzarote, but the luminosity of it all was even more enhanced, he really had worked on the whiteness, and there was no longer any music, just a few light, quavering sounds, a little like vague atmospheric vibrations. I had the impression of moving inside a milky, isotropic space, which sometimes condensed, suddenly, into granular micro-formations – on moving closer I could make out mountains, valleys and whole landscapes, which became rapidly more complex, then disappeared almost immediately, and the decor fell back into a vague homogeneity, criss-crossed by oscillating potentialities. Strangely, I could no longer see my hands, nor any other part of my body. I quickly lost all sense of direction, and I then had the impression of hearing footsteps echoing mine: when I stopped, the steps stopped as well, but slightly afterwards. Looking right I caught sight of a silhouette that replicated every one of my movements, and that was only distinguished from the dazzling whiteness of the atmosphere by being a slightly duller white. I felt rather worried: the silhouette disappeared immediately. I stopped worrying: the silhouette rematerialised, looming out of nothingness. Gradually I became used to its presence, and continued my exploration; it became increasingly obvious to me that Vincent had used fractal structures, I recognised Sierpinski Triangles, Mandelbrot Sets, and the installation itself seemed to evolve as I became conscious of it. Just as I had the impression that the space around me was fragmenting into Cantor's triadic sets, the silhouette disappeared, and there was total silence. I could no longer even hear my own breath, and I then understood that I had *become* the space; I was the universe and I was phenomenal existence, the sparkling micro-structures that appeared, froze, then dissolved in space were part of me, and I felt them to be mine, producing themselves inside my body, both every one of their apparitions and every one of their cessations. I was then seized by an intense desire to disappear, to melt into a luminous, active nothingness, vibrating with perpetual potentialities; the luminosity became blinding, the space around me seemed to explode and diffract into shards of light, but it was not a space in the usual sense of the term, it included many dimensions, and any other form of perception had disappeared – this space contained, in the conventional sense of the word, nothing. I remained like this, among the formless potentialities – beyond even form and absence of form – for a period of time that I couldn't define; then something arose in me, at first almost imperceptibly, like the memory or dream of the sensation of gravity; then I became conscious again of my breathing, and of the three dimensions of the space, which gradually became still; objects reappeared around me, like discrete emanations from the whiteness, and I was able to leave the room.

It was, in fact, impossible, I told Vincent a little later, to stay alive in such a place for more than ten minutes. 'I call this space *love*,' he said. 'Man has never been able to love, apart from in immortality; it is undoubtedly why women were closer to love when their mission was to give life. We have discovered immortality, and presence in the world; the world no longer has the power to destroy us, it is we, rather, who have the power to create through the power of our vision. If we remain in a state of innocence, and under the approving gaze of one pair of eyes, we also remain in love.'

Having taken my leave of Vincent, once I was in the taxi, I gradually calmed down; my state of mind as I crossed the Parisian suburbs remained, however, quite chaotic, and it was only after Porte d'Italie that I regained my sense of irony, and was able to repeat to myself mentally: 'Could this be possible? This immense artist, this creator of ethics, he hasn't yet learned that love is *dead*!' At once I felt a certain sadness as I realised that I had still not given up being what I had been for my entire career: a sort of Zarathustra of the middle classes.

The receptionist at the Lutétia asked me if my stay had been fine. 'Impeccable,' I told him as I looked for my Premier credit card, 'things are really humming.' He then wanted to know if they would have the privilege of seeing me again sometime soon. 'No, I don't think so . . .' I replied, 'I don't think I will be back here for a long time.'

'We turn our eyes to the heavens, and the heavens are empty,' writes Ferdinand12 in his commentary. It was around the twelfth neohuman generation that the first doubts regarding the coming of the Future Ones appeared – that is to say a millennium after the events related by Daniel1; it was at almost the same time that the first defections were heard of.

Another millennium has passed, and the situation has remained stable, the proportion of defections unchanged. Inaugurating a tradition of nonchalance in relation to scientific data that was to lead to the demise of philosophy, the human thinker Friedrich Nietzsche saw in man 'the species whose type is not yet fixed'. If humans in no way merited such an assessment – less so than most of the animal species in any case – it certainly no longer applies to the neohumans who followed them. It can even be said that what characterises us best, in relation to our predecessors, is undoubtedly a certain conservatism. Humans, or at least humans of the last period, adhered, it seems very easily, to any new project, quite independently of the direction of the proposed movement; *change* in itself was apparently, in their eyes, a value. On the contrary, we greet innovation with the utmost reticence, and only adopt it if it seems to us to constitute an undeniable improvement. Since the Standard Genetic Rectification, which made us the first autotrophic animal species, no modification of any real significance has been developed. Projects have been submitted for our approval by the scientific authorities of the Central City, proposing for example, to develop our aptitude for flight, or for survival in underwater environments; they have been debated, debated at length, before finally being rejected. The only genetic characteristics that separate me from Daniel2, my first neohuman predecessor, are minimal improvements, guided by common sense, for example an increase in metabolic efficiency in our use of minerals, or a slight decrease in sensitivity to pain of the nervous fibres. Our collective history, like our individual destinies, therefore appears, compared to that of the humans of the last period, peculiarly calm. Sometimes, at night, I get up to observe the stars. Huge climatic and geological transformations have remodelled the physiognomy of this region, as they have most of the regions of the world, over the course of the two last millennia; the brightness and position of the stars, their constellations, are undoubtedly the only natural elements that have, since the time of Daniel1, undergone no transformation. As I consider the night sky my thoughts turn to the Elohim, to that strange belief that was finally, in a roundabout away, to unleash the Great Transformation. Daniel1 lives again in me, his body knows in mine a new incarnation, his thoughts are mine; his memories are mine; his existence actually prolongs itself in me, far more than man ever dreamed of prolonging himself through his descendants. My own life, however, I often think, is far from the one he would have liked to live.

Back in San Jose I *kept on going*, that's about all there is to say. On the whole, things went rather well, for a suicide that is, and it was with surprising ease that I completed, during July and August, the narration of events that were, nonetheless, the most significant and atrocious of my life. I was an author venturing into the field of autobiography, although I wasn't really an author at all, which no doubt explains why I never realised, in the course of those days, that it was the simple fact of writing, which gave me the illusion of having control over events, that prevented me sinking into states which justified what psychiatrists, in their charming jargon, call *shock treatment*. It is surprising that I didn't realise I was walking along the edge of a precipice; and all the more so as my dreams should have alerted me. Esther reappeared in them more and more often, more and more friendly and *coquettish*, and they took a naively pornographic turn, becoming the veritable *hallucinations of a starving man*, which boded nothing good. I had to go out, from time to time, to buy beer and biscuits, generally I would come back along the beach, obviously I would come across naked young girls, a lot of them even: they would turn up again at night in the middle of pathetically unrealistic orgies, in which I was the hero and Esther the organiser; I thought increasingly often about the *nocturnal emissions* of old men that drive the auxiliary nurses to despair – whilst telling myself over and over again that I would never reach that point, that I would carry out the fatal gesture in time, that I still had, all the same, a certain *dignity* (of which, however, nothing, in my life, had yet to offer an example). Perhaps it was not completely certain that I would commit suicide, perhaps I might be one of those individuals who *piss people off* right up until the end, all the more so because I had enough cash to ensure I could piss off a considerable number of people. I hated mankind, it's true, I had hated it since the beginning, and as misfortune makes you nasty, I now hated it even more. At the same time, I had become a right little pooch, for whom just one lump of sugar would have been enough to appease him (I wasn't even thinking of Esther's body especially, anything would have done: breasts, a bush); but no one would hand me this sugar lump, and I was well on the way to ending my life as I had begun it: in dereliction and rage, in a state of hateful panic, further exacerbated by the summer heat. It is under the influence of an ancient animal sense of belonging that people have so many conversations about meteorology and the climate, influenced by a primitive memory, inscribed in the sense organs, and linked to the conditions of survival in the prehistoric era. These circumscribed, clichéd conversations are, however, the symptom of a real issue: even when we live in apartments, in conditions of thermal stability guaranteed by reliable and well-honed technology, it remains impossible for us to rid ourselves of this animal atavism; it is thus that a full awareness of our ignominy and misfortune, and of their complete and definitive nature, can only manifest itself in sufficiently favourable climatic conditions.

Gradually, the chronology of my narration caught up with the chronology of my real life; on 17 August, in scorching heat, I gave a shape to my memories of the birthday party in Madrid – which had taken place a year before, to the day. I passed quickly over my last stay in Paris, and the death of Isabelle: all this seemed to me to be already inscribed in the previous pages, it was predictable, part of the common fate of mankind, and I wanted, on the contrary, to do the work of a pioneer, to bring about something surprising and new.

   The full scale of the lie was now apparent to me: it extended to all aspects of human existence, and its usage was universal; philosophers without exception had swallowed it, as well as almost all writers; it was probably necessary for the survival of the species, and Vincent was right: my life story, once distributed and commented on, was going to put an end to mankind as we knew it. My *godfather*, to speak in mafia terms (and we were dealing, well and truly, with a crime, and even, strictly speaking, a *crime against humanity*) would be satisfied. Mankind was going to change direction; it was going to convert.

Before putting the final stop to my story I thought back for the last time to Vincent, the true inspiration of this book, and the only human being who had ever inspired in me the feeling that was so foreign to my nature: admiration. Vincent had been right to discern in me the abilities of a *spy* or a *traitor*. There have always been spies and traitors in human history (not as many as you might think, however, just a few, at well-spaced intervals, it was quite remarkable to observe on the whole how much men had behaved as *nice guys*, with the good will of the bull, who climbs joyfully into the lorry that will take it to the abattoir); but I was no doubt the first to be living at a time when technological conditions could give my treason its full impact. Besides, I would only accelerate, by conceptualising it, an inevitable historical development. More and more, men were going to want to live freely, irresponsibly, on a wild quest for pleasure; they were going to want to live like those who were already living amongst them, the *kids*, and when old age would make its weight felt, when it would become impossible for them to continue the struggle, they would put an end to it all; but in the meantime they would have joined the Elohimite Church, their genetic code would have been safeguarded, and they would die in the hope of an indefinite continuation of that same existence that was devoted to pleasure. Such was the direction of the movement of history, which would not only be limited to the West, the West was just happy to take the lead and scout out the road ahead, as it had been doing since the end of the Middle Ages.

After that the species, in its current form, would disappear; after that, something different would emerge, whose name could not yet be spoken, and which would perhaps be worse, perhaps better, but certainly more limited in its ambitions, and in any case more calm, the importance of impatience and frenzy should not be under-estimated in human history. Perhaps that crude imbecile Hegel had, at the end of the day, seen things correctly, perhaps I was a servant of *the cunning of reason*. It was scarcely plausible that the species destined to succeed us would be, to the same degree, a *social species*; since my childhood the idea that concluded all discussions, that put an end to all disagreements, the idea around which I had most often seen an absolute peaceful consensus form, could be summed up pretty much as follows: 'Essentially, you're born alone, you live alone and you die alone.' Accessible to even the simplest minds, this sentence was also the conclusion of the nimblest thinkers; it provoked in all circumstances unanimous approval, and it seemed to everyone, once these words were uttered, that they had never heard anything so beautiful, profound and true – this, regardless of the age, sex and social position of the inter-locutors. The fact was already clear to my generation, and even more to Esther's. A frame of mind such as this can scarcely, in the long term, favour a rich sociability. Sociability had had its day, it had played its historic role; it was indispensable in the early years of the appearance of human intelligence, but it was today just a useless and encumbering vestige. The same could be said of sexuality, since the spread of artificial procreation. 'To masturbate is to make love with someone you truly love': the phrase was attributed to various celebrities, from Keith Richards to Jacques Lacan; it was, in any case, at the moment it was uttered, ahead of its time, and could not therefore have a real impact. Besides, sexual relations were certainly going to continue for some time, as an advertising ploy and prin-ciple of narcissistic differentiation, whilst increasingly becoming the reserve of specialists, a certain *erotic elite*. The narcissistic battle would last for as long as it could feed upon consenting victims, eagerly seeking their ration of humiliation within it, it would prob-ably last as long as sociability itself, it would be its last vestige, but would end up dying with it. As for *love*, it could no longer be counted on: I was undoubtedly one of the last men of my generation to love myself sufficiently little to be able to love someone else, although I had only been in love rarely, twice in my life to be exact. There is no love in individual freedom, in independence, that's quite simply a lie, and one of the crudest lies you can imagine; love is only in the desire for annihilation, fusion, the disappearance of the individual, in a sort of what used to be called *oceanic feeling*, in something anyway that was, at least in the near future, condemned.

Three years before, I had cut out of *Gente Libre* a photo in which the sex of a man, of whom you could only make out the pelvis, was stuck halfway, effortlessly so, into a woman of about twenty-five, who had long curly chestnut hair. All the photographs in this magazine aimed at 'liberal couples' revolved more or less around the same theme: why did this image charm me so much? Leaning on her knees and forearms, the young women turned her face to the lens as if she was surprised by this unexpected intromission, which came at a moment when she was thinking of something completely different, like washing her tiled floor; she seemed, however, rather pleasantly surprised, her eyes betrayed a bland and impersonal satisfaction, as if it was her mucous membrane that was reacting to this unexpected contact, rather than her mind. Her sex itself seemed supple and soft, with good dimensions, comfortable, it was in any case pleasantly open, and gave the impression of being able to open easily, on demand. This friendly hospitality, without tragedy, without any kind of fuss, was now all I asked of the world, I realised it week after week as I looked at this photograph; I also realised that I would never manage to obtain it, that I would no longer really even try to obtain it, and that Esther's departure hadn't been a painful transition, but an absolute end. Perhaps by then she had come back from the United States, it was even quite likely, it seemed scarcely plausible to me that her career as a pianist would experience any great developments, besides she didn't have the necessary talent, nor the dose of madness that accompanies it, she was basically a very reasonable little creature. Whether she was back home or not, I knew it wouldn't change anything, she wouldn't want to see me again, for her I was ancient history, and, frankly, I was ancient history for me as well, any idea of embarking again on a public career, or more generally of having relations with my fellow men, had this time definitively left me, with her I had used up the last of my strength, I had surrendered to the present; she had been my happiness, but she had also been, as I had sensed from the beginning, the death of me; this premonition hadn't, for all that, made me hesitate, in as much as we all have to meet our own death, see it in front of us at least once, and each one of us, in our heart of hearts, knows this, it is, when you think of it, preferable that death, rather than being clad normally in boredom and attrition, should wear the rare robes of pleasure.

In the beginning was created the Supreme Sister, who is the first. Then were created the Seven Founders, who created the Central City. If the teachings of the Supreme Sister are the basis of our philosophical theories, the political organisation of the neohuman communities owes almost everything to the Seven Founders; but it was only, by their own admission, an inessential parameter, conditioned by biological evolutions, which had increased the functional autonomy of the neohumans, as much as by the historical shifts, already widely begun in previous societies, that led to the withering away of relationship functions. The reasons that led to a radical separation between neohumans have nothing absolute about them and everything indicates that this took place only in a gradual manner, probably over the course of several generations. To tell the truth, total physical separation constitutes a possible social con-figuration, compatible with the teachings of the Supreme Sister, and generally along the same lines as them, rather than being a consequence of them in the strict sense of the word.

The disappearance of contact was followed by that of desire. I had felt no physical attraction to Marie23 – no more naturally than I hadn't felt it for Esther31, who had, anyway, passed the age of arousing those kinds of manifestations. I was convinced that neither Marie23, despite her departure, nor Marie22, despite the strange episode preceding her end, related by my predecessor, had known desire either. On the other hand what they had known, and in a singularly painful way, was nostalgia for desire, the wish to experi-ence it again, to be irradiated like their distant ancestors with that force that seemed so powerful. Although Daniel1 shows himself, on this theme of nostalgia for desire, particularly eloquent, I have for my part been spared the phenomenon up until now, and it is with the greatest calm that I discuss with Esther31 the detail of the relations between our respective predecessors; on her part she displays a coolness that is at least equivalent to mine, and it is without regret, without distress, that we leave one another at the end of our occasional intermediations, and return to our calm, contemplative lives, which would probably have appeared, to humans of the classical age, unbelievably boring.

The existence of a residual mental activity, detached from all everyday concerns and oriented towards pure knowledge, constitutes one of the key points of the teachings of the Supreme Sister; up until now nothing has allowed its existence to be put into doubt.

A limited calendar, punctuated by sufficient episodes of mini-grace (such as are offered by the sun slipping across the shutters, or the sudden retreat, under the influence of violent wind from the north, of a threatening cloud formation) organises my existence, the precise duration of which is an indifferent parameter. Identical to Daniel24, I know that I will have, in Daniel26, an equivalent successor; the limited, respectable memories we keep of existences that have identical contours do not have any of the pregnancy that would be necessary for an individual fiction to take hold. The life of each man, in its broad brushstrokes, is similar, and this secret truth, hidden throughout the historical periods, was able to find expression only in the neohumans. Rejecting the incomplete paradigm of form, we aspire to rejoin the universe of countless potentialities. Closing the brackets on becoming, we are from now on in unlimited, indefinite stasis.

We are in September, the last holidaymakers are about to leave; with them the last breasts, the last bushes; the last accessible micro-worlds. An endless autumn awaits me, followed by a sidereal winter; and this time I really have finished my task, I am well past the very last minutes, there is no more justification for my presence here, no more human contact, no more assignable objective. There is, however, something else, something terrible, which floats in space, and seems to want to approach me. Before any sadness, any sorrow or any clearly definable loss, there is something else, which might be called the *pure terror of space*. Was this the last stage? What had I done to deserve such a fate? And what had men, in general, done? I no longer feel any hate in me, nothing to cling to any more, no more landmarks or clues; only fear is out there, the truth of all things, the only physical horizon, indistinguishable from the observable world. There is no longer any real world, no world, no human world, I am outside time, I no longer have any past or future, I have no more sadness, plans, nostalgia, loss or hope; there is only fear.

The space is coming, it approaches and seeks to devour me. The ghosts are there, they constitute the space, they surround me. They feed upon the gouged-out eyes of men.

Thus ended the life story of Daniel1; I regretted, for my part, this abrupt ending. His final predictions on the psychology of the species destined to replace mankind were quite curious; if he had developed them, we could, it seems to me, have drawn useful information from them.

This feeling is not shared by my predecessors. An individual who was certainly honest but limited, blinkered, quite representative of the limitations and contradictions that were to drive the species to ruin; such was, on the whole, the harsh judgement that they, following Vincent1, have passed on our common ancestor. If he had lived, they claim, he would, given the aporias that constituted his nature, only have continued in his mood swings between discouragement and hope, whilst evolving in general towards a state of increasing decrepitude linked to the ageing process and the loss of vital energy; his last poem, written on the plane from Almeria to Paris, is, they observe, symptomatic of the state of mind of the humans of the period to such an extent that it could serve as an epigraph to the classic book by Tatchett and Rawlins, *Decrepitude, Senioritude*.

I was aware of the strength of their arguments, and it was, to be honest, a slight, almost impalpable intuition that pushed me to try and find out a little more about it. Esther31 blankly and abruptly refused my requests. Of course, she had read the life story of Esther1, she had even finished her commentary; but she did not think it was appropriate for me to learn about it.

'You know . . .' I wrote to her (we had for a long time been back in non-visual mode), 'I still feel very far from my ancestor . . .'

'You are never as far as you think,' she snapped.

I did not understand what made her think that this two-millennia-old story, concerning humans of the former race, could still have an impact today. 'It did have an impact, however, and a powerfully negative one . . .' she replied, enigmatically.

At my insistence, however, she finally gave in, and recounted what she knew of the last moments of the relationship between Daniel1 and Esther1. On 23 September, two weeks after he finished his life story, he had phoned her. In the end they had never seen each other again, but he had called back several times, she had responded, gently at first, then in an irrevocable way, saying that she did not want to see him again. Realising that this method had failed, he tried SMS, then e-mails, in fact he had gone step by step through the bleak stages of the disappearance of real contact. As the possibility of receiving a reply evaporated he became more and more audacious, he accepted, frankly, Esther's sexual freedom, and went as far as congratulating her on it, multiplying the licentious allusions, recalling the most erotic moments of their liaison, suggesting that they could frequent swingers' clubs together, make naughty videos, live new experiences; it was pathetic, and a little repugnant. He wrote her many letters, to which he received no reply. 'He humiliated himself . . .' commented Esther31. 'He wallowed in humiliation, and in the most abject manner possible. He went as far as offering her money, lots of money, just to spend a last night with her; it was all the more absurd as she herself was beginning to earn quite a lot as an actress. At the end, he started hanging around her home in Madrid – she spotted him several times in bars, and began to be afraid. She had a new boyfriend at the time, with whom things were going well – she felt a lot of pleasure when making love with him, which had not always been the case with your predecessor. She had even thought of contacting the police, but he just hung around the area, without ever trying to make contact with her, and finally he disappeared.'

I wasn't completely surprised, all this corresponded more or less with what I had been able to learn about the personality of Daniel1. I asked Esther31 what had happened next – whilst conscious, in this too, that I already knew the answer.

'He committed suicide. He committed suicide after having seen her

in a film, *Une Mujer Desnuda*, where she played the lead – it was a
film taken from the novel by a young Italian woman, that had had a
certain success at the time, in which the latter recounted how she
had had multiple sexual experiences without ever feeling the slightest emotion. Before committing suicide, he wrote a last letter – in
which he didn't speak at all about his suicide, she only learned
about it through the press; on the contrary, it was a letter written in
an extremely joyful, almost euphoric tone, in which he declared
himself confident in their love, and in the superficial nature of the
difficulties they had been going through for a year or two. It is this
letter that has had a catastrophic effect on Marie23, and drove her
to leave, to imagine that a social community – of humans and
neohumans, basically she didn't really know – had formed somewhere, and that she had discovered a new mode of relational
organisation; that the radical individual separation we now know
could be abolished immediately, without waiting for the coming of
the Future Ones. I tried to talk her out of it, to explain to her that
this letter simply bore witness to an alteration in the mental capacities of your predecessor, a last and pathetic attempt to deny reality,
that this love without end that he speaks of existed only in his
imagination, that Esther in reality had never loved him. It had no
effect: Marie23 attributed to this letter, in particular to the poem
that ends it, an enormous importance.'

'Are you not of this view?'

'I must acknowledge that it is a curious text, as devoid of irony as
it is of sarcasm, not at all in his usual manner; I find it even quite
moving. But to go from there to giving it such importance . . . No, I
don't agree. Marie23 herself was probably not very balanced, it is
the only reason that can explain why she gave the final verse the
meaning of a concrete, practical piece of information.'

Esther31 was no doubt expecting my following request, and I had
to wait only two minutes, the time it took for her to tap on her
keyboard, to discover the last poem that Daniel had addressed to
Esther before taking his life; the very one that had driven Marie23
to abandon her home, her habits, her life, and leave in search of a
hypothetical neohuman community:

My life, my life, my very old one
My first badly healed desire,
My first crippled love,
You had to return.

It was necessary to know
What is best in our lives,
When two bodies play at happiness,
Unite, reborn without end.

Entered into complete dependency,
I know the trembling of being,
The hesitation to disappear,
Sunlight upon the forest's edge

And love, where all is easy,
Where all is given in the instant;
There exists in the midst of time
The possibility of an island.

PART THREE

FINAL COMMENTARY,
EPILOGUE

'What was outside the world?'

At this period of the beginning of the month of May, the sun began to appear at four o'clock, despite the rather low latitude; the modification of the axis of the Earth had had, in addition to the Great Drying Up, several consequences of this nature.

Like all dogs, Fox did not have any precise sleeping pattern: he slept with me, and woke likewise. He followed me with curiosity when I went through the rooms preparing a light rucksack, which I attached to my shoulders, and wagged his tail joyfully when I left the residence to walk up to the protective fence; our first walk of the day was normally later.

When I activated the unlocking mechanism, he looked at me in surprise. The metal wheels turned slowly on their axis, making an opening of three metres; I took a few steps and found myself outside. Fox again sent me a hesitant, interrogative look: nothing in the memories of his previous life, nor in his genetic memory, had prepared him for an event of this nature; nothing had prepared me for it either, it is true. He still hesitated for a few seconds, then trotted gently up to my feet.

I had first to cross a flat space, devoid of vegetation, for about ten kilometres; then there was the start of a very gentle wooded slope that extended to the horizon. I had no other plan than to make for the west, preferably west-south-west; a neohuman, human or indeterminate community might have settled on the site of Lanzarote, or in a nearby area; I would perhaps manage to find it; that is what my intentions boiled down to. The population of the regions I had to cross was scarcely known; their topography, on the other hand, had been the object of recent and precise surveys.

I walked for almost two hours, over stony but easy terrain, before returning once again to the cover of the trees; Fox trotted at my side, visibly happy with this prolonged walk, and exercising the muscles of his little paws. During all this time I remained conscious that my departure was a failure, and probably a suicide. I had filled my rucksack with capsules of mineral salts, I could hold out for several months, for I would certainly not lack drinking water, nor solar light, during my journey; of course, my reserves would eventually run out, but the very immediate problem was feeding Fox; I could hunt, I had taken a pistol and several boxes of lead cartridges, but I had never shot a gun before, and knew absolutely nothing about what types of animals I would be likely to meet in the regions I was about to cross.

Around the end of the afternoon the forest began to thin out, then I reached a patch of short grass that marked the top of the slope I had been following since the start of the day. To the west the slope descended, clearly more steeply, then I made out a succession of hills and steep valleys, still covered with dense forest, as far as I could see. Since my departure I had seen no trace of a human presence, nor of animal life in general. I decided to stop for the night near a pond where a stream bubbled up before descending southwards. Fox drank lengthily and then stretched out at my feet. I took the three daily pills necessary for my metabolism, then unfolded the light survival blanket I had brought; it would no doubt be sufficient, I knew that I could expect to cross no high-altitude area.

Towards the middle of the night, the temperature became slightly cooler; Fox huddled against me, breathing regularly. His sleep was occasionally disturbed by dreams; at those moments, he twitched his paws, as if getting over an obstacle. I slept very badly; my enterprise seemed to me more and more starkly unreasonable, and destined for certain failure. I had, however, no regrets; I could have easily turned back. No control was exerted by the Central City; defections were, in general, only noticed by accident, after a delivery or necessary repair, and sometimes only several years later. I could return, but I had no intention of it: that solitary routine, intercut solely by intellectual exchanges, which had constituted my life, which should have constituted it until the end, now seemed unbearable. Happiness should have come, the happiness felt by good children, guaranteed by the respect of small procedures, by the security that flowed from them, by the absence of pain and risk;

but happiness had not come, and equanimity had led to torpor. Among the feeble joys of the neohumans, the most constant revolved around organisation and classification, the constitution of small ordered sets, the meticulous and rational displacement of small objects; these had proved insufficient. Planning the extinction of desire in Buddhist-like terms, the Supreme Sister had banked on the maintenance of a weakened, non-tragic, energy, purely conservative in nature, which would have continued to enable the functioning of thought – a thought less quick but more exact because more lucid, a thought that knew *deliverance*. This phenomenon had only been produced in insignificant proportions, and it was, on the contrary sadness, melancholy, languid and finally mortal apathy that had submerged our disincarnated generations. The most patent indicator of failure was that I had ended up envying the destiny of Daniel1, his violent and contradictory journey, the amorous passions that had shaken him – whatever his suffering and tragic end.

Every morning for years, following the Supreme Sister's recommendations, I had practised, on waking, the exercises defined by the Buddha in his sermon on the establishment of attention. 'Thus he stays, observing the body from within; he stays, observing the body from outside; he stays, observing the body from inside and outside. He stays, observing the appearance of the body; he stays, observing the disappearance of the body; he stays, observing the appearance and disappearance of the body. "This is the body": this introspection is present to him, only for knowledge, only for reflection, thus he stays free, and is attached to nothing in the world.' At every minute of my life, since its beginning, I had remained conscious of my breathing, of the kinaesthetic equilibrium of my organism, of its fluctuating central state. That immense joy, that transfiguration of his physical being by which Daniel1 was submerged at the moment of the fulfilment of his desires, that impression in particular of being transported to another universe that he knew at the moment of his carnal penetrations, I had never known, I hadn't even any notion of them at all, it seemed to me now that, under these conditions, I could not go on living.

*

The dawn broke, humid, over the forest landscape, there came with it dreams of gentleness, which I was unable to comprehend. Tears came as well, and their salty contact seemed very strange to me. Then the sun appeared, and with it the insects; I began, then, to understand what the life of men had been. The palms of my hands and the soles of my feet were covered with hundreds of little blisters; the itching was terrible, and I scratched myself furiously, for about ten minutes, until I was covered in blood.

Later, when we started out across a dense prairie, Fox managed to capture a rabbit; in a clean motion, he broke its cervical vertebrae, then brought the little animal to my feet, dripping with blood. I turned away when he began to devour its internal organs; thus was the natural world.

During the following week, we crossed over a steep area, which, according to my map, corresponded to the Gador sierra; my itching decreased, or rather I ended up getting used to the constant pain, which was stronger at the end of day, just as I got used to the layer of filth that covered my skin, and a more pronounced body odour.

One morning, just after dawn, I woke up without feeling the heat of Fox's body. I leaped up, terrified. He was a few metres away, and was rubbing against a tree, sneezing furiously; the source of pain was apparently situated behind his ears, at the base of the neck. I approached and gently took his head in my hands. By smoothing his fur I quickly discovered a small, grey, bumpy surface, a few millimetres wide: it was a tick. I recognised it from the descriptions in books I had read on animal biology. The extraction of this parasite was, I knew, delicate; I returned to my rucksack, and took out some tweezers and a compress soaked in alcohol. Fox moaned softly, but remained still as I operated: slowly, millimetre by millimetre, I managed to extract the animal from his flesh; it was a grey, fat cylinder, a quite repugnant sight, which had grown fat on his blood. Thus was the natural world.

On the first day of the second week, in the middle of the morning, I found myself in front of an immense fault line, which blocked my path westwards. I knew of its existence through satellite surveys, but I had imagined that it would be possible to cross it to continue my journey. The cliffs of bluish basalt, absolutely vertical, plunged down for several hundreds of metres to an indistinct, slightly uneven surface, the soil of which appeared to be a juxtaposition of black stones and lakes of mud. In the limpid air, I could make out the smallest details on the cliff face opposite, which must have been about ten kilometres away: it too was just as vertical.

If the maps drawn from the surveys did not allow you to foresee at all the uncrossable nature of this unevenness in the ground, they did on the other hand give you a precise idea of its route: beginning in a zone that corresponded to the former site of Madrid (the city had been destroyed by a succession of nuclear explosions, during the last phases of the inter-human conflicts), the fault crossed the whole of the south of Spain, then the marshy zone corresponding to what had been the Mediterranean, before plunging deep into the heart of the African continent; that meant a detour of a thousand kilometres. I sat down for a few minutes, discouraged, my feet dangling in the void, while the sun climbed up the summits; Fox sat down at my side, looking at me inquisitively. The problem of his food, at least, was resolved: the rabbits, which were very numerous in the region, let themselves be approached and killed without displaying the slightest suspicion; no doubt their natural predators had disappeared many generations ago. I was surprised by the speed with which Fox rediscovered the instincts of his wild ancestors; surprised also by the manifest joy he exhibited, he who had only known the mildness of an apartment, sniffing the mountain air and gambolling across the mountain prairies.

The days were mild and already warm; it was without difficulty that we crossed the ranges of the Sierra Nevada through the Perto de la Ragua, at an altitude of two thousand metres; in the distance, I could see the snowy summit of the Mulhacen, which had been – and remained, despite the intervening geological upheavals – the culminating point of the Iberian peninsula.

Further to the north extended a zone of plateaus and limestone peaks, the surface of which had been bored with numerous caves. They had served as shelter for the prehistoric men who had first inhabited the region; later, they had been used as refuges by the last

Muslims hunted by the Spanish Reconquista, before being transformed in the twentieth century into recreation zones and hotels; I got used to resting in them during the day, and continuing my journey at nightfall. It was on the morning of the third day that I saw, for the first time, indications of the presence of savages – a fire, some small animal bones. They had lit a fire on the floor of one of the bedrooms installed in the caves, charring the carpet, despite the fact the hotel kitchens contained a battery of vitroceramic cookers – that they were incapable of understanding how to use. It was a constant surprise for me to observe that a large part of the equipment constructed by men was still, several centuries later, in working order – the electric power stations themselves continued to churn out thousand of kilowatts that were no longer used by anyone. Deeply hostile to anything that could have come from mankind, wanting to establish a radical break with the species that had preceded us, the Supreme Sister had very quickly decided to develop an autonomous technology in the enclaves intended for inhabitation by neohumans, which she had progressively bought from bankrupt nations who were incapable of balancing their budgets and soon after of satisfying the health needs of their populations. The previous installations had been neglected; the fact they could still function was all the more remarkable for this: whatever he might have been otherwise, man had undoubtedly been an *ingenious* mammal.

On reaching the top of the reservoir of Negretin, I made a brief stop. The gigantic turbines of the dam turned slowly; they now only powered a row of sodium lamps that stretched, uselessly, along the motorway between Granada and Alicante. The road, crevassed and covered with sand, had been invaded here and there by grass, and bushes. Sitting on the terrace of a former café-restaurant overlooking the turquoise surface of the reservoir, amidst metal chairs and tables gnawed by rust, I found myself once again seized by a fit of nostalgia as I thought of the parties, dinners and family reunions that must have taken place there, many centuries before. I was however, and more than ever, conscious that mankind *did not deserve* to live, that the death of this species could, from all points of view, be considered only good news; its spoilt and deteriorated vestiges were nonetheless upsetting.

'Until when will the conditions of unhappiness last?' wondered the Supreme Sister in her *Second Refutation of Humanism*. 'They will last,' she replies straight away, 'for so long as women continue to have children.' No human problem, teaches the Supreme Sister, could have found the merest hint of a solution without a drastic reduction in the density of the Earth's population. An exceptional historic opportunity for rational depopulation had been offered at the beginning of the twenty-first century, she went on, both in Europe through the falling birth rate, and in Africa thanks to epidemics and AIDS. Mankind had preferred to waste this chance through the adoption of a policy of mass immigration, and bore complete responsibility for the ethnic and religious wars that ensued, and that constituted the prelude to the First Decrease.

Long and confused, the history of the First Decrease is now only known by rare specialists, who rely essentially on the monumental, three-volume *History of Boreal Civilisations*, by Ravensberger and Dickinson. An incomparable source of information, this work has sometimes been considered to be lacking in empirical rigour; the authors have especially been reproached for devoting too much space to the relation of Horsa, which, according to Penrose, owes more to the literary influence of *chansons de geste* rather than strict historical truth. Its critics have, for example, focused on the following passage:

> *The three islands of the north are blocked with ice;*
> *The finest theories refuse to make sense;*
> *It is said somewhere a lake has collapsed*
> *And dead continents rise back to the surface.*
>
> *Obscure astrologists criss-cross our provinces,*
> *Proclaiming the return of the Hyperborean God;*
> *They announce the glory of Alpha Centaurus*
> *And swear obedience to the blood of old princes.*

This passage, it is argued, manifestly contradicts what we know about the climatic history of the globe. Deeper research has, however, shown that the beginning of the collapse of the human civilisations was indeed marked by variations in temperature that were as sudden as they were unpredictable. The First Decrease itself, that is to say the melting of the ice, which, produced by the explosion of two thermonuclear bombs at the Arctic and Antarctic poles, was to cause the immersion of the entire Asian continent, with the exception of Tibet, and divide by twenty the population of the Earth, occurred only a century later.

Other research has shown the resurgence, over the course of this troubled period, of beliefs and behaviours from the most ancient folkloric past of Western mankind, such as astrology, divining magic, and fidelity to hierarchies of a dynastic type. Reconstitution of rural or urban tribes, reappearance of barbarian cults and customs: the disappearance of the human civilisations, at least in its first phase, slightly resembles what had been predicted, at the end of the twentieth century, by various authors of speculative fiction. A violent, savage future was what awaited men, many were aware of it even before the unleashing of the first troubles; certain publications such as *Screaming Metal* display a quite troubling prescience. This anticipatory awareness, however, did not enable men in any way to put into action, or even to imagine any kind of solution. Mankind, teaches the Supreme Sister, was to fulfil its destiny of violence, right up until its final destruction; nothing could have saved it, even supposing such a rescue could have been considered desirable. The small neohuman community, gathered in enclaves protected by a failsafe security system, equipped with a reliable system of reproduction and an autonomous communications network, was to have no difficulty passing through this period of ordeal. It was to survive just as easily the Second Decrease, correlative to the Great Drying Up. Sheltering from destruction and pillage the whole sum of human knowledge, complementing it when the occasion arose, it was to play almost the same role as the monasteries during the Middle Ages – with the caveat that it had absolutely no intention of preparing a future resurrection of mankind, but rather it favoured, in all ways possible, its extinction.

*

During the three days that followed, we crossed a dry, white plateau, with anaemic vegetation; water and prey became scarcer, and I decided to shift eastwards, moving away from the line of the fault. Following the course of the Rio Guardal, we reached the reservoir of San Clemente, then it was with pleasure that we found ourselves in the cool shade, abounding with game, of the Segura sierra. As we continued along our journey, I became aware that my own biochemical constitution gave me an exceptional hardiness, an ease in adapting to different environments that had no equivalent in the animal world. Up until now I had seen no trace of the big predators, and it was rather in homage to an ancient human tradition that I lit a fire every evening, after setting up camp. Fox had no difficulty rediscovering the atavisms that were those of the dog before it had decided first to be a companion to man, now many millennia ago, then to retake its place beside the neohumans. Cool air came down from the summits, we were at an altitude of about two thousand metres, and Fox contemplated the flames, before stretching out at my feet as the embers glowed. I knew that he would sleep with one eye open, ready to get up at the first alert, and kill and die if necessary to protect his master and his home. Despite my close reading of the narrative by Daniel1, I had still not totally understood what men meant by *love*, I had not grasped all the multiple and contradictory meanings they gave to this term; I had grasped the brutality of sexual combat, the unbearable pain of emotional isolation, but I still could not see what it was that enabled them to hope that they could establish between these contradictory aspirations a form of synthesis. However, at the end of those few weeks of travel in the sierras of inland Spain I had never felt as close to loving, in the most elevated sense that they had given to this word; I had never been as close to understanding 'what is best in our lives', to use the words of Daniel1 in his final poem. I understood that nostalgia for this feeling could have started Marie23 out on the road, far from here, on the other side of the Atlantic. I was myself drawn along a path that was just as hypothetical, but it had become a matter of indifference to me whether or not I reached my destination: basically, what I wanted to do was to continue to travel with Fox across the prairies and mountains, to experience the awakenings, the baths in a freezing river, the minutes spent drying in the sun, the evenings spent around the fire in the starlight. I had attained innocence, in an absolute and non-conflictual state, I no longer had any plan, nor any objective, and my individuality dissolved into an indefinite series of days; I was happy.

After the Segura sierra, we began to climb the sierra of Alacaraz, which was not as high; I had given up counting the exact number of days we had been on our march, but it was around the start of August, I think, that we arrived in sight of Albacete. The heat was oppressive. I had strayed far away from the line of the fault; if I wanted to rejoin it I would now have to head straight west, and cross the plateau of La Mancha, which was over two hundred kilometres, and where I would find neither vegetation nor shelter. I could also, by turning to the north, head for the more wooded areas that extended around Cuenca, then, crossing Catalonia, rejoin the Pyrenean range. In my entire neohuman existence, I had never had to take any decision or initiative, it was a process that was completely foreign to me. Individual initiative, teaches the Supreme Sister in her *Instructions for a Peaceful Life*, is the matrix for will, attachment and desire; thus the Seven Founders, continuing her work, strove to create an exhaustive cartography of all imaginable life situations. Their aim, of course, was first to do away with money and sex, two pernicious factors of which they had been able to recognise the importance through the collective human life stories. It was equally a question of casting aside any notion of political choice, the source, they write, of 'false but violent' passions. These preconditions for a negative order, indispensable as they were, were not, however, sufficient in their eyes, to enable neohumanity to rejoin the 'obvious neutrality of the real', to use their frequently cited expression; it was also necessary to provide a concrete catalogue of positive prescriptions. Individual behaviour, they note in *Prolegomena to the Construction of the Central City* (significantly, the first neohuman work not to have a named author) was to become 'as predictable as the functioning of a refrigerator'. Indeed, while writing down their instructions, they acknowledged as a main source of stylistic inspiration, indeed more than any other human literary production, 'the manual for electrical appliances of medium size and complexity, in particular the video player JVC HR-DV3S/MS'. The neohumans, they inform us at the outset, can, just like the humans, be considered as rational animals of medium size and complexity; thus it was permissible, in a stabilised life, to establish a complete repertoire of behaviours.

By quitting the path of a standardised life, I had at the same time moved away from any applicable pattern. Thus, in the space of a few minutes, crouching on my heels at the top of a limestone mound, contemplating the endless white plain that stretched out at my feet, I discovered the torments of personal choice. I also realised, definitively this time, that my desire was no longer, and probably never had been, to join some kind of primate community. It was, without any real hesitation, a little like being under the influence of some kind of internal force of gravity, a little like the way one ends up leaning to the heaviest side, that I decided to turn towards the north. Just after La Roda, catching sight of the forests and the first shimmering of the waters of the reservoir at Alarcon, while Fox trotted joyfully at my feet, I realised that I would never meet Marie23, nor any other female neohuman, and that I did not feel any real regret about this.

I reached the village of Alarcon shortly after nightfall: the moon was reflected in the waters of the lake, animated by a light rippling. As I came to the first houses, Fox froze and growled softly. I stopped; I could hear no sound, but I trusted his sense of hearing, which was more acute than mine. Clouds passed across the moon, and I heard a slight scraping noise to my right; when the light became brighter I made out a human form – which appeared to be curved and deformed – as it slipped between two houses. I held back Fox, who was preparing to run after it, and continued to climb the main street. This was perhaps careless on my part; but, according to all the testimonies of those who had been in contact with them, the savages exhibited real terror of the neohumans, their first reaction in all cases was to flee.

The stronghold of Alarcon had been built in the twelfth century then turned into a luxury hotel in the twentieth, I learned from the faded letters of a tourist noticeboard; its mass remained impressive, it dominated the village and enabled one to survey the surroundings for kilometres around; I decided to stay there for the night, regardless of the noises and silhouettes that flitted around in the darkness. Fox was growling continually, I ended up taking him in my arms to calm him down; I was more and more convinced that the savages would avoid any confrontation if I made enough noise to warn them of my approach.

The interior of the castle bore all the traces of recent occupation; there was even a fire in the great fireplace, and a reserve of wood; so they had not lost that secret, one of the most ancient human inventions. I realised after a quick inspection of the bedrooms that this was about all you could say in their favour: the savages' occupation of the building translated above all into disorder, stink, and piles of dried excrement on the floor. There was no sign of mental, intellectual or artistic activity; this corresponded to the conclusions of the few researchers who had looked into the history of the savages: in the absence of any cultural transmission, the collapse had occurred with amazing speed.

The thick walls kept the heat in well, and I decided to set up camp in the main hall, contenting myself with pulling a mattress near to the fire; in a stockroom, I discovered a pile of clean sheets. I also found two automatic rifles, as well as an impressive reserve of cartridges and all the necessary kit for cleaning and lubricating the weapons. The region, which was hilly and wooded, must have abounded with game in the time of the humans; I did not know what was in it at present, but my first days on the road had revealed to me that at least some species had survived the succession of tidal waves and extreme droughts, the clouds of atomic radiation, the poisoning of the water supply, in fact all of the cataclysms that had ravaged the planet for the last two millennia. The last centuries of human civilisation, it is a little known but significant fact, had seen the appearance in western Europe of movements inspired by a strangely masochistic ideology, known as 'ecologism', although it bore little relation to the science of that name. These movements emphasised the necessity of protecting 'nature' from human ac- tivity, and pleaded for the idea that all species, whatever their degree of development, had an equal 'right' to occupy the planet; some followers of these movements even seemed to systematically take the side of the animals against men, to feel more sorrow at the news of the disappearance of a species of invertebrates than at that of a famine ravaging the population of a continent. Today we have some difficulty understanding these concepts of 'nature' and 'rights' that they manipulated so casually, and we simply see in these terminal ideologies one of the symptoms of mankind's desire to turn against itself, to put an end to an existence that it considered inadequate. Whatever the case may be, the 'ecologists' had greatly underestimated the living world's capacity for adaptation, the speed at which it reconstituted new equilibriums on top of the ruins of a destroyed world, and my first neohuman predecessors, such as Daniel13 and Daniel14 emphasise the sense of slight irony with which they watch dense forests, populated by wolves and bears, spreading rapidly over the old industrial complexes. It is also comical, at a time when humans have practically disappeared, when their past domination is only manifested in nostalgic vestiges, to observe the remarkable hardiness of mites and insects.

I spent a peaceful night, and woke up just before dawn. With Fox at my heels, I took the path around the battlements, watching the sun rising over the waters of the lake; the savages, having abandoned the village, had probably retreated to its shores. I then began a complete exploration of the castle, where I discovered numerous objects manufactured by man, some in a good state of preservation. All those that contained electronic components and lithium batteries intended to preserve data during power cuts had deteriorated irreversibly as a result of the passage of centuries; I thus left to one side the mobile telephones, computers and electronic pagers. The machines, however, that were made up of only mechanical and optical components, had for the most part stood up well. For some time I played with a camera, a double-lensed Rolleiflex with matt-black metalwork: the crank that enabled the movement of the film turned faultlessly; the glass of the shutter opened and closed with a small silky sound, at a speed that varied according to the number selected on the focusing knob. If photographic films had still existed, and developing laboratories, I was sure that I could have taken some excellent photographs. As the sun began to warm up, to illuminate the surface of the lake with golden reflections, I meditated for some time on grace, and forgetting; on what was best about mankind: its technological ingenuity. Nothing now remained of those literary and artistic productions of which mankind had been so proud; the themes that had given birth to them had lost all their relevance, their power to move had evaporated. Nothing was left, either, of those philosophical or theological systems for which men had fought, and sometimes died, and had even more often killed for; all that no longer aroused the slightest echo in a neo-human, we could no longer see in it anything more than the arbitrary ravings of limited and confused minds, unable to produce the slightest precise or simply practical concept. Man's technological predictions, on the other hand, could still inspire respect: it was in this field that man had been at his best, that he had expressed his deepest nature, *there* he had attained from the outset an operational excellence to which the neohumans had been able to add nothing of significance.

That said, my own technological needs were very limited; I helped myself only to a pair of powerful binoculars and a knife with a wide blade, which I slipped under my belt. It was possible, after all, that I might come across some dangerous animals in the course of my journey, and I might even pursue them. In the afternoon, clouds gathered above the plain, and a little later the rain began to fall, in slow and heavy curtains, the drops landed in the castle courtyard with a dull thud. I went out just after sunset: the paths were soaked and impassable; I understood that summer was giving way to autumn, and I also realised that I was going to stay there a few weeks, maybe a few months; I would wait for the beginning of winter, for the days to become cold and dry again. I could hunt, kill stags or deer that I would roast in the fireplace, lead that simple life that I was familiar with through various human life stories. Fox, I knew, would be happy with it, its memory was inscribed in his genes; for my part I needed capsules of mineral salts, but I still had six months' reserve left. Then I would have to find sea water, if the sea still existed, if I could reach it; otherwise

I would die. My attachment to life was not very strong, by the standards of human criteria, everything in the teachings of the Supreme Sister was oriented towards the idea of detachment; on rediscovering the original world, I had the impression of being an incongruous, contingent presence, in the middle of a universe where everything was oriented towards survival and perpetuation of the species.

Late that night I awoke, and saw a fire on the banks of the lake. Aiming my binoculars in this direction, I felt a shock at the sight of the savages: I had never seen them so close-up, they were different from those who populated the region of Almeria, they were more robust and their skin fairer; the deformed specimen I had seen on my arrival in the village was probably an exception. There were about thirty of them, gathered around a fire, dressed in leather rags that were probably of human manufacture. I couldn't bear to look at them for very long, and went back to stretch out in the darkness, trembling slightly; Fox nuzzled against me, pushing my shoulder with his muzzle, until I calmed down.

The following morning, at the gate of the castle, I discovered a suitcase made of stiff plastic, also of human manufacture; unable to produce any kind of object, having developed no technology, the savages lived on the debris of human industry, and contented themselves with using the objects they found here and there in the ruins of the ancient dwellings, at least those they understood how to work. I opened the suitcase: it contained roots, the nature of which I was not able to determine, and a piece of roasted meat. This confirmed how ignorant the savages were of neohumans: they were apparently not even aware that my metabolism was different from theirs and that this food was useless to me; Fox, on the other hand, tucked into the piece of meat. This also confirmed that they looked upon me with great fear, and wished to gain my goodwill, or at least my neutrality. When evening came, I put the empty suitcase at the entrance to show that I accepted the offering.

The same scene played out the following day, then the days after that. In the daytime, I observed through my binoculars the behaviour of the savages; I had almost got used to their appearance, their crude, craggy features, their exposed sexual organs. When they did not hunt they seemed to spend most of the time asleep, or coupling – at least those to whom the possibility was offered. The tribe was organised along a strict hierarchical system, which became clear to me after my first days of observation. The chief was a male of about forty, with greying hair; he was assisted by two young males who had rather broad chests, by far the biggest and most robust individuals in the group; copulation with the females was reserved for them: when the females encountered one of the three dominant males, they crouched down on all fours and presented their vulva; by contrast, they violently rejected the advances of the other males. The chief had in all cases precedence over the two subordinates, but there did not seem to be any hierarchy between *them*: in the absence of the chief they benefited in turn, and sometimes simultaneously, from the favours of the various females. The tribe comprised no elderly members, and fifty seemed to be about the maximum age they could reach. In short, it was a mode of organisation that quite closely recalled that of human societies, in particular those of the last periods after the disappearance of the great unifying systems. I was certain that Daniel1 would not have been homesick in this universe, and that he would have found his bearings easily.

A week after my arrival, as I was opening, as usual, the gate of the castle, I discovered next to the suitcase a young savage girl, hairy with very white skin and black hair. She was naked except for a leather miniskirt, her skin was crudely adorned with strokes of blue and yellow paint. On seeing me approach, she turned around, then rucked up her skirt and arched her back to present her rear. When Fox approached to sniff at her, she began to tremble all over, but did not change position. As I was still not moving, she finally turned her head in my direction; I gestured to her to follow me inside the castle. I was quite annoyed; if I accepted this new type of offering, it would probably be repeated in the following days; on the other hand, to send the female away would have been to expose her to reprisals from the other members of the tribe. She was visibly terrified, and watched my reactions with a gleam of panic in her eyes. I knew the procedures of human sexuality, even if my knowledge was purely theoretical. I pointed the mattress out to her; she went down on all fours and waited. I signalled for her to turn around; she obeyed, spreading her thighs wide, and began to pass a hand across her hole, which was astonishingly hairy. The mechanisms of desire had remained more or less the same among the neohumans, although they had weakened considerably, and I knew that certain neohumans were accustomed to lavish on themselves manual excitement. I had for my part tried once, several years before, trying to concentrate my mind upon tactile sensations – which had remained moderate, and which had dissuaded me from repeating the experiment. Nevertheless I took down my trousers, with the aim of manipulating my organ in order to give it the requisite rigidity. The young savage let out a moan of satisfaction, and rubbed her hole with redoubled energy. As I approached, I was overwhelmed by the pestilential odour that emanated from between her thighs. Since my departure, I had lost the neohuman habit of hygiene, my body odour was slightly more pronounced, but this was nothing compared to the stink emanating from the sex of the savage, a mixture of the musty smell of shit and rotten fish. I retreated despite myself; she got back up immediately, her fear aroused, and crawled towards me; once she was level with my sex, she approached it with her mouth. The stink was less unbearable but still it was very strong, her teeth were small, rotten and black. I gently pushed her away, got dressed again, and accompanied her to the castle gate, signalling to her not to come back. The following day, I neglected to take in the suitcase that had been left for me; overall, it seemed preferable to avoid developing too great a familiarity with the savages. I could hunt to satisfy the needs of Fox, the game was abundant and unwary; the savages, who were small in number, did not use any weapons other than the bow and arrow, my two automatic rifles would be a decisive advantage. The following day I made a first sortie and, to Fox's great joy, I shot two does that were grazing in the moat. With the help of a short axe I cut off two haunches, leaving the rest of the corpses to rot. These beasts were only imperfect, approximate machines, with a very limited lifespan; they had neither the robustness, nor the elegance and perfection of the workings of a double-lensed Rolleiflex, I thought as I observed their protruding eyes, deserted by life. It was still raining but more gently, the paths were becoming passable once more; when the frost began, it would be time to set off again towards the west.

In the days that followed, I ventured further into the forest around the lake; under the cover of the tall trees there grew short grass, illuminated here and there by sheets of sunlight. From time to time I could hear rustling noises in a denser thicket, or I was alerted by a growl from Fox. I knew that the savages were there, that I was crossing their territory, but that they would not dare show themselves; the shots must have terrified them. With good cause, as it turns out: I now had a good mastery of the workings of my rifles, I was able to reload very quickly, and I could have massacred them. The doubts that had occasionally, throughout my abstract and solitary life, assailed me, had now disappeared: I knew that I was dealing with baleful, unhappy and cruel creatures; it was not among them that I would find love, or its possibility, nor any of the ideals that fuelled the daydreams of our human predecessors; they were only the caricature-like residues of the worst tendencies of ordinary mankind, the kind that Daniel1 knew already, the one whose death he had wished for, planned and to a large extent accomplished. I had further confirmation of this in the course of a sort of party organised a few days later by the savages. It was a full moon and I was awakened by Fox's howling; the rhythm of the drums was of an obsessive violence. I climbed to the top of the central tower, the binoculars in my hand. The whole of the tribe was gathered in the clearing, they had lit a great fire and appeared overexcited. The chief presided over the meeting, in what resembled a sunken car seat. He was wearing an 'Ibiza Beach' T-shirt and a pair of high boots; his legs and sexual organs were exposed. At a sign from him, the music slowed and the members of the tribe formed a circle, delimiting a sort of arena in the centre, into which the two assistants of the chief brought – pushing and dragging them unceremoniously – two older savages, the oldest of the tribe, they had perhaps reached sixty. They were completely naked and armed with wide, short-bladed daggers – identical to those I had found in a reserve of the castle. At first the fight took place in the utmost silence; but from the first sight of blood the savages began to shout and whistle to encourage the antagonists. I understood immediately that it would be a fight to the death, with the aim of eliminating the individual least able to survive; the combatants struck each other without inhibition, trying to reach the face or other sensitive parts of the body. After the first three minutes, there was a pause, and they crouched at the edges of the arena, wiping themselves and drinking great gulps of water. The most corpulent one seemed in difficulty, he had lost a lot of blood. On a signal from the chief, the fight resumed. The fat one staggered to his feet; without wasting a second, his adversary leaped on to him and plunged his dagger into his eye. He fell to the ground, his face spattered with blood, and the scramble for the spoils began. With lifted daggers, the males and females of the tribe threw themselves screaming on to the wounded man who was trying to crawl out of sight; at the same time, the drums started to beat again. At first they cut off bits of flesh that they roasted in the embers, but as the frenzy increased they began to devour the body of the victim directly, to lap his blood, the smell of which seemed to intoxicate them. A few minutes later, the fat savage was reduced to bloody residue, scattered over a few metres in the prairie. The head lay at the side, intact except for the gouged eye. One of the assistants picked it up and handed it to the chief, who brandished it under the stars, as the music was silenced again and the members of the tribe sang an inarticulate threnody, slowly clapping their hands. I supposed that it was a rite of union, a way of strengthening bonds in the group – at the same time as eliminating weakened or sick members; all of this seemed to conform to what I had been taught about mankind.

I woke to a thin film of frost covering the prairies. I devoted the rest of the morning to preparing for what I hoped would be the last stage of my journey, Fox gambolled behind me from room to room. As I continued westwards, I knew that I would cross flatter and warmer regions; the survival blanket had become useless. I do not exactly know why I had returned to my initial idea of heading for

Lanzarote; the notion of rejoining a neohuman community still did not inspire much enthusiasm in me, besides I had found no further indication of the existence of such a community. No doubt it was the prospect of living out the rest of my existence in areas infested by savages, even in the company of Fox, even though I knew that they were terrified of me, far more than I was terrified of them, and they would do all they could to keep a respectful distance, that had, after that night, become intolerable. I became aware then that, little by little, I was cutting myself off from all possibilities; maybe, in this world, there was no place for me.

I hesitated, at length, in front of my automatic rifles. They were a burden, and would slow down my progress; I had absolutely no fears for my personal safety. On the other hand, it was not certain that Fox would find food as easily, in the regions we were going to cross. His head on his front paws, he followed me with his eyes, as if he understood my hesitation. When I stood up, holding the shortest rifle, after having stuffed a reserve of cartridges into my rucksack, he got up wagging his tail joyfully. He had, visibly, acquired a taste for the hunt, and to a certain extent so had I. I now experienced a certain joy in killing animals, in delivering them from phenomenal existence; intellectually, I knew I was wrong, for deliverance can only be obtained through asceticism, on this point the teachings of the Supreme Sister seemed to me more irrefutable than ever; but perhaps I had, in the worst sense of the term, become human. Any destruction of an organic form of life, of whatever kind, was a step towards the accomplishment of moral law; living still in hope of the Future Ones, I had at the same time to try and rejoin my fellow beings, or at least whatever it was that came close to resembling them. On closing my rucksack, I thought again of Marie23, who had departed in search of love, and doubtless had not found it. Fox was bounding around me, mad with joy at the idea of setting off again. I looked around at the forest and the plain and in my mind I recited the prayer for the deliverance of creatures.

It was the end of the morning and outside it was mild, almost warm; the frost had not lasted, we were only at the start of winter, and I was definitively going to leave the cold regions behind. Why was I alive? I was hardly of any importance. Before leaving I decided to take a final walk around the lake, my rifle in my hand, not to hunt really, for I would not be able to take the game with me, but to offer Fox the satisfaction of frolicking in the moat, sniffing the smells of the forest floor, one last time before we started out across the plains.

The world was there, with its forests, prairies, and its animals in all their innocence – digestive tubes on paws, with teeth at the end of them, whose life amounted to finding other digestive tubes in order to devour them and reconstitute their energy reserves. Earlier in the day, I had observed the savages' encampment; most of them were sleeping, slaked with strong emotions after their bloody orgy of the night before. They were at the top of the food chain, their natural predators were scarce; so they had to take on themselves the elimination of the ageing or sick, in order to preserve the good health of the tribe. Unable to count on natural competition, they also had to organise a social system of control of access to the vulva of the females, in order to maintain the genetic make-up of the species. All this was in accordance with the order of things, and the afternoon was strangely pleasant. I sat down by the lake whilst Fox ferreted around in the thicket. Sometimes a fish jumped out of the water, sending out slight ripples, which eventually died at its edges. I had more and more difficulty understanding why I had left the abstract and virtual community of the neohumans. Our existence, devoid of passions, had been that of the elderly; we looked on the world with a gaze characterised by lucidity without benevolence. The animal world was known, human societies were known; no mystery was hidden in it, and nothing could be expected from it, except the repetition of carnage. 'This is this and that is that,' I repeated to myself mechanically, many times, until I achieved a slightly hypnotic state.

After a little more than two hours I got up, perhaps a little calmer, in any case ready to pursue my quest – having nonetheless accepted its probable failure, and the death that would follow. I noticed then that Fox had disappeared – he must have scented a trail, and ventured further along the forest floor.

*

I beat at the bushes around the lake for more than three hours, calling out from time to time, at regular intervals, into an agonising silence, as the light began to fade. I found his body at nightfall, pierced by an arrow. His death must have been terrible: his already vitreous eyes reflected an expression of panic. In a final gesture of cruelty, the savages had cut off his ear; they must have acted quickly for fear of me arriving, the cut was crude, blood had spattered across his muzzle and chest.

My legs gave way under me, I fell to my knees before the still warm corpse of my little companion; it would perhaps have been enough, had I arrived five or ten minutes earlier, to have kept the savages at a distance. I was going to have to dig a grave, but for the moment I did not have the strength. Night was falling, patches of cold mist were beginning to form around the lake. I contemplated, for a long time, the mutilated body of Fox; then the flies arrived, in small numbers.

'It was a concealed place, and the password was: elentherin.'

Now I was alone. Night was falling on the lake, and my solitude was definitive. Fox would never live again, neither him, nor any dog with the same genetic make-up, he had sunk into the total annihilation towards which I in my turn was headed. I now knew with certainty that I had known love, because I knew suffering. Fleetingly, I thought again of Daniel's life story, now conscious that these few weeks of travel had given me a simplified, but exhaustive view of human life. I walked all night, then the following day, and a great part of the third day. From time to time I stopped, absorbed a capsule of mineral salts, drank some water and started off again; I felt no fatigue. I did not have much biochemical nor physiological knowledge, the line of Daniels was not a line of scientists; however, I knew that the passage to autotrophy had, with the neohumans, been accompanied by various modifications in the structure and workings of the smooth muscles. Compared with a human, I benefited from a suppleness, endurance and functional autonomy that were greatly enhanced. My psychology, of course, was also different; I did not comprehend fear, and whilst I was able to suffer, I felt none of the dimensions of what humans called regret; this feeling existed in me, but it was accompanied by no mental projection. I already felt a sense of loss when I thought of Fox's caresses, of the way he had of nuzzling against my knees; of his baths, his races, above all the joy that could be read in his eyes, this joy that overwhelmed me because it was so foreign; but this suffering, this loss seemed to me inevitable, because of the simple fact that *they existed*. The idea that things could have been different did not cross my mind, no more than a mountain range, present before my eyes, could vanish to be replaced by a plain. Consciousness of a total determinism was without doubt what differentiated us most clearly from our human predecessors. Like them, we were only conscious machines; but, unlike them, we were aware of only being machines.

*

I had walked without thinking for around forty hours, in a complete mental fog, guided solely by a vague memory of the journey on the map. I do not know what made me stop, and brought me back to full consciousness; no doubt the strange character of the landscape around me. I now had to be near the ruins of old Madrid, I was in any case in the middle of an immense tarmac space, which extended almost as far as I could see, it was only in the distance that I could vaguely make out a landscape of dry, low hills. Here and there the earth had been pushed up for several metres, forming monstrous blisters, as if under the influence of a terrifying underground heatwave. Ribbons of tarmacadam rose towards the sky, climbing for several dozens of metres before stopping abruptly and ending in a mass of gravel and black stones. Metal debris and blasted windows were strewn on the ground. At first I thought I was on a toll motorway, but there were no roadsigns, anywhere, and in the end I understood that I was in the middle of what remained of Baraja airport. As I continued westwards, I noticed a few indications of ancient human activity: flat-screen televisions, piles of shattered CDs, an immense point-of-sale advertisement depicting the singer David Bisbal. Radiation must still have been strong in this area, it had been one of the places most bombed during the last phases of the interhuman conflict. I studied the map; I had to be near the epicentre of the fault, if I wanted to stay on course I had to turn southwards, which meant I would pass through the former city centre.

Carcasses of agglomerated, melted cars slowed down my progress as I reached the M45–R2 interchange. It was while crossing the old IVECO warehouses that I caught sight of the first urban savages. There were about fifteen of them, grouped under the metal canopy of a hangar, about fifty metres away. I lifted my rifle to my shoulder and fired rapidly: one of the silhouettes collapsed, whilst the others fell back inside the hangar. A little later, on turning around, I saw that two of them were carefully venturing out to drag their companion inside – no doubt with the intention of feeding on him. I had taken out my binoculars and could observe that they were smaller and more deformed than those I had observed in the region of Alarcon; their dark-grey skin was pockmarked with excrescences and spots – no doubt a consequence of the radiation, I imagined. They displayed, in any case, the same terror at neohumans, and all those that I came across in the ruins of the city fled immediately, without giving me the time to take aim; I had, however, the satisfaction of killing five or six of them. Although most were limping, they moved quickly, sometimes helping themselves along with their forelimbs; I was surprised, and even appalled by this unexpected multitude.

With the life story of Daniel1 at the front of my mind, it was with a strange emotion that I found myself in the Calle Obispo de León, where his first meeting with Esther had taken place. Of the bar he mentioned there remained no trace, in fact the street was reduced to two sides of blackened wall, one of which, by chance, displayed a street sign. I had the idea of looking for the Calle San Isidor where, on the top floor of number 3, the birthday party marking the end of their relationship had taken place. I remembered fairly well the map of the centre of Madrid as it had been at the time of Daniel: some streets were completely deserted, whilst others, following no apparent logic, were intact. It took me about half an hour to find the building I was looking for; it was still standing. I climbed to the top floor, raising clouds of concrete dust with each step. The furniture, curtains and carpets had completely disappeared; there were, on the filthy floor, only a few piles of dried excrement. Pensively, I went through the rooms where no doubt one of the worst moments in Daniel's life had taken place. I walked as far as the terrace from which he had contemplated the urban landscape before entering what he called the 'home straight'. Of course, I could not stop myself meditating once more on the passion of love in humans, its terrifying violence, its importance to the genetic economy of the species. Today the landscape of burned-out blasted buildings, the piles of gravel and dust produced a calming impression, inviting a sad detachment, with their dark-grey dilapidation. The sight before me was almost the same in all directions; but I knew that to the south-west, once the fault had been crossed, from the heights of Leganes or maybe Fuenlabrada, I was going to have to make my way across the Great Grey Space. Estremadura and Portugal had disappeared as differentiated places. The succession of nuclear explosions, of tidal waves, of cyclones that had battered this geographical zone for several centuries had ended up completely flattening its surface and transforming it into one vast sloping plane, of weak declivity, which appeared in the satellite photos as uniformly composed of pulverulent ashes of a very light grey colour. This sloping plane continued for about two and a half thousand kilometres before opening out upon a little-known region of the world, whose sky was almost continually saturated with light clouds and vapours, situated on the site of the former Canary Islands. Obstructed by the layer of clouds, the rarely available satellite pictures were unreliable. Lanzarote may have remained an isthmus, or become an island, or have completely disappeared; such were, on the geographical level, the uncertain givens of my journey. On the physiological level, it was certain that I was going to be short of water. By walking twenty hours per day, I could cover daily a distance of one hundred and fifty kilometres; it would take me a little more than two weeks to reach the maritime zones, if they actually existed. I did not know exactly how much my organism could withstand desiccation; it had, I think, never been tested in extreme conditions. Before setting off I spared a brief thought for Marie23, who must have had to confront, coming from New York, comparable difficulties; I also spared a thought for the former humans, who under such circumstances would commend their souls to God; I regretted the absence of God, or of an entity of the same order; I finally raised my mind towards hope in the coming of the Future Ones.

The Future Ones, unlike us, will not be machines, nor truly separate beings. They will be one, whilst also being many. Nothing can give us an exact image of the nature of the Future Ones. Light is one, but its rays are innumerable. I have rediscovered the meaning of the Word; corpses and ashes will guide my feet, as will the memory of the good dog Fox.

I left at dawn, surrounded by the multiplied rustling of fleeing savages. Crossing the ruined suburbs, I approached the Great Grey Space just before midday. I put down my rifle, which was no longer of any use to me; there had been no sign of life, animal or vegetable, beyond the great fault. Straight away, my progress became easier than expected: the layer of ashes was only a few centimetres thick, it covered the hard ground, which looked like clinker, and my feet gripped easily. The sun was high in an immutable blue sky, there was no difficult terrain, no obstacle that could have made me change direction. Progressively, while walking, I slipped into a peaceful daydream in which were blended images of modified neohumans, more slender and frail, almost abstract, with the memory of the silky, velvety visions that, a long time before, in my previous life, Marie23 had made appear on my screen as a way of paraphrasing the absence of God.

Just before sunset, I stopped for a brief while. With the help of a few trigonometric observations, I was able to determine the declivity at about 1 per cent. If the slope stayed the same to the end, the surface of the ocean was situated at twenty-five thousand metres below the level of the continental plate. One would, at that point, be no longer very far from the asthenosphere; I should expect a significant increase in the temperature over the course of the following days.

In reality the heat became oppressive only a week later, at the same time as I began to feel the first attacks of thirst. The sky had an immutable purity and was of a smalt blue, increasingly intense, almost dark. One by one I took off my clothes; my rucksack now contained only a few capsules of mineral salts; at this point I had difficulty taking them, the production of saliva was becoming insufficient. Physically I was suffering, which was a new sensation for me. Entirely placed beneath the power of nature, the life of wild animals consisted only of pain, with a few moments of brief relaxation, of happy mindlessness linked to the satisfaction of instincts – for food or sex. The life of man had been, in gross terms, similar, dominated by suffering, with brief moments of pleasure, linked to the conscientisation of instinct, which manifested itself as desire in the human species. The life of the neohumans was intended to be peaceful, rational, remote from pleasure as well as suffering, and my departure would bear witness to its failure. The Future Ones, perhaps, would know joy, another name for continuous pleasure. I walked without resting, still at the rate of twenty hours a day, conscious that my survival depended now on the banal issue of regulation of the osmotic pressure, on the balance between my levels of mineral salts and the quantity of water my cells had been able to store. I was not, strictly speaking, certain I wanted to live, but the idea of death had no substance. I saw my body as a vehicle, but it was a vehicle for nothing. I had not been able to reach the Spirit; I continued, however, to wait for a sign.

Under my feet the ashes became white, and the sky took on ultramarine tones. It was two days later that I found the message from Marie23. Written in a clear, taut hand, it had been traced on pages made of a fine, transparent, untearable plastic; these had been rolled up and placed in a tube of black metal, which made a slight sound when I opened it. This message was not specifically addressed to me, it was in truth addressed to no one: it was only a further display of this absurd or sublime determination, present in humans and remaining identical in their successors, to bear witness, to leave a trace.

The general tenor of the message was profoundly sad. To get out of the ruins of New York, Marie23 had had to mix with many savages, sometimes grouped in large tribes; unlike me, she had sought to establish contact with them. Protected by the fear she inspired in them, she had been no less distressed by the brutality of their social relations, by their absence of pity for the old or weak, by their constantly renewed appetite for violence, for hierarchical or sexual humiliations, for cruelty pure and simple. The scenes I had observed near Alarcon she had seen repeated, almost identically, in New York – even though the tribes were situated at considerable distances from one another, and had been unable for seven or eight centuries, to have any contact. No feast among the savages could be imagined without violence, the spilling of blood, and the spectacle of torture; the invention of complicated and atrocious tortures seemed to be the only area in which they had preserved something of the ingeniousness of the ancient humans; that was the limit of their civilisation. If you believed in the heredity of moral character, this was nothing of a surprise: it was natural that it would be the most brutal and cruel individuals, having a higher potential for aggressiveness, who survived in greater number a succession of lengthy conflicts, and transmitted their character to their descendants. Nothing, in regard to moral heredity, had ever been proved – or refuted; but Marie23's testimony, like mine, amply confirmed the definitive verdict that the Supreme Sister had passed on mankind, and justified her decision to do nothing to stop the process of extermination that she, two millennia ago, had committed herself to.

You may wonder why Marie23 had continued along her path; indeed, it seemed on reading certain passages that she had thought of giving up, but there had doubtless developed in her, as in me, as in all neohumans, a certain fatalism, linked to an awareness of our own immortality, that brought us closer to the ancient human peoples, amongst whom religious beliefs had taken root. Mental configurations generally survive the reality that gave rise to them. Having become technically immortal, having at least reached a stage that was similar to reincarnation, Daniel1 had behaved until the end with no less impatience, frenzy and greed than a mere mortal. Similarly, although I had left on my own initiative the system of reproduction that ensured my immortality or, more exactly, the indefinite reproduction of my genes, I knew that I would never manage to become completely conscious of death; I would never know boredom, desire or fear to the same extent as a human being.

As I was preparing to put the pages back in the tube I noticed that it contained a last object, which I had some difficulty extracting. It was a page torn from a human paperback book, folded and folded again to form a strip of paper, which fell into pieces when I tried to unfold it. On the biggest of the fragments I read these phrases, in which I recognised the dialogue of Plato's *Symposium* where Aristophanes expounds his theory of love:

When therefore a man, whether attracted to boys or to women, meets the one who is his other half, the feeling of tenderness, trust and love with which they are gripped is a miracle; they no longer want to be apart, even for an instant. And this way people spend all their lives together, without being able moreover to say what they expect from one another; for it does not appear to be uniquely the pleasure of the senses that makes them find so much charm in the company of the other. It is obvious that the soul of each desires something else, *what* it cannot say, but it guesses it, and lets you guess.

I remembered perfectly what happened next: Hephaestos the blacksmith appeared to the two mortals 'while they were sleeping together', proposing to melt them and weld them together, 'so that from two they become only one, and that after their death, down there, in Hades, they will no longer be two, but one, having died a common death.' I remembered especially the final sentences: 'And the reason for this is that our former nature was such that we formed a complete whole. It is the desire and pursuit of this whole that is called love.' It was this book that had intoxicated Western mankind, then mankind as a whole, which had inspired in it disgust at its condition of a rational animal, which had engendered in it a dream that it had taken two millennia to try and rid itself of, without completely succeeding. Christianity itself, St Paul himself, had been unable to resist bowing before this force. 'Two will become one flesh; this mystery is great, I proclaim it, in relation to Christ and the Church.' Right up until the last human life stories, one could detect an incurable nostalgia for it. When I tried to fold the fragment back up, it crumbled between my fingers; I closed the tube and put it back on the ground. Before setting off again I gave a final thought to Marie23, who was still human, so human; I remembered the image of her body, that I would never have the chance to know intimately. Suddenly, I became worryingly aware that if I had found her message it meant that one of us had deviated from our path.

The uniform white surface offered no landmark, but there was the sun, and a rapid examination of my shadow told me that I had in fact gone too far to the west. I now had to turn due south. I had not drunk water for two days, I was no longer able to feed myself, and this simple moment of distraction risked being fatal. I no longer suffered much in actual fact, the pain signal had faded, but I felt immensely tired. The survival instinct still existed among neo-humans, it was simply more moderate; I tracked inside me, for a few minutes, its struggle with fatigue, knowing that it would end in victory. I set off again, more slowly, in the direction of the south.

I walked all day, then the following night, guiding myself by the constellations. It was three days later, in the early hours, that I saw the clouds. Their silky surface appeared to be just a modulation of the horizon, a trembling of light, and I first thought of a mirage, but on closer approach I made out more clearly cumulus clouds of beautiful matt white, separated by supernaturally still, thin curls of vapour. Around midday I passed through the layer of cloud, and found myself facing the sea. I had reached the end of my journey.

This landscape, it must be said, hardly resembled the ocean as man had known it; it was a string of puddles and ponds of almost still water, separated by sand banks; everything was bathed in an opal, even light. I no longer had the strength to run, and it was with wavering steps that I made for the source of life. The mineral content of the first shallow pools was very weak; the whole of my body, however, greeted the salty bath with gratitude, I had the impression of being swept by a nutritive, benevolent wave. I understood and almost managed to feel the phenomena that were taking place inside me: the osmotic pressure returning to normal, the metabolic chains beginning to turn again, producing the ATP necessary for the operation of the muscles, the proteins and fatty acids required for cellular regeneration. It was like the continuation of a dream after a moment of anxious awakening, like a machine's sigh of satisfaction.

Two hours later I got up, my strength already quite reconstituted; the temperature of the air and the water were equal, and must have been close to 37°C, for I could feel no sensation of cold, nor of heat; the luminosity was bright without being dazzling. Between the pools, the sand was pitted with shallow excavations that resembled little graves. I lay down in one of them; the sand was tepid and silky. Then I realised that I was going to live here, and that my days would be many. The diurnal and nocturnal periods had an equal duration of twelve hours, and I could sense that it would be the same all the year round, that the astronomical modifications that occurred at the time of the Great Drying Up had created here a zone that did not experience any seasons, where there reigned the conditions of an endless early summer.

Quite quickly I lost the habit of having regular hours of sleep; I slept for periods of one or two hours, during the day as well as the night, but, without knowing why, I felt each time the need to huddle in one of the crevices. There was no trace of animal or vegetable life. Any kind of landmark in general in the landscape was rare: sandbanks, ponds and lakes of variable size stretched out as far as I could see. The layer of cloud, which was very dense, most of the time prevented me from making out the sky; it was not, however, completely immobile, but its movements were extremely slow. Occasionally, a small space opened between two cloud masses, through which I caught sight of the sun, or the constellations; it was the only event, the only modification in the passing of the days, the universe was enclosed in a sort of cocoon or stasis, fairly close to the archetypal image of eternity. I was, like all neohumans, immune to boredom; some limited memories, some pointless daydreams occupied my detached, floating consciousness. I was, however, a long way away from joy, and even from real peace; the sole fact of existing is already a misfortune. Departing from, at my own free will, the cycle of rebirths and deaths, I was making my way towards a simple nothingness, a pure absence of content. Only the Future Ones would perhaps succeed in joining the realm of countless potentialities.

In the course of the following weeks, I ventured further into my new domain. I noticed that the size of the ponds and lakes increased as I headed south, until I could, in some of them, observe a slight tidal phenomenon; they remained, however, very shallow, and I could swim out as far as their centres, with the certainty of rejoining a sand bank without any difficulty. There was still no trace of life. I thought I remembered that life had appeared on Earth under very particular conditions, in an atmosphere saturated with ammonia and methane, due to the intense volcanic activity of the first ages, and that it was implausible that the process could be reproduced on the same planet. Organic life, anyway, a prisoner of the limited conditions imposed by the laws of thermodynamics, could not, even if it managed to be reborn, do other than repeat the same patterns: constitution of isolated individuals, predation, selective transmission of the genetic code; nothing new could be expected from it. According to certain hypotheses, carbon biology had had its day, and the Future Ones would be beings made of silicon, whose civilisation would be built through the progressive interconnection of cognitive and memory processors; the work of Pierce, basing itself solely at the level of formal logic, enabled us neither to confirm nor refute this hypothesis.

If the zone where I found myself was inhabited, it could in any case only be by neohumans; the organism of a savage could never have stood up to the journey I had made. I now anticipated without joy, and even with a certain annoyance, an encounter with one of my fellow creatures. The death of Fox, then the crossing of the Great Grey Space, had desiccated me inside; I no longer felt any desire, and certainly not the one, described by Spinoza, of persevering in my being; I regretted, however, that the world would survive me. The inanity of the world, evident in the life story of Daniel, had ceased to appear acceptable to me; I saw in it only a dull place, devoid of potentialities, from which light was absent.

One morning, immediately after waking, I felt for no perceptible reason less oppressed. After walking for a few minutes I arrived in front of a lake that was much bigger than the others, where, for the first time, I could not make out the other bank. Its water, too, was slightly saltier.

So this was what men had called the sea, what they had considered the great consoler, the great destroyer as well, the one that erodes, that gently puts an end to things. I was impressed, and the last elements missing from my comprehension of the species fell finally into place. I understood better, now, how the idea of the infinite had been able to germinate in the brain of these primates; the idea of an infinity that was accessible through slow transitions that had their origins in the finite; I understood, also, how a first theory of love had been able to form in the brain of Plato. I thought again of Daniel, of his residence in Almeria, which had been mine,

344   ~ *The Possibility of an Island*

of the young women on the beach, of his destruction by Esther; and, for the first time, I was tempted to pity him, without, however, respecting him. Of two selfish and rational animals, the most selfish and rational of the two had ended up surviving, as was always the case among human beings. I then understood why the Supreme Sister insisted upon the study of the life story of our human predecessors. I understood the goal she was trying to reach: I understood, also, why this goal would never be reached.

I had not found deliverance.

Later I walked, making my feet follow the movement of the waves. I walked for whole days, without feeling any fatigue, and at night I was rocked by a gentle surf. On the third day I discerned alleys of black stone that sank into the sea and disappeared into the distance. Were they a passage, a human or neohuman construction? It was of little importance to me now, the idea of going down them left me very quickly.

    At the same instant, without anything that could have allowed me to predict it, two masses of cloud parted, and a ray of light sparkled on the surface of the water. Fleetingly, I thought of the great sun of the moral law, which, according to the Word, would finally shine on. the surface of the world; but it would be a world from which I would be absent, and of which I did not even have the ability to imagine the essence. No neohuman, I now knew, would be able to find a solution for the constituent aporia; those who had tried to, if indeed there were any, had probably already died. As for me, I would continue, as much as was possible, my obscure existence as an improved monkey, and my last regret would be of having caused the death of Fox, the only being worthy of survival I had had the chance to encounter; for his gaze had already contained, occasionally, the spark announcing the coming of the Future Ones.

I had perhaps sixty years left to live; more than twenty thousand days that would be identical. I would avoid thought in the same way I would avoid suffering. The pitfalls of life were far behind me; I had now entered a peaceful space from which only the lethal process would separate me.

I bathed for a long time under the sun and the starlight, and I felt nothing other than a slightly obscure and nutritive sensation. Happiness was not a possible horizon. The world had betrayed. My body belonged to me for only a brief lapse of time; I would never reach the goal I had been set. The future was empty; it was the mountain. My dreams were populated with emotional presences. I was, I was no longer. Life was real.